HARRIGAN'S APPEAL

The Story of a Refugee Newspaper

by

Patricia Walker

And

Barbara Deatherage

www.harrigansappeal.com

Cover design and cover photo by Michael Van Buskirk

Historic newspaper images sourced from Chronicling America: Historic American Newspapers. Lib. of Congress. http://chroniclingamerica.loc.gov

ISBN: 978-0-9977498-0-9

First Edition: July 2016

10 9 8 7 6 5 4 3 2 1

Harrigan's Appeal
is dedicated with love to Ray Walker, Michael Van
Buskirk, John Deatherage, and all the rest of my family
who helped and encouraged me in so many ways.

PROLOGUE

On a summer night in 1862, just before the Yankees occupied Memphis, Tennessee, the staff of the Memphis Appeal loaded their press, steam engine, and supplies on a freight train and fled south to become a refugee newspaper. This novel, based on true facts, brings to life this almost forgotten page of history. For three years, the Appeal traveled the war-torn South, printing vital news in advance of enemy lines. The Yankees called the little paper "a thorn in their side", and pursued them at every opportunity. The Harrigans, a fictional Memphis family, join the Appeal's adventure, eager to do their part to preserve their homeland.

CHAPTER ONE

BELLS TOLLED, THEIR TONE DEEP and sorrowful, as Patrick Harrigan was lowered into his grave. Mourners crowded into the village cemetery in Shannonbridge, Ireland, spilling out over the lane and down the hill. A blustery wind whipped their cloaks and scarves and sent a few hats soaring skyward. The people shivered and moved closer to Joseph. Joseph, Patrick's six-year-old son, stood with his hands shoved into the pockets of his jacket, staring at the raw mound of dirt beside the open grave. Joseph was remembering how, less than a year ago, the bells had rung at the funeral of his mother and infant sister. To hear them again, ringing now for his father, was like getting punched in a stomach still sore from the last blow.

After the funeral, Joseph was taken to the nearby farm of his Uncle Duffy and Aunt Nora, where Patrick's wake had been held.

The wake had lasted for three days and the little cottage smelled of whiskey, stale tobacco and the remains of roasted lamb. The women tossed their coats and cloaks on a bench in a corner, donned aprons, and began cleaning the mess. Men rolled up their sleeves, offering assistance.

Joseph went to the bench and burrowed down among the discarded wraps with their familiar odor of damp wool. He could hear his cousins playing outside, but he did not want to join them. He hoped no one would notice him there so he could be alone. For the past few days, he had been smothered with attention. The relatives had fussed over him, clutching him to heaving bosoms, stroking his cheeks with leathery hands.

It had not helped.

The aunts and uncles hurried about, opening windows to air out the room, returning chairs and tables to their rightful places, scraping cheese and melted butter from bowls. There was a great deal of talk about dividing the leftover lamb, cutting it up in such a way that each family might take home a bit.

In the midst of this discussion, someone spoke of Joseph. Ah, the poor lad. What was to be done with him? Sure they must care for him. It was the least they could do for their brave brother, Patrick, hero that he was. Somehow they must help Joseph recover and go on with life after he had witnessed the worst thing a wee lad could possibly see.

Joseph put his hands over his ears and squeezed his eyes shut. He didn't want to hear any more, didn't want to be reminded of that terrible afternoon. But it was no use. Every time he closed his eyes, the afternoon was there again, happening over and over in his head.

He and his father were in their own cottage, just the two of them. His father was working at his printing and Joseph sat on a stool beside the table, helping fold the papers as soon as the ink was dry. He folded each paper carefully, folded it twice so that the printing was hidden inside, the way his father had taught him to do. As he worked, he listened to the wind howling across the moors, slamming against the thick sod walls of the cottage, banging shutters and whistling around the chimney. It must be very cold, he thought, but inside, the cottage was warm. Warm and cozy. A fine rabbit stew bubbled in the big iron pot hanging above the fire. And on the hearth, a fat loaf of potato bread was browning on the baking board.

After they had worked for what seemed to him a very long time, Joseph asked his father, "Would we be having our dinner soon?"

The press stopped thumping as Patrick stood and smiled down at Joseph. "Hungry, lad?" He pushed the press to one side of the table, then went to the fireplace and filled two bowls with the steaming stew. They tore off chunks of the warm potato bread and sat side by side, eating and talking. They had become very close since Joseph's mother and tiny sister had both become ill and died.

When they had eaten their fill, Patrick leaned back in his chair and lit his clay pipe. "Would you like it if I took time to read to you before we go back to work?"

"Oh, Da, would you? I'll go get a book and ---"

A sudden crash tore the door of the cottage from its hinges. Wind swept through the room. A group of burly men crowded in, stomping their feet, yelling, cursing. Patrick stood and demanded that they leave. One of the men lunged at him, grabbing him around the neck.

Joseph ran to wrap his arms about his father's legs. "Leave me Da alone," he cried.

Rough hands pulled the boy away from his father, shoving him against the wall. Two men threw the press on the floor, lifted huge clubs. Chips of wood flew about the room as the press was pounded until it was entirely destroyed. Other men dragged Patrick outside and wrestled him to the ground.

Joseph was so dazed that he could only stumble to the doorway to watch as the men circled his father, kicked him with heavy brogans and beat his face, his body, with fists and clubs until he no longer moved. They paused, examined him briefly, nudged him with booted toes. "Looks done in to me," one said. "We'd best be getting our arses out of here." They hurried off, disappearing around a bend in the road.

Joseph ran out, kneeled beside his father and stared at a face now bloody and crushed, at hands twisted and torn. He rocked back and forth, his arms wrapped about his stomach. "Please, Da, talk to me. I don't know what I should be doing."

There was no sound but the spatter of sleet on the ground.

I found him there, half frozen," Joseph's Uncle Duffy was saying now. He'd told the story over and over. And Joseph, now huddled on the bench among warm cloaks and coats, could still feel how it was to be so scared, so cold, so numb.

The relatives all murmured sympathetically. Oh, the pity of it. Shouldn't they, the brothers and sisters of brave Patrick, bless his soul, take care of his son now that he was all alone? It was the least they could do for a man who had died trying to keep the rebels informed. Aye, they must take him in. But which home should he go to first?

Joseph wanted to ask if he couldn't stay with Uncle Duffy and Aunt Nora, where he had visited often and already knew everyone. But he heard his Aunt Fionna say, "Since Nora will soon have a new babe to care for, I'll offer to have him now. I could keep him until next summer."

"And we could take him then, could we not?" Uncle Kevin asked, with an inquiring look at his wife, who hesitated a second, then nodded.

So Joseph went to live with first one relative, then another. Everyone was kind to him but in time, after he had been passed among several families, he realized what a burden he was. He couldn't help noticing how crowded the lofts were where the children slept, how difficult it was to make a place for another chair at the table, how carefully the food must be divided.

Often, as Joseph lay on his bog fir mattress, tucked beneath eaves and wedged between whatever cousins who might be sharing the loft, he would hear murmured discussions in the room below, discussions which always seemed to begin with "Ah, the poor lad....," And soon he would be sent off again to become part of yet another household.

He always felt he had to be better than the family's other children. Quieter. Less messy. More helpful. What if someday, when it was time to move on, there would be no one willing to take him?

Joseph was grateful that his father had taught him how to sound out letters, for during the lonely days when he was getting acquainted in a new place, he spent hours teaching himself to read. Each family had a few treasured books, most of them sent from relatives and friends in America, and he read all he could get his hands on, no matter how unsuitable for his age.

He was eager to learn and took advantage of any schooling he was lucky enough to receive. He had been told that, for almost a hundred years, the British had forbidden Catholics to educate their children. But some of Joseph's uncles and aunts had attended "hedgerow schools", classes conducted on the sunny side of hedges by traveling teachers who risked death to teach reading, writing, arithmetic, and a bit of geography and history. The uncles and aunts passed what they had learned along to their children, Joseph included.

When Joseph was eleven, he was sent to his Aunt Clare in Kilkenny, a widow with nine children. Joseph felt sorry for adding to her troubles. However, she gathered him into her fold and somehow spread her ample, cheerful self equally among them, making him feel as wanted as the others. When a year passed and there was no mention of sending him away, he relaxed and for the first time, made friends among neighboring children. He even found himself admiring a certain lass, Bridget Anna O'Ryan.

He couldn't imagine why he was so taken with her. Such a one she was for tossing her thick auburn hair about and having her say. What was it about her that made him so aware of her presence, made his heart pound when she was near? She was lovely, to be sure, but there were others as fine-looking and he barely noticed them.

And more amazing, why did she fancy him? Her father was the town's only doctor and the O'Ryans lived in a grand home. Sure a girl so well-off could have her choice of any boy. Why was she keen on him, a poor orphan with an ordinary face and shaggy hair the color of straw?

But they seemed meant for one another, Bridget and Joseph. They had long conversations, talking of their hopes and disappointments, the things they were unhappy about. Their plans for the future. Joseph told her all about his father, how he wanted more than anything to be a printer like his father, though he knew how unlikely reaching such a goal would be for an orphan. But he would be someone that mattered, someone his father would be proud of, he insisted. Bridget said she was sure he would be. She believed in him.

Bridget's goal was simpler. She wanted to make her own decisions. To do what she wanted to do with her life. And that would be difficult, too, for she was an only child, their "eye-apple" they called her. They were busily planning her life for her. Her father was the worst, she said. He doted on her. There was, for instance, the matter of her name. Bridget wished she could have been named after her mother, who was from France and had a lovely name, Maria Emilie. But she was told that her father had insisted she was an Irish girl and must have an Irish name. He had named her after his own mother. And, said Bridget to Joseph, wasn't it a fact that you could hardly toss a stone in Ireland without it landing at the feet of a Bridget?

The spring that Joseph turned thirteen, Bridget suggested they take a walk through the meadow to enjoy the warm softness of the day. She was wearing a bright skirt and a flax-colored blouse trimmed with lace. The fact that he was dressed in shabby knickers, his shirt patched at the elbow, did not seem to make a difference as they walked along, talking, teasing one another, laughing. When they came to a tumble-down wall covered with brambles, he took her hand to help her climb over. And somehow, after the climbing was done and there was no longer a need to be assisting her, they continued to hold on to one another. Nothing in all Joseph's life had ever felt as wonderful as having her hand in his. He had always wondered why the older lads and lasses seemed to set such store on going off alone. Now he knew.

After that, there was more hand-holding and eventually, shy kisses. The village priest kept a watchful eye on any of the lads and lasses who seemed too friendly, so Joseph and Bridget were careful. But the fact that they were seen together so often earned from the village gossips disapproving frowns or knowing looks. Bridget's father lectured her, saying she would regret having her good name associated with what he referred to as "that shanty-boat Irish lad."

But Bridget would not be swayed. "I refuse to pay any mind to what others say," she assured Joseph. "They just don't know you the way I do."

One afternoon, as Joseph was about his chores in Aunt Clare's byre, milking Netty, the family's only cow, Bridget came to him with tears in her eyes. He stood up, knocking over the milking stool, and gathered her into his arms. "Ah now, what's troubling you so?" he asked.

She had to calm herself before she could tell him that her father was threatening to part them by having her sent to live with her grandmother in County Antrim, in the far north of Ireland.

"If he does that," Joseph said fiercely, "if he sends you away from me, I'll be coming after you. Even in the dark of the night. If I have to climb up to your bedroom window, I'll rescue you."

Bridget looked interested. "Would you truly do that?"

"I would. If you want me to."

"Aye, I do."

"Then I will."

"Promise?"

"I promise," he said, and added that he swore on his mother's grave that he would allow nothing to part them. He had never made such a statement before, but it seemed called for. "And I'll take care of you always, I will."

"Ah, Joseph, aren't you the darling boy?"

They kissed, a kiss that went on and on until Netty looked back at them and mooed an impatient demand for Joseph to continue the milking.

Bridget pushed away. "I'd best be going now."

He stared after her, ignoring Netty's continued complaints about her swollen teats. His head was in a whirl. Only minutes before, his life had been proceeding as he expected.

Now, he thought, alarmed, what had he gotten himself into? He supposed he was almost as good as married, having promised – no sworn on his mother's grave -- that he would take care of Bridget always. Sure, hadn't he all but proposed to her? And himself with no hope of providing her with the kind of future she would want -- in fact, without hope of any sort of future worth their while.

But he did want Bridget for a wife. He did. He would have no other. He reached for the milking stool and sat down to relieve Netty while he struggled to think of a way to make a life for them. He must find work, he decided, and start saving so they could have a home of their own.

The next day he set out to find Bridget, to reassure her that he would keep his promise. But she was not in any of the usual places. Not at the crossroads. Nor at the homes of any of her girlfriends. In fact, no one had seen her.

He decided her mother must have kept her in for some sort of studying. For some of the lessons in how to be a lady that Bridget had complained so much about – lessons she had to endure.

He didn't worry too much at first, for Sunday was only three days away and she would surely be going to mass with her family. But when Dr. and Mrs. O'Ryan went to church alone, he felt a stir of panic. Was Bridget ill? Or had the unthinkable actually happened?   Had she truly been sent off to live with her grandmother?   He could wait no longer to find out, and though he'd never dared go to Bridget's home, he gathered his courage and walked up to their front door to bang the big brass knocker.

It seemed forever before the door opened. But finally Dr. O'Ryan opened it slowly and said, "Yes, young man. What is it you're wanting?"

Joseph stammered a bit. "About Bridget. I...I haven't seen her about. Is she... is she not feeling well?"

Dr. Ryan's reply was cold and unfriendly. "She's gone to visit relatives. And no. I can't say when she'll be back." Having given this bare amount of information, he closed the door firmly.

Joseph stood there, stunned, thinking that a door that is closed in your face has a different sound. A sound that takes your breath away, hurts your stomach, and somehow, makes you feel much smaller.

For several weeks, Joseph went about, trying to act as if nothing were wrong, hiding his hurt. Then, one day, Aunt Clare brought the mail from town and told him kindly that there was a letter for him.

It was a letter from Bridget, saying how sorry she was that she hadn't been allowed to tell him goodbye. Saying how she missed him. She gave him the address of a cousin who, she said, he could write to. The cousin would keep their letters secret and see that she got them.

Joseph wrote back that he was also sorry that they hadn't had a chance to say goodbye. He would keep the promise he had made to her in Aunt Clare's byre. "But I wish I'd had more time to get meself prepared." Now, he would find work as soon as possible and would save to come get her. They wrote letters back and forth, both looking forward to the day they would again be together. Joseph told her of his efforts to find work, so far unsuccessful. "But I won't be giving up."

He hoped he would be allowed to stay with Aunt Clare in Kilkenny until he could accomplish his goals.

But the discussions began again.

"Ah, the poor lad . . ."

Joseph got out of bed, taking care not to disturb his sleeping cousins, and crept toward an open trap door. He didn't want to miss any words spoken softly. He had become an expert at eavesdropping, for how else could he learn the things he needed to know? He leaned over the trap door until he could see down into the room below.

The gathering was larger than usual. Aunts and uncles had come from as far away as Donegal. They were settling themselves around the fireplace, the men tilted back in their chairs, puffing clay pipes, filling the air with fragrant smoke. The women bent over their handiwork, keeping busy as they talked. Voices hummed and sentences overlapped, so eager was everyone to have his or her say.

"We must decide. Time is getting away . . ."

"Aye, he's toward his fifteenth year. Almost a man."

They all agreed that to be an orphan in Ireland was a sorry life. With no father to soften the way and no bit of land to be handed down to him, what sort of life awaited him but to join the poor souls who stood idly on street corners, wishing for work?

"We can't let that happen to him," Uncle Duffy said. "We must do better by him. We owe it to his brave father, rest his soul."

"Rest his soul," said the others, and pipes were taken from mouths, heads bowed briefly.

"I have a thought," said Timothy Shaughnessy. He was an uncle from Joseph's mother's side of the family. "As you know, me eldest son, Eamon, has been in America for several years now. He wrote to me, telling me of the fine job he has." A note of pride crept into Uncle Timothy's voice. "Working for a newspaper in a place called Memphis, Tennessee, he is. And 'tis my thinking that perhaps he could persuade his boss to hire Joseph. Maybe just to sweep floors and run errands and the like. Or if that doesn't work out, I'm sure Joseph could find something for himself. 'Tis said there are all manner of jobs to be had in America."

There was a general murmur of agreement.

Only Aunt Clare looked doubtful. "But how would we get him to America? Who has money for such a journey?"

"We could take up a collection among us," Uncle Duffy suggested. "I have a copper or two put by."

"Aye, we could all donate a mite."

And so Joseph's future in America was arranged.

No one thought to ask him if he wanted to go.

CHAPTER TWO

AMERICA - 1841

EAMON SHAUGHNESSY LEANED on the polished mahogany bar in Paddy Meaghan's Old Bell Tavern, sipping a pint and listening to the latest gossip. All around Memphis, folks were talking about the town's newest newspaper, laying odds it wouldn't survive. Giving it a year or two. Three at the most. Men stood on street corners, or sat in cafes and saloons, pouncing gleefully, giving the paper's founder, Colonel Henry Van Pelt, the treatment. After all, wasn't he a foreigner from way off in Kentucky? Why, if he were a local boy, he'd be onto the fact that no Democratic newspaper had ever lasted long in these Whig dominated parts.

"Poor man doesn't even have much money to keep him going, or so I've heard," one of the men at the bar said now, looking proud of himself for being privy to such inside information. "He ought to have more sense about him."

"How can you be so sure he has no sense about him?" Shaughnessy asked. A huge man, he was, with a mane of red hair. A man who liked to do his own thinking. And he thought they ought to give this new editor a chance. "I met him last week, when he came by to introduce himself to the Enquirer's staff and tell us about his plans to start a new paper, and I thought he had a fine, intelligent look about him."

"Looks can be deceiving," someone put in.

"I'll not argue that," said Shaughnessy. "But I still think we should wait and see what the man can accomplish. Faith and haven't we been needing someone with the gumption to give the Whigs their come-uppance?"

A man sitting on a stool at the end of the bar challenged Shaughnessy. "If you think so much of this here Colonel feller, why don't you quit the Enquirer and join up with him? I hear he's looking for a printer and he's going to have a hard time finding someone who'll be willing to take a chance with him. He'd likely be plumb grateful to you for jumping on his wagon."

"Sure and I may be doing that," said Shaughnessy.

He regretted immediately that he had been goaded into making such a rash statement. He was a married man. He couldn't give up a secure job with an established paper to go off on some risky venture – no matter how interesting it might be. He looked around the cavernous, beery-smelling barroom and wished he had gone home to his Molly, the way he should have, instead of stopping by to have just one drink with the boys. It was a habit that often seemed to get him into trouble. He told himself he ought to give it up. But he knew he wouldn't.

The next night, he decided to avoid the idle chatter at the bar and chose a table in a far corner of the room. He was enjoying the novelty of drinking alone when Colonel Van Pelt entered the tavern, causing a silence to fall over the place. Everyone stared at the newcomer. He was so obviously a gentleman, dressed as he was in a black broadcloth suit with a shirt so white it shone in the lamplight. He removed his broad-brimmed hat and made his way between tables.

Paddy Meaghan stood behind his bar, polishing and re-polishing a glass on his apron as the Colonel approached. "What's your pleasure?" he asked.

The Colonel appeared to consider. "Do you have any good whiskey?"

"Don't know how good it is," Paddy allowed. He took a bottle from a shelf behind him, poured amber liquid into a glass and pushed it and the bottle toward the Colonel.

"No, just the glass will do, thank you. How much?"

After laying the proper amount of silver on the bar, the Colonel looked around the room. "I was wondering. Does the man they call Shaughnessy happen to be here tonight?"

Paddy nodded toward Shaughnessy's corner, and the Colonel walked over, taking his glass with him. He introduced himself. "Henry Van Pelt's the name. I believe we met a few days ago at the Enquirer." He hesitated. "I'm not disturbing you, am I?"

"Not a bit of it." Shaughnessy murmured his name and stood to shake hands. "I just decided I'd like to get away from the usual blather at the bar. Won't you join me, sir?"

The two men settled into chairs, facing one another across the small table. The Colonel was even more distinguished looking up close, Shaughnessy thought, noting clear brown eyes, a high forehead and dark hair with a bit of silver at the sides. His beard was trimmed in a thin line along his jaw in the manner gaining favor with the ladies who, so it was said, considered this style more gentlemanly than a full beard. Shaughnessy himself was clean shaven. His Molly didn't like hair anywhere on a man's face.

Colonel Van Pelt took a swallow of his whiskey, then shuddered. "Can't seem to get good sipping whiskey here like you could in Kentucky." He paused, looking distressed. "Not that I'm disparaging Memphis. I find it an intriguing place, actually. Not genteel like most southern towns. But it has an interesting frontier atmosphere."

Shaughnessy grinned. "And lots of frontier hell-raising to go with it. Makes for lively newspaper columns."

"Sounds good to me." The Colonel pushed his drink aside and leaned forward. "And that, actually, is why I wanted to talk to you. I hear you expressed an interest in my new publication."

"Ah well, you know how it is. A fellow says something just on impulse and it gets bandied about, passed on, made into something it's not meant to be. Truth is, I wish you luck with your efforts, but I'm a married man and I've been working for the Enquirer for a number of years. Got myself in pretty good there. It would be foolish of me to change."

"I understand. Especially when there's no guarantee in what I'm setting out to do." He gave Shaughnessy a boyish grin. "And yes, I know what I'm up against. Not much gets past an old newspaper man. I'm aware of the talk that's going on. The wagers. And I know about the three Democratic papers that failed in the last three years."

"Aye. 'Tis all true. The Whig-loving Enquirer seems to have a strangle-hold on the town. Darn shame, too. Most Whigs I know are self-serving scalawags. Always catering to the rich and taking advantage of the working man. That's my own opinion, of course."

"An opinion shared by many. Myself included."

Van Pelt reached for his whiskey, this time getting several swallows down. "Actually, I knew about the newspaper situation in Memphis before I came here and it occurred to me someone should do something about it. I don't expect an easy time of it, but I believe a man can do anything if he's determined enough."

As the Colonel warmed to his subject, Shaughnessy found his enthusiasm contagious. Wouldn't it be grand to work for such a man? A man who actually cared, who seemed willing to spend his life's savings to give the plain man a chance to have a say in things? More and more, Shaughnessy found himself longing to be part of the new paper. He heard himself saying that maybe, just maybe, he might consider leaving the Enquirer. "I'll talk to the missus," he said, "and see if she's up to the risk that's in it."

Two days later, the Colonel took Shaughnessy to see the place he had chosen for his first office. He steered his buggy through tall black trees, then followed a narrow road beside a river bank until they came to a small clapboard building.

"We're not exactly in the heart of town out here with the Wolfe River flowing right by our front door and on into the Mississippi," he admitted, as he unlocked the door of the building and went about opening windows. "But we'll be moving to a more business–like area as soon as I can afford it. This will have to do for now. What do you think? Are you with me?"

Shaughnessy hesitated. "Well, Mrs. Shaughnessy said I should follow my own inclinations. But there is one more thing that wants discussing before I resign from the Enquirer." As he talked, Shaughnessy was wandering about a large room, mentally measuring, deciding where walls should be built. "I need to have a talk about the one thing that didn't occur to me at first. You see, I have this young cousin – Joseph, he's called - who is at this very moment traveling across the ocean on his way to America. The lad is about fourteen, almost fifteen, and is orphaned – his father was killed while printing leaflets for the Irish cause – and I promised my father I would take care of him. I had made arrangements for him to work for the Enquirer but now" -- Shaughnessy shrugged – "if I change papers, they'll likely look upon me as a deserter and won't be wanting to hire any kin of mine. Do you think we could use him here?"

The Colonel tugged at a sideburn as he thought the matter over. "No doubt we could use him. In fact, we need him. But the trouble is, the paper can't afford another employee until we get more subscribers. Have you thought of finding something else for the boy to do? I hear Mr. Gilhooley is looking for a stable boy."

"Ah -- but Joseph has his heart set on newspaper work, or so I was informed."

"I see. Well, perhaps in time we could take him on as an apprentice."

"Aye, and I could train him to be a printer. I haven't seen Joseph since he was a lad of six or so but I understand he's a bright one. Eager to learn."

"Well then, it sounds like you've made your decision. You'll be coming to work for me?"

"It's a deal."

"A deal." They shook hands.

With great enthusiasm, they went to work. Shaughnessy built walls and tall book shelves to divide the building into offices and pressroom. The Colonel furnished his office with a used desk and old cabinets. He also made final arrangements for buying an old press from the Western World, the most recent Democratic newspaper to fail. Several boxes of type had been included in the deal along with a list of two hundred subscribers.

The Colonel planned to put out one newspaper a week at first. Even that, he admitted, would be a financial strain. By comparison, their rival was an established semi-weekly with more than a thousand subscribers.

The town gossips were right, of course. The odds were against the new newspaper, no denying that. To make matters worse, the Whigs were riding even higher and mightier than usual. Their prestige had been boosted by the recent victory of the Whig party at the polls – the election of their candidate, William Henry Harrison, to the presidency of the United States.

"A most gloomy hour for the Democratic party," the Colonel told Shaughnessy as they sat in his office discussing the election. "I put my heart into campaigning for Van Buren's re-election. I never cared much for that confounded Whig, William Henry Harrison. A boastful, self-centered man, to my way of thinking. I fought to keep him out of power and I intend to continue fighting him every way I can." The Colonel rose from his desk to pace about the room. "Do you see now, why our newspaper must succeed? We're giving Memphis Democrats the chance they deserve to have a voice in the country's affairs. And my first goal is to point out that a wrong choice was made in the last election. I intend to appeal to the sober second thoughts of the people."

From this idea came the name the Colonel had been searching for. He would call his paper The Memphis Appeal. He spent hours composing an editorial, explaining just why he had chosen this name.

When the newly-bought Washington hand-press arrived, Shaughnessy constructed a platform for it and assembled the iron and wood machine. As he worked, he thought often of Joseph, hoping he was having a safe journey. He ought to be almost across the ocean by now, Shaughnessy figured. Soon he would board a steamboat in New Orleans and travel up the Mississippi to Memphis. Though Shaughnessy had looked forward to Joseph's arrival, he was a bit apprehensive about the bad news he had for him. He had heard just how much Joseph wanted to work for a newspaper. How would he take it when he heard he would have to start out as a stable boy?

CHAPTER THREE

JOSEPH OPENED HIS EYES to look up at a wide sky filled with fading morning stars. An American sky, he thought. Only half-awake, he had to remind himself that he, Joseph Harrigan, was traveling up a river in a strange land, stretched out on the steamboat called the Delta Star. He lay for a while, listening to the creak of the boat's paddle wheel as it turned, splashing in and out of the water. As a deck passenger, he had no cabin, no bed of his own, but he thought it pleasant to be sleeping in the open, on rough boards with his head pillowed on his knapsack.

He was surrounded by the shadowy mounds of other passengers, huddled together in family groups, their possessions piled around them. It would be hours before everyone was awake, hours before breakfast would be served, but he was too excited for more sleep. He stood, stretched, then strapped his knapsack to his back. He would go down to the texas-deck, he decided, and wait for Jeremiah to come out of the galley and perhaps slip him a bit of buttered bread as he sometimes did.

Joseph and Jeremiah, the Delta Star's cabin boy, had become friends. As they were leaving New Orleans, Joseph had seen Jeremiah shaking a tablecloth over the railing. Joseph had never known a black person, and he was curious. He wanted to find out more about this boy who, like him, was not quite man-sized and probably about the same age, and yet so different. One day, after he had helped Jeremiah dump a large sack of garbage over the stern, their friendship had begun.

Joseph felt he couldn't have chosen anyone better for his first friend in America. They seemed made for one another, the way Joseph was bursting with questions and Jeremiah so eager to show off his knowledge.

Joseph had asked about the giant birds with huge filmy wings wandering about the marshes and was informed airily that they were great blue herons. And the birds with wrinkled brown pouches under their chins -- pelicans. Jeremiah knew the names of every tree and bush along the riverside, from the gnarly old, moss-hung cypress trees growing out of the water to the paw-paws. Whenever they tied up at a settlement, he knew not only the name of the town but much of its history.

Joseph asked about the strange, ark-like rafts he had seen bobbing down the wide brown river. Some were keelboats, Jeremiah told him, but those without keels were called flatboats. And the men who steered these boats with long poles--the 'flatboatmans' he called them--were an ornery lot.

"I stays away from them," said Jeremiah. "And you be smart to do the same."

Joseph learned that Jeremiah was a slave. "I belongs to the Cap'n," he told Joseph, sounding proud of the fact. Joseph, who had seen pictures of slaves working in cotton fields, had trouble fitting his friend into that role. More like a part owner of the boat, he seemed, the way he showed Joseph around. Let him see the fancy dining room with real silver where the rich folks ate. Took him down to the engine room, led him along the row of furnaces with flames leaping from their open doors. Got him invited into the pilot house to meet the captain and the pilot.

"I could run this old boat if'n they'd allow me," Jeremiah confided to Joseph. "Steer it all the way up to the Ohio all by myself. I knows every inch of this here Mississippi river. Knows all its shallows and snags and sand-bars." He grinned and stretched himself so he would look taller. "The Delta Star would be in mighty safe hands if'n I could take her wheel for a spell."

Now, as Joseph made his way down to the texas-deck in the pre-dawn light, he smiled, remembering Jeremiah's boast. He had a feeling his friend could do anything if he put his mind to it. The captain himself had said that Jeremiah was the best cabin boy he'd ever had.

While Joseph waited for Jeremiah to come out of the galley, he leaned over the railing, trying to forget the rumbling in his empty stomach. The sun was rising now, turning the sky above the trees pink and gold. Mist drifted up from the river. Finally, Jeremiah appeared on deck carrying a tray covered with a cloth. "Hey there, Joseph," he said. "You up mighty early. Wish I had time to stop and visit but the cap'n, he's in the worstest mood. Fit to be tied about something. But," he added, before he hurried off, "I have good news. Today be the day you been waiting for. Ought to be in Memphis 'fore noontime."

Delighted to hear this, Joseph turned his attention back to the passing scenery. He had been fretting over the possibility of getting carried past his destination and he intended to keep a careful eye out until they docked at Memphis. The steamboat was gliding past a thick forest growing close to the edge of the river. Tangled shrubbery with bright colored flowers covered the bank and the air was musty and heavy with the smell of blossoms and damp earth. The sun was beginning to send out rays of light but the tall trees, draped with ropey vines, blocked out most of it out. Peering into the gloom, Joseph thought it had the look of a forest which had been there forever. A wild, strange, untamed land he had come to, but there was no going back now.

His relatives had sacrificed too much to get him here, scraping together almost three pounds for his fare across the sea and another pound to pay for his passage up the Mississippi, money Joseph knew came hard to them. But they seemed pleased to be helping him. Aunt Clare had sewn a knapsack out of scraps of linen from an old bed coverlet. In the knapsack, he had packed all his belongings: an extra set of clothes, a sweater, some lumpy socks knitted by his young cousins, a kerchief or two, and an older cousin's outgrown shoes that Aunt Clare insisted he take. He would be growing into them soon, she said, and he would be glad for the good still in them.

To these things, Joseph had added a small daguerreotype of Bridget, his most prized possession. He hoped Bridget wouldn't be in trouble if her parents discovered it missing. She had been devastated when he had written to tell her he was going to America, even though he had reassured her over and over that he would send for her as soon as he could earn money for her passage.

Just before he set out on his journey, Aunt Clare had added a package to his knapsack. It contained some salt pork, dried beef, oranges and onions. "And I've baked you a supply of oaten 'journey cakes'. See, I have them wrapped in this cloth."

She made room for the white bundle in his knapsack. "They're hard to chew, I'll admit – made of oats and water and a wee bit of ginger, they are – but they have a lasting quality and can be a great blessing when the weather is rough or the food on the ship is not fit to eat."

She brushed his hair from his eyes and settled his old cap on his head. "Ah, don't look so sad, Joseph. I know you're frightened to be making such a fearsome voyage alone, but it won't be as desperate as you expect. And when you get to Memphis, your cousin Eamon Shaughnessy will be meeting you at the wharf."

"But how will I recognize him if he's among a crowd of strangers?"

Aunt Clare had smiled. "Ah, you'll have no trouble knowing him. A great show of a man he is, much taller than most, with flaming red hair. A man not easily overlooked. Everything will be fine when you get to America, I just know it will."

Joseph hoped Aunt Clare was right. She had certainly been right about the journey cakes, for they had kept him well while he was crossing the stormy seas confined in an over-crowded, stinking hold beneath closed hatches. He wished he had one of the cakes now, he thought, for he didn't want to leave the railing and stand in the long line to get the tea and toast offered to deck passengers.

Just after noon, there was a stir of excitement as the Delta Star cruised slowly around a bend in the river.

"There's Chickasaw bluff," someone cried, pointing toward a mound of red earth rising beside the river.

Passengers bound for Memphis began to hurry about getting their belongings together. Since Joseph wore his knapsack strapped to his back at all times, he had nothing to gather. He was free to watch as the steamboat drew alongside the bluff and cruised beneath its steep banks. The great wall of red clay fascinated him. He noted with interest that layers of purple and violet made irregular, horizontal stripes across the red clay. Gullies cut deep swaths from top to bottom.

Jeremiah joined Joseph at the railing. "Ain't it the beatenist sight ever?" he asked, his voice hushed. "Ever see clay all colors like that? And those gullies. They's put there by buckets of rain running down its sides during the rainy season."

"Holy Moses," was all Joseph could think of to say.

After a moment, Jeremiah cleared his throat. "I come to tell you something. It 'pears we might not be stopping at Memphis."

"Why? Why not?" Joseph asked, his voice rising.

"'Cause the flatboatmans are on a rampage. Heard the Cap'n say they were raising cain because Memphis has started charging a wharf fee, trying to keep them from landing and hanging around. The cap'n says he won't be stopping there this time if it looks like there's gonna be real trouble. He mighty upset about it. Says we oughta just by-pass Memphis this time. But don't worry, you can get off at Randolph and make your way back."

Having delivered this shattering message, Jeremiah said he had to get back to work and disappeared. Joseph slumped against the railing, his heart pounding. If they didn't stop at Memphis, how could he get off there? His greatest fear seemed about to come true. And where was this place Jeremiah had called Randolph? How would he get back to Memphis? How would he find his cousin?

As the steamboat traveled on upriver, Joseph saw an assortment of ramshackle buildings clinging to the crest of the bluff. Rough shacks were also built along the river bank. Nothing grand of course, but there must be more to this Memphis, things he wouldn't see until he climbed to the top of the bluff.

Joseph breathed a sigh of relief when the Delta Star sounded its landing bell after all, and headed shoreward. He went to the bow, shaded his eyes from the glaring sun, and studied the waiting crowd. He didn't see anyone he could rightly count on as being his cousin. The wharf was teeming with men, and at least half of them were huge. Bigger than most. Which one would be Eamon Shaughnessy? He struggled to remain confident, telling himself that his cousin would no doubt recognize him when he saw him. Putting his hands in the pockets of his knickers, he stood tall. His fine life in America was about to begin.

Once ashore, however, he felt his confidence slipping away. All but buried in a swirling rush of humanity, he edged his way forward, uncertain, confused. After a while he began to wonder. Was this the answer to his dreams, this country that brushed him aside, ignored him, stepped on his toes? To save himself from more trampling, he moved to the edge of the wharf. There, he saw men with long poles propelling a flatboat toward shore. The boat was roofed over with weathered boards. Under its roof, a cow and two pigs were tethered. Like Noah's Ark, thought Joseph. When the flatboat reached the wharf, the men jumped ashore.

"Where's that wharf-master?" one of them demanded, swinging his pole above his head. "Who does he think he is, charging us a fee just for landing here?"

"Yeah, we'll give him a fee to remember us by." With menacing snarls, the men shoved their way forward and gathered around a stocky bald man.

Murmurs of concern spread through the crowd. Were the flatboatmen aiming to cause the poor wharf-master trouble? Would they be going on a rampage again?

People scurried to get away from the brewing conflict. In the confusion, Joseph was almost knocked into the river. He decided it would be wise to wait for his cousin somewhere else.

He would climb up the rutted road to the top of the bluff.

Sure, he thought, he would be easier to find if he wasn't hidden in a crowd.

Mud clutched at his brogans as he hurried up the steep road, eager to have a look at his new home. "Memphis, Tennessee," he murmured, liking the way the name rolled off his tongue, liking the way it reminded him of strange, mysterious hideaways, the kind he'd read about in books. Sure, a name so fine must belong to a grand city.

But when he reached the crest of the bluff, he was sorely disappointed. "Why 'tis no more than a wee hamlet," he thought, "A wee hamlet scratched into raw land." All brown and gray angles, it was, with rough buildings squatting in rows beside muddy streets.

Overcome by a sudden aching wave of homesickness, he yearned for Ireland with her soft, rolling green hills, for cottages with thatched roofs, for easy, friendly people. For Bridget.

He turned away from the town. Below him, the Delta Star – his boat, he considered it – was preparing to leave. Clouds of black smoke billowed from its chimney, wafting up the sweet scent of burning wood. Joseph heard the steamship sound its parting bell, saw it back into the center of the wide river, then turn north. Even though he and Jeremiah had assured one another they would get together whenever the Delta Star tied up at Memphis, he was sad to see his friend leaving. And sad to see the boat which had become like a home to him travel on without him.

He grasped the straps which bound his knapsack to his back, drawing comfort from the familiar feel of the rough cloth. Small comfort to be sure, but somehow the soft nubby cotton made it less painful to watch the Delta Star disappear around a bend in the river. It was foolish, he knew, but he felt deserted. Abandoned.

Where was the cousin who was supposed to meet him?

Perhaps he shouldn't have left the wharf. Maybe, if he went back, it would be less crowded. But when he started down the road toward the river, he noted two more flatboats had joined the first, their crews as rambunctious as the first. Joseph hesitated, then spotted a grassy mound beside the road. It was halfway up the bluff where he could be seen from above and below. He would wait there.

He settled on the grass, untied his knapsack and laid it on the ground beside him. Wearing it so constantly had driven painful raw marks on his shoulders.

Several times during his journey he had considered lightening his load by throwing away the heavy shoes he was supposed to grow into, but every time he tried to do so, he saw Aunt Clare's soft eyes chastising him for wastefulness. He had always obeyed his aunts and uncles, especially Aunt Clare. He supposed that was why he hadn't protested when the relatives had told him of their plans to send him away. He was accustomed to letting others have charge of his life. And he was lured by the promise of a job on a newspaper. He hadn't dared to hope for such good fortune, but as soon as he heard about his cousin's offer, he knew that fate meant to be kind to him. He could hardly wait to begin his new job.

His thoughts were interrupted as more shouts arose from the wharf. Loud, angry shouts. Several boatmen waved their poles at the poor wharf-master, who darted away from them and scrambled up the side of the bluff. The boatmen followed, lashing their cane poles toward the fleeing man. Joseph heard a thwack of wood against backside, heard the wharf-master's yelps of pain.

"We'll give you your fee, you egg-sucking son of a mud turtle," one of the boatmen shouted.

"Gol-danged flea-bitten dawg."

Intrigued by the angry men and their colorful curses, Joseph failed to notice they were headed straight toward him.

Too late, much too late, he scrambled to his feet, snatched up his knapsack and tried to get out of their way. The wharf-master managed to dodge him, puffing by, eyes wide with fear, but a boatman skidded into Joseph, knocking him to the ground. Others pounded over him. When he tried to stand he was shoved down again. As the last man ran toward him, Joseph swung his knapsack and slammed it into the man's shin.

"Why you dirty little bastard," the man yelled. "Who do ya think ya are?"

"Leave me be," Joseph said. "You—you—" -- What were those words he had heard? --"You gol-danged flea-bitten mud turtle."

"Mud turtle is it yer calling me?" A sneer twisted the pock-marked face. "You insolent pup." He grabbed Joseph's arm. Joseph swung his knapsack again, this time landing a blow square in his foe's stomach. The man doubled over, his breath going out with a whoosh. When he recovered enough to straighten up, he grabbed the knapsack, held its straps in large, knobby hands, swung it in a circle about his head. He let go and the bag sailed through the air.

"Me possessions!" Joseph cried out. He watched as the small bundle rolled end over end down the hill until it splashed in the water beside the wharf and sank rapidly. "Tis all I have in the world," he moaned softly. "I'll get you for this," he shouted, and dashed after the disappearing flatboatmen. He was too distraught to realize at first that his legs were churning through air, that someone had grabbed him around the middle and his feet were no longer on the ground.

"Hold it, me lad," said a voice, close to his ear.

Though he twisted and turned, Joseph couldn't break away. "Put me down," he demanded. "Put me down or I'll break your arm."

His captor laughed. "Break me arm, will you now? 'Tis spunky you are. But those are mean critters you were fooling with. You're going to get yourself killed chasing after the likes of them."

The lilting words cut through Joseph's anger. He stopped struggling and hung limp. "You're Irish," he said.

"So I am." The man put Joseph down and extended a hand in greeting. "And would you be Joseph?"

"Aye."

"Then I'm your cousin, Eamon Shaughnessy. But folks around here call me Shaughnessy."

"Shaughnessy," repeated Joseph. His hand disappeared in his cousin's huge paw. He tried not to wince as Shaughnessy's vigorous pumping brought to mind recently acquired wounds. He looked up at his cousin. He was, as Aunt Clare had put it, a great show of a man, with flaming hair. He wore a vest and a striped, collarless shirt with elastic bands above the elbows of his long sleeves. The clothes of a man of medium importance, thought Joseph. A man with respectable work to do.

"'Tis a pleasure to be shaking the hand of a lad who has the backbone to tangle with the fearsome flatboat men," Shaughnessy said.

Abashed at the praise, Joseph lowered his head. "Aw, I only went after them because they knocked me down. And they threw all me belongings in the river. My hand-knitted socks. Me extra sweater. Everything I had, even—" he faltered and drew in a long breath—"even me only picture of Bridget."

"A dirty shame. And this Bridget? Would she not be your sweetheart?"

"Aye." He was silent for a moment, figuring ways to recover his loss. "Is the river deep near the wharf?"

"Deep enough. And the current is swift. By now, your lass's picture is no doubt on its way to Vicksburg. You'd have a devil of a time finding anything in all that murky water and you'd likely get yourself drowned in the trying." He paused. "And I'd say you've had enough punishment. You're going to have a dandy shiner. And your cheek needs doctoring."

Joseph looked down, saw that blood had dripped on his jacket and the sleeve was torn. "Me jacket is ruined. Me only jacket."

"Never mind. I'll take you to Molly. My wife is a kind soul. She'll fix you up and find pleasure in it. Now, I ought to be thinking about getting back to the office. I've only to stop by the Wells Fargo office and collect the mail, then I'll be finished with my errands and I'll take you to meet my boss, the Colonel." He sighed. "It will be a help when we can hire you so I can turn over these chores to you. And the Colonel promised he would hire you as soon as he can afford it. I can hardly wait for the day to come."

Joseph looked at him, puzzled. "Would I not be starting right away?"

Shaughnessy hesitated. "Ah well, I'm afraid I have a wee bit of bad news. You see, since I wrote to my father about getting you a job at the Enquirer, I've gone to work for a new publication. A newspaper newly born, it is. And we can't afford to hire anyone right away. But don't fret. I've found you a job at Gilhooley's Livery Stable."

"A stable?"

"Aye." They had reached the top of the bluff and were now walking down the main street. Shaughnessy pointed out a huge barn of a building with a weathered sign. 'Gilhooley's Livery Stable' was printed above the barn doors in large black letters. And in smaller letters, 'Horses and rigs to rent. Also board horses.' "Of course, you can look for something else if you wish. But the job pays well. Better than most. Gilhooley is always looking for stable boys."

Joseph felt a sudden need for more air. He took a deep shaky breath. A stable boy? Had he traveled all this way, left everything and everyone he loved to become a stable boy? Did that mean, he wondered, that it might be years before he would be working for a newspaper? And most important, would Bridget still wait for him? He shook his head, wanting desperately to make Shaughnessy's words go away.

CHAPTER FOUR

SHAUGHNESSY PUT A HAND on his shoulder. "Now don't feel bad, son. It's only temporary. I promise you'll be a part of the Memphis Appeal before too long."

Promises, thought Joseph. Even though people meant well, a promise wasn't a thing you could depend on. But he said nothing else – what was the use?

He followed as Shaughnessy hurried down the boardwalk. "I'm in a bit of a hurry," he told Joseph. "Still have to get the Appeal printed so it can be delivered on time. 'Tis the twenty-first of April, the day the very first issue of our little paper is due to make its appearance. My boss will be very upset if it's put out late."

Joseph could only nod. He was getting out of breath trying to keep up with Shaughnessy's long-legged steps. He was glad when the big man paused to pat the nose of an ancient sway-back mule hitched to a rickety wagon at the side of the road. "This is Old

Abby," he told Joseph. "Helps me deliver papers. She's not much to look at, I'll admit. Almost blind, she is, but she can still pull a load if she's handled right."   Shaughnessy removed a pile of rolled up newspapers from the front seat of the wagon. "Just occurred to me, Joseph, you've had a hard day. Would you like to sit and rest a bit while I go pick up the mail?"

"Aye, I would." Gratefully, Joseph climbed into the wagon.

"Won't take me long and you can keep Old Abby company." Shaughnessy said. He crossed the road and hurried toward a building which bore the sign, "Wells Fargo Office", returning soon with a packet of mail. Dropping the mail in the back of the wagon beside the newspapers, he untied the reins from a hitching post and settled into the seat beside Joseph. He had to give Old Abby several light taps with the reins before she decided to move. "Come on now, Old Abby," he urged. "We've got a ways to go." He explained to Joseph that the Appeal's office was located out on the banks of a little river. "The Wolfe River, it is. Runs through the woods into the Mississippi."

Joseph only nodded. He was adding up facts in his head – an office stuck out somewhere on a river bank, a rickety wagon and a half-blind mule for transportation. Sure, it did not have the sound of a thriving business that might soon be taking on more workers.

They moved slowly down the muddy street between log buildings and turned on a road which led away from town. As they continued on, the dwellings grew farther and farther apart. They traveled along a rutted road. On each side of the road, thick trees with vines draped over their gnarled limbs almost blotted out the afternoon sun. In the gloom, bright colored birds flitted from tree to tree. Shaughnessy slipped the reins beneath his leg and reached for a wicker basket behind him. As he set it on the floor between them and removed a white cloth, a tempting cinnamon-apple aroma arose. To be polite, Joseph looked away. He didn't want to seem a beggar but he couldn't resist looking at the food.

"Hungry are you?" Shaughnessy asked.

"Aye," Joseph admitted.

"I'll share what I have with you. Me Molly makes a delicious apple pie and churns the sweetest butter in all of Tennessee. Here, try one of her bread and butter sandwiches. The bread's fresh baked."

Joseph bit into thick slabs of bread, generously buttered. "Yummm," he muttered, mouth full. "You must have a fine wife."

"I do, indeed. She's a tiny thing, me Molly, but there's few with a bigger heart. She'll likely take you right under her wing, she's that tender." Shaughnessy took another bite of bread, chewed and swallowed before adding in a soft voice, speaking almost as if he had forgotten Joseph was there, "I just don't see how God can keep doing her thataway."

Joseph wondered what God was doing to Molly, but a glance at Shaughnessy's profile, grim, unsmiling now, told him he mustn't ask. They finished the bread and Shaughnessy divided a large slice of apple pie, laid the pieces on napkins. Joseph ate his share with dreamy appreciation.

When Shaughnessy was ready to talk again, he spoke of impersonal things. "Something should be done about those flatboat men," he said. "They're the scourge of Memphis. Like maggots in a cabbage patch, they are." He picked up the reins. "Oh, some are harmless enough, just farmers setting out to make a few extra dollars between planting time, wanting to raise a bit of hell while the home-folks aren't looking. But the others, those who live on the river the year round, they can be meaner'n striped snakes. They'd as soon kill a person as look at him. A shame it is the way they terrorize the decent folks of Memphis." Joseph only nodded in reply. He'd heard enough of flatboat men for one day and didn't want to hear more. He saw that they were now traveling along the bank of a small lazy river. Lulled by the hum of insects and the thud of the mule's feet on the spongy ground, he was soon asleep. He slept until they came to a stop. Blinking his eyes open, he saw a white building facing the river, trees rising around it. "Is this the Appeal's office?" he asked. "Right here in the middle of nowhere?"

"'Tis," said Shaughnessy. "I guess it doesn't look too inviting but we'll no doubt move into town later on. Come along now and meet the Colonel."

Joseph followed Shaughnessy into the building and through a large room containing an iron press and work tables. He paused beside the press, admired it, almost reached out a hand to touch it.

"Have a look at this, Joseph," Shaughnessy said. "These are the galleys all ready for the press. I have all the type set for four pages. Our paper will be a small weekly but it's been carefully planned. The Colonel wanted to make his first issue as impressive as possible. The birth of a great newspaper, he called it. He's chosen the masthead with care, written and re-written editorials and gathered material for seven columns on each of the four pages. Can't you see what a fine newspaper we're going to have?"

"I can," Joseph said with a smile.

"Colonel's office is back here behind the book shelves," Shaughnessy said. He knocked on an unpainted door and was told to enter. Joseph hung back, waiting politely to be asked in. He could see the Colonel sitting behind a cluttered desk.

"Ah Shaughnessy, you're here with the mail. Good." The Colonel pushed paste pot and shears aside to make room for the newspapers and mail pouch. Then he saw Joseph. "And this is, I suppose, your cousin just off the boat. Come in, lad."

Joseph hesitated. Seeing the neatly dressed Colonel made him aware of how dirty and ragged he was. Shaughnessy nudged him forward. "Aye, I'd like you to meet Joseph Harrigan," he said. "And Joseph, this is Colonel Henry Van Pelt, editor of the Memphis Weekly Appeal." His introduction of the Colonel seemed almost accompanied by a flourish of trumpets, so proud he obviously was of his boss.

"How do you do, Joseph," Colonel Van Pelt said, standing to reach over his desk and shake Joseph's rather grimy hand. He looked at Shaughnessy, a question on his face.

"Had a bit of a haymaker with some flatboat men," Shaughnessy said. "He was going after them with fists flying when I got there. Had to drag him away."

The Colonel studied Joseph. "Well, young fellow, I'm impressed that you stood up to those scoundrels. Most of the folks around here tend to go into hiding whenever they come ashore. Just let them take over the town. We could use more like you."

"That we could," Shaughnessy agreed.

"It's too bad we can't hire the spunky lad right off." The Colonel tugged at one of his sideburns, seeming to ponder the problem. "Well, we'll hope for better times so we can take on an apprentice soon."

Joseph's eyes lit up. "An apprentice? Are you saying I could learn to run the press? Sure and you wouldn't even have to pay me for that."

"Sounds like an offer a man could hardly turn down," the Colonel said. "But I'm afraid there's more to it than that. Someone would have to feed and clothe you and--"

"Why, Molly and I could take him in for a while if that's all we're lacking," Shaughnessy said, sounding surprised he hadn't thought of it before. "I'm sure Molly wouldn't mind setting an extra plate, at least until we can afford a boarding house room for our new apprentice."

And so it was settled. Joseph and Shaughnessy went back to the pressroom. Shaughnessy examined the galleys. "Want to be sure they don't contain any errors," he told Joseph. They were startled to hear a soft moan from the Colonel and rushed back to his office.

"What is it?" Shaughnessy asked.

The Colonel handed him a letter.

"This will inform you that President Harrison is dead," Shaughnessy read aloud. "The president caught a chill during the inauguration. Then he got pneumonia, lingered a bit, and died a month after taking office." Shaughnessy looked up. "Good grief, and we're just receiving the news."

Elbows on desk, the Colonel held his head as if he had suddenly developed a terrible headache. "Don't know why we didn't hear sooner. But then, I do know, considering how slow news travels across the country. Someone needs to solve that problem. And someday they no doubt will. But right now, we have other things to consider. It seems that our very first issue may be late."

"No it won't." Shaughnessy was firm. "We can still get it out on time."

The Colonel sighed. "I don't know. We'll have to tear out the columns you've already set so nicely. Re-write editorials to make them smaller. But we have no choice. Scoundrel or not, Harrison was the president of our country. And though it leaves a bitter taste in my mouth, we must pay the proper respect to a fallen leader."

"Let's get to it," Shaughnessy said. "Joseph, can you read?"

"Of course," Joseph answered, looking insulted.

"Then you can help with the proofreading and the folding."

A flurry of activity followed. No one seemed to have time to explain to Joseph what they were trying to accomplish so he followed orders, helped where he could. He didn't understand until the Colonel held up the first copy of the printed paper. It was bordered in black.

"This," said the Colonel, "is the very first issue of the Appeal – dressed in a black border of mourning for our former enemy. I can just hear the talk in the pubs. But I say, if we can survive this, we can survive anything."

Without further discussion, Shaughnessy printed two-hundred issues of the paper. Joseph folded them as fast as he could.

The sun was just rising when they finally hitched up Old Abby and loaded the newspapers in the wagon. Joseph went along to help with the delivery.

"Hopefully, we're getting them delivered in time for the master of each house to enjoy while he has his coffee," said Shaughnessy. "And when we've finished I'll take you home. You're going to be a great surprise to Molly. But I'm thinking she'll enjoy having someone to mother and will be delighted to take you in."

CHAPTER FIVE

THE FIRST LETTER JOSEPH WROTE to Bridget after he arrived in Memphis was filled with cheerful optimism. He assured her that he had arrived safely and in good health. "The trip was difficult, but well worth the taking," he wrote. "Would you believe, I'm already working for a newspaper? A newspaper called 'The Weekly Appeal'.

"I almost didn't get the job, but my new boss, Colonel Van Pelt, hired me after I proved my worth in a most unexpected way." He told her about working all night to help change the borders of the newspaper's very first edition in order to meet its deadline, and how the Colonel had decided to hire him even though he couldn't afford to pay him. At least not right away. "But I'd work for nothing for such a fine man, so I would," he wrote.

"Don't be fretting, though. As soon as I start getting paid, I'll save money for your fare so we can be together again. For the present, Shaughnessy and his wife, Molly, have agreed to give me shelter. Molly is a lovely lady with dark eyes and hair and skin white as milk. She says she'll be more than pleased to have me as a guest until I can get a room in a boarding house. She's recovering from the birth of a wee son who lived only two hours and she says the tragedy has made a great hole in her heart. She insists it will help take her mind off her sorrow if she has someone to mother. And mother me, she does. Reminds me of Aunt Clare. I'm grateful not to have to live alone, for I miss you so very much."

" I'd like to think of some flowery words to tell you how much, but I must get back to work. Had a hard time finding a spare moment to write this letter, but I will write again soon. And often. Just know that I long for you with all my heart. Yours forever, Joseph."

Joseph loved working for the Appeal. He enjoyed folding papers and tying them into bundles. Even enjoyed straightening supplies and sweeping the floors, for he liked to be close by while the Colonel scribbled editorials and Shaughnessy set the type and printed the weekly edition of the Appeal. For Joseph, it reminded him of the days when he had watched his father operate the small hand-press on their dining table.

It seemed to Joseph that the Colonel was very much like his father. And Shaughnessy was a great teacher. Each day, he taught Joseph more about putting out a newspaper, how to make ink out of mineral oil and lamp black, how to set type. It was also Joseph's job to see to it that newsprint and other supplies were always on hand.

Joseph's letters to Bridget were filled with happy descriptions of his work. "Shaughnessy says I'm his apprentice," he wrote. "Or as some call it, a 'printer's devil'. The hours are long and the work hard and grubby--so grubby that I often look in a mirror and see the blackened face of a creature from some devil's world. But I don't mind a bit. I'm training to become a journeyman printer so I can soon afford to send for you."

A few weeks later, he wrote, "I'm actually learning how to operate the press now. With Shaughnessy at my side, of course. Today I learned how to apply 'kiss pressure'. That's a term that newspapermen use. It means applying the exact amount of pressure needed to make a mark without tearing the paper. I like the term 'kiss pressure'. Brings to mind how I was pleasured when applying the exact amount of pressure to your soft lips. How I long to kiss you again. Well, I'm sounding a bit mush-mouthed so -- back to work."

As Shaughnessy gained confidence in Joseph, he began to allow him to hitch up Old Abby and go into town to gather supplies and fetch the mail.

Joseph found these trips exciting. There was so much going on, so much to see. He loved the bustle of city life and looked forward to the day when the Appeal could move into town.

Whenever the Delta Star came to town, Joseph and Jeremiah met on the wharf to visit. Once he even took Jeremiah out to show him around the Appeal building and introduce him to Shaughnessy and the Colonel.

The letter Joseph wrote to Bridget on his fifteenth birthday glowed with praise for the Appeal and Memphis. "The Appeal has made great progress in the past year," he wrote. "Keeping pace with Memphis, it is. And such a town Memphis is for growing. Every time I go into town to pick up supplies and fetch the mail, I ride along to the sound of screeching saws, pounding hammers and axes, the crash of falling trees. The forest is being pushed farther and farther back and new buildings are sprouting like weeds. Ah, you're going to enjoy living in such a fine place."

As usual, he didn't mention the muddy streets. Or the saloons. Or the occasional bears he saw rummaging in trash cans on the edge of town. Or the flatboat men.

As he sealed the envelope, he felt a twinge of guilt. Was it right not to tell her about the problems she would be facing in Memphis? Should he not be preparing her for the town as it really was? Ah well, there was always hope for improvement. He'd heard Shaughnessy and the Colonel talking, saying that the new mayor, Will Speckernagle had the guts to tame the boatmen and civilize Memphis.

Any day now, the flatboat men were threatening to gather for another riot, but "Old Speck", as admiring constituents called him, had promised he would take care of the matter. Recently, he had organized a volunteer militia to uphold the laws. He'd appointed Captain Ruth, a retired army man, to be their leader. It was said by those in the know, that Captain Ruth was a daring and experienced fighter, completely fearless no matter how overwhelming his enemy might be.

Sure, Memphis was in good hands and Joseph had decided there was no use alarming Bridget about troubles that would no doubt be taken care of by the time she got there.

On a warm day in late May, Joseph hitched Old Abby to the wagon, climbed aboard, and set out for his weekly trip into town. He was in a fine mood, hoping for a chance to meet with Jeremiah. He hadn't seen him in quite a while and he figured the Delta Star ought to be stopping at Memphis before too much longer. As he rode along, he noticed that the woods were unusually quiet. Birds were singing but he heard no hammering or sawing. The building projects he passed seemed to be deserted. When he reached Main Street, he discovered other puzzling changes. Though men crowded the streets, there wasn't a woman or child in sight. Many merchants had shut their doors and put up 'closed for the day' signs.

Since he was unable to navigate his wagon through the crowded streets, Joseph tied Old Abby to a hitching post and set out on foot. The men around him were grumbling, everyone talking at once. He had to strain to decipher bits of information --- that a hoard of flatboat men had descended on Memphis. Obviously in a foul mood, they were threatening to make good their warning that they would put an end to the wharf fee once and for all. Someone estimated there must be at least five hundred flatboats gathered in the river beneath the bluff. They had crept in during the night and trapped two steamboats at the wharf, or so it was rumored.

"What were the steamboat's names?" Joseph asked, but his question was lost in the clamor. He hoped the Delta Star wasn't one of them. He walked faster, threading his way between the men. At the edge of the bluff, he stopped and stared, amazed. Hundreds of flatboats filled the river. He could hear the boats banging together, hear the shouts and curses of the boatmen. Joseph noticed that the Delta Star was indeed one of the trapped steamboats. Also, a ferryboat waited beside the shore, unable to move.

Joseph decided to go down to the shore to see if he could find Jeremiah. He went down the winding road now dried into crusty ruts by weeks of sunny weather. Just as he reached the shoreline, he saw a bearded man standing in the center of the wharf, waving a huge club in the air. The club was made of a large branch from which limbs had been whittled, leaving half-inch spikes.

"Come on, Mr. Wharf Master," the man taunted. "Come here and I'll comb your hair with this here club." The branch made a whistling noise as it sliced the air.

"Someone go fetch the militia," the wharf master shouted.

"Yeah, go get Captain Ruth," another man yelled.

Joseph hesitated. He realized he ought to give up visiting Jeremiah and get back to the top of the bluff before things on the riverside got worse. But as he turned, he felt a tug on the leg of his britches. He looked down and saw Jeremiah hiding beneath the wharf. He motioned for Joseph to join him.

"I was running an errand for my boss and got caught," he said. "Had to hide out to keep from getting smashed by the crowd. You better do the same."

Joseph crouched down beside his friend but leaned outward so he could see what was going on. Above them, boards vibrated under the force of stamping, whirling footsteps.

"Bring on your militia. See if I care," the bearded man yelled, waving his club.

Jeremiah told Joseph, "The man with the club be named John Tester. Comes down here every spring from Indiana. Gives Cap'n Ruth all kinds of trouble. They say John Tester be one of the meanest men on the Mississippi."

"Maybe we should get away from here," Joseph said. But he could see their way was now completely blocked by both citizens of Memphis and boatmen. They had no choice but to stay where they were.

After a time, the crowd parted to allow the militia, dressed in their new uniforms, to march down the bluff.

'I have a warrant for you, John Tester," Captain Ruth called out.

"And I've got something for you," Tester answered. Once more the huge club whistled through the air.

The militia continued to advance and Tester retreated to the deck of one of the flatboats and shoved it away from the wharf. "Come out here, if'n you want a good fight," Tester yelled. Other men on his boat echoed the invitation.

The men of the militia commandeered the ferry boat. As they drew alongside Tester's boat, Captain Ruth jumped on board and was immediately knocked senseless by one blow of the haw club.

"Uh, oh," Jeremy said to Joseph.

"Yeah," Joseph said. "Now there's really gonna be trouble." They moved closer to one another.

Tester leaned over the fallen captain and lifted his club. Obviously, he intended to finish him off.

From the ferry, someone in the militia yelled, "Fire." The crack of a single rifle rang out. Tester dropped his club, grabbed his chest and sprawled backwards. He lay limp and still. His crew fled into the flatboat's rickety cabin.

The ferryboat attached a rope to Tester's boat and pulled it ashore. There, they were met by an angry mob of boatmen. A crowd of citizens began to swarm down the side of the bluff. Joseph heard the ominous clicks of the militia's rifles, saw the sun glint on fixed bayonets. A stillness settled over the scene. No one moved for a long moment, a moment when it seemed anything might happen.

Then, as if they had conferred and agreed on the matter, the boatmen gave way. Meekly, they returned to their rafts, took up their poles and began to cast off.

"Wow," said Joseph. He couldn't wait to get back to the office to tell Shaughnessy and the Colonel about what he had seen. He felt as if he had witnessed something momentous. And, as it turned out, he was right.

John Tester's death seemed to mark the end of the flatboat men's reign of terror in Memphis. Though not entirely subdued, they were far less aggressive. Sometimes they crept in at night and caused a bit of trouble in the saloons, but by day, they either remained on their boats or blended unobtrusively with the regular citizens. The city prospered in the peaceful atmosphere. Construction crews took up their tools and soon a hotel and the white spires of two churches appeared on the horizon. And as the town became a civilized metropolis, the weekly Appeal also progressed. They began to publish two editions a week. The Colonel raised the price of a yearly subscription from three dollars to five. He hired two compositors and Joseph had heard him tell Shaughnessy they would soon need a new printer. Joseph hoped he would be chosen for the job, although he now earned a satisfactory salary as an assistant to Shaughnessy.

The Colonel liked to say Joseph had grown up with the Appeal and it was true enough. He was now quite tall. His shoulders were wide and strong and his arms knotted with muscles from lifting bundles of newsprint and boxes of supplies. Sure, he was ready to be a journeyman printer.

The Appeal, the Colonel pointed out, had outgrown the little house on the banks of the Wolfe River. He began to search for larger quarters.

At first, he could find nothing suitable. Offices were being snatched up as fast as they were built. Then one day, he entered the pressroom to announce he'd found an ideal place. "It's on the corner of Poplar and Main. Right in the center of the business district. Only one problem though. It's located above Browning's grocery store. It won't be easy getting the press up those stairs."

Everyone assured him they wouldn't mind. They were eager to work in town where proper newspapers were published.

On a sultry day in mid-July, they moved to the new building. Joseph was straightening and stacking bundles of newsprint when Shaughnessy approached him. "And this is Joseph Harrigan," he said. "Joseph, I want you to meet someone."

With two bundles of paper in his arms, Joseph paused to observe the stranger. He was a scrawny man with slicked back hair and watery eyes.

"This," said Shaughnessy "is Norm Willard. He's going to be our new printer."

Surely he hadn't heard right?" Joseph thought, continuing to stare.

"Joseph, where are your manners? Can't you stop long enough to welcome a new employee?"

Still struggling to absorb what he'd heard, Joseph put down the bundles and reached out to shake Norm Willard's hand, a hand as ink-stained as his own.

CHAPTER SIX

THE APPEAL was now giving the Enquirer real competition. In the year that had passed since they'd moved into the new building, the paper had become a bi-weekly with more than 800 regular subscribers. Its staff had increased steadily. Things were humming.

Joseph had not yet been promoted to journeyman printer, but he was confident that if he worked long enough, hard enough, he soon would be. He hurried about the pressroom, adding oil to the press's spit handle, checking the consistency of the ink, making sure everything was ready before Shaughnessy and the rest of the night crew arrived. *The nights we put out the paper are me favorite time*, he thought. He loved the bustle and clamor, the sense of a worthwhile job being done, loved the closeness which developed between men who sweated by the light of gas lamps while the town slept.

Compared to this, the rest of the world seemed dull. Unworthy of notice. If Shaughnessy didn't insist that he do so, he would probably never take time off.

"You'll let your younger days get away from you entirely if you don't have a holiday now and then," his cousin had scolded as they were finishing up one night. He had insisted that Joseph have the next night off, pointing out that he was a growing boy and must eat and rest properly.

Now, Joseph noted, the rosy glow of sunset filtered through the grimy panes set high in the barn-like room. The rest of the crew would be arriving any minute and the work of putting out the Thursday edition would begin. He hoped Shaughnessy would forget he wasn't supposed to be working.

But Shaughnessy hadn't forgotten. "What are you doing here, Joseph?" he demanded as he entered the pressroom. "And this your night off, the first you've had in almost a month. If you get worn down, you'll be coming down with the grippe like the rest of the crew."

"But I'm fine," Joseph protested. "Honest. I'm not at all worn down."

"And you wouldn't be admitting it if you were, I'm thinking."

"But we're short-handed, are we not? And isn't the Colonel depending on us to keep things going while he's gone?"

"Aye, that's all true enough." The big man's shoulder's sagged. "But it won't help matters to have you ailing along with the others. So, mind what I say and go have yourself a steak and a good night's sleep. And Joseph – ah – you could do with a haircut."

Joseph wanted to say that he was almost a man now and didn't need anyone to tell him when he should rest or cut his hair. But he kept those words to himself.

"I've only your best interest in mind, Joseph." Shaughnessy's voice was fatherly, though he was only twelve years older than Joseph. "One night away from here will do you a world of good."

Reluctantly, Joseph stopped arguing, but hung around for a while, like a child sent early to bed. What if something interesting happened while he was gone? He tried not to feel banished as he left.

He went to Will's Steak House and ate the prescribed steak -— a huge chunk of beef which covered an entire platter. He hadn't realized he was so hungry. As he ate, his mind was on the Appeal, going over a matter which continued to puzzle him. He couldn't understand why the Colonel had been hiring a succession of strangers instead of promoting him. Why would he be wanting such undependable men, "tramp printers" they were called, these men who drifted into town with their printing skills, worked for a while then moved on when the notion took them?

Norm Willard, who had seemed such a threat when Joseph first met him, had lasted less than two months. Another printer had come and gone in a week. Now they had two printers, both of them efficient but crotchety. Spending far too much time arguing among themselves about who was doing the most work. Wasn't it obvious, Joseph thought, that he was much more dedicated? And far more loyal?

Why didn't the Colonel see this and stop passing him by? Though Joseph went over and over the problem, the answer seemed just out of reach. With an impatient shrug, he finished his steak, considered smoking a cigar and decided against it. They still made his stomach queasy and he didn't have time for that. He decided to get his hair cut, as directed. After that, he spent several hours playing snooker. Finally, when he could think of nothing else to do, he started home to write a letter to Bridget before he went to bed. But the thought of going back to his boarding house room depressed him. And for some reason he had an uneasy feeling, a feeling he might be needed, though why he thought the night's edition couldn't be gotten out without him --and himself a mere printer's devil -- was hard to explain. He only knew he would not get a wink of sleep unless he stopped by to make sure everything was going well.

He hurried down Union Avenue and bounded up the steps which led to the Memphis Appeal's pressroom. As he opened the door, he was greeted by familiar odors of newsprint, ink and oil-stained wood. Ah, he sighed, was there a smell in all the world that pleasured him more?

He stepped inside the room and paused, frowning. He looked about while he hung his coat and cap on a peg, noting that only one whale-oil lamp glowed feebly in a far corner.

Why was it so dark? And why so quiet? Usually, no matter what time he arrived for work, he would hear some kind of noise--the soft click of type being set, the scratching of a quill against paper, the murmur of voices--sounds which meant newsmen with owlish ways were getting last minute news ready for the press.

Tonight he heard nothing. Where was the crew? It was after midnight and they should be hard at work on the edition due to hit the streets by four a.m. the next morning.

He groped his way past shadowy forms. Past roll-top desks, long work tables and wooden benches, past the ancient, sprawling Washington hand-press. At the pot-bellied stove in the rear, he hoped to come upon a few back-side warmers bent on reviving themselves with mugs of coffee. But the fire in the stove was almost out. No one had even set the big enamel coffee pot to boiling.

He heard a small sound in the composing room, saw a sliver of light beneath the closed door. He hurried over to knock and call out, "Where is everybody?"

"I'm all there is," was the answer, followed by footsteps. The door opened and Shaughnessy towered there, looking rumpled and cross. "Ah, Joseph"--his expression brightened--"you're here. Finally."

"It's me night off," Joseph reminded him.

"I know, but I've been waiting for you."

Shaughnessy motioned for Joseph to follow him. "I've much to tell you and little time," he said over his shoulder as he hustled about lighting more lamps.

He led Joseph to a table where four galleys were lined up, each filled with neat rows of printing. "I have these ready for the press. Maury and Bates didn't even set the type before they deserted."

"Maury and Bates are gone?"

"Deserted like rats. They decided to catch a freight train to Kansas, and left without giving any notice a'tall. You know how tramp printers are."

Joseph nodded.

"And the rest of the men, those who weren't already taken, have come down with the grippe. Every one of them. Never saw the like. Half of Memphis has it, or so 'tis said. I hate to be telling you this, me lad, but I'm afraid there will be no one to help with the press tonight. Not to mention the folding and baling that wants doing."

"But what about the Colonel? Wasn't he supposed to be back from his meeting in Nashville?"

"He was indeed. But he sent word he's had a slight accident. Nothing serious. Sprained ankle, I believe is all. And his buggy lost a wheel. He's getting it fixed and will try to make it back by tomorrow morning. But that won't help tonight."

Joseph's eyes widened. "Then you and I -- we're the only ones left?"

"I'm afraid it's worse than that. Molly has started to have her child. I've got to go to her as soon as I can get you settled. Do you think you could handle things without me?"

"You mean--all alone?"

"Well, you know what's to be done, don't you?" Shaughnessy was edging past him as he spoke, working his way toward the door of the pressroom. He took his coat from its hook and slipped it on, then held his cap in his hands, nervously twisting it round and round. "Faith, and haven't you run the press a thousand times?"

Joseph hesitated only a moment. He had run the press many times, though never without Shaughnessy at his side. Actually, he had been waiting for the chance. "Sure," he said. "I can do it."

Shaughnessy's cap took a few more turns as he gave Joseph a look of appraisal, a long look which ended in a sigh. "If me Molly weren't in such need, I would never consider leaving a mere tadpole to get out the day's edition."

A mere tadpole? Joseph was miffed. Would Shaughnessy ever notice he had grown up? In the past year, he had sprouted to a decent size for a man. Still he had to admit, there was a spindliness about him, an unfinished look. Silently, he cursed his boyish face, cursed the curves that hadn't yet hardened into manly contours, the fuzz on his lip which refused to become a proper mustache, the sprinkle of freckles on a nose striving to assert itself. Things time would take care of, of course. But when?

Well, he couldn't hurry the process. It wasn't his fault he was young.

He was suddenly angry, realizing he had found the answer to the problem he had fretted over while eating his steak. Shaughnessy was forever calling him "lad" and the Colonel liked to refer to him as "son". No wonder they hadn't noticed he was a man.

"Seems you'd have more confidence in me," he told Shaughnessy, "and yourself the one who taught me all I know. Go to Molly and stop fretting. You've worries enough."

Shaughnessy settled his cap on his thick red mane. "Indeed, I have. I've got to be with her. Though 'tis said the husband is looked upon as useless at such times. But things--things are not going well, as usual."

"I'm sorry to be hearing that. But maybe this time."

"That's what Molly always says. You would think after burying four infants, she would just give up. And yet, whenever there's a new one on the way, she starts hoping again. She sews little garments, makes plans, considers names. She even manages a few brave smiles through her final pain. And then---every time---every time---" For a moment, he seemed unable to go on. "But what am I doing standing here talking and her needing me? I leave the Appeal in your hands."

He hurried out, letting the door slam behind him. For a moment, Joseph stood there alone, feeling some of his confidence slipping away. Hastily, he shoved doubts from his mind.

He went to the press and put out a hand to touch wood worn smooth with use. "It's up to us, isn't it now?" he told the machine, conversationally. "And don't forget, I know all your ways, so you needn't be trying to give me trouble."

But no more talk. He was suddenly in a frenzy to get started. Carrying the four galleys to a table near the press, he began to lock them into metal frames. He fumbled a bit--all thumbs he was-

-but forced himself to adopt a steady pace. To stay calm in spite of lingering doubts.

Suppose he didn't get the paper out in time? If he missed the deadline, the Colonel would be upset. Not that Joseph was afraid of him, kind man that he was, but he wanted more than anything to please him. To amaze him, in fact. To make him realize that if he could put out an entire edition with no help, surely he was ready to be certified as a journeyman printer.

The thought that he might receive his long dreamed of promotion filled Joseph with tantalizing thoughts. With the raise in pay, could he not afford to send for his Bridget at last? He had saved every cent he could, and he had enough--barely enough--to pay for her fare.

To be sure, he conceded, there were other things needing consideration, like where to keep her when he got her here. His boarding house room shared with two other lads wouldn't do, of course. A more sensible man, a man of patience, would be a wee bit leery of taking on a wife until he was sure he could care for her properly. But patience was not one of Joseph's virtues.

He wanted Bridget now.

Each night as he lay on his narrow cot alone, he longed for her, picturing the way her golden brown hair fell soft about her shoulders. He imagined putting his arms about her tiny waist and pulling her close. The thought almost made him stop breathing. He had to have her now.

"Sure then, you'd better get your mind back on what you're supposed to be doing," he scolded himself aloud. His voice echoed in the big room.

With great care, he took two leather balls attached to short sticks and began to ink the letters contained in one of the galleys.

This done, he set the framed galley in the hand-press and secured a sheet of paper to the padded tympan above it.

As he worked, he felt the old press working along with him. A partner it was. A friend. Its inky, metallic breath warmed the air around him. As he turned the spit handle to roll text and paper beneath a thick wooden platen, its joints creaked and groaned with effort.

When all was aligned, he grasped the lever which lowered the platen, forcing galley and tympan together, and the first page of the October 13, 1844, issue of the Memphis Appeal was printed. He removed the damp paper and examined it. The letters were unsmudged, their edges crisp.

"Aye," he murmured, nodding approval. "A fine professional job if I do say so meself."

He suppressed a grin and set the paper aside to dry. He had no time to stand there beaming at his handiwork. He didn't even have time for proofreading. He would just have to put his trust in Shaughnessy, though his mind must have been mighty burdened when he set the type.

After the papers were printed, Joseph still faced the task of folding and binding. Then he must carry them down to the loading dock where they would be put in wagons and delivered. Delivered, as Shaughnessy had once put it, in time for the master of each house to find his paper set out beside his morning coffee. If all went well...

Just before noon the next day, the Colonel limped into the office, his ankle swathed in bandages. Joseph ran to assist him.

The Colonel hobbled on, insisting he was all right. "It's only a sprain," he said as he balanced his big frame against one of the tables and looked around. "Where is everyone?"

"I'm all there is," Joseph said, just as Shaughnessy had said the night before.

"What happened?"

Joseph told his story, aware that the Colonel's intelligent eyes were on him, taking him in, assessing him. "Well done," he said, when he had heard it all.

"Thank you, sir."

"You know, I've been thinking for some time, Joseph, that it's time we took steps toward getting you certified. And I'm gratified to find you living up to my expectations. How would you like to be a journeyman printer?"

"Aye, I'd like that more than you could ever imagine. And I thank you kindly."

The Colonel held up a hand. "Don't thank me. You've earned it. And you'd better go home and get some sleep. You look exhausted."

But Joseph was too excited to sleep. If he was soon to be a journeyman, couldn't he do the things he had dreamed of so long? He went to the bank and withdrew his savings. He didn't want to send the money to Bridget directly--suppose her father took it away from her?--so he went to the small office of a steamship company on Main Street. There, he was able to arrange for Bridget's passage to America. The agent assured him that tickets, with arrangements made for transfer to a steamboat in New Orleans, would be waiting in Liverpool to be claimed by a Bridget Anna O'Ryan.

Coming out of the steamship office, the deed done, Joseph found his mood changing. An uncomfortable feeling seemed to be settling over him, a feeling of responsibility for his soon-to-be wife. It was almost as if she were there, walking beside him. And right off, she seemed to be causing trouble. Somehow he couldn't fit the memory of her into his present surroundings.

What would she think of this untamed town with its frontier atmosphere, its rows of log buildings and wooden sidewalks?

As Joseph walked along Main, he came upon a Memphis matron starting across the muddy road. Carefully, the young woman lifted her skirt and stepped over puddles, choosing mounds which seemed most solid. As she did so she revealed high-buttoned kid shoes, lacy pantalets, ruffled petticoats and even a bit of black-stockinged leg. Joseph tried to picture Bridget crossing a street in such a manner but he could bring no such vision to mind. Try as he might to imagine otherwise, Bridget remained at the side of the road, refusing to lift her skirt an inch or stick so much as a toe in the mud. The arch of her slender neck stated her refusal clearly.

"Niver in all me life have I seen such durtee mud," He could hear her sharp little voice exclaim with distaste.

In his mind, he answered her back with the reminder that 'whither thou goest go I' was the proper attitude for a wife. And if she was going to live in Memphis, sure and she had better be getting used to mud.

He supposed it was one of the hazards of knowing someone well, of having grown up childhood sweethearts, which made it possible to get a grand argument going without so much as being in one another's presence. And perhaps he should be thankful for the chance to practice outsmarting her, for there was no doubting the difficulties he faced when she arrived. One look at the little river town was likely to win her disapproval -- and she was quite capable, he knew, of taking the next boat back to Ireland. Somehow he must find a way to prevent this from happening.

That night he wrote two letters. One to Bridget telling her the good news. Another, much more difficult to write, was a request to Bridget's father for her hand in marriage. After composing a few lines, he tore up his first attempts. Why did he find it so difficult to ask for permission to marry Bridget? He wondered. He was a man now, a man with a responsible job, perfectly capable of providing for a wife. Yet he had only to write her father's name and he felt like a small lad again. A "shanty-boat Irish lad", as Dr. O'Ryan called him. He could still see the disdain in the man's eyes as he looked him over, still hear the slam of that door.

He must get over that. He squared his shoulders and began a new letter, a brief, formal letter ---almost business-like, it was --- but it would have to do. He sent it off, hoping desperately that it would receive a positive response.

Joseph and the Colonel put out the next edition of the Appeal without assistance. Then, gradually, things got back to normal in the pressroom. One by one, the ailing employees came back.

Shaughnessy returned to work as soon as he was able to leave Molly. They'd had a girl, he told them. A lass with Molly's sweet face, and the fuzz on her wee head promised her father's red hair. "Kathleen, we called her," he said, stopping briefly to compose himself, "And she lived four days, which made it more difficult when she was taken from us."

Joseph could barely endure seeing his friend hurting so.

"But," said Shaughnessy, "life must continue. And we've a paper due out tomorrow, have we not?"

In mid-November, Joseph ripped open two envelopes. Bridget's letter was grand to read. She sounded delighted, excited. "Ah Joseph, at last we will be together again," she wrote in her small, precise hand. "America will surely be a fine place to live and I am counting the days until I get there." She promised to love him forever, no matter what difficulties they encountered, and added, almost as an afterthought, that she would be arriving on the morning of February twenty-seven on a steamboat called the Natchez.

As Joseph had expected, her father didn't share her enthusiasm.

"Bridget's mother and I had hoped for a more substantial match for our daughter," he wrote, "but it seems she has her head set on you. Since she has refused to even consider other likely lads, we have no choice but to give our consent." He added that he planned to make sure the poor lass carried enough money to pay for her return fare should she need it at any time.

A dirty trick, thought Joseph. To allow her to come to America but give her money to leave him and go back to Ireland.

Well, he could connive as well as any. A plan hatched in the back of his mind. We'll see who has the last say about this, he muttered to himself.

To take the sting from her father's obvious disapproval, he read Bridget's letter a dozen or more times

Aye, she does love me, he thought, though heaven alone knows why, with meself so poor I don't even have a roof to put over her head.

Shaughnessy and Molly came to his rescue.

"If you think Bridget wouldn't mind living out in the Pinchtown area," Shaughnessy told him, "there's a shack standing empty just down the road from my house. 'Twas built with lumber from old flatboats that someone scavenged from the shores of Catfish Bay. Made themselves a small shanty, then deserted it, so it could be had for the taking. It's in bad shape but if we work hard, we could make it quite nice. And there'd be no rent payments to worry about."

They went to work on the little shanty, Shaughnessy and Molly and Joseph. The men replaced rotted boards and painted, while Molly sewed curtains, made a fine quilt and donated dishes, an odd table or two and several chairs.

"'Tis a pleasure to have such a happy project to be working on," Molly said. She was still pale, but determined to at least appear cheerful.

She was like that, Molly, a fine lady, sweet, pretty, with ample curves and gentle ways. With a tinge of regret, Joseph found himself thinking, *So different from Bridget*. Still, he hoped the two would be friends in spite of their differences.

The stormy days of January came to an end and February brought almost spring-like weather. Only traces of snow remained in shaded areas beneath bushes and along the north side of buildings. The nice weather made it possible to add the finishing touch to the shanty, a coat of buttercup yellow paint to brighten the outside and cover some of its flaws.

"Ah," said Shaughnessy. "And now we're ready for Miss Bridget's arrival."

Joseph nodded and smiled, his head full of plans.

CHAPTER SEVEN

THE SUN WAS JUST VISIBLE above the trees when Joseph stationed himself on the wharf beside the Mississippi to await the arrival of the Natchez. The big day had arrived and he intended to be there to welcome Bridget the moment she stepped off the boat.

He looked about him, trying to picture the scene as it would appear to her -- the wooden wharf swarming with people of every description -- the muddy Mississippi lapping at its moorings -- bales of cotton and other freight stacked high on one end -- wagons, drays and carts bouncing along the rutted road which meandered up the steep side of Chickasaw Bluff.

How different it all seemed when compared to the thatched cottages, soft rolling hills and misty colors of their homeland. Altogether an overwhelming sight, he decided.

No matter how long he had to wait, he must be here to reassure Bridget when the *Natchez* arrived.

He knew, of course, that steamboats weren't noted for keeping to schedule. But this fact had somehow escaped him when he was making his careful plans. It came back to him as the day wore on. Morning passed. The sun moved relentlessly westward. Shadows began to lengthen. He fumed. If the *Natchez* didn't get there soon, Bridget wouldn't have time to freshen up before the wedding he had planned for eight o'clock that evening.

The others who waited with him on the wharf were people he did not know, a fact he appreciated. He was much too tense to be carrying on idle conversations. Sweat formed beneath his tight collar. He tried to remain calm, for if he got into a dither, his wedding finery would surely wilt.

Molly had tried to talk him out of getting fancily dressed so early, pointing out that he could change while Bridget was freshening from her travels. But Joseph was afraid he would have other last-minute arrangements to make. "I'll be more at ease if I have meself ready to go," he had insisted stubbornly.

And so he had donned the striped trousers, the linen shirt with celluloid collar, the broadcloth frock coat and, to top it off, a beaver stovepipe hat -- garments the like of which he had never worn before in his life. The clothes were, for the most part, either borrowed or rented. They made him feel stiff and self-conscious, as if he were someone else. But were not such sacrifices required of a man about to become a husband?

Now he wished he had listened to Molly and started out in his regular clothes. With nothing to do but wait, he had plenty of time for regrets. He found himself worrying about everything.

Suppose, as various friends had thoughtfully pointed out, Bridget had changed so much he wouldn't recognize her? No doubt after the passage of four years, he would find her transformed from lass to woman, just as he had become a man.

But would she be that different? What if they had grown into strangers who no longer wanted one another?

They had been so young when they parted. It came to him now that the natural order of their courting days had been taken from them. According to his plans, they would be going from the first shy kisses of very young lovers to the marriage bed, with no time allowed for a gradual closeness developing in between. Why hadn't he thought of that?

Because, he admitted to himself now, he had been too busy scheming to think.

When he had first hatched his plot to take Bridget straight to the marrying priest on the day of her arrival, it had seemed a fine, sensible idea. He would make her his wife before she had a chance to look about her and change her mind.

Without revealing his true motivation, he had sought Shaughnessy and Molly's approval for his scheme. He had presented it to them one Sunday morning as the three of them sat around the breakfast table.

Basking in the warmth of the cook stove, savoring Molly's good cooking, he had leaned back in his chair and chatted away about the arrangements he'd made for his wedding.

"Whoa, back up," Shaughnessy had said, looking up from the biscuit he was buttering. "Did I hear right? Are you saying you want to be married the very night Bridget arrives on the boat?"

"Well, yes," Joseph said in what he hoped was a mature and sincere voice. "I was just thinking of her welfare, so I was, of getting her settled quickly without a great fuss."

"But I don't think what you're planning can be done. You know how the Church is about rules. And with weddings, there's procedures to be followed which will take time."

"I know, but I'm going to talk to Father Murray about it. He'll alter a few rules for a good cause. Sure, and he's a considerate man, the way he can complete a mass, sermon and all, and have you back on the street in an hour, your Sunday duty done?"

"So that's what you're counting on? Father Murray's soft heart?" Shaughnessy bit into a strip of bacon, looking at Joseph thoughtfully as he chewed. "Well, I hate to be the bearer of bad news, but Father Murray's been transferred elsewhere."

"Go on with you. I've heard no such news."

"That's because you never pay attention to announcements from the pulpit, me lad. This very morning Father let it be known he's transferred to Baton Rouge. Until the new pastor arrives, Father Angelo will be running the church alone."

Joseph groaned and pushed his plate away, his appetite gone. "Are you saying Father Angelo's me only choice? How could God do this to me?"

"I doubt He had you foremost in mind at the time," Shaughnessy pointed out.

"'Tis a dark turn of events." Joseph got up to pace around the room. Father Angelo was the last person he wanted to have in charge of his wedding. "He makes every ceremony twice as long as need be," he complained. "Even fretful babes can't hurry him along with a baptism. And his sermons are endless, with himself carried away, waving his arms about, shouting that the whole parish is taking the downward road."

"I'm sure he wouldn't do that at a wedding, dear," Molly said. "Now, sit down and stop fretting or you'll be ailing on the most important day of your life. Here, have another biscuit."

He sat down and began pushing food about on his plate.

"And we shouldn't be criticizing the ways of others, should we now?" Molly scolded gently.

Joseph ducked his head, a bit ashamed of himself. Father Angelo was no doubt a fine holy man. As was the way with his church, Joseph had been taught to respect the cloth and to leave matters of faith in the hands of the experts. But still, did he not have a right to his own version of God? And he saw God as a friendly, sensible Being who would never be so inconsiderate as to blather on and keep a working man from his duties.

"Ah well," he sighed. "I suppose I'll have to make do with what's been handed me. Sure, there must be a way around Father Angelo, a way to make him understand my needs."

"There may be," said Shaughnessy, barely suppressing a smile. "Though it would take a small miracle. I say it's not possible."

But Shaughnessy had been wrong. "You must have done some grand talking," he had observed, a bit awed. "How did you get him to agree to marry you before he'd given you the series of little pre-nuptial talks he sets such store by?"

"Oh," said Joseph, with a shrug, "I just promised we would stop by for them afterwards."

Actually, for once, Joseph hadn't had to do a lot of talking. He had merely mentioned casually, sort of as if he were thinking aloud, that he would have no choice but to take Bridget straight home from the boat, for he didn't have the money to be putting her up in a hotel. He had trusted the good Father's fertile imagination to conjure up visions of a marriage consummated in sin. After that, he'd had no more trouble with the difficult priest.

The sound of paddle wheels splashing up the river brought Joseph back to the present. He leaned over a piling and strained to see through the mist now gathering on the river. He made out the red glow of torch baskets swinging from the hurricane deck of a great white steamboat. The *Natchez* had arrived. Finally.

He felt a surge of relief, but panic quickly followed. He wished Shaughnessy and Molly had come with him to help welcome Bridget, but they had refused to do so, saying the young lovers would need time alone to talk and get re-acquainted.

Talk. Sure there was a need for that. But what would he say? Should he ask the usual questions: Had the ocean been rough? The boat crowded? The journey pleasant? No. He did not want to resort to such commonplace remarks, trivial matters expressed to one another by casual acquaintances.

He searched his mind for something original, endearing, maybe even humorous, to open the conversation, but his head seemed full of mush.

The *Natchez* sounded its landing bell and turned shoreward. With pent steam hissing through safety valves, its side wheels stopped, then reversed themselves, churning water to foam as the boat drew alongside the wharf.

Joseph scanned the passengers who crowded the lower deck, his heart pounding, but he saw no one familiar. He felt desperate.

But then he saw a slender form with a small, straight back, directing two deck hands on the proper stacking of her trunks beside the railing, and he knew immediately, instinctively, that this busy little figure could be none other than Bridget.

The gangplank was lowered and the passengers scrambled to leave the ship while, at the same time, others hurried aboard. Joseph kept his eyes on Bridget for, having found her, he certainly didn't want to risk losing her in the confusion.

And it was indeed her he had singled out. He was sure now. Even though she was dressed somberly for travel--a gray frock buttoned high at the neck, white gloves, a wee, lace-trimmed bonnet subduing her wealth of dark hair, a reticule over one arm and a shawl draped over the other--even thus encumbered and obviously weary, she was still the same comely lass he remembered. He noticed with pride how the men took in her fine looks, cornering their eyes as they passed her.

She came ashore, followed by the deck hands with two large trunks balanced on their shoulders. Joseph couldn't help comparing it with his own arrival in America, with himself dressed shabbily and only a knapsack needed to carry his possessions. Aye, we're made of varied cloth, he thought.

He approached her. "Bridget?"

She stopped and looked at him, saying nothing.

"'Tis meself. Joseph."

"Joseph?"

Once again, he wished he was wearing his old cap and regular clothes. No wonder she couldn't recognize him when he looked a stranger to himself. Maybe if he took off the ridiculous stovepipe hat. He removed it and smoothed his unruly hair.

"Aye, 'tis you, Joseph." She extended her hand. He shook it nervously until his manners came to him. Gentlemen usually kissed a lady's hand, did they not? He lifted a white glove and brushed it with his lips.

That's better, her expression said.

He found himself asking all the questions he had scorned.

"Was the ocean rough?"

"Aye, a great part of the time."

"And the ship was no doubt ancient and overcrowded?"

She shook her head. "Sure and it was that."

"I hope it didn't make you--unwell."

"I survived," she said, lowering her eyes.

"Did anyone accompany you? To see that you were kept safe as I requested?"

"A young man and his wife traveled with me as far as New Orleans."

"Ah. Well then. We'd better relieve these fellows of your baggage. I have the loan of the Colonel's buggy. And we're in a great hurry." He took her elbow and propelled her toward the edge of the wharf, looking back to make sure the deck hands were following.

"Did you say we're in a great hurry?" she asked. "And why would that be?"

"Well, uh, we're supposed to be at the church by eight. We'll be getting ourselves married tonight."

She stopped so suddenly they were almost run down. "Tonight? Did you say tonight?"

"Aye, tonight." Joseph looked around nervously. "But should we go on to the buggy? Then, I'll explain everything to you, why we're having to go at it so willy-nilly."

"Willy-nilly? We're getting married willy-nilly?" Her voice rose and a few passersby stared at them with interest.

"Here, let's be getting to a place more suited for talking this over."

She followed him, clearly a bit dazed.

She remained silent as he urged the horse up the side of the bluff. He wondered what she was thinking. It was just as he had feared--he didn't know her. And obviously she found him equally baffling.

Now, he could see what a mistake he had made, not planning for a time spent getting used to one another again before being joined for life. But, alas, what was done, was done.

He tried to explain how it had all come about, hoping to make her think he'd had no choice in the matter, that somehow everything had just turned out this way. "Can't you see how it was?" he pleaded. "I only wanted us to be properly wed so I could take you home with me tonight."

"And where would that be? Home."

"'Tis a surprise I have for you. You'll see when we get there."

"Joseph, how can we marry this very night? 'Tis the most important thing anyone could do -- and we should be preparing ourselves for it. Besides, there's the reading of the Banns to be done. And there should be a rehearsal. How will I know what to do or say, if we don't practice first?"

He had forgotten what a determined lass she was, how she had always insisted on doing things her way and getting away with it because she was the taller.

Well, saint's be praised, he had finally caught up with her growing. She was still tall and willowy--and to be sure he would not be able to tuck her under his arm the way Shaughnessy did Molly--but at least he could look eye to eye to her when they talked. And a blessing this was, for he was going to need every advantage to claim his rightful place as head of the household.

Didn't she trust him to handle things? He asked her now. He had tended to having the Banns read as they should be. And the reason he had not planned a fancy church wedding was because he thought it might be a burden to her, her being so new to the land. He had decided it would be best to have a small ceremony in the priest's study.

"And we shouldn't be needing a rehearsal," he said. "Have you not been to such weddings before?"

"Not recently. Not for some time. I've forgotten what's to be said."

"It will come to you. When the priest says 'repeat after me', you merely have to say whatever he tells you. Doesn't that sound simple?"

She continued to look doubtful. "There's one other matter to be discussed, Joseph Harrigan. I'll not be marrying you in me traveling clothes. I've brought me ma's wedding gown--all satin and homemade lace it is--and I have it packed in one of the trunks I brought and I'll not be marrying a'tall unless it's on me."

"I understand your feeling," he said, although he didn't. "That's why I arranged to stop by Mrs. Finian's place. She's an older woman who keeps the rectory clean for the priests. She offered to let you freshen up in her little cottage. But since the boat was so late and Father Angelo said he'd not be waiting for us past eight-thirty, I've decided we haven't time to stop by Mrs. Finian's."

Bridget looked at him steadily, then leaned back in the buggy and folded her arms. "And I've decided we'll marry some other day."

Was he hearing right? Joseph thought. Would all his careful plans be ruined by something so unimportant?

He controlled his voice with effort. "How can you do that to me after all the trouble I've gone to? And why does it matter so much what you're wearing? A lovely lass like you, sure and you couldn't look other than beautiful were you wearing . . .”

"Joseph, stop blathering. I'll not be swayed by your blarney. I've had me say and you're not listening. Why do you ignore me wishes this way?"

He opened his mouth to say something, then shut it. What was he doing? It hadn't been his intention to ignore her wishes. The trouble, he thought, is that she's wanting a wedding to remember and I'm wanting a quick one.

They were nearing the church and they had to come to an agreement. Calling forth every bit of persuasive powers he possessed, he described the lovely ceremony prepared for them and the care gone into planning it. He told her how Molly had arranged flowers and set them out in the study among the shelves of fine old books. "And in the corner of the room," he went on, in a honeyed voice meant to beguile, "there'll be a fire crackling in the wee fireplace, sending out a soft glow."

"And," she said, her voice equally beguiling, "the glow reflecting off the satin sheen of me mither's wedding gown."

Ah, she was the difficult one. But wasn't this the moment he should be letting her know he would be making the decisions? He looked at her. The moon shown softly on her upturned face. So earnest. So lovely.

CHAPTER EIGHT

"DEARLY BELOVED," Father Angelo intoned, "we are gathered here in the presence of God to join this man and this woman in Holy Matrimony." His Sunday-sermon voice, much too loud, resounded around the small room, rattling the panes of its one window. "Holy Marriage is instituted of God, regulated by His commandments, blessed by our Lord Jesus Christ, and to be held in honor by our Lord. Let us therefore reverently remember that God has established and sanctified marriage."

Were all those words really in that little Missal, Joseph wondered, looking suspiciously at the leather-bound book clutched in the priest's pudgy hands. Or was Father Angelo adding things here and there to fancy it up? Lingering over every phrase, he was, stressing every syllable, beguiled as usual by the sound of himself.

Joseph was irritated, though he suspected the speechifying impressed Bridget. And could he not endure it on her account? Was it not sinful of him to be criticizing the priest who was taking the time to get his marriage properly sanctified? He ran a finger around the rim of his celluloid collar, hoping to loosen it. His neck seemed to be swelling. A body could be mortally wounded by such a contraption and wouldn't it serve him right, heathen that he was?

"Let us pray," said Father. Shaughnessy, Molly and the Colonel, along with Joseph and Bridget, bowed their heads and the prayer was begun. "Gratia agamous domino Deo nostro..."

The grand thing about Latin, to Joseph's way of thinking, was that hardly a word of it could be understood. It flowed over and about him, soft and soothing, leaving his mind free to roam.

He opened his eyes and, after making sure everyone else had theirs closed, stole a glance at Bridget. So beautiful she was, shimmering in her mother's satin dress, her face glowing with reverence. She smelled of spring flowers, fresh and faintly sweet. Ah, he thought, and wasn't he as proud as a white-washed pig to have captured such a bride?

The prayer ended at last. Father Angelo fastened his dark gaze on Joseph and Bridget and returned to his sermon voice. "I now charge you both before God, the searcher of all hearts, that if either of you know any reason why ye may not lawfully be joined together in marriage, I charge ye to confess it now."

"Me conscience is clear," Joseph mumbled, a bit insulted by what he felt was an accusatory tone.

Father Angelo ignored him. "For be ye well assured that if any persons are joined together otherwise than as God's Word allows, their union is not blessed by Him."

Bridget lifted her head, looking suddenly alarmed.

Confound it, Joseph thought, the man is getting her all upset. He could just see how it might be, with himself forced to devote his entire wedding night to convincing his new wife their marriage was truly blessed by God and, thus, official. He should have warned Father Angelo beforehand, let him know how fretful Bridget was.

He reached out, took her icy hand and held it tightly as the ceremony droned on.

Finally, he heard the question he'd been waiting for: "Do you, Joseph Patrick Harrigan, take this woman..."

"Aye, I do indeed," Joseph burst out.

"Oh, shhh," said Bridget, looking embarrassed.

Father scowled and after waiting a moment, began the question again.

Each in turn, Joseph and Bridget repeated the solemn oath to forsake all others, to cherish each other in plenty and want, in sickness and health, til death parted them.

"And now--" began Father Angelo.

There was an urgent knock at the door and the nightwatchman entered, his eyes wild, the lantern he held aloft set swinging by his abrupt stop. "Father," he cried. "I thought you should know. There's a turrible fire a-happenin'. Don't know if anyone's hurt yet but likely there will be afore it's over. The whole corner of Poplar and Main is ablaze."

"Poplar and Main?" the Colonel gasped. "The Appeal? Is it burning?"

"It's about to go up. The whole block's going if you ask me. I've never seen..."

The Colonel did not wait for further talk. He bolted from the room, followed by Shaughnessy, Joseph and the ponderous priest.

The nightwatchman tipped his hat at the ladies and went out, closing the door softly.

Bridget and Molly were alone.

For a moment they stared at one another. Then Molly shrugged. From a chair in the corner of the room, she fetched two shawls and wrapped one around the confused almost-bride.

"Come along, dear," she said, gently. "Let's go to the fire. We may be needed."

"God have mercy," Joseph gasped, as he ran down the road. The smell of burning wood stung his throat. Ahead, the western half of the sky glowed red. They turned off Adams Street onto Main and he caught his first sight of flames leaping high in the air, orange and red demons dancing against the night sky. As they drew closer, he could feel the heat against his skin.

Shaughnessy tore his celluloid collar from his neck. "Better get that thing off your neck or it'll melt and be a part of you forever."

Joseph obeyed.

The intersection of Main and Poplar was jammed with volunteer fireman, some shouting orders, some working on the hand-pumped fire engine, drawing water from public cisterns to spray on the fire. Roaring flames enveloped the building beside Browning's grocery store. Browning's itself had the look of a pot-bellied stove with a cozy fire spreading rapidly behind its bay window. Miraculously, the upper part of the building seemed untouched as yet.

"We'd better save what equipment we can," Shaughnessy yelled, and Joseph nodded. They dashed up the stairway. When the door to the pressroom resisted their attempts to enter,

Shaughnessy rammed it open with a powerful shove of his shoulder. Without hesitation, they rushed inside.

It was like stepping into a furnace, Joseph thought. Smoke stung his eyes, blinded him. He couldn't see the back of his hand, let alone find equipment to be saved. Panic swept over him. They'd been fools to enter the building. And if they didn't leave immediately, they'd be dead fools.

"Got to get out," he gasped, barely able to breathe. He fought to overcome dizziness, to remain conscious. "Shaughnessy," he called. No answer. Then he heard the sound of a body falling. "Shaughnessy. Where are you?""

Still no answer. Burning wood crackled ominously below Joseph's feet. Dropping to his knees, he crawled across the floor until he found the fallen man. He shook him but got no response. Flames shot through a crack in the floor. Joseph wanted to run but he would not leave Shaughnessy behind.

Oh God, he prayed now, without actually saying words. Please help us. He gripped Shaughnessy beneath his arms and pulled but could not budge him. Oh, please, God, me cousin is a big man--so heavy--Oh, God, please help. He pulled with all his strength and began, inch by inch, to drag the limp body across the room. Please God. Please. Help.

He became disoriented. Where was the door? He ought to have something tied around his face to protect him from the smoke. But did he dare stop? He staggered on.

"Hey, in there," called a voice. "Say something so we can find you."

"We're here," Joseph called back.

In moments, three firemen were beside them. Two of the men grasped Shaughnessy by the shoulders. Joseph and the other man each held a leg. They made it out the door. Hungry tongues of flame broke through the walls, reached out for them as they started down the stairs. When they were near the bottom, the stairway collapsed. They had to leap clear of flaming debris. Immediately after that, the upper floor of the building went up with a great whoosh, like fireworks exploding.

It seemed to Joseph that he was living a nightmare: Shaughnessy being loaded into an ambulance; Molly weeping beside him; shouting men thrusting a leather bucket into Joseph's hands; he and Bridget finding themselves working side by side, part of a human chain passing buckets of water up the levee from the river; everyone straining, doing their best to keep the water moving, desperate to prevent the fire from spreading and devouring the entire town.

A storm of white ashes and glowing embers swirled in the air around them.

Each bucket passed through Joseph's hands seemed such a pitifully small thing, so hopelessly ineffectual. But bucket after bucket moved along the chain. While the little fire engine continued to spray the fire with water drawn from cisterns, the water in the buckets was used to immediately douse sparks on the roofs of surrounding buildings.

Gradually, the firefighters gained control. Newcomers arrived to relieve the exhausted men and women of the bucket brigade.

Above the noise, Joseph yelled to Bridget. "Now we can find out about Shaughnessy." He led her through the crowd and down the street toward the hospital. As they passed beneath a street lamp, he saw that her face was blackened by soot, and her hair and clothes so damp she was shivering like a wet pup. Then he saw what had happened to her dress. Her beautiful dress. Oh, the pity of it.

"'Tis sorry I am to be telling you that your dress is ruined. There's wee holes burned into it."

Bridget didn't seem worried about the dress. She was staring at Joseph's face. "And I'm sorry to be telling you, Joseph, that you only have one eyebrow."

He passed his hand over his eyes and felt stubbles. "Aye, 'tis lucky I am to still have hair."

A carriage drew to a stop beside them and the Colonel leaned out. "There you are, you two. Been looking everywhere for you. I just returned from the hospital. Shaughnessy is awake and grumbling."

"Thank the good Lord," Joseph said. "We're on our way to see him now."

"No use doing that. They won't let anyone in except Molly. She's staying the night with her man. She's the only one who can keep him quiet. You ought to hear him complaining."

"A good sign," Joseph said.

"Yes, a welcome sign. He'll probably be hollering to be let out tomorrow. Doc said he's in fair shape, that the smoke just got to him, felled him first because he was the taller. He did a fool thing going into that burning building. Foolish. Both of you."

"I know," said Joseph. "I can't imagine what we were thinking."

"I'd say you weren't thinking at all, but I'll save my lecture for later. Right now you need to get your poor bride and yourself into dry clothes. Here, climb in and I'll take you home."

"I'm that grateful to you," Joseph said as he helped Bridget into the carriage. The men sat on either side of her and the Colonel gave his horse a light flip with the reins.

"Could we go by Mrs. Finian's first?" Joseph asked. "Bridget's trunks are there. I meant for her to change clothes before we went to Paddy Meaghan's for the party." How distant his happy wedding plans seemed now. "We need to gather up her things and take them home."

But when they got to Mrs. Finian's, the house was dark and locked up tight. And either the ancient lady was sound asleep on her good ear or she'd gone elsewhere, for pounding as hard as they could did not bring her to the door.

Joseph returned to the buggy. "I guess we'll have to go on home and come back in the morning for your baggage."

Bridget merely nodded. As they drove along, she slumped against him, not saying a word. The town was growing quiet again, lulled to sleep, after the excitement of the fire. A thick fog had settled over everything.

"We'll be there soon," Joseph said. They bounced up Jackson Street toward Catfish Bay. She sat up and peered about.

"You won't be able to see much until morning," Joseph told her. "The wind has blown a lot of smoke our way and 'tis mixed with fog. Made it dark as the inside of a cow."

When they reached the muddy shores of Catfish Bay, Joseph helped Bridget alight.

"I'll be going back to the fire," the Colonel said. "I plan to stay there the rest of the night. Or at least until the danger of more fires breaking out is over."

"Thank you kindly for the ride home," Joseph said. He and Bridget stood and watched silently until the carriage was out of sight.

Joseph turned and smiled at Bridget. "Come me darlin'. Let me carry you over the threshold of our new home like a proper bride."

He lifted her easily and started up the wooden walkway. "This is my surprise--our new home." He indicated a bulky shadow barely visible in the fog.

She looked but gave no indication of what might be going on in her mind.

He chattered on. "Shaughnessy and Molly helped me get it ready. A wee cabin on the shores of a bay, it is. A fine home for us to start our life together." He was glad the lingering smoke covered the usual odors of dead fish and rotting wood.

He set her down just inside the doorway of the cabin. "Don't move, me darlin', until I light a candle." After a moment a flame flickered, casting a faint glow about a sparsely furnished room with beamed ceilings and white-washed walls. In one corner, was a fireplace made of natural stone, in the other, a home-made bed with feather mattress, covered with a bright flowered quilt.

"Molly made the quilt," Joseph said. "'Tis her wedding gift to us. And she gave us the little table and chairs. Now this, is the main room,"--there was pride in his voice as he showed her about--"and we've a fine big kitchen. And above, in the loft, there's plenty of space to add sleeping room as--as our family grows."

Bridget looked about doubtfully. She couldn't stop shivering.

"Here now, we've got to get you out of those wet clothes."

She backed away from him and folded her arms across her breasts. "If you'll recall, I have no other clothes to put on."

"But you can't stay as you are the whole night. You'll catch your death."

"Then I'll have to die, Joseph, for I just remembered, Father Angelo didn't finish marrying us. He didn't get the pronouncing done. So we're not properly married."

He stared at her. "Nonsense. Did we not make our promises to each other? And what is marriage, the real part of marriage, but the promising? If you wish, we'll go back tomorrow and have him say the pronouncing part."

"Sure and we must do that. But tonight"--she sighed deeply--"tonight I'm just too weary to think about anything."

"Aye, we've been through enough, so we have. We should get some rest. And I have an idea. You could wear me night shirt. I have an extra one."

She shook her head and backed even farther away from him.

"No, wait. Me night shirt is made of flannel and 'tis modest as a nun's habit. And I'll go into the kitchen while you freshen up and change. There's water in the pitcher yonder and a chamber pot neath the bed. And if you like, I could build a nice fire in the fireplace."

"No," she said quickly. "No fire."

"Aye, I get your meaning. Well then, the fire in the cook stove should take the chill off. And I'll make us some hot tea." He took two night shirts out of the chest at the foot of the bed and gave her one.

In the kitchen, he washed as much of the soot off himself as he could and put on the other night shirt. And to think he'd considered it a waste to own two.

He returned with cups of tea on a tray. She had washed and changed. Her hair, unbraided now, fell thick and soft about her shoulders. He swallowed hard and set the tray on the small table.

"'Tis not the way I thought this night would be," he said as they sat at the little table and sipped their tea. "I had plans for a bit of festivities following the ceremony but--" He gazed into her eyes and forgot to continue.

She stood abruptly, trembling once again.

"You're still cold, me poor sweet," he said, coming to stand beside her. Gently, he put his arms about her and pulled her close.

If he lived to be a hundred and eighty, he thought, he'd always remember the way she felt this night with her slim body lost in the folds of his night shirt, her bones small and pliant. He was suddenly set wild by emotions he could barely control.

Steady. Steady. He must not startle her.

But it was she who surprised him, throwing her arms about him, burying her face in his neck and bursting into tears.

"Oh, Joseph, Joseph," she gasped between sobs, "when you were in that building with the flames crawling up the stairway, I thought I was going to lose you forever."

"There, there, me darlin'." He stroked her back. "'Tis all over now."

She continued to cry. He carried her to bed and lay beside her, pulling the soft quilt over them. When she'd cried herself out, she lay quite still, as if lulled by the warmth surrounding them.

His arms tightened about her. "Don't you see we're already one and no words can cause us to be more so?" he asked softly. He wanted to make her feel as he felt, make her understand that she was a part of his very soul. Bone of his bone and flesh of his flesh--as was said in the Bible. He kissed her, beginning with a tender lingering kiss.

"Joseph, me love--"

When they finally thought of sleep, a misty dawn was swirling about the windows. Their bodies were entwined in a cocoon of bedclothes. The night shirts lay tossed on the floor, forgotten.

Just before Joseph drifted off to sleep, the horror of the fire came back to him. The Appeal burned to the ground. Gone.

Bridget stirred drowsily, snuggled closer into his embrace. *Ah well*, he thought, when *love is this grand, sure and there's no problem can't be solved.*

CHAPTER NINE

SHAUGNESSY WAS OUT OF THE HOSPITAL in a matter of days with only a warning from the doctor to rest a bit and give his lungs a chance to repair themselves.

The Appeal's recovery was far more difficult.

"We've got to get back into circulation," the Colonel fretted. "And soon. We don't want our readers to get attached to the Enquirer again, do we?"

"Sure and we won't let that happen," Shaughnessy insisted in a somewhat croaky voice. And the rest of the staff agreed.

But in spite of their optimism, it was obvious that recovering from the fire was going to be a great struggle for the Appeal. A small insurance policy paid for a new press and helped lease another building, but it did not cover replacing lost equipment and supplies. Nor did it meet the payroll of men who were working extra hours to put the paper back into production. To solve these problems, the Colonel reluctantly applied for loans and accepted donations from loyal readers.

"I wish I could think of a polite way to tell everyone that, if they would just pay the money they owe for past subscriptions, we wouldn't need donations," the Colonel said during a staff meeting in his new office. "But the whole matter has me over a barrel. Canceling subscriptions doesn't seem the answer. We have to keep our circulation up or we won't be able to charge for advertising. We'd be worse off than ever."

"Why don't we do some horse trading?" Shaughnessy suggested.

The Colonel lifted an inquiring eyebrow.

"Well, horse trading in a manner of speaking. Why don't we put a small announcement in the paper saying that if the reader is unable to come up with money, we'll accept produce as payment for subscriptions. Chickens, for instance."

"Chickens?" The eyebrow lifted higher.

"Well, chickens, vegetables, milk, things like that. Anything that might be used by our employees to feed their families. Just to tide us over."

The Colonel saw Shaughnessy's point. "By jingle, that just might work."

And so it was done. The announcement was placed in the next edition and people were quick to respond.

Joseph was slightly nervous the first time he brought home two chickens, some sweet potatoes and turnips instead of a paycheck. What would Bridget have to say about that? He watched her closely for signs that she was she beginning to regret marrying him. He had meant to take some time off to get her settled in America and instead he had been forced to work even longer hours.

She had not complained at first, agreeing with him that troublesome times called for such sacrifices. And their few hours spent together each day were so wonderful, they made up for his absences. Bridget seemed quite content--until the sickness began.

"I can't be that way already," she said.

But she was, and they hurried back to Father Angelo to have him complete their wedding ceremony properly.

Joseph was aware of the morning illnesses suffered by women who were expecting a child, especially a first one. He had seen aunts laid low by the affliction, but somehow he had thought his finicky and always-in-control Bridget would not put up with such an indignity. This, however, was not the way of things, for she was taken even harder than anyone he had ever known or heard about. Not only was she sick on awakening, but it continued throughout the day and night. Sometimes she awoke from a sound sleep reaching frantically for the chamber pot.

"Is there nothing can be done for her?" Joseph asked Molly.

Molly brought ginger tea for Bridget to sip and gave her drops of peppermint on lumps of sugar. "Go along to work," she told Joseph.

Joseph hurried away, trying hard not to show how relieved he was to leave things in Molly's experienced hands and return to tasks he understood.

Approximately nine months after their wedding day, Bridget gave birth to a daughter. They named her Joanna, a combination of a shortened 'Joseph' and Bridget's middle name, Anna. Joseph was entranced by the wee morsel. Once again, life seemed grand until, in almost no time, the sickness began again. Eleven months after their first child's birth, they were again blessed, this time with a solemn and fretful boy.

Though everyone was charmed by baby Joanna's sunny smiles and red-gold curls, it was the boy who caused the most excitement. Bridget named him Thomas O'Ryan after her father. Joseph, not at all pleased to have a son named for the man who disapproved of him so heartily, refused to call him Tom; he would be Ryan.

The entire staff of the Appeal came to call on the Harrigan's new son. Holding the infant in his arms, the Colonel was quite obviously impressed as he and Ryan exchanged stares. "He's got the making of a fine newspaperman," the Colonel pronounced. "See those sharp eyes, looking right at me instead of wandering aimlessly about like the eyes of most newborns. Yes sir, you can just tell, this little fellow is destined for the news business."

No one but Joseph seemed to notice how the statement brought a look of alarm to Bridget's face. Nor did they take note of how quickly she rose from her chair and, ever so politely but firmly, removed her son from the Colonel's arms.

CHAPTER TEN

O N A JUNE MORNING, more than three years after the fire, the Colonel locked the door of the Appeal's office and strolled toward the railroad station. Joseph, Shaughnessy and the rest of the staff followed him, all of the men smiling, their steps jaunty.

'Tis a memorable day for the Appeal," Shaughnessy said.

"Aye," agreed Joseph.

The newspaper was now one of the city's leading publications. And today, they had been given proof of the respect the Appeal commanded, for the Colonel had been chosen to exchange a message with an editor in Boliver, Tennessee. It was the first such message to be exchanged in the state.

The railroad station was filled with people who pressed to get inside the little room which had been set aside to accommodate the amazing new telegraph machine.

"Let us through, please," the Colonel said. "I'm going to give this thing a try."

The crowd parted respectfully.

Once inside the room, they were silent, all of them staring at the curious conglomeration of wood and iron --- a box, wheel and tap hammer set up on a counter. Joseph thought it looked more like a rudely made child's toy than the instrument supposedly responsible for great miracles.

From behind the counter, Mr. Peevey, the new telegrapher, smiled and greeted the Appeal's staff. "Ah, come in, gentlemen. The marvel awaits you. What message do you wish to send?"

The Colonel hesitated. "I suppose I should have prepared something momentous, but like everyone else, I've thought only of seeing it work."

More spectators pushed their way into the room and Mr. Peevey, a stooped-shouldered, pale little man, held out a protective arm. "Please, folks, move back. I don't want you getting too close to my machine. And no touching."

Joseph studied the strange machine with interest. He had read about it and heard much talk. Invented by a man named Samuel Morse, it was said to be able to send messages over thin copper wires with the speed of lightning. Word was that the first message had been sent from the Supreme Court chamber in Washington. Samuel Morse had tapped out: "What hath God wrought?" A receiver in Baltimore repeated the message.

After that, Joseph had followed reports of the network of copper wires spreading across the country, connecting first the cities of the east, then spreading south and west. Now, finally, Memphis had been connected to the main trunk line in the east.

Everyone waited for the Colonel to decide what he wanted to say, knowing he was as capable of coming up with a fine biblical line as anyone in Washington. But he was not a pretentious man.

"After all, we're only perpetuating, and not ushering in this great era," he said. He settled on asking for news of the Mexican War and for the name of the candidate nominated at the Democratic Convention.

Mr. Peevey shot his cuffs and lifted a hand above the machine. There was a dramatic pause as he appeared to be concentrating. Then he tapped out the message.

In a few moments, the telegraph box began to rattle out a series of squeaky noises. The telegrapher listened, scribbled words on a sheet of paper and handed it to Van Pelt.

"What does it say?" everyone wanted to know.

"Read it to us."

"Excuse me, folks." The Colonel made his way toward the door. "I've got to get this to the office. And if you want to know what it says" -- he flashed a grin -- "you can read it all in the Appeal."

Next morning, the caption 'By Telegraph' headed the column containing the telegraphed items.

"The opening session of the Democratic Convention nominated Andrew Stevenson of Virginia for president," Joseph read. "Why, 'tis almost as if we were there as it happened."

It was indeed the beginning of a new era. From this point on, they would not be wholly dependent upon steamboats, stagecoaches and post riders to bring them news of the outside world. Cotton quotations from New York and river elevations from St. Louis could be printed within a few hours after they had been recorded.

What would it mean to the world when everyone would know everything that happened in the same few moments? Joseph wondered. He wished his father could be alive to witness this incredible invention. For him it would no doubt be a great source of pleasure. And it was amazing so it was. More than ever, Joseph was convinced there was nothing more interesting, more satisfying, than being a part of the news business.

"Except, of course, my family," he amended.

He did love his little family and did not mean to be more devoted to his work than to Bridget.

She was once again spending her days and nights over the chamber pot and his heart went out to her. The constant production of little Harrigans was beginning to wear her down. But wasn't that nature's way? What could he, a mere man, do about it?

How lucky they were to have Molly to help Bridget, he thought. Joanna and Ryan were running about now and had to be watched every second. Joseph and Shaughnessy had built a fenced-in area for them to play in, but the rascals were already trying to climb the fence so they could go down to wade in Catfish Bay. Joseph realized Bridget wasn't too happy about raising her children in Pinchtown but, so far, hadn't protested, a fact for which he was grateful. Probably gave Molly an earful, though.

Bridget did indeed confide in Molly about her concerns. They had become close friends and shared their troubles with one another. At first, Bridget had been put off by Molly's goodness. She'd anticipated a boring companion, but found that a light heart and a fine mind accompanied the generous, caring nature. And a sense of humor. Who could know Molly and not love her?

Aye, 'tis grand to have Molly here with me, she thought. She was feeling a bit better and they were sitting out in the yard, watching the children and sewing for the new baby.

She sighed. "And wouldn't I be completely happy, if we had a garden?" she asked Molly. "With a bit of grass for the children to play in. I know, my complaining to you is a bother and what can you do about it?" But I don't like to say anything to Joseph--and himself so proud of the home he's made for us."

Molly smiled. "Well, you can say such things to me and I'll understand, though I can't do anything about it."

"And I know Joseph can't do anything either, since he has no money to move to a better place."

"Aye, unless he was willing to use the bit of money he's been saving to buy a share of the Appeal."

"The what? He has money saved? To buy a newspaper?"

Molly put a hand to her mouth, looking distressed. "Oh dear, I thought you knew. I thought Joseph ---"

"Seems Joseph only tells me what he wants me to know."

"But if wouldn't have said that if ---oh, you must promise me you won't let Joseph know I told you."

Reluctantly, Bridget promised.

Frustrated, she turned her attention to cleaning every inch of their little shanty, though the steamy heat of summer was almost unbearable.

"I'll not be having my children living in a dirty home, even if it is in Pinchtown," she insisted when Molly pointed out that in her condition she shouldn't be working so hard.

"But for the sake of the infant, you must rest more," Molly persisted.

Bridget remained on her hands and knees, scrubbing floors with a large brush, dusting and sweeping. Throughout July and on into an equally hot August, she continued her obsessive cleaning.

Joseph was surprised when he returned home early one morning to find that Molly had called in the midwife sometime during the night.

"It's at least a month before her time," he protested. "Is she all right?"

"She's fine," Molly assured him. "And your new son seems quite healthy."

Bridget was overcome with remorse. "He'll probably not live to grow up, the way it is with Molly's infants. And meself the blame, getting all taken up with me housework and forcing him into the world before he was ready."

She named the child Connor, after a favored uncle. And she was in a constant dither over him.

Joseph thought she worried needlessly. As far as he could see, Connor was as healthy as any newborn he had ever observed. No one in danger of expiring could yell <u>that</u> loud, he reasoned.

When he expressed this opinion to Bridget she was furious.

"Now aren't you the one, Joseph Harrigan? A fine concerned father you are. Well, you needn't be bothering yourself. I'll tend to the poor wee lad meself."

Joseph looked stricken. "But I didn't mean to sound uncaring. Here, let me hold him."

He lifted the tiny infant and put him on his shoulder. To their surprise, Connor settled against his father's rough shirt and stopped crying. Joseph walked back and forth. "There now, wee Connor. There now." After a few sniffles and a tiny hiccup, Connor drifted off to sleep.

And for some reason, Joseph's shoulder became Connor's favorite spot. When no one else could quiet him, his father could. Joseph would come home after long hours of hard work, take the fussy baby from Bridget and begin to walk.

There was one problem, however. Connor always woke up as soon as he was put back in his cradle. Joseph got very little sleep. Sometimes he could hardly keep his eyes open while he did his job in the noisy pressroom, a room that was becoming busier and busier as the days passed.

CHAPTER ELEVEN

THE APPEAL'S STAFF was now putting out an issue of the daily newspaper every day except Monday, besides printing weekly and tri-weekly editions. There was hardly a moment when some kind of work wasn't going on at their new location on Front Street, and the Adams power press, acquired after the fire, was in use almost constantly. Even an editor as dedicated and hardworking as the Colonel found it difficult to keep up with the newspaper's demands. Reluctantly, he announced he would have to take on a partner as soon as possible. He began to advertise, asking anyone who was interested to contact him.

"Wish I was ready to take advantage of this," Joseph told Shaughnessy. "But I have a thought. Why don't you and I pool our resources and buy enough shares to become part owners?" Shaughnessy shook his head. "Can't do that, Joseph. I have doctor bills to pay. And I'm planning to buy a horse and carriage. I'm hoping occasional rides through the countryside and perhaps stopping for a dinner somewhere will cheer Molly."

"I understand," Joseph said. He knew that Molly was recovering from the loss of yet another infant. Though Shaughnessy had insisted on having the new doctor in town attend her this time, instead of a midwife, the birth had ended as tragically as ever. "Sure an outing in a new carriage might divert her. She deserves to be considered first of all."

"Aye. Maybe I could help you buy a few shares of the paper at some later date. After all, Joseph, you're only twenty-four."

"Twenty-four-and-a-half."

"And a half then. You're still very young. What I'm saying is, your time will be coming, lad. The Appeal will no doubt have other shares to sell later on. Just be patient. A bit more seasoning is what you're needing."

"When it comes to the news business, I'm as seasoned as any man twice my age," Joseph protested.

But he realized Shaughnessy was right about waiting. What could he do but hope that the Colonel would be unable to find anyone he considered worthy of becoming part owner of the Appeal? Perhaps Joseph's willingness to work long hours and his constant dedication would be taken into consideration--and the money he had to give would be found acceptable.

Sadly, Joseph's hopes died as a string of promising newspapermen arrived for interviews. The Colonel chose John McClanahan, a thirty-year-old journalist from Jackson, Tennessee, a man who had the money as well as the needed experience.

Most of the staff approved the Colonel's choice. A robust, jovial man, McClanahan was. He went about greeting each employee with a hearty handshake and saying --boastfully,

Joseph thought--that the Appeal would be surging ahead in the months to come.

"Acts like he owns the whole place," Joseph grumbled.

Shaughnessy shushed him. "He's the man the Colonel wanted. You'd best mind your manners and accept him as your boss. And learn to like him."

"I'll let him boss me," said Joseph, with a fierce scowl, "but I won't like him."

The forceful McClanahan was like a fresh wind blowing through the organization. Colonel Van Pelt still maintained control, but he worked quietly, diligently. His drudgery was easily buried beneath the good-humored blustering presence of McClanahan.

More men were hired. Printers, typesetters, compositors, reporters and editors worked interchangeably, helping one another whenever and wherever they could. Besides being Shaughnessy's assistant, Joseph was now the River News Editor, gathering news three mornings a week and writing a short column. Also, the entire staff served as salesmen, soliciting ads and selling subscriptions while going about their other tasks.

As the staff grew, Joseph couldn't help feeling that he and Shaughnessy were being sifted down through the ranks. No longer did they seem to be Van Pelt's good right hand men, as he had often called them.

"I've a mind to take my money and go buy a press, maybe move to a small town that has no newspaper and start one of my own," Joseph fumed. He began to watch for ads offering such opportunities. After all, the *Appeal* wasn't the only newspaper in the world.

On April 21, 1851, there was a festive atmosphere in the *Appeal's* pressroom as it printed an edition announcing the completion of its first decade in business. Drinks were served and toasts made.

"Here's to the next ten years," Van Pelt said, lifting his glass.

"Hell, here's to the next one hundred years," one of the new men said.

The celebrating continued for days. No one seemed to notice Joseph's lack of enthusiasm. Sure, he was proud of the newspaper for its survival, he thought, and he did wish it well, but he still felt that he and Shaughnessy had been pushed into the background. More than ever, he considered having his own paper. But somehow he was beginning to feel disloyal. After all, if it weren't for the Colonel giving him his start in the business, he might still be cleaning stables. At least he ought to let the man know what he was planning. See how he felt about it.

Joseph watched for a moment when he might talk to the Colonel alone, moments that were becoming quite rare. He found his chance one night when the Colonel had stayed late to work on an editorial that needed last minute changes before it went to press. Shaughnessy and his crew were busy getting ready for the night's run as Joseph slipped away and went to knock on the Colonel's door. "It's me, Joseph," he called out. "Can I come in to talk to you about something?"

There was no answer. The door was ajar, so he pushed it a bit wider and looked inside. He was surprised to find the Colonel slumped over his desk. He withdrew quietly and walked away, thinking that the poor man must be exhausted and in need of a bit of rest. But something nagged at him. Had he ever seen his hard-driven boss asleep on the job? And his sprawled position seemed so--so uncolonel like. So wrong.

With pounding heart, he turned and rushed back into the office. He shook the Colonel's shoulder, calling out his name.

Joseph's cries summoned Shaughnessy and the rest of the men. Gently, they removed the pen still clutched in the Colonel's hand and laid him out on the floor.

"He's gone from us," said Shaughnessy.

The Colonel was buried in Winchester Cemetery. Huge crowds attended the funeral. They came from all over Tennessee, Mississippi and Kentucky. Letters and telegrams poured in from across the country, from lands across the sea, expressing sorrow and regret, saying the world had lost a great man.

After the service, Joseph and Shaughnessy helped Molly and Bridget into their carriage. They were the last to leave the cemetery. Joseph looked back and could hardly bear the lonely look of the grave. "We can't just leave him," he thought. "Just leave him out here all by himself." The irrational words rose in him. He clamped his mouth shut and reached for Bridget's hand.

"There now, hush now," she whispered, though he hadn't said anything aloud. Or had he?

That night Joseph borrowed Shaughnessy's horse and buggy and returned to Winchester Cemetery alone. Mist swirled just above the ground as he urged the horse forward along the deserted lane. Moonlight cast an eerie glow on the rows of stone monuments. It was so quiet, he thought. He heard nothing in the graveyard but the soft thuds of his horse's hooves. A mournful blast from a steamboat's whistle drifted up from the river and somewhere a dog barked, but somehow these sounds seemed to deepen the silence around him.

Joseph supposed it was his Irish ancestry that made him leery of the spirit world. He peered into the darkness, searching for the newly-covered grave. He wanted to be with the Colonel once more. Today, when the crowd had trampled about, there had been no quiet space for deep emotions to find expression. And there was something bothering Joseph. The Colonel had died without warning, leaving much that needed saying. "I didn't even get to say a proper goodbye," he thought, his heart aching over the lack.

When he found the rectangle of loose sod he searched for, he climbed from his buggy and walked over to kneel beside the grave, one knee pressing into the soft soil. What should he say first? Where should he begin? Like a father to him, this good man was. This kind intelligent man. How could he have thought of leaving him? In the dim light, Joseph saw that a small flat tombstone had already been set in place at the head of the grave. The inscription had been requested by the Colonel -- "H.V.P., Editor of the *Appeal*. Died April 23, 1851" – an inscription as simple and unassuming as the man himself. He hadn't even wanted his name spelled out, just wanted it known that he was editor of the *Appeal*.

As Joseph pondered the words on the tombstone, he sensed a burden settling about his shoulders. He knew now that he must stay no matter what. Though McClanahan would be taking over, the newspaper would always be the Colonel's monument.

"I'll not be going away after all, not until the day I die," Joseph vowed. "I'll be staying to help make the *Appeal* the grandest newspaper in all of Tennessee." He put a hand on the grave of the man he'd loved since he was a lad. "'Tis me promise to you."

CHAPTER TWELVE

F OR A TIME THE *APPEAL* FLOUNDERED about, rudderless. McClanahan was biding his time, saying that it didn't seem decent to be taking the Colonel's place too eagerly. Nothing was decided, nothing written, no new policies adopted until the staff had first discussed how the Colonel would have handled the matter. What opinion would he want the *Appeal* to express? Which side of an issue would he wish them to take?

But McClanahan was a natural leader. Gradually, the men began to look to him for direction. To trust him. Some even called him 'Mack' when he mentioned he preferred the informal title. Mack was likable, generous, good-natured and fair in all his dealings. He did, however, have one fault -- he was overly fond of the bottle -- but this was a fault soon overlooked in a newspaperman. Who could object to a man's enjoyment when he was so willing to share what he called his supply of the best vintage of Europe?

"Would you be joining me?" he'd ask, and the men would gather around.

Even Shaughnessy. The traitor.

Joseph was aware of the need to accept McClanahan. Wasn't it said that the death of an editor often meant the end of his newspaper? The Colonel had died so young, only fifty-four, he was, and he had devoted most of his short life to his paper. And hadn't Joseph promised he would do all he could to see that the *Appeal* survived and prospered? With this in mind, he forced himself to continue in his job, to do it well.

Still, he just couldn't get accustomed to seeing McClanahan sitting at the Colonel's desk, using his paste pot, his scissors, his favorite quill.

He was displeased when, after a time, the staff began to consult with McClanahan, to ask deferentially whether all the news was in before they locked up an issue and began a press run. Joseph refused to conform, kept his distance. Refused to call him Mack. And whenever things went well, or there was a small triumph to celebrate, Joseph had to swallow his resentment. Shouldn't the Colonel be here to see his dreams realized, to see that the *Appeal* had not only survived the Whigs, but appeared to have outlasted them?

By the early eighteen fifties the Whigs were said to be dead or dying. However, Joseph began to read accounts of a new political movement, now threatening the power of the Democrats. Known as 'Nativists' at first, the new party presented itself as the 'American Party', though it was a well-known fact that they had begun as a secret society opposed to the waves of immigrants entering the country. When they continually denied this, often replying 'I don't know' when asked about their party's origins and goals, people began to call them the Know-Nothings. How scornful the Colonel would have been of their selfish ideals, Joseph thought. How displeased he would have been with the many Memphians who welcomed them into the territory.

The city's population was now over twenty thousand and more than a fourth of these – Germans, Italians and Irish -- were considered "foreigners."   "Old families" who had been in America for several generations, looked down on the new arrivals. And Pinchtown, made up mostly of Irish laborers, became a favored target for the Know-Nothing plot to rid the country of what they considered "those upstarts."

Joseph hoped Bridget wouldn't find out about this new threat to their neighborhood.

But he hoped in vain, for Bridget had developed a most unladylike habit. She read the newspapers. Not just the women's section in the Sunday Appeal that he always brought home to her, but other weekly and daily papers as well. He wasn't sure where she got them. Molly, perhaps? But whatever the source, he often came upon her reading earnestly as she sipped her tea. To Joseph, it seemed unnatural to see a woman holding up a newspaper just as a man would do. Most women he had known in his life had been too busy with their household concerns to have time for such things. And if they did have leisure, didn't they always have their handwork and a basket piled high with mending?

Joseph blamed the changes in his wife and her new independence on the fact that there had been no new babies to care for. Molly had passed on information she'd gotten from her fancy new doctor, ways to avoid having a child every few years. The doctor had told Molly that bearing children so often took a harsh toll on a woman's health and compromised her ability to produce a healthy child.

What blather. Joseph didn't believe a word of it. But Bridget did. And now she followed the doctor's methods as faithfully as Molly did, no matter how much Joseph protested that they were unnatural.

The strangest thing about the doctor's weird advice was that, thus far, it had worked. Connor was almost six years old and there'd been no sign of a new wee brother or sister. Joseph felt sure the freedom this provided Bridget gave her more time and energy to find reasons they must move from Pinchtown.

Besides reading the newspapers, she had begun wandering about town, making the acquaintance of blathering biddies who were only too happy to put a flea in her ear.

Sometimes Joseph suspected Bridget knew more than he did about what was going on. She was always informing him of things she thought might have escaped his attention.

"Did you know, Joseph," she asked him one evening, "that the mayor is warning all citizens to keep alert? 'Tis said a gang of Irish laborers will be approaching the city this very night for a mass attack on the Know-Nothings. The police will be on duty all through the night, or so 'tis said. There's sure to be trouble, Joseph, and what if the fighting comes this way?"

"Should I stay home, do you think?" She considered. "I suppose that won't be necessary. Molly is going to come stay with us. And actually, they'll not likely be wanting to harm women and children."

"No, that's not who they're after. Anyway, nothing is going to happen. 'Tis all a lot of nonsense." He did not tell her that he had also heard rumors of a possible conflict. However, the rumors had come from the mayor's office and he was a Know-Nothing himself, glad to promote anything that would cast a bad light on the Irish.

"Just stay inside," Joseph advised Bridget when he left for work.

He noticed, as he walked along, that lamps were burning in most of the houses he passed, though it was almost midnight. And groups of angry men were gathering on street corners, armed with shovels and picks and whatever else they thought would cause damage to another. Sentiment against foreigners seemed to be nearing hysteria. The mayor had indeed done a fine job of stirring up the town.

But in spite of all the threats, the night remained peaceful. Obviously, the problem existed only in the minds of the Know-Nothings.

And the next day, McClanahan wrote an editorial expressing the *Appeal's* opinion of the event.

"Away with such humbuggery and nonsense," the editorial began. To chide the city, McClanahan turned to sarcasm. Tongue-in-cheek, he concluded with: "Three native Americans were seen in our city last week. They were engaged in selling beaded moccasins and were of a dark copper color. We learned that there were quite a large number of them in the territories west of the United States, whither they have been driven by the foreigners and Christians. They are at present gravely debating the question as to whether it would not be a good policy to take steps prohibiting the further immigration of foreigners into the country."

Joseph felt a great surge of pride as he read the editorial.

What a clever come-uppance for the Know-Nothings. How the Colonel would have loved what was written. No wonder he'd chosen McClanahan for a partner. For it was obvious to Joseph now. McClanahan was a fighter with heart.

And he didn't back down.

Those who were in league with the Know-Nothings were angry with the *Appeal's* stand. They wrote vicious letters of protest. But McClanahan refused to print the letters, declaring that he was "unwilling and unprepared to be made the instruments of such alienation of one class of our citizens from another."

Some Memphians tried to force the *Appeal* to find itself a new editor. McClanahan held fast, ignoring the storm. "What good is a newspaper if it isn't allowed to stir up the complacent and puncture the pompous?" he asked.

Joseph found his respect for the man growing stronger each day. "Never thought I'd say this," he told Shaughnessy, "but I'm beginning to think the Colonel couldn't have made a better choice for his successor. With Mack as our editor, sure and we'll soon have a grand battle going. Those Know-Nothings will wish they'd never fooled with the *Appeal*."

CHAPTER THIRTEEN

"**N**EVER HAVE I SEEN such children for wandering," Bridget complained to Joseph one evening as he set out for work. Every time I take my eye off them, they're gone who knows where. And who knows what kind of danger they'll encounter."

"Ah now," Joseph soothed. "Aren't we surrounded by friendly neighbors who'll come to their rescue if they need it?"

"Am I supposed to depend on others to keep my children safe?"

"Well---" He decided it would be wise not to say more. She looked exhausted. He had not noticed how thin she'd become. And there were dark circles under her eyes, circles which didn't belong on a face so young. "I've been intending to tell you," he said, his voice so gentle he hardly recognized it, "if you'll just be patient, I'm going to buy you the grand home you're wanting."

"And when would that be?"

"Soon," he said. And he really meant it. As soon as he got his share of the newspaper paid for, he would begin saving for Bridget's new house.

She turned away. "If you'll haul some water up from the river before you leave, I'll give the children a cool bath." There was only resignation in her voice.

Several mornings later, he returned home from a morning spent gathering news for his river column to find her packing.

"I'm waiting no longer," she told him. "I'll either have a proper place to raise my children or I'm going back to Ireland. I've already sent a letter to my father."

Though it was only mid-morning, her day had gone badly, she told him. Joanna and Ryan had run away, gone clear up to Market Street, and of course, Connor had followed them. There, they met some children, probably offspring of Know-Nothings, who had thrown rocks at them and Connor had come home with a gash in his head. "The poor wee thing was all bloody. I thought at first his eye had been damaged but it's bad enough, it is. He'll have a scar above his eyebrow. I tell you, Joseph, I will endure no more."

Boxes were piled up in the room and she was filling them rapidly. Joseph knew there would be no use arguing, she had always been as fierce as a mother bear where Connor was concerned. He was going to lose her if he didn't do something. Now.

"Well then, I suppose you could begin looking, just looking mind you, for a new place to live." His words came slowly, as if they caused great pain. "But it must be a wee house. A small cottage located in the south part of town. Somewhere close in so I can still walk to work. Maybe you and Molly could see what's available."

Later in the day, he watched unhappily as Bridget, Molly and the children set out in the carriage. He had hoped to live in Pinchtown a few more years. She didn't understand how he felt. Sure, Pinchtown wasn't quality like she was accustomed to, but hadn't she known from the beginning that he was shanty Irish and content to remain so?

He thought moving to some fine neighborhood in south Memphis might be the ruination of him, might change him into a pompous waistcoat-wearer with nothing but serious thoughts in his head. As far as he was concerned, living in Pinchtown among so many of his fellow countrymen was grand. And he loved the little shack he and Shaughnessy and Molly had fixed up because it was the first home he'd had of his own since he was a wee lad, although he was too proud to mention this to Bridget. Ah well, he would let her look. Maybe she wouldn't find anything suitable that they could afford.

But less than a week later, Bridget told him she had fallen in love with what she called "a fine family home." She insisted that Joseph must see it as soon as possible. Molly offered to keep the children and they set out in Shaughnessy's carriage. They drove to the outer limits of south Memphis and then, to Joseph's dismay, continued onward.

"Where are we going?" he asked, looking about at the meadows they passed, at the big elm trees whose branches met over the road. "We're practically in the wilderness. Sure, you're not thinking of living way out here."

"Don't worry." She patted his hand. "The horse-car stops within a half mile of the house. And as you often point out, Memphis is growing fast. 'Tis only a matter of time before the town will be all around us. Here," she said, pointing to a driveway. "Turn in here."

Joseph pulled back on the reins. He saw a large gray house at the end of a curving driveway. "Is this the house you've chosen? What were you thinking of? We could never afford such a place."

"But we can. Do you remember that, when I came to America, my father provided money so I could return to Ireland should I wish to do so?"

Joseph grumbled an answer. He did indeed remember.

"Well then, after Joanna was born, he allowed as how I'd not be coming back."

"True enough."

"But he still wanted me to have that choice – if it became necessary."

"Grand of him to be trying to make off with my wife."

"Ah Joseph, he just had my well-being at heart. And he told me that if I sent the money back, he would put it in the bank where it could earn interest. And it did earn interest, Joseph. You'd be surprised how much. After more than ten years, I -- we – have quite a sum."

She seemed so pleased that he had to look away from the happy glow of her face in order to remain firm and businesslike. "I'll grant that the money would have added up over the years. But still, it couldn't be enough to buy this. Why, it's almost an estate."

"'Tis," said Bridget calmly. "At least that's what Mrs. Claybrook calls it. She's the widow who owns the house, and she said we could make a payment on it and the bank would fix it so we could pay the rest with yearly payments. And she's selling it for a very reasonable price because she's anxious to move closer to her family. Oh Joseph, can't you at least let me show you around inside? Mrs. Claybrook has given me a key. Come on. It can't hurt to just look."

Reluctantly, he urged the horse up the driveway. "Gray was never my favorite color." He was in no mood to approve anything. "But it has plenty of lacy white trimming to brighten it. 'Tis like icing on a cake, don't you think?"

"A gray cake?"

"Oh, shhh. Don't go judging it before you've seen it all."

They stopped before the stairs leading to a wide veranda. She climbed down from the carriage without his help and waited while he tied the horse to a hitching post. As they walked across the veranda, Bridget removed a key from her reticule. "Now remember, give it a chance," she pleaded.

Grudgingly, Joseph admired the massive front door with narrow etched glass windows on each side. Inside, he was impressed by the graceful stairway which followed the curving wall of a large entryway. But as he looked closer, he noted that the air of elegance did not hold up. There was a sad, neglected look about the place. Sagging wallpaper. Peeling paint.

"It needs a bit of fixing," Bridget admitted. "Mrs. Claybrook's husband was bedridden for years before he passed on, rest his soul. But don't worry. I have the money to make needed repairs. And Molly is going to help make curtains and draperies. In no time, we'll have the place looking like a real home."

He could no longer ignore the happy note in her voice as she showed him the front and back parlor, the dining room with its charming wainscoting, the huge kitchen, a sunroom and a study (for him, she said.)

When they returned to the foot of the stairway, she stood for a moment, admiring it, a faraway look in her eyes. "I can just picture our daughters floating down the stairs in their wedding finery," she said.

Daughters? Had she made the word plural or had he imagined it?

Upstairs, six large rooms needed paint and wall paper--even more than those downstairs. She was pleased with the large linen closet, though. Seemed to think that made up for everything.

"There's more to see," she said, taking him down a narrow back stairway, through the kitchen and out into the rear of the house. "There's several outbuildings. A wash room. A carriage house. And behind that, there's three small cabins. Oh, and two acres of land come with the house."

He whistled softly. "What in the name of heaven would we do with all this?"

She lowered her eyes. "There'll be a use found for it, you'll see. Such a house is meant for a large family. And you know I'm wanting more children."

He knew no such thing. He thought of the kettle of warm water which waited in their bedroom each night. Was he to assume that, in this house, the teakettle would no longer hover about to put an end to their closeness? He gave her an intent look. She blushed.

"'Tis a grand house," he decided.

They met Mrs. Claybrook at the Farmer's and Merchant Bank and Joseph signed the papers which made him the owner of the house. He refused to use the money Bridget's father had given them. Instead, he invested a large part of his savings. He hoped he would be able to save more soon for it if Mack made good his stated intention of taking on a partner in the near future, he hoped to at least make an offer.

The bank loaned them the money needed to pay the balance on the house. In turn, Joseph agreed to pay them back at the rate of six hundred dollars a year for the next ten years.

Mrs. Claybrook had tears in her eyes as she handed the keys over to Joseph. "I do hope you and your family will be happy in my home," she said, dabbing at her tiny nose with a lace handkerchief. "Such a house should be filled with children, don't you think?"

Bridget patted the woman's plump shoulder. "I do indeed. And don't you fret about the house being lonely. I've always intended to have at least seven. Maybe more."

"Well then," – Mrs. Claybrook brightened – "I can leave with visions of a happy family in my beloved home. I have no choice, it seems, but to go up north and live with my sister in Chicago. But, oh dear, it's so different. Like another country almost."

"So I've heard," said Joseph.

"Oh and there's one more thing," said Mrs. Claybrook, as if suddenly recalling a matter of small consequence. "I've left my remaining slaves in the slave's quarters. I hope you'll be able to spare them one of the cabins until I'm able to send for them."

"Slaves?" said Joseph.

"Just two. A woman and her husband."

"Oh. Well then, I suppose . . ."

"I'll send for them as soon as I've convinced my sister to accept them. She doesn't believe in slavery but, you see, Viney is more like a friend. I've had her for years. And no telling where she'll end up if I don't see to her."

Well, if it's all right with my wife," -- Joseph gave Bridget a questioning look and she nodded -- "they can make themselves welcome until you're ready for them. I would never consider owning slaves, so we have no use for the cabins." Or the other outbuildings and the two acres, he thought. But he said nothing. The house was now theirs. And he was a man with a mortgage to be paid. The responsibility rested uneasily on his not quite thirty-year-old shoulders.

CHAPTER FOURTEEN

CARPENTERS AND PAINTERS SWARMED over the new house, making necessary repairs, giving its outside a fresh coat of gray paint with white trim. Inside, another crew refinished the woodwork and adorned the walls with pleasing patterns of wallpaper. As promised, Bridget paid for all repairs with her savings. Meanwhile, she and Molly shopped for furniture and made draperies for the many windows. When all painting and repair work was done, the floors newly varnished and the furniture delivered, the Harrigans moved into the house.

The first morning, Joanna awakened at sunrise and looked about, admiring her surroundings. In all her ten years, she had never had a room of her own. It was a perfect room, she decided. Light and airy, with cheerful daisy wallpaper and white furniture. She lay in bed for a while, feeling contented. Then, she threw back the coverlet Molly had made her and hopped out of bed. She was eager to start exploring the neighborhood.

She dressed hurriedly, tiptoed past the bedroom where her mother slept and entered the sleeping porch to wake her brothers.

"Get up sleepy-heads," she whispered. "And be quiet so you won't wake, Mama. I heard her tell Papa she was tired to the bone. But I'm not tired in the least and I want to go see the slaves Mama said were living out back."

Ryan reached for his knickers and stepped into them. "I thought Mama told us not to bother them."

"I'm not going to bother them. I'm just going to look."

"I want to see, too," Connor said.

"Well come on. And don't make any noise."

They crossed the dew-covered back yard, went around the carriage house and approached the cabins.

"Maybe we can keep them," Connor said.

"Don't be silly," Ryan told him. "Papa would never allow us to have slaves."

"Then why did we get up so early to go look at them?"

"No one said you had to come with us. Now stop talking. They'll hear us."

When they neared the cabins, the three children walked softly, creeping from bush to bush, stopping when they came upon a man building a fire in front of an open doorway. When the man stood, he was quite impressive. Tall, slender and dark with silvery hair. He hummed to himself as he worked on the fire, throwing on more wood. After a while, he stopped humming. Without turning in their direction, he said, "Y'all can come out and say good mornin' now."

The Harrigans pushed their way out of the bushes.

"We just came here to meet you," Ryan said. "We're your -- your new neighbors. From up at the big house."

Joanna felt a need to explain the size of their house, lest Ryan seem to be bragging. "The house is big because Mama said we're going to be a big family."

He smiled at them. "That so?"

They heard a soft chuckle from within the cabin and a woman appeared in the doorway.

"Will, why you not askin' our new neighbors to set for a spell?" she asked.

Joanna looked around. There were several logs in the yard but no furniture.

"That's right, young miss," the woman said, in a cheery voice. "Pull yourself up a log and set. We'll be havin' coffee soon. And some mighty fine hoe cakes and molasses. You're welcome to join us."

Hesitantly, Joanna, Ryan and Connor sat in a row on one of the logs.

"Would you fetch some water, Will? The woman asked.

She turned to the children. "I hope your Mama don't mind us using your well."

"Oh no, ma'am," Ryan said.

"You can call me Viney," she said. "And my husband, he be called Will. We won't be here long and Miz. Claybrook, she told me your Mama said for us to make ourselves to home." She bent over to place an iron frying pan on rocks that held it above the fire. "Reckon the fire's about right now for cooking those hoe cakes. I'll bring the batter out." She returned to the cabin and came out carrying a large bowl, stirring its contents with a wooden spoon as she walked.

She's beautiful, Joanna thought. She was tall and big-boned and graceful. Her skin had a reddish tinge. Joanna decided it was about the color of mama's new mahogany dining table. A bright printed cloth was tied around her head, and a homespun dress flapped about her ankles.

"Now let's get those hoe cakes to cookin'." She said. Will returned with a pail of water and busied himself, stacking wood beside the cabin.

The young Harrigans thought they'd never eaten a tastier meal. The hoe cakes, made of corn meal and water, were fried to a perfect crispness. Then Viney filled their tin plates with molasses until the hoe cakes were thoroughly sopped. She handed each child a cup of steaming, black coffee, also sweetened with molasses. Eagerly, they accepted. They weren't usually allowed to have coffee.

They had just finished eating when Bridget appeared. "Well, there you are." She stopped and fanned her flushed face with the bottom of the white apron she wore. "I thought I'd find you here. When am I going to learn that telling you children not to go somewhere only makes you more determined to go?" Bridget paused, out of breath. She swayed and reached out a hand to steady herself on one of the trees. "I – I'm a bit dizzy. I guess I walked too fast. Do you suppose I might sit down?"

Viney hurried to guide her toward one of the logs. "There now, rest yourself."

Bridget sat down, then remembering something, tried to stand again and abandoned the effort. "I ought to be seeing to the peach cobbler I left cooking," she said. "Meant to finish it and bring it out here as a neighborly gesture. Then I discovered the children weren't in their beds and forgot all about it. I hope it doesn't burn."

Viney suggested that Ryan go up to check on the cobbler. "You sure don't look too good, Miz ---"

"Bridget."

"Miz Bridget. Viney is what folks call me. And funny thing, I was just thinking I ought to go up and see about you today. See how you're getting along. And offer my help."

"Oh, I wouldn't want to take advantage of ---"

Viney lifted a hand. "Hush now. Don't talk about taking advantage when my man and I would likely be having to camp out if it weren't for you. I mean to repay you somehow."

"Oh, that won't be necessary. I have Joanna and the boys and ---."

"We wants to earn our keep," Will insisted. "That's a big house you've taken on. You'll be needin' a bit of help."

"And I'm 'spectin' you might be feeling poorly these next months," Viney said, her voice kind. "I'm mighty experienced at guessin' such things. So, if you'll allow me, I could lighten your load. I could help you clean and do some cookin' for your man and your young'uns." Viney stood taller, looking proud. Folks say I'm a mighty good cook."

"I'm sure you are. But you see, the house was, well, quite expensive for us and we won't be able to afford any help. Not yet."

"Who says nothin' about affordin'? I mean to do it in return for you bein' so kind and lettin' my Will and me have a place to stay until Miz Claybrook sends for us. So let's just think of me as a friend, a friend helpin' out a neighbor."

Bridget smiled. "A friend. Aye, I do need a friend."

Early the next morning, Bridget hurried to answer a knock on her back door. She found Viney standing there, a woven basket over one arm and a cloth bundle on the other. "Brought you some a Will's green onions and tomatoes from the garden. And some butter beans. If you like, I could set them to simmerin' with a nice ham hock."

"That sounds delicious, Viney. Please come in. I'll get you a kettle to use."

After that Viney came every day to cook and clean. She swept and polished the house until it was spotless and shining. It seemed to Joseph that she enjoyed her tasks as much as if the house were her own. As she worked, she sang spirituals in a soft, pleasing voice. However, Joseph noticed there was a mournful quality beneath the singing as if it rose from a well of sorrow deep inside. He wondered about the sadness for, otherwise, Viney seemed happy and cheerful.

Molly and Bridget finished the draperies they were sewing, and began to ready the nursery for the new baby.

"I'm getting spoiled," Bridget told Joseph. "And I know Viney and Will won't be here forever. Mrs. Claybrook is sure to send for them soon."

"Well, enjoy them while you can," Joseph said. "You deserve a bit of spoiling."

It was wonderful to see Bridget so happy, he thought. So content.

He didn't regret the move from Pinchtown as much as he had expected. The new house was beyond the fancy part of town, out in the country. His only complaint was the horse-car he had to ride to work. It was inconvenient, for it seldom matched his work schedule.

When he mentioned this to Bridget, she offered to buy a horse and carriage with the rest of the money her father had saved for her. They went to Gilhooley's and purchased a new carriage and a filly, a beautiful chestnut sorrel. Joseph named the beautiful horse "Kilkenny" after the beautiful land he still carried in his memory.

Bridget also suggested they buy a pair of goats to help Will keep the lawn trimmed. "He has so much work to do, with his garden and all," she said. "He even helps me keep an eye on the children. He always seems to know just where to look for them."

Joseph noted that Bridget now seemed much more relaxed about the children. In Pinchtown, they had never been allowed the freedom they presently enjoyed. They soon made friends with other children in the neighborhood.

Often, when Joseph returned from work in mid-morning and found the veranda filled with small visitors, he stopped to get acquainted. Asked them what they would be doing on such a fine day. They always had plans. Picking blackberries in a patch growing near the forest. Wading in a little creek. Catching crawdads. Joseph grew especially fond of Ryan's new best friend, Nate Walsh. Nate reminded him of his cousins back in Ireland. Nate loved being with the happy, boisterous Harrigans and arrived to spend time with the family as soon as he finished his chores at home.

When fall arrived, Joseph enrolled his children in one of the new free schools which Memphis had recently started. Each morning, they gathered with the other nearby children and rode the horse car into town.

"Sure is quiet around here now, with everyone gone off to school." Joseph observed.

"Tis." Bridget smiled at him. But we'll soon get accustomed to it. And Molly and I have so much to get done before we have a wee infant to care for."

The new baby arrived in March, a little girl that Bridget named Maria Emilie, after her mother.

Emilie charmed them all. Even Joseph found her bewitching. He was feeling more fatherly now that he was older. And Bridget was so pleased with the baby that she didn't seem to mind at all when she discovered another child was on the way.

Joseph dreaded the day when Mrs. Claybrook would send for Viney and Will. Will cared for the grounds, milked the goats and groomed Kilkenny. He supervised the children, taught Ryan and Conner to groom the horse and weed the garden. Without being told, Joseph knew that Will was preparing them for the day when he and Viney would have to leave.

But months and then a year passed and they heard nothing from Mrs. Claybrook. Bridget had sent a letter telling her about the new baby, but she had not answered.

Viney shook her head. "Sure don't sound like Miz Claybrook. She told me she was lookin' to hear about havin' little children in her house again."

Finally, a letter arrived from Mrs. Claybrook's sister.

"My poor sister has been quite ill ever since she arrived here," she wrote. "But you'll be hearing from her when she is better."

Joseph and Bridget were sorry to hear that Mrs. Claybrook was ill. But Joseph felt sure it meant they would soon be needing Viney and Will to care for her.

And how would he and Bridget ever manage without them?

CHAPTER FIFTEEN

O NE EVENING, JOSEPH NOTICED there was a letter from Chicago in the mail that he picked up from Wells Fargo. He did not open it up immediately, just stuck it in a pocket and continued on his way to work. He supposed it contained funds or traveling fare for Viney and Will, sad news he was not eager to receive. Bridget would be expecting the new child any day and she had grown increasingly dependent on Viney.

When he reached the pressroom, Joseph forgot about the letter. There was a buzz of excitement in the composing room. The *Appeal* was now being distributed in four states, Arkansas, Mississippi, Alabama, and Tennessee, and its staff had grown to twenty-nine, not counting apprentices. Mack had declared their present building 'crowded and inadequate' and had decided to have a building constructed which would meet the newspaper's special needs. Now, the recently-completed plans for the building were spread out on a table in the composing room. Mack invited everyone to look them over and make any suggestions that might prove helpful.

Joseph studied the blueprints. He was impressed, for there seemed to be an area designated for every activity required in putting out a paper. First floor offices in the front of the building would take orders for advertising. The composing room would be in the basement beside the press room, where a new printing press would be installed. The news room would be on the top floor, along with several large rooms designated "executive offices." A small row of offices in the basement were marked "semi-executive." Joseph supposed he and Shaughnessy would be assigned these.

Joseph didn't remember the letter until he was on the way home the next morning. He read it as he traveled and found it wasn't what he had expected. It was not from Mrs. Claybrook after all, but from an attorney in Chicago. It informed him in impersonal language, that Mrs. Claybrook had "expired", an expression he disliked. To him, it sounded as if a person had simply lapsed because her subscription hadn't been renewed. Mrs. Claybrook, he remembered, had been a dear lady.

When he got home, he told Bridget of Mrs. Claybrook's death. Reluctantly, he gave her the letter, let her read that Viney and Will were now part of Mrs. Claybrook's estate and would be sold so that the money could be divided among the heirs.

"It's not right," he said. "No one should be considered part of an estate to be sold off along with the furniture and livestock."

Bridget was devastated. "Poor Viney and Will. Isn't there anything you can do about it?"

Joseph shook his head. "I'm afraid not."

That evening, Joseph and Bridget walked down to the cabins to tell Viney and Will the sad news. They did not react as Joseph had expected.

Viney murmured "Oh, the poor, poor lady." She put both hands over her mouth but her eyes held terror, not sorrow.

Will brought her a cup of water, which she refused. Then he strode up and down the small room, shaking his head as if he were refusing to believe what he'd heard. Finally, he sat in the chair beside Viney, held her hand, and invited Joseph and Bridget to please have a seat.

"Forgive our manners," he said, but this brings on painful memories."

"What memories?" Joseph asked. "Can we help in any way?"

Will looked at Viney. "All right if I tells them?"

She nodded. "Guess I can stand to hear it one more time."

Will began pacing again. "Know we been actin' strange, but a terrible thing happened to our family. Long time ago we worked for a family in New Orleans and had four fine sons. We was so happy but the man that owned us, he had to go back to France to take care a family business. He left all his slaves to be sold. Made the seller promise not to break up any families. But the scoundrel broke his promise. Separated children from their parents right away. Sold us all separate. Viney and I never saw our boys again."

Will paused, drew in a long breath. "Viney was bought by Mr. Claybrook and a man in Mobile purchased me. Viney and I might never been together again, but Mr. Claybrook, he hunted me up and bought me. Never could find the boys, though. We all looked and looked. Viney and I are still hopin', but it's been ten years so----." He struggled to hold back tears but several rolled down his cheeks.

"Oh, you poor dears," Bridget said. "Oh my, how did you manage to go on with so much sorrow in your heart?"

"Had to," Viney said.

Joseph and Bridget left soon after so the two could be alone to comfort one another. They held hands as they walked back to the house.

"How do they live with such sorrow?" Bridget wondered.

"I don't know," he said. But a thought occurred to him. He now knew why there was so much sadness beneath Viney's singing.

The new infant was born the next day. A boy, it was. They named him Patrick to honor Joseph's father.

Viney seemed especially happy to have another boy to help care for.

Several days later, a man arrived at the Harrigan's front door saying that he'd come to "collect" Mrs. Claybrook's assets.

Joseph took exception to his attitude. "What do you mean her assets? You are talking about people, are you not? Two real live people?"

"Well, I didn't mean to sound callous. I just have a job to do. Now if you will tell me where they are…?"

"I'll tell you. But first I want your promise that the two of them will not be separated."

"Oh, I couldn't assure you of that. The matter is out of my hands entirely."

"And also out of your heart," Joseph said, glaring. "How can you take them away without even saying you'll make no effort to do the right thing?"

The man stuck out his big chin. "I don't think I need anyone to tell me what the right thing is. And anyway, if you're so concerned, why don't you do something? You could buy them yourself. But I don't suppose you'd do that, would you?"

To his surprise, Joseph heard himself saying he would.

The transaction was made. It took almost all of Joseph's money to become the last thing on earth he wanted to be – a slave owner.

He was surprised at how easily he slipped into his role. How convenient it was to leave his family in such caring hands while he devoted his time to the newspaper.

The *Appeal* was now one of the leading newspapers in the south. When Mack was ready to take on a new partner, the asking price was $20,000. Joseph realized this amount would be far above his means, even if he hadn't spent all his money rescuing Viney and Will.

The partnership went to Benjamin Dill, an attorney who decided he would rather be in the news business. Dill, a portly, distinguished-looking man, was welcomed by the rest of the staff.

"Gives the place a bit more class," was Shaughnessy's assessment of the man. "He's sensible, methodical. Just what Mack needs to calm him down when he's off on a tangent, wouldn't you say?"

Reluctantly, Joseph agreed. He told himself firmly that he was not going to sulk and shun Dill as he had Mack. He merely started saving again. No doubt, some day there would be other stock for sale.

The new building was nearing completion. Offices were being assigned. Shaughnessy wanted to be head of the composing room. Mack offered Joseph a promotion. He could choose to become the new city desk editor. Or, would he rather be foreman of the pressroom?   Joseph wasn't sure. He loved the challenge of printing daily issues, but he also enjoyed writing editorials. He told Mack he would have to give it some thought.

CHAPTER SIXTEEN

IN THE FALL OF 1860, the *Appeal's* new building was finally completed. Moving in seemed a great milestone to the staff. They reorganized their departments, taking advantage of the added space, accepting additional responsibilities. As Shaughnessy pointed out, they'd come a long way from the little house beside Wolf River.

Joseph sat in the office assigned to him, feeling a sense of contentment that surprised him. He was glad he had chosen to be foreman of the pressroom. Sure, the large, carpeted offices on the top floor with their wide windows overlooking the river had tempted him. And he might have enjoyed being the City Desk Editor. But this was where he belonged, he decided, here in this small room with its bare cement floor and brick walls, with its single window offering a view of the feet of passers-by on Front Alley. Maybe he would feel out of place in a fancy office.

The *Appeal* was big business now. The new building was said to be worth $40,000. It was rumored that Benjamin Dill had offered $10,000 for a fourth of the newspaper. Out of my league, Joseph thought. And for now, shares of the Appeal weren't available for any price.

Ah well, he would begin saving again. Who knew what the future might bring. And there were compensations in being the foreman of the pressroom. The main attraction was that he would be in charge of the Hoe single cylinder, steam-operated press Mack had ordered for the new building. Joseph had been told that it was a huge marvel of a machine, twenty feet long, six feet tall and eight feet wide, cast of iron, steel and smelt. He could hardly wait to see it.

Just before noon, he heard a commotion out on the loading dock and rushed outside to watch two hefty men unload crates and shove them into the pressroom.

Joseph and his crew went to work immediately, removing the crates and assembling the machine. They intended to have it ready for the night's run.

The job required more time than they had expected. For one thing, there were constant interruptions as other members of the staff took time off from their duties and wandered down to the basement to have a look. Everyone wanted an explanation of how the machine, with its big cylinder actually worked. More than ever, Joseph thought the pressroom an exciting place to work.

In midafternoon, Ryan stopped by on his way home from school, wanting to see the new press, too.

His eyes were shining as he circled it. "Wow, Pa, I'd love to learn how to run a press like this."

Joseph smiled, murmured, "Maybe someday."

"But couldn't I start as an apprentice now? I'll soon be fourteen. Wasn't that your age when you first started working for the *Appeal*?"

Joseph said indeed it was, but the circumstances were different.

"You mean, Mama?"

"Well, yes. You'd have to have her approval."

Would you talk to her about it? Just ask her?"

Joseph studied the boy. He was thin, intense, quietly confident. Tall for his age. And obviously, they shared a great love for the news business.

Joseph felt a stab of hope. How long he had waited for the day when he could begin training one of his sons to work for the *Appeal*. It was part of his dream. He recalled a long ago memory of the Colonel holding infant Ryan in his arms, remarking on his steady gaze and saying that the boy seemed to have the makings of a newsman.

Ryan still had the same eyes the Colonel had admired, gray eyes that looked directly at you. Sure, good eyes for a newsman. Maybe, now that Ryan was older, he could convince Bridget to change her mind about keeping her boys away from the newspaper.

"Well, all right Ryan, I'll talk to your mother," Joseph said. "But don't get your hopes up. I can't promise you anything."

It was late evening before they had the press assembled and installed. Ready to go! The boiler was lit, steam hissed through the engine and the cylinder clicked into action. The crew cheered. As the cylinder turned, it printed papers much, much faster than the old press.

Tom Ebey, the assistant foreman, was scheduled to take over so Joseph and Shaughnessy could have a much needed night off. Shaughnessy left immediately, but Joseph, as usual, lingered to make sure no unexpected problems developed.

As he sat in his office, feet once more propped on his desk while he kept an eye on the men, he was plagued by the notion that he had forgotten something important. But what?

Mentally, he reviewed the day.

"Saints alive," he exclaimed, grabbing his cap and jacket and bolting from the building. "I've forgotten Bridget's birthday dinner."

He hitched Kilkenny to the carriage and urged the horse forward at a fast trot.

He was filled with guilt. Once more he had let Bridget down. She set great store in birthdays, he knew – a person's "special day" she called it. – and she always planned family gatherings for the others no matter how busy she was. And now he had forgotten hers.

"I've planned a wee dinner," she had told him before he left for work that morning. "And the children and I were hoping you could be there. 'Tis not for myself I'm asking, mind you. I'd as soon let the day go unnoticed, being as I'm past my prime. But you know how children set their hearts on such things."

Joseph had promised to be there. And he had intended to keep that promise. He tapped Kilkenny with the reins.

What a neglectful husband he was. But at least he had a present for her, he thought, feeling somewhat better. Several weeks ago, he had bought a tiny ring and had it hidden away in his bureau drawer beneath his long-johns, ready to accomplish its purpose. He hoped her pleasure over the trinket would soften her up for a little spooning in bed.

Lately, she had been stand-offish, turning her back on him and gathering her nightgown tightly about her knees, saying she didn't want to risk having another child, at least not so soon. She had added two more girls to their brood, little Molly Kate and the baby Clare. (It had made Molly very happy to have a child named after her.)

But after Clare was born, Bridget had announced she didn't plan to have another child. Seven children were quite enough, she insisted.

He couldn't argue with that. Still he was much in need of a bit of spooning. The denial, which had been going on for some time now, had made him tense and cross. But, of course, he couldn't expect a woman to understand how such things affected a man.

If only he had gotten home earlier, he thought. Maybe they might have had a private celebration after the children were in bed. Now, the most he could hope for was that everyone would be asleep and he could slip in unnoticed.

But alas, Bridget was waiting up.

"Recalled you had a family, did you now?" she asked, opening the door a mere crack to let him squeeze through into the hall.

She didn't want to hear about the problems he'd had installing the new press. "Always that paper," she said. "Sure and all the saints in heaven know a bit o' printing is more important than a man's wife and children."

Weariness spread through Joseph. "Could we be sitting down to have this conversation?"

She looked him over with distaste and said she refused to be sitting anywhere with someone who appeared as if he had come in through the coal chute.

Joseph felt sudden embarrassment. In the pressroom, it seemed natural to be covered with grease and ink. "I'll be that happy to be taking a bath if you've remembered to leave any pots of hot water on the back of the stove for me."

"Do you think I'd be neglecting my wifely duties?"

He felt the sting in that. She had been a good wife. Better than he deserved. But he was in no mood to admit it. "Do you happen to be knowing if we have any Epsom salts?"

With a sigh, she said she would see if she could find some even if it was the wee hours of the morning and she hadn't yet had a wink of sleep.

"Never mind. I'll soak plain," he said, edging toward the kitchen.

When he finished his bath, he climbed the stairs to their bedroom dressed in a night shirt and robe.

Bridget had put on a long nightgown and released her hair from the bun she usually wore at the nape of her neck. Her hair was now woven into one fat braid which hung down her back and switched about as she hurried around the room, folding the bed clothes and repositioning the chamber pot. She said she couldn't sleep in a disordered room. It was something she said every night.

Joseph stood barefoot by the door, watching her. He wouldn't quite agree with her claim that she was past her prime, he observed, but mothering seven children had left its mark. When had her dark auburn hair become salted with silver strands?

Her face, though still lovely, had a careworn look. Wistfully, he thought of the young Bridget, the lass he had scrimped and saved for so he could send money to have her join him in America. How he'd longed for her then. He'd dreamed of her thick hair hanging about her shoulders and her eyes with their sparks of green.

Now, they were always serious and gray. He couldn't recall the last time they had sparked with green. Aye, the years had taken a toll on his lass.

Noting this made him realize he was no longer a young lad himself. Just recently, he had begun to notice that the whiskers which stuck to the basin when he shaved each morning were showing quite a bit of gray.

It was a sad, sad thing that everyone had to get old, he thought. He leaned against the frame of the door to his bedroom, waiting for his wife to stop frittering about, and a fine Irish melancholy settled upon him.

Then he recalled the ring he had meant to give her.

"What's this now?" she asked as he slipped it on her finger.

"Your birthday gift."

She was silent a moment, holding her slender hand up to the lamp, admiring the tiny sapphire. "'Tis a pretty thing," she allowed. "And 'tis with pride I'll be wearing it."

His heart leapt with hope when she let him place a kiss on her cheek. Maybe after the lights were out ---

Ah, he wasn't so old after all, he noticed as he settled himself in bed. But when he put his arm around her and pressed close to her in the darkness, she freed herself and moved to the edge of the bed.

"You needn't be thinking I'm the type of woman whose favors can be bought," she murmured. "A store bought gift doesn't take the place of a man's giving of his time to his family."

He sighed and turned over on his back, all the youthful feelings going out of him.

For a long while, he turned this way and that, unable to sleep. What a foolish man he was, almost thirty-seven and still getting excited over the possibility of a little spooning.

He made himself think of other things. Was the new press still clicking along? Maybe he shouldn't have left so soon, left it in such uncaring hands. Tom Ebey had several apprentices working with him. But most apprentices, Joseph had noticed, did not have the proper dedication. It was just another job for them. The *Appeal* needed lads who cared the way he did. Another Harrigan.

He recalled his promise to talk to Bridget about Ryan. And if he waited until morning, she would be busy tending the children and would have no time for serious talk.

With a swift movement that shook the bed, he got up and re-lit the lamp.

She blinked at him in the sudden brightness. "What is it Joseph?"

"I have a need to discuss something with you."

"Now?" She pulled the quilt closer about her shoulders. "Can't it wait till morning?"

Pacing about the bed, he began to talk, hardly stopping for breath so she couldn't interrupt. First, he spoke of the new building, of how it had brought a new refinement to the *Appeal*. Then he brought up the war, though he knew she hated hearing about it. Still, it loomed on the horizon, a distinct possibility. And the men of the *Appeal* were beginning to speak of joining the fight. If they did, there must be other men trained to take the place of those gone soldiering or the paper would be in serious trouble.

"We'll be needing younger men," he concluded. "Boys."

She sat up propped in bed. The look of wariness in her eyes told him she knew what he was going to ask. He continued anyway.

"So my thinking is that during these troubled times, what the Appeal needs is some new blood. We must begin training new lads to carry on. Lads who will be truly dedicated." He paused, then plunged ahead. "I was just realizing today that Ryan and Connor are old enough to begin training for-"

"But," she protested, "Connor is only eleven. And Ryan not quite fourteen. They belong in school."

"That's true enough during ordinary times. But if a war comes, they'll be shutting the schools down anyway."

Bridget clutched the beribboned front of her gown. Her voice was low, a dangerous sign. She reminded him that she had never wanted her boys to be newspapermen under any circumstances.

"Ryan is a lad who's loftier of mind. He would make a fine doctor, or maybe a professor or a scientist. And Connor has a gentle soul. He's much too tender to be associating with --- with those newspaper types."

Joseph held up an impatient hand. "I was talking about Ryan, not Connor. And as for Connor being tender, he's only so because of the strong mother-hold you keep on him. He'll soon benefit from the company of real men."

"Haven't we discussed this before, Joseph? Haven't I made it very clear? I don't want my boys to be in the news business."

Joseph was silent, thinking that she was being unfair. After all, didn't she have a house full of children now? Couldn't she share her bounty and allow him to have the say of his older son?

As if she had read his mind, she defended her decision. "I'm only thinking of Ryan's future." She was firm about it. "His teacher says he has a fine mind."

Joseph considered asking why she thought a fine mind wasn't needed by a newsman, but he decided he would rather not hear her answer.

With a sigh, he blew out the lamp and crawled into bed.

He awoke the next morning, frustrated and angry, and left while she was tending to the baby.

He expected everyone to be surprised when he reported for work by mid-morning. Actually, he wasn't due in until midnight.

But no one even noticed him. The entire staff was gathered in the telegraph room, waiting for the election results to come in over the wires. Like most Southerners, they were convinced that if Lincoln won the election, there would be war. The men were glum, fidgety. And the news, when it came was not good.

Lincoln had been elected president.

Now South Carolina would surely carry out its threat to secede. And other states had indicated their intention to follow.

At first, the staff of the Appeal was not happy over the prospect of a southern confederacy. Like most of the folks in Tennessee, they seemed undecided as to which side they owed allegiance. The state was divided into sections, each according to their interests.

The upper east section was devoted to the Union. The agricultural center of the state favored secession. Citizens of the western section, especially Memphis, a city of commerce and trade, figured they had little to gain from becoming a separate nation. Mack's editorials urged everyone to remain calm.

Then, in April, shortly after Fort Sumter was fired upon, Lincoln called for troops from Tennessee to "quell the rebellion." Union sentiment disappeared.

In Memphis, a mass rally cheered a resolution that Memphis should secede from the Union. And in Nashville, a special session of the legislature voted.

Tennessee became the last state in the Union to secede.

Now that the matter was settled, the Appeal published fiery editorials about state's right. A rebel flag, a homemade gift from a group of Secesh women, flew from the roof of the Appeal building.

Stump orations rang out in Court Square. Crowds cheered, growing more and more belligerent.

Each evening, torchlight parades marched through the streets accompanied by bands playing "Dixie". Street bonfires added to the excitement, and that excitement was contagious. Especially, Joseph noted, among the young folks.

He was not surprised when Ryan and his friend, Nate joined the parade. But Joanna and Connor, who had never seemed too interested in politics, also insisted on taking part in the demonstrations. As Joseph and Shaughnessy watched from the Appeal's second floor, Joseph saw them marching along with Ryan, Nate and other youngsters he knew.

The citizens of Memphis continued to ready themselves for war. *The Appeal* recruited an artillery battery bearing its own name and sent it to fight with the confederate armies. They contributed to a fund which placed a cannon on the bank of the river to defend the city. And the *Appeal*'s editorials grew even more belligerent.

People throughout the South praised the *Memphis Daily Appeal*, referring to it as "the voice of the Confederacy." Soon the North was calling the newspaper "the hornet's nest of the rebellion." And the rumor was that General Sherman considered them "a thorn in his side" and was determined to silence them.

"Well, let him try!" Joseph thought

CHAPTER SEVENTEEN

A S JOSEPH STOOD beside his bedroom window early one morning in June, he heard a distant rumble, like rolls of thunder announcing a summer storm, a sound he had always loved. But this, he knew, was no storm approaching Memphis. For weeks, scouts and pickets had been skirmishing east of the city. And to the north, Federal gunboats were lining up on the river. Excitement stirred in his gut, a longing to be part of the coming conflict. But Bridget had been firm from the beginning, that he needed to remain home for the family's safety. Who knew what would happen if the Yankees captured Memphis.

'Tis the reaction of a fool, he told himself sternly, getting all fired up by heroic notions. Why couldn't he be content himself with looking after his family?

He turned from the window and went to the bed where Bridget slept. She lay on her side with her dark hair spread over the pillow. There was a small frown between her brows and her hands were drawn into fists. Lately she'd been sleeping like that, in a business-like manner, as if it were a chore on her list of things to do: sleep seven hours.

She stirred as he stood looking down at her, opened her eyes and sat up quickly. "Joseph, what are you doing home at this hour?"

He went back to the window, answering over his shoulder. "We got the paper out early and Mack sent us home to get ready to go, at least those of us who will be going. The *Appeal* plans to print its last home-based issue tonight and then -- well, the Yankees may be here by tonight. Or tomorrow at the latest."

"That soon?" In a swift moment, she was out of bed, wrapping her robe about her. When she came to stand beside him at the window, he put his arms around her and pulled her close. They stood so for a long moment. If he was going off to war, he thought, this would be their parting. Their final embrace before the children woke to claim her. But of course, he wouldn't be leaving her. He held her closer, she kissed him lightly and moved away from him.

"I have breakfast to fix," she said, "And you should be gathering the equipment and clothing you'll be needing to take with you when the *Appeal* leaves."

He shook his head, not believing what he'd heard. "To take with me? Are you saying you've changed your thinking?"

A shadow of pain passed over her face and she did not answer immediately.

"I thought--" he began.

"I know. I was so sure. Until yesterday."

"And yesterday?"

"Oh, Joseph, 'tis terrible news I've been bracing myself to tell you. Ernie Nelson is dead."

He felt a shock run through him. "Our Ernie?" He had a momentary vision of Ernie, the son of one of their neighbors, a cheerful, friendly lad who often sat on their porch strumming an old guitar. Strumming songs of love. And happiness. "Are you sure? Because sometimes there's mix-ups on the reports from the front, you know."

She shook her head. "This wasn't a report I heard. I was" -- she swallowed hard -- "I was at the hospital doing what comforting I could, when someone called my name. I turned and saw Ernie lying just outside the operating room. When I sat beside his cot, he tried to smile. I could see he was bad off with a wound in his shoulder and a leg that looked as if it might have to come off. He asked me to hold his hand, so I did, and he clung to me. And suddenly, he died. His hand was so -- so still in mine." Tears welled in her eyes but she blinked them away. "That's when wars really begin." Her voice was low, intense. "Before then they're a lot of foolish talk, a lot of men swaggering about. And I could ignore that. Even scorn it. But yesterday I understood for the first time."

He remained silent, holding his breath.

"I didn't want this war, Joseph, but the Yankees are here, killing our children and ruining our homeland. And if war has come to us, I can see why you find it so hard to stand by and do nothing. I wouldn't want a man who felt otherwise. So get whatever you'll need packed while I start breakfast."

As she hurried out of the room, he stood looking after her, trying to adjust his thinking to new circumstances. Was he actually going after all? He moved about, aimlessly at first. What was it they'd been told to bring? He'd take his gun of course – an ancient musket, not in the best condition, but he hoped he'd only need it for foraging. He gathered up an extra set of clothing. And his winter coat and gum shoes. And his knife. No telling how long they'd be gone, or what kind of conditions they might encounter. Pulling the old woolen blanket he used for occasional hunting trips from the back of the linen closet, he wrapped everything in it, then rolled it tightly and tied it. He was so involved with his packing that he didn't notice he had an audience until he looked up and saw three-year-old Molly Kate scowling at him.

"Papa, don't go away to the war." She dug her fists into tear-filled eyes.

He leaned back on his heels and invited her into his lap. "Papa doesn't want to go but he has to."

"But you might get killed."

"Now, who told you such a thing?"

"I hear talking. And I don't want you to go."

She settled into his arms and began to sob. He took a deep breath and held her close, rocking her gently. "Aye," he said, "Aye, 'tis sad." Her face was covered with tears and he wiped them from her cheeks with his thumbs, forgetting that, for some reason, she disliked having them wiped away.

"Put my tears back," she demanded with a fierce frown and he had to pretend to press them back into place. Oh, he was going to miss her. For a moment, he actually considered staying. But only for a moment.

He lifted the child from his lap. "Go tell Mama I'll be wanting my breakfast soon." She liked having tasks to perform so she kissed him and hurried away.

He finished his packing and went down to eat the bowl of wheat shorts Bridget had set out for him. And then it was time for him to set forth. He was surprised by the rush of emotion he felt, the sharp pain which lodged itself in his stomach and refused to go away. For the first time he considered the possibility he might not see his family again. Who knew what might happen?

He gave Ryan and Connor last minute instructions.

"Can't you change your mind and let me go?" Ryan asked. "Connor could look after things here."

"Hey," Connor protested. "If you go, I get to go, too. There's not that much difference in our ages, you know."

"I know, Connor. Fact is we're both going to be drafted if the war goes on much longer."

"They won't have to draft me. I want to fight."

Joseph frowned at them. "Here now, you'll be upsetting your mother with such talk. Anyway, we've discussed this enough and 'tis settled. The both of you will be staying here and there'll be no more said about it."

An understanding squeeze of each boy's shoulder softened his words. He unwrapped little Patrick's arms from around his legs and kissed the top of his head. Then, he embraced each daughter - - how clean they smelled, how silken their hair, how vulnerable their small bodies seemed.

He wanted to hold Bridget close one more time, but she was hurrying about the kitchen, preparing food for him to take. She allowed only a brief embrace. "Now go along with you," she said," in a voice that almost betrayed emotion. "I've much to do. I'll not have it said that I sent my man off to war with no provisions in his haversack." She continued to fill the sack with dried beef, biscuits and a few precious oranges, then handed it to him. As he tied it on his back, picked up his gun and blanket roll, she assigned chores to the children. Chopping wood went to Ryan and Connor. Emilie, helping Viney with the dishes. And Joanna could see to the little ones, give them something else to think about. "It will be easier for them to take your leaving if they're all kept busy," Bridget said.

So Joseph climbed the hill alone to catch the horse-car. Near the top, he turned to look back at his home. Ah, it was a lovely home, with its wide veranda and tree-shaded lawn. He watched as Joanna came around the corner of the house, pulling Patrick and Molly Kate in a red wagon. He hesitated, letting the scene take hold, sensing that no matter where he went or what he did, he need only close his eyes and this moment would be there for him: the house drowsing in sun, the children laughing as the wagon bumped across the lawn toward the elm tree, the wind whipping Joanna's long blond hair about her face. After a while, he gave his shoulders a shake, and reminded himself he had things that must be done.

That night, as Federal gunboats gathered in the Mississippi River above Memphis and the Confederate fleet waited below the bluff, the staff of the *Appeal* ran off the last edition they would issue from their own building. Then, they began loading the Hoe press, the boiler, steam engine, boxes of type and other supplies into wagons.

When they were ready to go, Joseph performed one last task. He nailed a copy of an *Appeal* editorial to the front door of the building. It was the editorial proclaiming that they would rather sink their press into the bottom of the river than submit to the Yankees. The editorial would be there for the Yankees to read when they arrived to take over.

Nine members of the *Appeal's* staff climbed into the wagons to go to the station, though many more had expressed a wish to go. The final count included Mack and Dill and Dill's wife who would be helping Vernon with the bookkeeping. Vernon himself surprised them by volunteering in the final week of their preparations. Shaughnessy, Ed Goins had been in at the start, as had Joshua, a slave loaned to the Appeal by a wealthy Memphis slave-holder. Joseph was still a bit dazed over the fact that he was going too. He half expected Bridget to catch up with him and say she'd had another change of mind.

At the depot, they saw that the freight car the Mississippi & Tennessee Railroad Company had promised was waiting on a nearby track. Without delay, the rebel newspapermen began to push the press and other equipment up a ramp onto the train. Then they carried the boxes aboard, moving quietly, stealthily. It was, Joseph thought, almost as if they could feel the Yankees' breath on the back of their necks.

It was nearing four a.m. when they rolled out of the railroad yard. Standing at the door of the freight car, Joseph saw flames leap up on the river front, saw a red glow spread across the sky. That, he knew, would be the warehouses on Front Alley, set afire to keep the Yankees from gaining possession of large amounts of cotton awaiting shipment to England. The fires cast an eerie glow over the city's skyline. As Memphis faded in the distance, Joseph struggled with a mixture of feelings. Excitement. A sense of awe that he was actually going. And unexpectedly, regret over leaving his loved ones. Ah well, too late for such thoughts, he told himself. No matter the consequences, the refugee newspaper was on its way.

CHAPTER EIGHTEEN

I T WAS AMAZING THAT THE HORSE-CARS were still running, Ryan thought, as he, Connor and his friend Nate rode into town at sunrise. Everything else in Memphis seemed out of control. Or shut down entirely. Many stores had their windows boarded up. And the streets had never been so crowded, at least not so early in the morning. Wagons and buggies hurried in every direction. Some were piled with household possessions, their occupants obviously fleeing the city. Others headed in the direction of the river. And the Bluff swarmed with people.

"There must be hundreds here," Connor said as they walked toward two wagons filled with issues of the *Appeal*.

"We have plenty of bags here," the man who was handing out the papers said. "Any of you boys who want to earn a little money, just grab one. Won't have any trouble selling to that mob."

Ryan, Nate and Connor accepted a bag, then picked up a stack of papers. As they folded them and put them into the bags, Ryan looked around at the crowd. "You know I think there's more like thousands of people here. When I heard everyone talking about wanting to see our gunboats chase the Yankees away, I didn't think they'd actually come this close to the battle site. But just look at them. They're spread out all along the levee. Sure, there must be thousands of them."

"Yeah," Nate agreed. "Seems like they think they're going to see a parade -- or a grand boat race."

Ryan folded a paper with a snapping sound. "Thought grown people were supposed to have some sense. Wonder if they know the Yankee fleet spent the night anchored a few miles up the river? They'll be moving down any time now and bullets are gonna fly."

They settled the straps of their sacks over their shoulders and set out to sell their newspapers.

As Ryan shoved the *Appeal* into outstretched hands and pocketed coins automatically, he was amazed to see that many of the spectators had brought their children. The women were calmly preparing picnics, spreading blankets on the ground, putting jam on bread, peeling hard-boiled eggs. The men were gathered in groups, discussing the coming event excitedly, like boastful boys. Let 'em come. We'll show 'em. Yeah, our boats are the fastest, we'll run circles around them.

"And if they come ashore, we'll make them wish they hadn't."

The editorials in the *Appeal's* two-page farewell issue advised against such rash action. Ryan had read what Mack and Dill had written, had read their warning the people to expect the worst. And if the city fell into enemy hands, Dill had told them that open resistance on the part of the citizens would be useless. "Keep aloof from your conquerors," they urged. But as the men on the Bluff read those words, they swore softly, grumbled that they would do no such thing. Were they supposed to just let the Yankees come ashore without a fight? Welcome them with open arms? No, they said. They would fight, fight to the last man. Fight with sticks and rocks if they had no guns.

When Ryan had sold all his papers, he went back to the wagon to get a new supply. Connor and Nate were already there and Joanna and her friend, Sarah, were with them. "I thought Mama told you not to come here today," Ryan said to Joanna.

Joanna's eyes were bright. "Oh but, Ryan, I couldn't stay away. This is history. I had to see it."

There was a sudden stir among the crowd, shouts of "Here they come." The Harrigans and Sarah made their way to the edge of the Bluff. Ryan's heart skipped a beat when he caught his first glimpse of Confederate gunboats, sitting low in the water, bristling with guns, their bows sheathed with armor plate. Smoke rolled from their smokestacks as they positioned themselves across the river -- eight boats in all, their names painted on their bows – *Colonel Lovell, Little Rebel, Jeff Thompson, Van Dorn*, and three vessels which were named after generals, *General Beauregard, General Bragg* and *General Price*.

Joanna looked down and pointed to the boat closest to them, the Little Rebel. "What are those men doing?" she asked. "Why are they spreading sand on the decks?"

"Because--" Ryan began, then paused. "I don't think I want to answer that question."

But Connor took the matter up with boyish enthusiasm. "The sand is supposed to soak up the blood so the deck won't get too slippery for the men to stand on. It's hard to fight when you're slipping around in blood."

"That's awful," Sarah said, looking ill.

Joanna glared at Connor. "I don't believe you. You're just making that up to be disgusting."

"No, I'm not. It's the God's truth I'm telling you. And if you don't believe me, ask--"

Connor abandoned conversation as the gunboats began to move upstream. Then, a large steamer bearing the name "*Queen of the West*" rounded a bend in the river. The stars and stripes waved from her flag pole.

The Confederates fired a shot, the Yankees returned fire and the battle began. Cannons boomed and shells shrieked through the air. As the smell of gunpowder drifted upward, the crowd cheered. Ryan heard, for the first time, the rebel yell. It was primitive, aggressive. He felt its wild call, felt a sudden desire to join in the battle.

In spite of the opposition awaiting them, the Rebel gunboats continued to move toward the Yankees. Ryan held his breath when he saw that the *Colonel Lovell* and the *Queen of the West* seemed headed for certain collision. At the last minute, the *Lovell* veered shoreward, exposing its side. With a huge crash and tearing of wood, the *Queen* rammed into the *Lovell*, cutting her almost in half. For a moment, the ships locked together, the *Lovell* harpooned like a giant whale. Her smokestack leaned crazily, threatening to fall on the deck of the *Queen*. But the *Queen* shook free and the *Lovell* sank almost immediately, carrying most of her crew to their deaths.

On the bluff, there were gasps, cries of disbelief. Men shouted, "Make them pay." "Go after 'em." Destroy their whole fleet."

But the Yankees were on a rampage. The *USS Monarch* joined the *Queen of the West* and they charged into the remaining Confederate boats. A shot pierced the Beauregard's boiler. It exploded with a deafening roar. Bodies flew through the air. Men jumped overboard. Hissing steam and roaring flames mingled with the screams of scalded crewmen.

The people on the bluff were silent now, their faces filled with disbelief. Ryan put his arm about Joanna to comfort her. And himself.

When the *General Thompson* was set on fire by shells, the crew abandoned ship. The boat burned to the water's surface, then exploded with a force that rocked the entire Bluff. Heat and black smoke engulfed everyone. It was now impossible to see what was happening. But sounds could be heard. Gunboats ramming, blasting, steam hissing. Shells ripping into wood. Gunners firing round after round. Wounded men calling for help.

Soon, the fight moved down stream, the Yankees chasing after the fleeing Rebels.

As the smoke began to clear, Ryan strained to see through the haze that hung over the battle scene. Charred remains of destroyed vessels bobbed about, settling among mud covered fragments along the shore. Bodies floated amid the wreckage. The Yankees were now busy taking possession of captured vessels, securing prisoners and helping the wounded. They were the victors. Feeling sick inside, Ryan turned away and saw that a white flag of surrender had been raised over the post office. The final humiliation.

The crowd on the bluff began to leave, clutching frightened children in their arms. The women wept openly. Men were ashen faced, their grim tightly-sealed lips giving evidence to the bitter aftertaste of their boasts.

"Well, that was history," Joanna said. "But I'm sorry I saw it. I don't think I'll ever be able to forget it."

Later that morning, after Connor and the girls had gone home, Ryan and Nate wandered among the crowd, trying to sell the rest of the papers the Appeal had printed. As Ryan moved about, he kept his ears opened, listened to talk about the battle's outcome and learned that only one of their own gunboats, the *Van Dorn*, had managed to flee undamaged. The rest of the Confederate boats were burned or blown up, or damaged and captured. "Didn't take much over an hour," one man kept repeating, his face gray with shock. "One hour and they destroyed our entire river navy."

At noon, four Federal officers came ashore carrying rolled-up flags. A crowd of angry men followed them to the post office, shouting insults and tossing stones. The Yankees entered the building and reappeared on the roof. As they lowered the Rebel flag, shots rang out. More rocks were thrown. But the men who had boasted of fighting to the last man soon lost heart. Defeat caved in once defiant faces. When the stars and stripes were raised, they stood watching in silence.

More Yankees came ashore and an officer raised a hand in Ryan's direction. "Here boy, I'll have one of your papers."

He and his companion approached and Ryan held out a paper. He did not ask for payment but a dime was pressed into his hand. He stared at the men, curious to see the enemy up close, noted that they looked tired and needed a shave. Hard to believe that a short time ago, they were attacking the Rebel fleet and killing southern men.

The officer opened the newspaper he'd bought and shared it with his companion. "The *Memphis Appeal*, eh? I've heard of that one."

"Where's the *Appeal's* office, young man?" the other officer asked.

Ryan merely pointed in the general direction of Union Street.

The men looked at one another. "Let's pay them a call."

You'll just find an empty building, thought Ryan, as they walked away. A building with the Confederate flag still flying from its staff. But there would also be message for them, he remembered. He and Connor had stopped by the *Appeal* building early that morning and had seen the newspaper Joseph had nailed to the door. Ryan's heart lifted as he recalled the defiant words waiting for the Yankees. If only he could have gone into exile with the Appeal, he thought. If only . . .

THE MEMPHIS DAILY APPEAL.

BY M'CLANAHAN & DILL.   MONDAY EVENING, JUNE 9, 1862.   VOLUME XIII NO. 130.

Daily Appeal.

BY McCLANAHAN & DILL.

GRENADA.

MONDAY EVENING, JUNE 9, 1862.

TO OUR READERS.

The occupation of Memphis by the Federal forces, has convinced us of the necessity of removing our office of publication to Granada, Miss. In taking this step our principal motive has been to continue in a position wherein we may be able to render efficient service to the cause we advocate, hereafter as heretofore; and in accomplishing this, should we succeed, we will find our greatest reward. Our fate is indissolubly connected with that of the Confederacy. Our political action in the past is well understood. We cannot desert the one or change as to the other. Our political ideas were not formed to be cast aside under any exigency that can possibly happen; and so long as two or three States are gathered together in the name of the Confederate States, so long will we be found advocating, as zealously as ever, a continued resistance to the tyranny which a haughty foe are endeavoring to establish over us. The APPEAL will not swerve from its course, come what will, no matter how great the sacrifices we may find it necessary to make. We have an abiding faith in the success of the South, and trust that at no distant day we shall be able to again address our readers from our old stand point. Until we are enabled to do so, the general will find our columns equal y as interesting and very particular as heretofore.

In issuing our lot temporarily among the people of Mississippi, we feel that we are in the midst of friends who will not fail to appreciate our motives. The future will demonstrate to them in the spirit with which they have entered into this contest cannot fail to be subservient; and to aid in the accomplishment of the purpose of all we only desire to continue our mission.

TO OUR EXCHANGES.

THE FALL OF MEMPHIS!

NAVAL BATTLE ON THE MISSISSIPPI.

Destruction of the Confederate Fleet!

Escape of the Gen. Van Dorn With $300,000 Worth of Property!

The Federals in the City!

Incidents of the Day, Etc., Etc

Memphis has fallen. But it is a source of pride to us, in this our first issue from another theater of operations, to record the fact, that she fell honorably, and with her "flag nailed to the mast head." For months the city has been the object of Federal hopes and aspirations, not only because of its important position with reference to the Mississippi valley, but because it was believed that there existed among its people a Union sentiment which would extend, and give tone to the community of the entire State. At last they have succeeded in attaining their object. Their gunboats now swarm before her portals; the stars and stripes are now flaunting from her public edifices; her streets are guarded with Federal soldiery, and a Federal commander has usurped the powers which belong to her municipal rulers. Yet not one voice, to our knowledge, has been raised in behalf of the new administration—not one heart has throbbed in sympathy with the invader.

In order to convey to our readers a comprehensive account of the surrender, we should observe that the evacuation of Forts Pillow and Randolph had taken place two days before. All of the ammunition, stores, and many of the guns had been brought away. Yet, so quietly was this done, that notwithstanding the close proximity of the enemy, they were not aware of the fact until the last man was miles away from the position, "en route" for Memphis, and the last dollar's worth of Confederate property either removed or rendered valueless.

Thursday morning found the troops all in Memphis, about to depart for another sphere of action. Thursday night the Federal fleet fol-

CHAPTER NINETEEN

*The Appeal will not swerve from its course,
come what will, no matter how great the
sacrifices we may find it necessary to make.*
– June 9, 1862

MEMPHIS DAILY APPEAL's first issue
as a refugee newspaper

ONE HUNDRED MILES AWAY in Granada, Mississippi, the refugees carried equipment into their new location. They were surrounded by friends of the newspaper, offering assistance. When their train had first chugged into the depot, the staff had been met by a crowd of citizens who greeted them with hearty handshakes and words of welcome. It's an honor to have the *Appeal* in our midst, they had said. An honor and a pleasure. Been reading the Appeal for years. Knew those Yankees couldn't stop you.

The mayor of Granada had come forward, introduced himself, then reminded the greeting committee they were there to help. "Just let these fellows know what they can do to be useful," he told Dill, "and it's as good as done."

Now willing hands pitched in to assist in unloading supplies and equipment from the freight wagon and transfer it to the new office. They worked with good-natured enthusiasm. The atmosphere was festive. Too festive. Finally, Mack lifted a hand and asked, "Could I have a word, friends? "I want to thank you for helping us. We're indebted to you. But I ask your understanding when I say that we each have our assigned tasks, tasks we must do alone in relative quiet. We need to get organized so we can get our first edition out as soon as possible".

The volunteers had grinned a bit sheepishly. Once more the mayor pushed his way to the head of the crowd. "We understand, of course. We just wanted to get you settled in. We'll leave you to do what you have to do."

The men murmured apologies. Didn't mean to get in the way, they said. But let us know if there's anything else you need us to do for you. Gradually, the men drifted away. Mack stood by the doorway, thanking them – more handshakes – and telling them they were welcome to drop around again any time they wished to do so. "Just don't all come at once, you hear?"

Friendly laughter and then blessed silence. The staff got down to business. Joseph and his crew assembled the press. Shaughnessy organized the composing room, readied dresses of type for the typesetters. Mack and Dill went to work on an editorial the moment their desks were in place. When the Appeal's correspondents sent a full account of the battle of Memphis over the wires, Mack edited the story. Joseph fired up the boiler, started the press and its one cylinder was soon rattling away.

The first edition of the exiled paper was two pages long. Before the ink was dry, Joseph held the paper up to examine it. On the front page, the MEMPHIS DAILY APPEAL nameplate was topped by a Grenada date-line. A graphic description of the battle of Memphis and the destruction of the Confederate fleet was printed side by side with an account of the sad evacuation of Corinth, Mississippi, the latest town to fall into Yankee hands. The issue also contained the editorial Mack and Dill had written to explain in full their reason for leaving Memphis.

"To our readers," it began. "The occupation of Memphis by the Federal forces has convinced us of the necessity of removing our office of publication to Grenada. In taking this step our principle motive has been to continue in a position wherein we may be able to render service to the cause we advocate. In accomplishing this, should we succeed, we will find our greatest reward." The paper's loyalty to the Confederacy was reaffirmed. "Our political ideas were not formed to be cast aside under any exigency that can possibly happen; and so long as two or three states are gathered together in the name of the Confederate States, so long will we be found advocating as zealously as ever, a continued resistance to the tyranny which a haughty foe are endeavoring to establish over us." The editorial ended with a promise that the Appeal would not swerve from its course, "come what will, no matter how great the sacrifices we may find it necessary to make."

As Joseph looked over the freshly printed issue, he was filled with a sense of history. Usually, a newspaper had a very short life, a fact he had always thought rather sad. One day it was sought after, read eagerly. Readers were informed, influenced, entertained by it. But soon that same paper was cast aside, used perhaps to insulate a wall, or to wrap garbage for the dust bin, or it might be cut up to become a pattern for some woman's sewing project. But this issue of the *Appeal*, he thought, would not be tossed aside so carelessly. There would be readers who would see its value, who would treasure it. Perhaps they'd put it away in a trunk or an attic so that, on a day far in the future, someone could turn its fragile, yellowed pages and know exactly how it felt to stand on the Bluff and watch a great battle rage on the river below.   Joseph had never before imagined himself as a grandfather, but for a moment, he saw himself surrounded by as yet unknown grandchildren, telling them how the *Appeal's* staff had fled the Yankees one dark night to produce a refugee newspaper.

Within a week, the *Appeal* was being issued on schedule as an afternoon paper. In spite of the disheartening news their first issue had contained, the staff remained optimistic. The Yankees were now referring to them as a "rebel sheet". A name that made them more eager than ever to succeed in their venture. Even though they no longer had their fine building to work in and their staff was much smaller, they continued to meet every deadline.

They soon settled into a busy routine. They had printed an invitation to those who had fled Memphis, offering to help them in whatever way they could. When Joseph arrived for work the next morning, he found two displaced families waiting beside the door of the office. After that, they had a steady stream of such visitors. Refugees came to ask about missing relatives or to leave messages for them. The *Appeal* became a center for handling mail for exiled Southerners who could not locate members of their scattered families. Letters were forwarded when possible and the names published in the newspaper. In turn, the families they helped often brought the *Appeal* copies of newspapers still being published in occupied cities. The staff devoured these papers, hungry for any news even if it was days or weeks old.

The mails were growing more unreliable every day. Joseph had not heard from Bridget since he'd arrived. Nor had Shaughnessy had any word from Molly. They received only general information about conditions in Memphis from refugees who had recently come from there. This news was not reassuring. Though Memphis had not been destroyed as other conquered cities had been, they still suffered mistreatment. Even ministers who prayed for the Southern Confederacy were being suspended and otherwise admonished. Those suspected of rebel sentiments were often banished from the city or locked up in the terrible Irving Block prison. Joseph hoped Bridget was all right. After all, she wasn't noted for keeping her opinions to herself. Once again, he wondered if he should have left her. Perhaps, he thought, he should have brought her with him as Dill had brought his wife. But there were the many Harrigan children to consider. And, Joseph realized, no amount of insisting would have convinced Bridget to leave her home. No, they were all better off in Memphis.

Still, he did miss his family. Bridget would like Granada, he thought. It was a charming town, though the weather was hot and muggy. The townspeople treated them like royalty. Hotels and private homes offered them free living quarters and the town's best cooks supplied them with fried chicken, steamy shrimp dishes, fresh okra, candied yams, and rich, dark chocolate cakes.

"They're spoiling us," Shaughnessy observed, but no one really minded. Being an exile brought them attention and a freedom from family responsibilities, a freedom new to most of them. They made the most of it. Since no one had to be home at a certain time, a poker game became a fixture in the rear of the composing room. As each man finished his duties, he joined in and games went on day and night.

"There's one thing to be said about war," Shaughnessy said to Joseph as they walked toward their rooming house in the mist of dawn after a night of work and play, "It sure takes the ordinariness out of life."

"It does indeed," Joseph agreed. But of course, they had to remember their soft life in Granada could not go on forever. Soon they would have to move on. The Yankees were advancing, getting closer every day.

That night, shortly after midnight, Joseph was scowling at the unpromising mixture of cards in his hand when he thought he heard Ryan's voice calling out, "Hi, Pop." He shook his head to clear it. His worrisome thoughts were getting him addled, he decided.

"Are you surprised to see us?" the voice continued as two dirty, scraggly, exhausted-looking boys materialized. Joseph stared, open mouthed at Ryan and his friend, Nate. Surprised wasn't the word. He put his cards on the table, face down.

"A sight to turn a man's hair white, the both of you are," he said with a heartfelt sigh. "How on earth did you get here?"

Ryan looked proud. "Came on horseback. Sneaked by right under the Yankee's noses."

"We almost got caught twice," Nate said, cheerfully. "But here we are."

"So you are." Joseph stood and gave each boy a bear hug which seemed to be the signal for the whole crew to gather around for hugs and back slapping. Mack and Dill came out of their office to add their greetings.

"We've brought news from home," Ryan said. "And other stuff."

"How's your mother?" Joseph asked. "And Molly and the children?"

"Everyone's fine as could be expected. And Mama's fine, Pa. Peppery as ever."

"What did she have to say about you and Nate taking off like this?"

There was a slight hesitation. "She didn't say anything-- exactly."

"And why is that."

"Well, we left at night. We figured we should go when it was dark. We didn't want to get her all upset so I just sort of left her a note on the kitchen table. Nate took two horses from his father's barn"

"Sort of left her a note," Joseph repeated, thinking, in spite of himself, that he was glad he hadn't been present when Bridget found that note. Then he got properly indignant. "Well, you are scoundrels, you young pups." He looked at the two of them thoughtfully. "I suppose you think you're going to stay. But you know I can't allow that, don't you now?"

Ryan's answer surprised him. "That's all right, Pa. We just came to bring you some mail. And some other important stuff. Come on, Nate, let's bring it in."

All the men waited expectantly as the boys disappeared, then returned with haversacks. "Here's some newspapers, sir," Nate said. He reached into his sack again. "And a packet of letters."

"I have mail, too," Ryan said. "And also this."

Carefully, he removed an object wrapped in an old towel. He unwound the towel and revealed Dill's much loved wool hat.

"My hat," Dill exclaimed. "How did you boys come by it?"

"You left it back on the shelf in your office, sir. Nate and I were looking around for things left behind and we spied it there. We knew what store you set by it, so we wrapped it ever so carefully. See, we even stuffed paper in the crown to keep it from being crushed." He removed the paper, brushed some lint from the smooth surface of the wide-brimmed hat and presented it to Dill.

Dill took the hat, looked it over, tried it on, then removed it to examine it again. "Hmm, it does appear to be in fine shape. You boys are to be commended. I can't imagine how my favorite hat got left. It's genuine wool, you know. I thought Mrs. Dill had it packed. But anyway, many thanks for getting it to me safely."

Ryan and Nate basked in his appreciative smile.

"I think this warrants a celebration," Dill proclaimed. He brought out a bottle of aged sherry a subscriber had donated to the staff.

The golden liquid was divided into an assortment of chipped and cracked cups and passed around. Dill lifted his drink. "Here's to a pair of clever boys."

"And to Dill's hat," someone added, irreverently.

The sherry was gone in no time but a convivial atmosphere remained. Ryan and Nate were allowed to join the poker game for a while and then Joseph took them to his room to rest up before starting back.

Before the boys left, there was a discussion about whether or not to allow them to take back a packet of mail and the latest editions of the paper.

"They could get caught," Dill warned. "I don't like to think about what might happen if they did."

Joseph didn't like to think about it either. But Ryan and Nate were unafraid.

"We got here safely, didn't we?" Ryan pointed out. "And no man is one hundred percent safe in war unless he hides at home with the women and children. And I sure don't intend to do that."

"Anyway, we know the way to Memphis much better than the Yankees do. We won't get caught."

Reluctantly, the Appeal's staff agreed. The boys were given letters and copies of the latest editions of the Appeal to take back to Memphis.

"Just take care," Joseph said, as he saw them off. "And I wouldn't want you to make a habit of this. Actually, I'd rather you stay here, but I suppose your mothers would have my hide if I kept you."

"We understand, Pa," Ryan said. Both boys mounted their horses and seemed anxious to be off. Still Joseph clung to the horses' reins.

"Take care now," he said once again. "Grant's men are swarming all over the countryside, or so I've been told. You'll want to stay off the main roads. But of course I suppose you already know that."

"We'll be careful, sir," Nate promised.

"Don't worry, Pa, we'll be fine." Ryan spurred his horse, and Joseph regretfully released the reins. "We'll see that Mama gets your letter," he called back as they started down the road.

For a long time after they'd ridden from sight, Joseph stood looking after them. He fought a strong urge to go after them, to keep them in his care, but the matter seemed to be out of his hands. They would get home all right, he tried to assure himself. It was true enough that they knew the shortcuts, the hiding places. They knew where a swamp would hold a horse's weight and when it would be best to go around. They had the advantage of the Yankees who were strangers to the land, did they not?

Damn, he thought. It seemed that no matter what he did, he was plagued by guilt. Was it an Irish curse, this melancholy certainty that whatever disasters occurred would happen because he, in his negligence, had failed to prevent them? A man going off to war ought to at least be able to feel he was doing the right, the noble thing. But having two young boys in harm's way had certainly put a damper on him, taken all his dash, his feeling of adventure, and returned him to the role of family man. His shoulders slumped under the burden. Ah well, perhaps the boys' mothers would tighten their hold and gather their sons back into the nest for at least another year. By then, the war would no doubt be over.

CHAPTER TWENTY

BRIDGET TURNED IN HER BED, twisting the sheet about her legs, kicking it loose, turning again. Worn down, body and soul she was. Exhausted. So many cares to struggle with. So many responsibilities. And herself only one person. She ought to be resting while she had the chance. But she could not quiet her mind. She kept wondering over and over: Had she done the right thing? Should she have joined the other refugees who had been fleeing southward for months? Now, she had no choice but to stay, for the Yankees were building a fort about the city. And General Sherman was on his way to take over control of the occupation of Memphis. He was a crazy man, Sherman. Or so it was said. He could not be trusted to treat a conquered city fairly. Considering this, Bridget was overcome with guilt. Had she put her desire to stay in her home above the safety of her family? Wasn't she the one now? But surely, surely, she told herself, this terrible Yankee General would not hurt children. He was a human being, was he not? She fell asleep at last, a fretful, tortured sleep. And the dream began again.

In the dream, she was trying to get out of Memphis. All ablaze it was, fire roaring everywhere, leaping from building to building. The streets were teeming with frantic drivers of wagons, buggies and carts. They scraped against her frail carriage and threatened to push her aside. Burned out skeletons of buildings collapsed, showering blazing debris. Kilkenny rose, terrified, and she laid a whip across his back to urge him onward.

"Hold tight to the small ones," she cried out. She looked over her shoulder to make sure everyone was all right. Molly and Viney and the children were huddled together. But wait. Someone was missing. Patrick. Where was Patrick?

Without knowing how she'd gotten there, she was now on foot, pushing her way back through the hordes in the street. She tried to tell them about Patrick but she couldn't make herself heard. She screamed, struggled. The crowd continued to push her forward, crushing the breath from her body. She awoke gasping, her heart pounding as if it would leap out of her.

It's only a dream, she told herself and gradually she calmed a bit. She'd not had such dreams until Joseph left. Funny, he was seldom home but just knowing he was nearby, that he could be summoned if needed, had made her feel secure. The realization that she was affected this way surprised her.

She moved to the other side of the bed, to Joseph's side, to find a spot not sweat-dampened and rumpled by her twisting and turning. But it did no good. No matter where she lay, she could feel yesterday's heat lingering in the feather mattress. The air was sultry, still. A black night it was, with only a sliver of moon and stars shrouded in mist. She got up and lit a lamp. She would look at the children, assure herself of their safety. Perhaps then she could get back to sleep.

She checked Patrick first, the troubling dream still fresh in her mind. He slept peacefully, clutching his beloved, ragged stuffed bear. Clare was in her crib, her lips moving around her thumb. Emilie, too, was asleep. Molly Kate wasn't in her bed but Bridget knew where to find her. Since Joseph had departed she'd taken to slipping out in the middle of the night and getting into bed with Joanna. Tonight she was snuggled close to her sister, her thin, sharp-boned little body curled into Joanna's soft curves.

Bridget allowed herself a peek into the sleeping porch where Connor slept. Just to make sure he was still there. For lately, she'd felt him slipping from her grasp. Pining to join his brother, to be part of the excitement. Afraid the war would pass by before he had a part in it. For just a second, she hoped to see Ryan back sleeping in his bed, safely back in her grasp. His bed – still empty. The foolishness of young boys. Or men, for that matter.

After she had returned to her room, blown out the lamp and got back in bed, she stared wide-eyed into the blackness. Would another nightmare come if she allowed herself to sleep? She lay awake for a long, long time, until the sky turned a rosy gray. Finally, she heard Viney come up the back steps and enter the house, heard her shake the stove's grate then clatter about, banging cabinet doors and pots and pans, humming a gospel song. Bridget settled against her pillow, relaxing finally. The sounds from the kitchen were so familiar, so normal. Viney was awake now, looking after the world. She thought of Molly sleeping in the next room. Thank goodness she had urged Molly to come stay with them while the men were gone. And she could sleep at last.

When she awoke again, the sun was shining through the lace curtains. Patrick was leaning over her, his face inches from hers.

"Wake up, Mama," he urged. "You're sleeping as long as a bear."

She sat up guiltily. "Mama had a bad night," she said.

"Well, I think Molly needs you."

"Why do you think that?"

"Because --- is it all right if she's sleeping on the floor?"

"On the floor?" Bridget jumped from her bed and ran down the hall. She found Molly sprawled on the floor beside the window. "Molly," she cried.

Molly's brown eyes blinked open. "Oh, what is the matter with me? I just got up because I wanted some fresh air and ---" She tried to sit up.

"No, lie still. I'll get a damp cloth." Bridget got a cloth, dipped it into the basin of water, then brought it over to bathe Molly's pale face. "Molly darling, you look terrible. Should we fetch a doctor?"

Molly waved a limp hand. "No, I don't need a doctor. I – I think I just need something to eat."

Bridget saw that Patrick had followed her and now stood at the door, his eyes saucer-like. "Go ask Viney to please bring us some tea and toast," she told him. He scampered away.

"I didn't want to admit it, even to myself," Molly said, "but I'm afraid I'm -- that way again."

"Oh Molly. Does Shaughnessy know?"

"Of course not."

"You didn't tell him?"

"And would he be leaving me if he knew? Anyway I wasn't really sure until the last few days." She took a deep breath, half a sigh. "Oh, I know, I know. I've been an idiot. It shouldn't have happened. But he was going away. And we didn't know if we'd ever see each other again. Ah yes, weren't we the fools?" Her voice was bitter, but her expression softened at the memory. She blushed and hurried on. "But how can I be keeping him from his duty to his country when I know, sure as there's a God in heaven, that this child won't live?"

"Hush, don't be talking so."

"But isn't it true? Isn't it the way it always is with me?"

Bridget was silent, remembering the bad times, remembering the sorrow over lost babies. But she mustn't go through it alone-- "We'll have to get word to Shaughnessy and---"

"No. Promise me you won't. Why bring him back to go through such a hopeless ordeal -- again? I know it won't be easy for me. Especially with the war." She hesitated and some of her assurance was gone when she continued. "This terrible war. And now that awful Sherman is coming to make things worse."

"Maybe he won't. Maybe ---"

"But I've heard he's going to make everyone of substance take an oath of allegiance to the North. If they refuse, it's said he'll make them leave town. And I know Dr. Doyle, how loyal he is to his homeland. He's lived here most of his life and he'd never take such an oath. I must accept the fact that he won't be here to help me, and himself the only doctor who understands my problem. Oh Bridget, don't women get themselves into the worst fixes?"

Bridget's eyes flashed angrily. "You didn't get into it alone, did you now?"

"Shhh. You mustn't say things like that. It isn't proper. Anyway it's my fault I'm such a failure at bearing children. Sure, it's something I should be facing up to by myself, is it not?"

Bridget bent down to put her arm around Molly's small tense body. "Not by yourself, Molly darling. You have me. We'll see it through together."

CHAPTER TWENTY-ONE

A PASSEL OF YANKEES weren't going to make her give up her wandering ways, Joanna vowed, as she saddled Kilkenny and rode off to meet Sarah. The two friends rode together each day, giving their horses needed exercise and getting a bit of fresh air for themselves. Although both their mothers had warned them that unescorted girls should remain close to home, they often ventured into town. As usual, Joanna was curious, eager to see what was going on, determined to find out what the enemy was doing to the city she loved. And Sarah, looking small and unsure of herself atop her father's huge horse, Buster, felt duty bound not to let her friend go alone.

In the days immediately following Yankee occupation, Joanna had grieved over the condition of her home town. Though it had been spared the shelling and burning other captured cities had endured, Memphis still seemed a sad sight. Smoke from the burning warships had lingered in the air. Flies swarmed over molasses oozing down the river banks, molasses poured there before the Yankees arrived to keep the scarce item from nourishing the enemy. Most of the shops remained closed, their windows still covered with boards. And soot had clung to everything, even the leaves of the trees.

Now, it was fall and the trees were bare. Sherman had arrived to become Military Administrator of Memphis, had been there since July. Joanna had fretted that he would cause further destruction, might even put a torch to some of the buildings. Instead, he seemed intent on reviving the city so he could use it as a base of operations for the Yankees.

At first, Joanna had thought this a blessing. Sherman made things hum. The owners of shops uncovered their windows and opened for business. Churches, schools and theaters had re-opened. But blue-coated soldiers walked about town as if they owned it and Joanna decided she hated Sherman. Who did this wild-eyed General think he was anyway, with his high-handed ways, making a Yankee city out of her Memphis?

"It doesn't seem like the same place," she complained as she and Sarah rode into town on a wintry day in late November. "The Yankees are just everywhere."

Sarah shivered and pulled the collar of her coat closer around her neck to keep out the wind. "Yes, and look how they're staring at us. Maybe we should go home."

"Indeed we won't. We have more right to be here than they have." The two girls rode in silence for a while, Joanna deep in thought. Almost a month had passed since Ryan and Nate had slipped away leaving only a note, and they hadn't yet heard from them. Didn't even know if they had reached Granada safely. Her mother and Nate's mother were frantic about it. Connor had taken the job delivering telegrams that was supposed to have gone to Ryan, and he always went by the post office before he came home, looking for mail that never arrived. If only the war would end and they could go back to normal living.

The girls rode past Court Square, past the Irving Block Prison with iron bars covering its windows. Joanna tried to imagine what it must be like to be locked inside such a place. When Nate was working there, he had told them the food he took to the prisoners was so awful that most of it was left uneaten. The prison was dirty, he'd said, wrinkling his nose at the thought of it, and it was smellier than a barnyard. He said he felt sorry for the fine ladies and gentlemen who were used to a grand life and now had to live like animals. It made Joanna furious to think about it. Most of the prisoners were guilty of nothing more than being a relative or friend of Confederate sympathizers. Or being the wife of a Confederate officer. When the Yankees were unable to get their hands on the victims they really wanted to punish, they settled on locking up innocent family members and friends.

Pigs, thought Joanna. The Yankees were nothing but dirty pigs. They'd turned everything topsy-turvy, putting admirable citizens in jail while painted women walked the streets, clinging to the arms of fuzzy-faced soldiers.

"I've seen enough of this for today," she decided. She pulled Kilkenny's reins about and headed out of town.

But even at the edge of town there was no escaping the enemy, for the Yankees were building a fort to shut Memphis away from the world. The structure, Fort Pickering it was called, was a zig-zag of earthworks large enough to accommodate ten thousand men. It surrounded the town on all sides except the west where the river formed a natural barrier.

Joanna and Sarah paused on a hilltop to see what progress had been made on the huge project. Men with pick and shovels were digging into the ground and tossing the dirt on rising mounds. Howitzers, Columbiads and other guns Joanna couldn't identify were positioned on top of the mounds at angles meant to sweep the ground should the Rebels attempt to retake the city. Or, she thought, to prevent those held captive within the fort's boundaries from leaving. And what did that accomplish? Did the Federals think they could imprison the entire city?

Wild shouts interrupted her thoughts. "Let's see what's going on," she said, and Sarah followed her as she galloped down a hill and up the next rise. They stopped there and looked down on a group of soldiers who were jumping around, yelling and cursing. And all for nothing as far as Joanna could determine. When the circle parted, she saw two roosters going after each other, wings spread, feathers flying. Squawking and pecking at one another.

"What is it?" Sarah asked, her hand at her throat, her eyes wide.

"Cock-fighting," Joanna said, scornfully. "Ryan told me such things were done, that some men enjoy setting roosters on each other for the sport of it."

Sarah turned away. "How can they be so cruel? Oh, I can't bear to watch."

"And who asked you to watch, miss?" a rough voice asked.

They turned to see that four Yankees had ridden up behind them. They surrounded the girls, moving in so close that Joanna caught the scent of body odor and cheap ale. Their blue uniforms were dirty and their forage caps were set at a jaunty angle.

"What are you doing riding into a restricted area anyway?" one demanded.

"Restricted?" Joanna's eyes flashed. "This happens to be my homeland."

"Not any more it ain't," a stocky soldier told her. "Ain't you heard we took Memphis way last June. So you better be moving along if you know what's good for you."

"Yeh," said another. "Get back to yer knittin'"

"Yeh," agreed the others. "Yeh."

"Or you'll be sorry," said one.

"What are you going to do?" Joanna demanded. "Shoot me?"

"Oh, shush," Sarah pleaded.

"The dark one has good sense," said the stocky man. "And ain't she a purty little thing?"

"They both are, matter of fact."

They moved in closer. One reached out to grab Kilkenny's bridle.

"Get your hand off my horse," Joanna snapped. "You Yankees think you can just have anything you want. And you ought to be ashamed of yourselves. It's bad enough to steal our livestock to feed your men. But to take chickens and make sport of the poor helpless creatures ---"

"Who says them chickens are yours?"

"Well, I suppose you brought them all the way from the North."

A soldier spit a stream of tobacco before answering. "Matter of fact, we did."

"You don't expect me to believe that, do you?"

"No, but it's true anyway."

"They're our pets," said the tobacco chewer. "Just because we're soldiering doesn't mean we can't take along a few animals to keep us amused."

"Those two roosters down there are real fine birds." A young soldier seemed intent on impressing them. "Better'n any old chickens you got around here. One's a Dorking and one a Bantam. Came with us all the way from Indiana."

For a moment, Joanna was interested. "How did you get them here?"

"They rode along on the top of our knapsacks. Or on the breech of our cannons. Or in the cook's wagon."

"I don't believe a word of that."

They threw back their heads, laughing.

"Who cares what you believe?"

"Now get out of here before we---"

One of the men took off his cap and flapped it in Joanna's face. They all hooted, jeered.

The sound of hooves pounding across the ground interrupted. Joanna saw another Yankee ride out of the woods and come toward them. This one, she noted with relief, had stripes on his sleeve. Someone with authority. The other men were obviously the scrapings from the bottom of a barrel.

"What's going on?" the new arrival asked, reining his horse. "Are these men bothering you ladies?"

"They surely are," Joanna said.

He turned on the men, demanding, "Didn't Sherman tell us not to cause unnecessary trouble?"

"But they're not supposed to be here." A sulky answer from a be-whiskered older man. "This being a restricted area and ---"

"I'll handle this." The new man spoke with authority. "Move along, all of you."

Reluctantly, they left. The men who'd been gathered about the cock-fight caught up their roosters and disappeared into the woods.

"Thank you, er, Corporal," Sarah said.

"Sergeant," he corrected. Sergeant-Major Andrew Bradley."

Joanna studied the stripes on the man's uniform. Three down topped by three curved above. Impressive for a man who seemed so young, younger in fact than the other men who had been so rude to them. But he was obviously superior. His uniform was spotless, his boots shone, and he wore his cap set straight on his head. "Sergeant, then," she said. "Whoever you are, we thank you for rescuing us from those awful soldiers."

"I apologize for my men," he said. "But they were right in a way. This is a restricted area. It's no place for women."

"I've always gone about Memphis as I pleased," Joanna said, scowling fiercely. "And I don't intend to have Yankees tell me where I can and cannot go."

Unexpectedly, he grinned. "I admire young ladies with spirit," he said. He removed his hat, revealing a wealth of brown hair above his thin, olive-skinned face and serious brown eyes. "But you still have to obey our rules. It will make it easier."

"And who will it be making it easier for? I can't see that we were doing any harm."

"Indeed we weren't," Sarah spoke up. "And we're leaving right now. Aren't we, Joanna?"

The Yankee looked at Joanna, his eyes lingering. Then he turned his attention to Sarah. He put out his hand to caress Buster's velvety nose. "You have some magnificent horses in these parts."

Joanna couldn't resist pointing out that they wouldn't have them long if the Yankees continued to slaughter them.

He removed his hand from Buster's nose. "It does seem a shame," he said, almost to himself. "But, after all, I didn't start the war."

"Nor did I," said Joanna. She pulled Kilkenny's reins, turning the horse away from the Yankee. She would not waste any more time talking to him. After all, he was the enemy. With her head held high, her back straight, she rode slowly away. Sarah followed.

"Good-bye," he called after them, then added in a soft voice. "Joanna."

CHAPTER TWENTY-TWO

A S THE HOLIDAY SEASON DREW NEAR, Bridget forced herself to keep even busier than usual. In idle moments, she was almost overcome by concern for her missing loved ones. Now almost two months had passed since Ryan and Nate had left and no word of their whereabouts had yet reached Memphis. Not a single letter from Joseph or Shaughnessy.

From the newspapers, she read only disturbing news. Yankee-edited papers boasted that Grant's men were swarming about northern Mississippi, closing in on Granada. Also, rumors brought unconfirmed reports that the Appeal had moved on to Jackson. If only Bridget could be sure the boys were safe with Joseph, but she didn't even know if they'd made it to Granada.

Nevertheless, she decided they should do something about the gloom which had settled over the household. "We'll have ourselves a Christmas tree," she declared. "Isn't it our custom to do so?"

Connor was slumped in a kitchen chair, exhausted from a day of delivering telegrams. "Aw, Mom---"

"I know, I know. It won't be the same without the others here." She rested a hand on his shoulder. "But it will cheer the wee ones and occupy us."

So Connor went alone to do a task he'd always shared with Ryan. Climbing the fir covered rise behind the house and cutting down a nicely-shaped tree had always seemed a pleasant task. Now, he went about it glumly, dragging the tree home and setting it up in the parlor. A fine choice, Bridget called it. Clare watched from her high chair while she and the other children decorated the tree with candles, strings of popcorn and brightly colored trinkets. While Emilie, Molly Kate and Patrick drew pictures to hang about the house, Joanna gathered holly and berries and mistletoe and draped them over the banisters and above doorways.

Bridget approved the results. "I do believe the decorations are the nicest we've ever had. The house looks grand, so it does."

Encouraged, they brought out pecans and the molasses they'd hidden in the basement. Viney baked pies, Bridget surprised them with her wonderful pralines, and the children made gingerbread men.

On Christmas day, they cooked the last of the hens, a scrawny bird, too old to supply them with eggs. Viney created a great meal with sweet potatoes, corn bread and a pot of field peas seasoned with a bit of fatback she'd saved for the occasion.

After dinner, they opened presents. Things made with odds and ends and loving hands, wrapped in scraps of paper. Rag dolls for the small girls, a carved wooden horse for Patrick, an apron for Viney. There were socks and mittens and scarves for all, items that once would have been admired politely were accepted with genuine words of appreciation.

"It's been a nice day, after all," Bridget said as she examined the tea cozy Molly had knitted for her.

Molly Kate suddenly threw her new doll aside and flung herself on the floor beside the tree. "I want Papa to be here," she told them, between sobs. "I want Papa."

Viney gathered her into her arms. "Shush," she whispered. "You'll make your Mama feel bad."

Connor went to the window and gazed longingly out the frosted panes. "You know what I'd like? A grand snow storm."

"Could we not pray for one?" Molly suggested.

"Indeed, why not?" Bridget said. Snow would lighten the gloomy day. The children could get out their sleds and go whooping down the hill behind the house and then come in for hot tea and cinnamon cookies. Oh, it did seem a fine idea.

But the weather refused to cooperate. An icy wind whipped the tops of the pine trees beneath a leaden sky. And everyone knew the truth: it was too cold for snow.

Late that Christmas afternoon, they gathered about the piano to sing the traditional carols, singing that ended abruptly when Molly slumped to the floor.

They carried her to the davenport and fussed about her until she opened troubled eyes. "I'm sorry," she murmured. "I can't imagine what's ailing me, I've never fainted so many times before. What a problem I am to all of you."

Bridget held Molly's limp cool hand. She and Viney exchanged looks of concern. Even in her condition, Molly shouldn't be fainting so often. Something was not right.

"We'll have to visit a doctor soon, Molly darling," Bridget said.

Molly protested. "Not yet. Let's wait a while longer."

Bridget didn't blame her for being reluctant. Dr. Bayless, the doctor she knew and trusted, was gone now, forced into exile along with other doctors who had refused to take an oath of allegiance to the North. There was no longer any guarantee that Molly would get the care she needed. The thought angered Bridget. Was there no end to the difficulties a war could cause?

The new year, 1863 it was now, did not offer encouragement.

The wind had died down a bit, the temperature rose a few notches but the gray sky -- ignoring their prayers for snow -- sent instead a nasty mixture of rain and sleet. Since the frozen ground was treacherous, they put off Molly's visit to the doctor. Bridget and Joanna also decided it would be best not to try to get to the hospital for their volunteer duties -- at least for a while. They worked at home, rolling bandages and knitting, although for some reason Bridget didn't understand, Joanna seemed to have developed an aversion to knitting. She tried to explain -- something about some awful Yankees telling her to get back to her knitting -- but it didn't make sense. Never had Bridget known such a child for having strange notions.

Connor was the only one who ventured out of the house. He was a man, he pointed out, and men couldn't let a little weather keep them from their work. "Besides who would deliver the telegrams, if I didn't?"

The sharp patter of sleet against the windows, the knee-deep mud on all the paths, the breath-taking cold seemed to shut out the world. To cheer everyone, Bridget lit lanterns in every room and built a fire in both kitchen and parlor. But in their hearts, they remained sad. Bridget ached for the poor soldiers forced to march and camp in the bitterest winter weather the South had experienced in years.

The frigid month reached the halfway mark and dragged on.

And then one evening, Connor burst in the front door shouting, "Look what I've got." He waved an envelope over his head. "A letter from Papa."

Footsteps pounded against hardwood floors, scrambled down stairways. Everyone gathered about Connor, asking questions. Where's it from? How'd you get it? Is it a telegram?"

"No, a letter. Not a fat one. But a letter posted sometime in December."

"Oh, is there one for me, too?" Molly asked.

Connor's smile disappeared. "I'm afraid not. But don't worry. Now that the mail is getting through---"

"It's all right," Molly said softly. "I'm sure I'll be hearing in a day or two."

"And I'll be sharing mine with you," Bridget said.

"Oh no, you mustn't. It may be private. You'll want a chance to read it alone first and then maybe share parts."

"Indeed not." Bridget took the envelope from Connor and tore it open. "Look." She held up a single page. The writing was tiny and crowded onto every inch of both sides of the paper.

"See, it begins with "Dear Loved Ones." It's for all of us.

Come along everyone, I'll read it aloud."

They settled in chairs about the fire, the children huddled on the floor, leaning against their mother's skirts. When Viney remained in the doorway, Bridget insisted she must join them beside the fire. She waited until they were all quiet.

"Dear Loved Ones," she began, turning the letter toward the firelight. "First of all, I must tell you that Ryan and Nate are safe with us."

"Praise the good Lord," said Viney, tears welling in her eyes. There were sounds of joy from the children, a sigh of relief from Bridget. After a moment, she continued reading.

> *"I've written other letters, of course, but I have no way of knowing whether you received them so I'll repeat vital information and hope it will get to you in one letter or another. Once again, I beg your forgiveness for being unable to get the boys back to Memphis. We had decided, after talking it over, to send them back and they were already on their way, had just ridden off in fact, when we got word that Grant was closing in on us. Shaughnessy and I grabbed horses and rode like wild men to overtake them and bring the boys back. They are safe here with us now so don't be fretting about them."*

"Lord be praised," Viney murmured again. "'Scuse me Miz Bridget. Don't mean to keep interrupting."

Bridget looked up and smiled. "That's all right, Viney. You speak for all of us."

She returned to the letter. "Perhaps you've heard by now that we had to leave Granada. It seemed a wise move and the good people of Jackson were more than happy to take us in. We have a fine office just a few doors below the post office, not that it gets us our mail any sooner. Most of the time, the news we receive by mail is too stale to print. And to make it even more difficult, the telegraph companies are swamped and the Appeal is limited to only one daily dispatch of five hundred words.

"But here now, I didn't mean for this letter to be an account of our difficulties. Just know that we are doing as well as can be expected and that we're managing to get out our daily edition no matter what the odds.

I've been thinking a lot about my family and how the children always made Christmas such a grand time. I hope you have managed to be at least a bit happy this year. Here in the Appeal's offices, we decided to ignore the jolly season. Mack struggled to write an encouraging editorial for our Christmas issue but after a dozen or so false starts, gave up. For the first time, our holiday editions have not contained a single cheery word. I hope our readers will understand. After today's paper was printed and put in the hands of the delivery boys, Dill suggested we take the rest of the afternoon off. He and most of the staff are gathered in his office reminiscing about happier times. Shaughnessy and I joined them for a while but decided we'd rather use the time to write home."

Bridget beamed at Molly. "See, darling, you'll be getting your letter soon since he wrote to you as Joseph was writing this."

Molly nodded and smiled.

"We are quite busy most of the time. Last week, two brothers from New Orleans joined our printing staff, and in Granada we took on another compositor. There are now fourteen of us, counting Mrs. Dill. She is a fine lady, much liked for her uncomplaining nature and willingness to pitch in with clerical work. I confess I sometimes envy Dill, having his wife with him while you and I must be separated. But Shaughnessy and I are both comforted by the thought that you and Molly are together. Give Viney and Will my best, and tell Nate's parents he is in great health, and assure all the children that I miss them more

than I can say and pray the war will end soon so we can be together again.

"I wish I could write more and oftener, but paper is hard to come by and we try to share it equally, if possible. Getting supplies is one of our biggest problems. Securing dry wood to fire up our boiler is a challenge but we're very resourceful. In Granada, we ran out of ink entirely and the last few issues were printed with boot blacking! Aye, we're a crafty bunch, determined as we are to keep our Southern friends informed.

I hope to get a letter from home soon. Haven't heard in over two months but I am sure you are writing and doing your best to get word to us. Shaughnessy and I keep hoping that, any day now, the sorry mail services will catch up with the wandering Appeal and we will hear that you and Molly and the children are safe and well.

Love to all,

Joseph

CHAPTER TWENTY-THREE

IN FEBRUARY, THE WEATHER IMPROVED enough for Bridget and Molly to make a trip to the doctor's office. They were dismayed to learn that the pleasant waiting room once reserved for Dr. Bayless's patients had been set aside for the use of Yankee officers and their families. Bridget supposed they should have been prepared for the worst, since Memphis had become a medical center for wounded Northern soldiers. Most of the remaining doctors were Yankees, inclined to favor their own.

Molly and Bridget were made aware of their second class status from the moment they entered an uncomfortable, shabby waiting room to be told that the doctor on duty would see them when he had the time.

"Let's just go home," Molly whispered.

"I'm wishing we could," Bridget said. "But we must have a doctor see you. Maybe it won't be too bad."

They found their place behind the last person on a narrow bench against a far wall. A woman who sat at the front of the room behind a battered desk rose and brought a paper for Molly to fill out. "Just put down your name, address and your complaint," she instructed in a tired voice. "That's all they want to know."

When Molly had complied, she took the paper up to the thin, defeated-looking woman who put it in a folder. "You'll probably be seeing a different doctor each time," the woman said, her accent soft and southern. "I'm afraid it's the best we can do under the circumstances. I'm sorry, truly sorry, but I have no control---" Abruptly, she cut off her words and looked fearfully about.

They sat on the hard crowded bench for three hours, surrounded by feverish, coughing sneezing patients. Children swung their feet, kicking the bench, jarring poor Molly. Flushed babies whimpered in their mother's arms.

"It won't be much longer," Bridget whispered, as they moved forward on the bench, inch by inch. Molly kept her bulging stomach covered with her shawl and held her head high.

It was late afternoon by the time they were ushered into the doctor's inner office. There, they waited an additional half hour in a small room which contained an examining table, a tall stool and cabinets filled with instruments and medicine. The room was unheated.

Sitting on the edge of the examining table, Molly began to shiver. "Oh, why did you insist that we come here?" she asked, mournfully. "I just can't take this. Come on. We're getting out of here."

She got down from the table and headed for the door but her exit was blocked by a large man in his middle years. With a reproving look, he waited for Molly to climb back on the table.

Then he opened the folder he carried and read the note Molly had written when she filled out her form.

"Hmmmm," he said. And, "Hmmmm."

"So--" he peered at Molly through small steel spectacles –" "I see that, war and all, we're having another child." His voice was gruff, faintly disapproving.

Molly only nodded.

He waited, appearing to expect more from her. Finally, he asked, "Well, are you having any particular problems at this time?"

"Just a bit of fainting now and then."

"Oh. Well that's common enough. They all do that. Don't know how many times I've picked my own wife up off the floor."

"But all women don't faint," Bridget burst out, unable to keep quiet any longer. "At least not so many times."

The doctor turned to stare at Bridget as if he'd noticed her for the first time. "Are you telling me how to do my business, Mrs--?

"Mrs. Harrigan. And sir, I didn't mean---"

"And who might you be, Mrs. Harrigan? A relative?"

"Molly and I are cousins. Cousins-in-law, that is."

"I see. Not exactly close relatives, I'd say." He set Molly's folder on a cabinet and drummed on it with short stubby fingers. "Perhaps you'd better wait outside."

"No," exclaimed Molly. "She stays." -- Bridget had never heard her speak so firmly -- "Or I go."

"Well now, Mrs." -- he opened the folder and consulted it again-- "Mrs. Shaughnessy, have it your way. Anyway the only thing I can do for you is perhaps give you a tonic for the fainting. It's a well-known fact in the medical profession that not much can actually be done for female complaints. But may I ask Mrs." – another peek in the folder -- "Mrs. Shaughnessy, why you don't go to a mid-wife? Don't you know how busy we doctors are in wartime? We have many patients who are in far more serious ---"

"I'm sure you do." Molly slid down from the table. "And I won't be troubling you again, unless I'm dying. And maybe not even then." Her voice was deadly quiet. " 'Tis a fact, I do sometimes have a problem -- but I won't take up your valuable time telling you about it."   She edged past him and went out the door.

Bridget had to hurry along to keep up with Molly as she left the building. She had conflicting emotions. She wanted to say "good for you Molly, for standing up to that rude man". And yet an icy fear crept into her heart. They must find another doctor. Someone who would know how important it was that Molly receive proper care, how dear she was to everyone.

And time was growing short. Six weeks, Bridget figured. Maybe less.

CHAPTER TWENTY-FOUR

T HE ATMOSPHERE IN THE PRESSROOM was tense. The staff hurried about, some printing the final edition of the paper for the citizens of Jackson, others snatching up and packing equipment and supplies as soon as they were no longer needed.

Joseph was fitting cases of type into a wooden box when he heard a low rumble roll across the sky. He paused a moment, lifted his head, listened. The rumble came again, far away, familiar sounding. Ah, he approved, we could use a bit of rain to cool us. But then, beneath the growling thunder, he heard another, more ominous sound. The sharp crack of howitzers. His heart thudded. The Yankees were closing in on the city. Couldn't be more than twenty miles away.

It had been pure foolishness to linger so long in Jackson. But then, everyone had agreed it was the honorable thing to do. They had promised to remain at their posts until there was no longer any hope, until they were certain the Yankees would take over the city. And it wasn't right that they should leave without putting out a farewell issue to thank the people who had been such kind and generous hosts. They deserved a few parting words of consolation and encouragement. And so the staff had risen early and fired up the press, knowing the Yankees might set upon them with yelps of triumph before the ink was dry on the May 14, 1863, edition.

As the sun rose higher, the morning grew warmer, muggier. Joseph felt his damp shirt sticking to his back. He continued packing, ignoring the sweat running down his face, dripping from his chin. He had no time to be concerned with matters so inconsequential as the weather. He was closing the lid on the last case of type when a sudden brisk breeze blew into the room. Everyone was forced to abandon their work and scramble after papers sent flying about.

"What the Sam Hill?" someone muttered.

"Storm's coming sure as cats have kittens," said Vernon.

Hurriedly, they recovered the papers and returned to work. As the press rattled on, they heard more gunfire mixed with thunder, heard the boom of cannons, getting louder, closer. Through an open door, Joseph noted thunderheads piling high in the sky. Soon clouds blotted out the sun. The bright day became dusk-like. Dill lit lamps in the darkened pressroom.

Ryan came over to stand beside his father. "Do you suppose that was just thunder we've been hearing? Or is it gunfire?"

"'Tis both," Joseph admitted. "Hard to tell one from the other, isn't it now? Are you frightened?"

"No. Well, maybe a little. Do you think we'll have time to get away before the Yankees come?"

"That's our aim."   Joseph saw a mixture of fear and excitement on his son's face. But then, he thought, looking around at the others, every man in the room was wearing a similar expression. "We're doing our best to be long gone by the time they get to State Street," he assured Ryan. "Come along, let's take these cases of type and load them on the wagons."

Outside, lightning zigzagged across the sky followed by a great blast of thunder. The air took on a musty smell, the smell of approaching rain. Joseph glanced up at the sky. "Lord, I know the land needs rain," he muttered, "but couldn't it have waited one more day?"

Thunder answered. Lightning sparked around them. The first drops of rain plopped on thirsty oak leaves. As they hurried inside, the world grew even darker. Rain splattered against the windows, then fell in a sudden torrent, pounding the roof.

Shaughnessy took the last page from the press and looked up momentarily, assessing the storm. "A regular frog strangler," he commented as he joined the other printers who were folding and stacking papers.

A violent crack of thunder shook the room. Not to be outdone, cannons boomed louder.

"Sounds like all Hell is breaking loose," Mack said. "Come on, men, hurry with the loading before things get any worse."

Four wagons were parked outside the building – one regular sized and two larger freight wagons designated to haul the twenty-foot press, the engine and boiler. They were hustling to get boxes of supplies loaded when Sheriff Chaney came galloping up the street. His oilskin slicker flapped around his thin body as he dismounted and entered the building.

"What the hell," he exclaimed. "Haven't ya'll finished your packing yet?"

"We have most of it done," Dill answered, "but we have to wait for the boiler to cool so we can handle it."

"It better cool fast," Chaney said. "You should have gotten out of here long ago."

"I know," Dill said. "What's the latest on Rebel positions."

"Our scouts tell us Grant and Sherman have combined forces and, as we speak, are coming up Raymond Road. We were no match for them, couldn't hold 'em back. And McPherson's men are fighting on Clinton Road. Our troops are retreating northward on Canton but they've run into opposition."

Dill nodded, digesting the information. "Sounds like we're trapped then. As I'm figuring it, there's no other way out."

"Don't be giving up hope," the sheriff said. "There's still the old Brandon road and--"

"But Pearl River..."

"Whoa now, let me finish. We've got it all planned. There's a heap of old boys who appreciate what the Appeal has done for Jackson. They're down there now getting a barge rigged to ferry you across. The river is out of its banks because of all the rain we've had this spring. But don't worry. I'm on my way to see everything gets done right so you'll have a safe crossing. Can you fellas make it to the river bank in a coupla hours?"

"We'll make it," Mack said.

Chaney looked around the room doubtfully. "The Yanks are sure gonna grab you if you don't move faster than this." He hurried back to his horse, mounted and galloped away.

"All right," Mack said. "Let's get the press dismantled and ready to go."

They were accustomed to the job by now. It was almost routine, separating press, boiler and steam engine, taking off removable parts and hammering crates about the bulky objects.

Finally, with much grunting and words of caution and encouragement -- "Steady men, steady." "Heave now, give it all you got." "All together now, let's go." -- they shoved the crates up a mud-slick ramp to the wagons.

"I think we've got it all now except for the safe," Mack said.

"Leave it," Dill ordered. "I've already removed everything important. And we have today's edition of the paper stacked beside the door so newsboys can pick them up and deliver them after things calm down."

There was a brief discussion. Who should ride in which wagon? "Mr. and Mrs. Dill in the first wagon with the press," Mack decided. "Ryan and Nate can ride their horses. And the rest of you can follow in the small wagon."

As they were climbing into their places, one of Chaney's deputies rode up, leading two mules. "Thought maybe a couple of your men could ride these," he offered, "Seeing as your wagons are loaded to the buckboards."

Joseph jumped from the last wagon, followed by Shaughnessy. They took the rope harnesses from the deputy and mounted the mules. Shaughnessy's feet almost dragged in a mud puddle.

"We'll be the rear guard," he said to Joseph, sounding almost jovial. "Sure, every military maneuver needs a rear guard."

"We'll be thinking up diversionary tactics," Joseph added, marveling that they could sound so playful while the war nipped at their heels.

Slowly, the four wagons made their way to the end of State Street and started down the long narrow road leading to Pearl River. The storm continued. Sheets of lightning set the sky on fire.

Riding along behind the wagons on the sway-back mule, Joseph looked back at the flashing, smoke-filled sky. He heard the roar of artillery, the shriek of shrapnel tearing through the air.

From the sound of it, he judged the fighting might have reached State Street. The Yankees would no doubt be sending out scouts to search for the Appeal office. For hadn't they hankered to capture the Appeal? If they found the final edition still damp from the press, they would be after them in short order. In fact, any minute now, they could come tearing over the rise and the lumbering wagons would be sitting ducks.

The condition of the rutted road worsened. In some places the mud almost reached the wagon beds. As they rounded a slight curve in the road, one of the wagons slipped into a ditch. The procession stopped. Nervously, Joseph turned on his mule to survey the hill behind them.

"Come on, men," Mack yelled, "Let's shove this wagon out of here."

The men put their shoulders to the side of the wagon, and with their combined strength, finally pushed it back on the road.

Just before they reached the river bank, the storm drifted off to the north. The sounds of battle, Joseph noted, had dwindled to occasional rifle shots. The silence seemed ominous for it meant that Jackson had been taken.

At the river, Sheriff Chaney showed them the set-up of ropes and pulleys which would drag them across the river. "Just drive right onto this barge, one wagon at a time," he directed.

The wagon containing the press and Mr. and Mrs. Dill was loaded first. Ryan and Nate followed on Tipper.

"Heave away," one of the men on the other side of the river shouted and horses strained at rope harnesses until the barge creaked forward over the churning water.

One by one, each wagon made the safety of the far bank. Joseph and Shaughnessy kept watch until everyone was across.

Then they dismounted and led their mules onto the barge. As they were pulled into the stream, they looked back to see a dozen mounted blue coats come over the hill. As they galloped down the road, the Yankees raised rifles, took aim, fired. Joseph and Shaughnessy lay low as their craft moved slowly across the river. Rounds of shell zipped overhead, churning the water around them. Just before they reached the far bank, the bullets began to fall short.

Shaughnessy took a deep breath. "I think we're out of their range. We're going to make it after all, Joseph."

They stepped ashore, pulling their frightened mules behind them and their rescuers cut the barge loose. It bounded down the river toward the gulf.

Most of the wagons had gone on. Chaney had led them up the road, toward a town called Brandon where, they had been told, a railroad car would be waiting. A wise move, thought Joseph, for any moment now, more Yankees might arrive with longer-ranged artillery.

From across the river, a Yankee shouted, "We're coming after you, you fool rebels." His voice carried well in the still air.

"Oh yeah," Joseph hollered back. "How are you gonna get over here? Swim?"

"Damn it to Hell," came the answer. Frustrated Yankees rode up and down the bank beside the swollen river, looking for a place where their horses could swim across. Finding none, they shook their fists and shouted curses.

"We'll get you next time you bastards."

"Damn fool traitors."

"Secesh sons of bitches."

Joseph and Shaughnessy grinned at one another. They could answer those volleys. They put their hands to their mouths and aimed.

"To hell with you and your horses, too," yelled Shaughnessy.

"Yankee white trash. Devils," Joseph added.

"Bloody rebels," was the return. "Sonsabitches."

"Bastards," replied Shaughnessy.

The Yankees were still hurling insults as Joseph and Shaughnessy mounted their mules and rode toward Brandon.

CHAPTER TWENTY-FIVE

"'Tis folly to say the people must have news."
General William Tecumseh Sherman
1863

FOR ALMOST THREE WEEKS, the weary newsmen traveled across the hot and humid land. In Meridian, they stopped to issue a few extras printed on handbills. There, Sheriff Chaney sent heartening news by courier. "Just thought you'd like to know that one of the first things Sherman's men did when they took over in Jackson was to ask where they could find a refugee newspaper called the *Appeal*. When I told them you were gone, they were furious. Seems Sherman is determined to get his hands on you. Keep moving, and good luck.

Taking Chaney's advice to keep moving, the Appeal traveled on. Generous offers of free transportation enabled them to take a rambling rail and river journey through Montgomery and on toward Georgia. On June 6, exactly one year after they had left Memphis, they arrived in Atlanta.

No one in the crowded depot even looked their way. The men seemed a bit lost as they gathered on the station platform.

Mack attempted to cheer them. "We don't need to be greeted royally everywhere we go, men. After all, we can't expect a town of more than eleven thousand people to be impressed with us."

"And newspapers are no novelty here," Dill said. "Atlanta has two thriving dailies of its own, as well as several small scale weeklies."

"That's all right with me." Mack's voice was a low growl. "I like competition."

"Well, let's not be standing here waiting for a welcoming committee," Shaughnessy said. We have to unload and find a place to put out our paper." He stepped off the platform, stirring up clouds of red dust as he walked toward the freight car which carried their equipment.

It was obvious from the beginning that, though the people of Atlanta accepted the Appeal's presence, they were not as delighted to have them as the friendlier natives of Mississippi had been. No eager citizens offered to help them get settled. No one opened homes to them.

They leased a building on Decatur Street, near the railroad. Once a dry-goods store, the building provided ample space. They delegated the large front area for the press, and smaller rooms near the rear for the composing room and the editorial offices. In the rear of the building, there was another room which they planned to use for storing supplies. They bought desks, tables and chairs from second-hand stores to replace what they'd left in

Jackson. Once again, Joseph and his crew assembled the press and connected boiler and steam engine. Within a week, they were organized enough to print the first edition.

To reassure Atlanta citizens, the editors included an editorial in their first issue, promising the paper would not interfere in the state's domestic affairs. "To the Confederacy we owe our first duty," the editorial stated, "and when we have faithfully performed that duty, we shall have accomplished the object of our highest ambition in the present unsettled condition of the country."

Only after the paper was printed and delivered, did the staff relax and consider their own needs. They gathered in Dill's new office, some sitting on available chairs, others on the floor. Joseph leaned against the wall, thinking that weeks of traveling, sleeping on bed rolls and eating very little could make a man feel his years.

"We'll need to find a place to live," Dill said. "And I regret to report the city is over-crowded. Mrs. Dill and Vernon have been scouting around and there's not much available. They did manage to reserve two rooms in a local hotel, and made arrangements for a few more to stay in a boarding house."

"Sounds fine to me," Shaughnessy said.

Dill looked uncomfortable. "But they haven't yet found enough rooms for all of us. And much as I hate to tell you this, men, I'm afraid the cost of your living quarters will have to come out of your salaries. I wish the Appeal could stand good for them, but our money is dwindling and we're going to have to save what remains for pure necessities. I won't even be able to give you your back pay until we get some money coming in again."

The men nodded. There was silence as each man seemed to be considering his personal financial woes. After a while, they began to discuss who should get the accommodations Mrs. Dill had found. The staff now included the two printers they'd taken on in Jackson, Billy Haney and Doyle Jenkins, and a compositor, an older man named Seth Latke. Dill said that, at least for the time being, some of the men would have to bed down in the storage room at the rear of the building.

Shaughnessy groaned. "More bed rolls. I'm afraid my bones won't tolerate it."

"And my bones are looking for a more civilized environment," Mack said.

The matter was settled when the younger men offered to take on the assignment. Mack, Dill and his wife were allotted the hotel rooms in Washington Hall. Vernon Weist, Ed Goins and Seth Latke agreed to share one of the rooming house vacancies. Shaughnessy and Joseph took the other. Ryan, Nate, Joshua, Billy and Doyle settled among stacks of newsprint and supplies in the rear of the office building.

"Where will we eat?" Doyle wondered. "And who'll do the cooking?"

"Don't you fellas be frettin'," Joshua said. You won't starve. We can build a campfire out back and take turns with the cooking."

"Sure," said Billy. "It will be sort of like tenting with troops."

The boys thought it might be fun.

Everyone was anxious to receive any mail that might be forwarded to them. The men haunted the post office, hoping letters long delayed would find their way to them.

Shaughnessy was particularly upset. "I keep reading the last letter I got from Molly back in January, reading it over and over, and somehow – maybe 'tis some notion that's come over me – I have a feeling something is wrong. Nothing Molly said, mind you. Just a sense that she was holding something back."

"Just your Irish imagination at work," Joseph told him. "Your next letter will no doubt be full of good news." But privately he worried too, wondering if Shaughnessy might be right.

Joseph was delighted when he stopped by the post office one morning and was given a packet of mail. He couldn't wait to get back to the office to open it, but began sifting through its contents as he walked along Peach Street. When he recognized Bridget's handwriting on a somewhat dirty and rumpled envelope, he grinned. But further searching turned up no letter from Molly. Shaughnessy would be more upset than ever, Joseph thought. He decided not to go directly to the office. Instead he turned down a side street and walked the block and a half to his boarding house room. He would not read Bridget's letter – at least, not the first reading – in Shaughnessy's presence. He entered the room he and Shaughnessy shared, typical bachelor's quarters, Joseph thought, with beds unmade and clothes piled on the room's only chair. The shades were still drawn. However, shafts of light streamed through small holes in the old shades so it was not entirely dark. Putting the bag of mail he'd picked up at the post office on the floor, Joseph sat on the edge of his bed to enjoy his letter in private. He turned it over, wondered how it had gotten so dirty and felt its thickness to see if perhaps it might contain a page from Molly as well.

"Blast," he said to himself. All of Shaughnessy's talk had made him afraid to even open his mail. He tore open the envelope and settled back to enjoy.

"Dear Joseph," Bridget had begun, and then there were several sentences scratched out, followed by, "Oh Joseph, my Joseph." He sat up straight, his heart pounding, for didn't Bridget always begin with these words when she had bad news to tell? He read on: "'Tis terrible news I have for you. My pen shakes in my hand but I must have it done with. We have lost our sweet Molly, God rest her soul. She died giving birth to yet another still-born child."

No," he cried out. "It's not fair. It can't be." He closed his eyes, and the words swam before him. Molly, God rest her soul. Dead? Molly?

The room was suddenly stifling. Joseph walked over to raise the ragged shade and open the window. The fact that people were hurrying by on the street below seemed a shock to him. How could life just go on as usual? How could it, with sweet Molly gone?

He returned to the letter. "I hope you are not reading this in Shaughnessy's presence. It was Molly's final wish that he not be told the sad news immediately. 'Let him live a bit longer,' was how she put it. But Joseph, Shaughnessy must be properly informed before someone blurts it out. She died the first week in March ---

March? Joseph tried to take that in. Molly had been dead for almost three months. Yes, of course Shaughnessy must be told at once.

"And as you know," the letter continued, "news travels by various methods these days. And 'tis a shock that could kill a man, hearing such a thing from a stranger. So Joseph, it falls on you to tell him, yourself being his best friend. You must somehow prepare him, tell it to him softly and be there to comfort him."

Tell it softly? Was there a soft way to say such a thing? And prepare him? How could that be done?

There was more to the letter, probably details Shaughnessy would eventually want to know. But for now, Joseph could take in no more. He turned the letter over, read the last few lines saying that Bridget, Viney and the children were doing well. But Molly, he thought. Molly.

There was a knock on the door and, without waiting for an answer, Vernon entered the room. "I thought I heard you call out ---" He looked closely at Joseph. "Say, you don't look so good. I'm on my way down to the office but – is there anything I could do for you?"

"Aye. Truth is I've never felt worse. Would you please find Shaughnessy for me and ask him to come to our room? Tell him – tell him that – that 'tis important he get here soon."

Joseph waited, pacing about the room until Shaughnessy finally arrived. "What is it, Joseph?" he asked as soon as he opened the door. "Vernon said you weren't feeling well and I --- His voice trailed away when he saw Joseph's expression and the letter in his hand. He took a deep shaky breath. "Molly?"

Joseph could only nod.

"Ah no," Shaughnessy said. "Ah, no,"

Joseph led him to the chair, pushed piles of clothing to the floor. "Would you be sitting now?" he asked gently.

CHAPTER TWENTY-SIX

EVEN BEFORE THE GRANDFATHER CLOCK chimed in the hall below, Joanna knew she had overslept. She lay in bed, counting each clang – eight there were — and she was always awake by seven. Of course, she had gone to bed very late the night before and had tossed about for hours. What must everyone think of her, sleeping half the day away like this? But she did need the rest, she thought, as she snuggled down, her pillow a great comfort.

She had almost drifted back to sleep when she heard the squeak and rattle of a vendor's cart. "Fresh corn, butter beans, black-eyed peas," the vendor chanted. "Blackberries, watermelons, nice ripe cantaloupe."

She untangled herself from the sheets and went to the window to watch a vegetable cart rumble along the road in front of the house. A second cart appeared, pushed by a man and woman she recognized from other mornings. They were favorites of hers, this tall, black, lanky man with his round little woman walking beside him, her skirts dragging in the dirt. In spite of their contrasting appearance, they sang well together, his baritone blending with her mellow soprano.

"Crowder peas, butter beans, fresh-picked snap beans. Honeydew melons right off the vine," they sang. Joy was in their voices, such ain't-this-a-fine-day-the-Lord-has-given-us joy. Patting a bare foot in time with their rhythm, Joanna agreed. Since she was a small child, she had loved the sound of vendors hawking their wares. She was grateful that the pleasant custom had survived the city's capture. Thinking about this made her happy, filled her with love -- love for the grand morning, for the hazy sunshine. For the breeze rustling the dusty leaves of the elm tree. For the vendors and their summer songs. And for-- She stopped herself before she added Andrew. She couldn't love a Yankee. How disloyal that would be. And yet she had to admit she had strange longings when she thought of him. He'd crept into her heart while she wasn't paying attention.

When he had first started coming to the hospital to visit an injured friend, she'd made it a point to ignore him, to go on with her duties as a volunteer. But when he nodded at her, nodding back seemed only polite. After all, hadn't he saved her from those disgusting soldiers out at Fort Pickering?

He came to the hospital often and read a book called "The Last of the Mohicans" to his friend. She began to look for excuses to work nearby so she could listen. But only, she assured herself, because she liked the story and admired how well he read, how he gave each word its rightful attention instead of sliding on to the next as Southerners were inclined to do.

She found other attractions about him -- the way his sun-bleached hair grew in swirls at the nape of his neck, his wide straight shoulders, his alert brown eyes. Eyes that she caught regarding her from time to time.

If only he weren't a Yankee.

One stormy evening, they had found themselves standing across from one another in the hall beside the front door of the hospital, waiting for the rain to stop. They exchanged polite 'good evenings', a few comments about the weather. Then she turned away to look out a small window. But she was curious, fairly bursting with questions. What were Yankees like? What did they think about? What part of the North was he from? Had he ever been to New York? The rain continued. He wondered aloud if it would ever stop or if it would go on for hours as it did in his home town. Impulsively, she asked where he lived. And had he ever been to New York.

He was from Philadelphia, a town in Pennsylvania. And he went often to New York. He loved to travel so much that his old Grandmother teased him and called him "journey-proud." He had four brothers and a sister and a lawyer father, he told her, now that they were talking. His mother was beautiful. Her hair was long and blond, like Joanna's.

He had questions, too. Did she have brothers and sisters? What were her interests? Was she planning to be a nurse?

A definite no to the last, with a little grimace that made him laugh. She told him about her family, about her father who was on the staff of a newspaper that was traveling about the South. The *Appeal*.

He said he'd heard about the *Appeal*. It was generally known, he said, that Sherman could be set raving by the mere mention of it. He saw that she did not find that fact comforting, so he added that Sherman was not fond of any newspaper, then changed the subject. Did she like the theater? And music?

When the rain stopped, he walked her to the corner where she caught the horse car. After that, he had timed his departures so they often left the hospital together. Walking her to the horse- car became a habit.

And why not? Joanna asked herself as the days passed and their friendship continued. The boys her age had all gone off to war. Andrew was lonely and far from home. It seemed natural that they should talk to one another.

She had confided in him when Molly died because she had to talk to someone about it. He was sympathetic. One day he talked about being a soldier, told her he'd been wounded in the Battle of the Wilderness. He admitted he was often afraid in battle, but he had refused to be a coward and run away from his duty. He hated the killing most of all. His face darkened at the memory. Fortunately, he had never had to shoot anyone at close range. That, he thought, would be the worst -- looking into the eyes of a man like himself, then having to kill him.

He was a good person, she decided. Even if he was a Yankee.

She was careful to keep their friendship casual. But sometimes thoughts came unbidden – thoughts of how his hand might feel brushing against hers. Or his steadying arm at her back as they crossed a street.

Though they avoided physical contact, their minds met in a hundred ways. Last night, after she had gotten off work, he had suggested that they take a walk along the bluff. It was quite a way to go and she would be even later getting home, but how could she say no?

"This has always been a favorite place of mine," she told him as they strolled along. "As a child I used to walk here alone and think about the people who were here long ago -- De Soto and Joliet and the Chickasaw Indians -- and sometimes I imagined, I was almost positive, I could feel them there with me. Isn't that silly?"

He didn't think it was silly at all. He liked history, too. She was very intelligent, he said. For a girl. And before she'd had time to protest that girls were just as intelligent as boys, he was telling her about a touring ballet company from the North that would be coming to Memphis soon, saying he would love to see their performance with her by his side. His voice was shy as he asked her to go with him.

That was what had caused her to oversleep, lying awake thinking about her answer to his invitation. He had to know in the next few days, he'd said, in order to get the tickets. She wanted very much to go, but didn't know if she would be allowed. Going for walks after she got off work was one thing. Getting dressed up to attend a show with him wouldn't be so easy. For one thing, she hadn't yet told her mother she was friendly with a Yankee. Bridget was still grieving over the loss of Molly and sometimes seemed hardly aware of what was going on around her. And obviously, she hadn't taken note of how often her daughter was late getting home from the hospital.

How should I begin, what should I say when I tell her? Joanna wondered as she arose from bed and dressed.

In the kitchen, she found leftover biscuits on the stove, poured molasses on them and took them to the table. She ate slowly so that, if Mama and Viney found her and assigned a task to her, she could truthfully say she hadn't yet finished her breakfast. She could see the two of them on the service porch, leaning forward in their wicker chairs, heads bent over a tub of snap beans they were getting ready to put up for the winter. They'd become very close since Molly's death. She heard them talking softly, companionably.

"Today is going to be a scorcher," Bridget observed. "It's not quite ten o'clock and already hot."

Viney assured her a summer storm would cool things off before the day was over, that she could tell by her bones a rain was brewing. Joanna looked out the window at the cloudless sky and was confident it would soon be raining. Viney's bones were seldom wrong.

The snap beans done with, Viney lifted a basket of tomatoes to the work table. "Aren't the tomatoes pretty?" she exclaimed. Bridget agreed and added that she had never seen them as firm and red as they were this year. Their enthusiastic voices brought a curious Molly Kate to the porch. She stood on tiptoe to see the top of the table. Obviously disappointed to find mere vegetables, she scowled and said, "I not going to eat those damn tomatoes."

Bridget and Viney stared at her.

"Where did you learn such language, young lady?" Bridget demanded.

The child backed away from the table and stuck her thumb in her mouth.

Hands on hips, Bridget frowned at her. "Well, little miss, if you're old enough to talk in such a manner, you're old enough to get your mouth washed out with soap." She tucked the child under one arm and carried her toward the back stairway. Molly Kate's bare feet kicked wildly beneath her ruffled skirt but she didn't make a sound. Joanna continued to listen, knowing the punishment would undoubtedly be carried out immediately. She heard no cries from her little sister.

After a while, Bridget came back to the service porch, looking flushed and exasperated. "I declare I never saw such a child. I washed her mouth out good and she didn't make a sound. Then I put her in bed to think it over but she didn't seem the least bit sorry."

Viney chuckled. "That Molly Kate – she's a sight. Of all the feisty Harrigans, sure looks like she might turn out the spunkiest of the lot."

"Well, I intend to tame her a bit. Except---" Bridget was silent a moment, staring off into the distance. "You know, Viney, when I consider the way things are, well, maybe it's a shame to squelch a little girl's spirit. I'm thinking we're all going to need whatever spunk we have. Who knows what it will be like after the war, how changed it will be. Maybe we should be prepared to change our way of thinking."

Joanna listened to this, smiling. Now wasn't it fortunate that she had heard exactly the words she would be needing when she spoke to her mother about Andrew?

CHAPTER TWENTY-SEVEN

JOSEPH FROWNED at the Appeal's stalled press. Since early morning he had been poking about its innards, examining bed wheel and cylinder, crank pin and grippers, prying into every crevice until his eyes felt like coals burned into his skull. What could be troubling it this time? So far he knew only that, during last night's run, it had developed a strange grinding sound. Then it had shuddered and shut itself down. Shut down for the third time in less than two weeks.

No doubt the rough treatment they had given the poor machine, dragging it about the country this past year, had taken its toll. Made an old man out of it before its time, Joseph thought. Nevertheless, he had to keep it in working order, no matter what the effort. Wouldn't it be a sorry thing if the newspaper known by such impressive names as "the Voice of the Confederacy" and "the hornet's nest of the rebellion" fell by the wayside? He must not allow that to happen. Their circulation was beginning to rise again after falling off sharply when they first arrived in Atlanta. But Joseph knew that a newspaper, to be truly successful, had to become a habit. And how could it achieve this if it didn't arrive on a regular basis?

"We can't be missing editions," he thought grimly. He wiped sweat from his face, took a deep breath and started over, inspecting each part of the press again.

He was still working when the night crew arrived.

"Haven't you got that thing fixed yet?" Ed Goins asked.

Joseph ignored him. A headache of a man, he was.

"Don't mean to be hurrying you," Goins said, "but we'll have to start printing within the next hour or we won't get tonight's edition out."

"I know. I'll have it ready. Just give me breathing room."

But Goins insisted on standing by to hand out needed tools along with unneeded advice.

Joseph was fumbling about, deep within the cogs of the cylinder, when he encountered a lump of metal. He gave it a yank and brought out what appeared to be a mangled chain. After a brief examination, he stuffed the grease-smeared object into his pocket, hoping no one else would catch sight of it.

A sly smile twisted Goins' thin lips. "That was a watch chain you put in your pocket, wasn't it? I bet anything I know who it belongs to."

"We're not here for betting," Joseph growled. "There's things more important to do. Why don't you tell Joshua to get the boiler fired up and we'll have a trial run?"

When all was ready, Joseph started the press. As it chugged into action, he held his breath, watching, waiting to see if the chain had caused further damage. He grew less anxious with each rhythmic whir of the cylinder. It didn't matter now that he was tired and dirty, his clothes, his face and hands blackened, as long as he heard no wayward clunks indicating more trouble. He inclined his shaggy head, listening intently. The old war horse was back on duty.

He put his tools away and went back to the boarding house for some much needed rest. Shaughnessy wasn't there, was probably at a local bar, for where else did the man spend his time these days?

Since he'd lost Molly, Shaughnessy had become more and more withdrawn. He drank too much, then wandered about the streets with blank eyes, his big shoulders bowed, shutting everyone, everything out. Doing what work had to be done, saying only what had to be said. No one had been able to get through to him, to draw him back.

Joseph had taken it upon himself to keep careful watch on Shaughnessy's work, for he often found mistakes had been made. Everyone, except Ed Goins who was hankering after Shaughnessy's job, pretended not to notice there was a problem.

"Shaughnessy will be all right in time," Joseph assured everyone, trying to believe his own words. But July passed in a shimmer of heat, a stifling August followed, and Shaughnessy continued to sleepwalk through his duties.

Joseph himself was depressed. He figured he wasn't the same man who had departed for war as if he were a boy going off on an adventure. He began to keep a journal. Not a serious one. Just something that might help him keep track of the passage of time. His entries were brief, usually a line or two about daily happenings, such as:

--- Newsboys hawking our paper take pleasure in shouting, "Fresh off the press, the Memphis-Grenada-Jackson-Meridian-Atlanta Appeal." Some find humor in this.

--- We receive numerous letters from homesick lads thanking us for our 'heroic' efforts in getting the Appeal to them. Don't know how heroic we are, but such letters make what we do seem worthwhile.

--- Learned today that the *Appeal* is one of less than fifty Southern newspapers remaining out of the more than eight hundred which were published before the war.

--- We're now putting out 8,000 copies of the morning edition and 6,000 copies in the evening. Paper costs twenty-five cents. Most newsboys ask for fifty. And get it.

And each day, just before he closed his journal, Joseph wrote a single observation about Shaughnessy: Still no smile.

CHAPTER TWENTY-EIGHT

GRADUALLY, THE *APPEAL* GAINED popularity in Atlanta. To keep up with the demand for the paper, extra typesetters, compositors and printers were hired. Still the staff was required to work long hours, a requirement Joseph considered a blessing. When working, a man had no time for brooding.

War brought the *Appeal* a new problem, a problem they'd never before encountered. For the first time in the history of warfare, newsmen were allowed to remain at the front with the troops. There, they became eye witnesses to every battle and gained unprecedented access to military information. An advantage to newspapers, of course, but also a responsibility. The editors of the *Appeal*, who had correspondents stationed wherever armies were fighting, called frequent meetings to warn their staff. They must remain alert, Mack told them. Every man must keep his eyes open and assist in the task of making sure that, while printing words of encouragement to the South, they did not reveal anything which might be of assistance to the enemy.

"It's a touchy subject," Dill said. "I don't like the idea of censoring what we tell the people. But we must be discrete."

Often the news received from the front was edited in such a manner that vague descriptions were substituted for numbers and positions of troops, such as: "Important movements are taking place at the front, but it would not be prudent for us to state their character at present." Or: "Other features of a gratifying character might, were it not imprudent, be noticed; but our readers may rest assured that affairs generally are in as prosperous a condition as the most sanguine could expect."

Joseph took it upon himself to give reports from correspondents a second reading as they came off the proof press. He often asked Ryan to help with the task, for the boy had a sharp eye and occasionally caught things others had missed.

"I think I'd make a great correspondent," Ryan announced one day and Joseph looked up from his work, vaguely alarmed. "Indeed you wouldn't. You're much too young."

Ryan scowled. "Actually that could be an advantage. No one would suspect me. I could go poking around almost anywhere and learn all manner of things. I could call myself -- hmmm, what is it that our correspondent, John Linebaugh, calls himself – Shadow? -- that's a good name. I could be -- let me think?"

"Never mind," Joseph said. "I'd not allow a lad your age to be placed in such a dangerous position."

"You're just saying that because I'm your son."

"Not at all. I'd feel the same about any young boy, but I still have the say of you. So you might as well forget it."

Ryan returned to his proof, his stubborn expression making it clear he didn't consider the matter closed.

In spite of the editor's vigilance and Joseph's extra proofing, the Appeal did eventually run into trouble with military authorities. John Linebaugh, who was assigned to the Army of Tennessee under General Bragg, was arrested in September and, for reasons not made clear, charged with treason. Mack obtained a writ of habeas corpus, but Linebaugh was held prisoner without a hearing. Eventually, the charge was dropped, again without explanation, and he was set free.

He came at once to the *Appeal's* office and the staff gathered around him, wanting to hear the truth about the matter. Linebaugh, a pleasant looking man, with the dash and swagger typical of reporters, admitted that perhaps he might have gotten into trouble over a dispatch which mentioned troop movements, but he was puzzled because he had gotten military clearance for everything he wired to the Appeal. "I'm more inclined to believe," – his voice was a slow drawl – "that I stepped in it when I stopped complimenting General Bragg and hinted that he seemed – er – a bit reluctant to engage the Yankees in battle."

"Sounds likely," Shaughnessy observed.

"Tell me," Linebaugh said, looking around at all the staff, "What should a man do in such a situation? Should he tell the truth as he sees it, or should he close his eyes to the facts when a general shows himself to be incompetent, thus allowing him to continue to send soldiers to their deaths?"

There was a silence while the staff mulled over the question.

"A tough decision to make," Mack said, exhaling a stream of cigar smoke. "A mighty tough decision. But frankly, when it comes to the life of our fighting men, I would prefer to err on the side of truth."

"Amen," said Dill. "And I suggest that the *Appeal* continue on as it has, dealing with each piece of news as it comes to us and making judgments as fairly as possible. It's the best we can do. The best, probably, that any newspaper can do."

Joseph was pleased when Linebaugh decided not to return to General Bragg's army and instead, remained to work in the *Appeal's* office. He was a good man to have around. His presence made the office livelier. Word spread around town that he had fascinating stories to tell about his experiences as a correspondent. Many a dreary fall afternoon was passed pleasantly as they sat around the pot-bellied stove, listening to Linebaugh's adventures, drinking the mixture that passed for coffee. Made of peanuts, corn and chicory, it was a poor substitute, but it was hot and the company was good. The *Appeal* had become a favorite gathering place for the editors of other papers, as well as for local business men, politicians, soldiers, preachers and shop keepers.

By the time winter arrived -- the second winter in exile for the refugee newsmen -- the *Appeal* was printing more than fourteen thousand morning and afternoon papers. Work continued day and night with little time for rest.

As Joseph walked along Peach Street late one afternoon in November, he reflected that the distance between his rooming house and the office on Whitehall seemed longer every day. Shivering, he pulled his shabby coat about him, a coat worn thin, patched and buttonless, but he was not likely to get a new one. It did a poor job of shutting out the fierce wind that now swept through Atlanta, a wind Southerners called a "blue norther." Leaves had been stripped from trees and replaced by a coating of ice. Once again, Joseph wished he had chosen to camp in the office with the younger men when they had first made their arrangements for living quarters. In the rooming house with Shaughnessy, each unbearably sad day followed another. But life in the *Appeal's* office – ah, nothing could dampen spirits entirely in such an atmosphere. The boys were having a grand time. Always busy, grabbing a few hours of sleep in the back room, then at it again. When they weren't working, darts and poker amused them, though by now the cards were so worn it was sometimes hard to determine just what they were. This brought about endless, good-natured arguments.

Meals were also jolly affairs, with everyone sitting around on the floor, eating from tin plates. At first they had taken turns cooking on an open fire behind the building, but they soon discovered that Joshua was the best cook among them, and so assigned him to commissary duty, a duty he seemed proud to accept. When food became scare, Joshua proved to be as proficient at foraging as he was at firing the boiler and cooking. He fed them sweet potatoes, turnips, field peas and johnny cakes. Now and then, he surprised them with a bit of meat.

"I'll swear," said Billy, "that Joshua could steal a chicken off a spit if a dozen Yankees were standing over it with fixed bayonets."

Joshua grinned, did not deny it.

When finally, the weather softened, the town became a wonderland of blossoms: dogwood, wisteria, honeysuckle, Judas trees. The newsboys picked ripe blackberries to bring to Joshua. As scarce as flour was, he managed to acquire some to make blackberry pies which he fried over the open fire in his big iron skillet.

Enjoying life was important, everyone agreed, for all signs pointed to bad times ahead. They were beginning to hear the sound of distant artillery which meant that Sherman was fighting his way toward Atlanta.

At a staff meeting, Joseph brought up for discussion the fact that they ought to stop trying to deliver the paper to soldiers in the outlying areas. "We're putting the lads who deliver the papers in harm's way," he said, not caring if they accused him of feeling this way because Ryan and Nate were among the boys.

He was almost shouted down by all the newsboys. They insisted that, since the men were fighting for them, the least they could do was to bring them their newspaper.

Linebaugh took their side. "If they want to see to it that our fighting men have their papers, they should be allowed to do so."

The boys gave him looks of pure admiration. He was their hero. Ryan said he wanted to be just like Linebaugh, a disturbing thought to Joseph.

But the matter was settled. At least for a while, the paper would be delivered as usual to the camps outside the city limits.

The atmosphere in Atlanta grew more tense as the days passed. The city was filled with military traffic. Horsemen and footmen dashed about. Wagon wheels screeched as drivers cracked whips on the backs of braying mules. Confused and frightened people huddled in their homes, or scurried about the streets.

The news from the front was confusing. General Johnston, who was commanding the Rebels, was now trading gunfire with General Sherman in the Kennesaw mountains. The Generals moved their troops like men playing on a giant chess board, a cautious Johnston giving ground slowly, Sherman striking, drawing back, waiting, then moving relentlessly forward.

CHAPTER TWENTY-NINE

ON A PLEASANT SUNDAY MORNING, Joseph was surprised to find himself wanting to attend church -- and Bridget not even there to prod him. In Memphis he had gone quite regularly, grumbling a bit about getting all fancied up and sitting on a hard pew between squirming children, but going anyway to please Bridget and to satisfy Aunt Clare's long ago teachings. But once off to war, he had abandoned the habit. Today, however, the peal of church bells blending with the distant boom of cannons filled him with a longing for family traditions. He decided he would take in Father O'Reilly's Sunday service. Father O'Reilly, a frequent visitor to the Appeal, was a pleasant young man much liked by Atlantans of all creeds. Joseph considered him a fine fellow, not nearly as long-winded as most men dedicated to preaching.

Joseph rolled out of bed, woke Shaughnessy and invited him to join him. Shaughnessy made a small noise, half moan, half growl. He hadn't been near a church since Molly's death and had refused to even acknowledge Father O'Reilly's attempts to console him.

So Joseph washed up as best he could, put on a clean shirt, shook the dust off his pants, spit-polished his shoes and set out alone. He would stop by and take Ryan and Nate with him, he decided. He would not allow them to grumble their way out of it.

But Nate was already out of his bed roll and off catching crawdads.   And Ryan protested, saying it was his turn to straighten the boxes of type and sweep the office floor.

Joseph remained firm. "A little churching now and then never hurt a fellow. And won't your Mama be pleased when I write that we've been attending mass? That is" -- he paused, momentarily glum -- "if she ever gets any of my letters, that is. "But come, lad. Get yourself dressed and hurry about it."

They were a bit late when they reached the small Church of the Immaculate Conception, but they tiptoed down the aisle and settled into a wooden pew. Joseph glanced at the worshipers around him. He concluded that his fear that he and Ryan might appear too ragged to mingle with the church goers was unfounded. Everyone in Atlanta was beginning to look seedy, with homespun clothes patched, turned inside out, and sometimes turned yet again to get more wear out of the garment. He and Ryan looked fine.

He knelt to pray, several prayers coming to mind immediately, one for Bridget and the children, one for Shaughnessy. And one for General Johnston who, according to a report from one of the Appeal's correspondents, was tangling with Sherman near Marietta just eighteen miles from the center of Atlanta.

When the congregation sang, Ryan joined in, his voice mellow and deep. Deep as a man's, Joseph noted in surprise. When had the lad's voice changed? What kind of father was he that he took no notice of his son's approaching manhood? He stole a sidewise glance at him and felt a surge of pride. Occasions for looking one's best were few these days. He didn't often get a chance to see Ryan with his hair combed, his face scrubbed, and the bit of fuzz he called his beard shaved away. And wasn't he grand looking? Handsome and tall, he was, almost taller than his father. Joseph was suddenly overwhelmed by a surge of love for this dark, intense son. He loved all his children, the whole passel of them, with their good looks and eager minds and lively ways. Who wouldn't be proud? But the bond which had developed between himself and Ryan since they'd gone to war together was different. They had become companions and friends as well as father and son. Joseph had not known a man could become so attached to a person. It made him aware of a terrible vulnerability. What if something happened to Ryan?

"Lord, don't take my son," he prayed silently, almost belligerently. "You've already taken my poor mother and my good brave father." He paused and quickly added, "Amen." He hadn't meant to sound angry and demanding, as if he were accusing God of wrong-doing. Sure, a prayer like that must be a mortal sin and wasn't it his policy to avoid sins that brought no pleasure?

He was glad when everyone stood and raised their voices in a rousing chorus of, "Holy God we praise thy name--" The singing was the part he liked about church going.

In the days that followed, summer rain storms made the weather as muggy and uncomfortable as steam baths. Everyone was on edge. Some insisted that Sherman would never cross the Chattahoochee River and, of course, would never be able to take the heavily fortified city of Atlanta. Others wondered why he hadn't already marched right on in. After all, wasn't it said that he had over one hundred thousand seasoned men? Why had he paused when he reached the bank of the river, a mere six miles away? Was he giving his men a chance to rest up for the big battle ahead? Or was he waiting to see what Grant wanted him to do before he pushed onward? The Rebels could only speculate and continue to work like beavers, building up fortifications around the city.

Most of the newspapers had already left Atlanta, or were preparing to do so. The *Confederacy* and the *Gate City Guardian* had ceased publication. The leading newspaper, the *Intelligencer*, was packing. Were it not for the *Appeal's* tendency to hang on as long as possible, the city would soon be without news. Even so, Dill had insisted that they dismantle their large press and boiler to have them prepared for a hasty getaway. This meant they had only the ramshackle proof press to put out small editions. Poor substitutes for the large metropolitan dailies the city was accustomed to, Joseph thought. It was taking all of his know-how and most of his time to keep the machine operating properly. As he struggled with it, he often thought of his father. Ah, wouldn't he approve of the *Appeal's* determination to continue bringing news to the people of Atlanta no matter what sacrifices it called for, himself being a man who would have done the same.

One night, Joseph took a break from his printing and went to the front door of the press room. As he stood there, leaning against the door jamb, taking advantage of a rare breeze stirring the hot night air, he was surprised to see Ryan and Nate riding down the street, both astride an old mule, the mule called Bessie. They looked tired and dirty and their shoes had been removed and tied across Bessie's back. Were they just now returning from delivering the day's edition? Joseph wondered. The other boys had been back for hours. He stood in the shadows, watching as they turned into an alley that led to the back of the building. He would have a talk with those two, he decided, heading for the back door.

A small campfire burned behind the building. A group of newsboys lounging about on the grass called a greeting to Ryan and Nate. Where you fellows been? See any more blue-coats today? Joseph hesitated, returned to the shadows to observe. Was something going on that he ought to know about?

As the boys climbed down from Bessie, Joshua lifted an old coffee pot from a rock beside the fire, poured each boy a cup of whatever he was serving that night.

"You're not going to believe what we saw today," Ryan said, his voice excited. He paused to blow steam from his cup. "But Nate can back me up."

Nate nodded. "Sure can. Just listen to this."

"We were riding Bessie near the shores of a small creek," Ryan began. "Staying sort of out of sight in the brush when we heard talking and laughing up ahead. Well, we got off the mule and crept forward on foot until we came upon a bunch of Yankees gathered on the opposite bank. Of course, we wouldn't have known they were Yankees if we hadn't seen their blue uniforms spread out on bushes to dry. The men, themselves, were naked as newborn babes."

A number of "Wows" interrupted.

"He's telling the truth," Nate insisted. "It's the God's truth."

All eyes were on Ryan as he paused for a sip from his cup. "Appeared as if they were doing their laundry because they'd built fires and were stirring tubs filled with water and bubbling suds.

Down the creek a bit, other men were washing themselves off. Taking a bath in the creek and hooting and hollering and splashing one another like a bunch of boys. Which was what they were. Boys. Maybe not much older than us. Nate and I moved along behind a line of bushes, and came upon a bunch of Rebels doing the same thing. We saw their uniforms drying on bushes, too. And across from these Rebels, not more than fifty yards away, more Yankees were swimming in the creek. We held our breaths, thinking fighting would break out any minute. But it didn't."

Ryan paused for breath and took another sip out of his cup while the others urged him to continue.

"It was strange," Ryan said, sounding awed. "The men on both sides of the river, Yankees and Rebels, were talking to one another just as polite as you please. The Yankees were saying that they were sure impressed with the size of our mosquitoes and asking was it always so hot here. Like they were just passing the time of day. And then they got to asking if they could trade coffee for tobacco, and some of the Rebels swam out to a log in the middle of the creek, holding a bundle over their head, and the Yankees came up from the other side and traded something in a pail. Coffee beans, I guess."

"Hey, why didn't you get us some coffee?" one of the newsboys asked.

"We weren't about to come out of hiding," Nate said.

Others clamored to know what had happened next. Joseph realized that he too wanted to hear more.

"We stayed where we were until the sun went down," Ryan continued. "Then the men began gathering their clothes from the bushes and getting dressed. While they were dressing, someone spied a firefly. The Rebels started catching fireflies, saying how they hadn't done that in years. The Yankees joined in the fun and we heard shouts of 'got one' and 'here's another' until it was completely dark and the fireflies quit lighting up. It was quiet after that. Nate and I waited a little longer, then felt sure they'd gone back to their outfits and we decided we'd best get back inside the city. As we started out, we heard rifle shots in the area, as if they'd started shooting at each other again." Ryan shook his head, looking completely confused. "I just can't understand this war."

"It's the beatenist thing," Nate agreed. "Seems like those boys actually liked each other when they weren't fighting. It's almost like they forgot about the war for a while. Maybe they're just tired of war. I know I am." Ryan shook his head, "Seems like the longer the war goes on, the less sense it makes to me."

Joseph remained in the doorway, no longer sure just what he wanted to say to Ryan.

Later he discussed the matter with Shaughnessy, knowing concern for Ryan and Nate was the only thing that might interest him these days. Also he needed advice. "How do you think I should handle this?" he asked. "I was caught up in every word Ryan said to those boys. I have to admit he does seem to have the makings of a good reporter."

"Sounds like it," Shaughnessy agreed.

"He told me he wanted to be a correspondent. And after all these years of wishing I had a son in the news business, it seems I'll have to stand in the way of his ambition. It's just too dangerous. Delivering papers to our troops camped outside the city is risky enough. But Ryan and Nate are venturing much further. They could run into real trouble. And I promised Bridget I'd keep her son safe and bring him home. She would never forgive me if I didn't do so. As a matter of fact, I'd never forgive myself. So, what should I do about this? Should I allow him to continue delivering papers to the troops?"

"I don't think it's your choice to make," Shaughnessy said.

"What do you mean?"

"Just that it's out of your hands. Ryan is nearing eighteen. He'll soon be a man and I think he'll feel he has a right to make his own decisions. You'll want to give him a word of caution, of course. Point out the risks he's taking. But if he's determined to be a correspondent, I have a feeling he'll consider the risks worthwhile."

Joseph only nodded. Shaughnessy was right, of course.

Early in July, the constant booming of Yankee artillery suddenly ceased. Only sounds of occasional skirmishes broke the uneasy stillness. For a short time Atlantans dared to hope. The men who gathered regularly at the Appeal office discussed rumors and theories. Had Sherman stretched himself too far? Sure, maybe he's been cut off from his supply lines and could be defeated yet. Things could take a turn for the better. Any time now.

But the fighting began again. And the news was all bad. Johnston had retreated once more. Sherman had advanced. It was said that, in one or two places, a few Yankees had even ventured across the river.

When Joseph heard this, he fretted, for the newsboys had already left to deliver the day's edition. He paced the floor, barely able to keep his mind on his duties, going often to the open door. The sun set and the other boys returned. Ryan and Nate were not with them.

Joseph slept not at all that night. Toward morning, an explosion lit up the sky. They learned, later that day, that Johnston had set fire to the Chattahoochee railroad bridge so the Yankees couldn't use it to march across the river.

Joseph, frantic now, asked Shaughnessy if he would go with him to help find Ryan and Nate.

"And where would you be looking?" Shaughnessy asked.

"In the woods. On the roads." Joseph did not speak of other places that came to mind. Among the wounded. Or worse. "Do you suppose they're caught behind enemy lines?

I should have warned them again not to go too far."

"And didn't we both agree that would have made no difference?" Anxiety replaced the listless tone in Shaughnessy's voice. "But they're smart boys, the both of them. They're probably hiding, looking for the right moment to slip back into the city. And if we went looking for them, what could we do but make it more difficult? We'll have to wait."

They stood in a patch of light streaming from the open door of the *Appeal* office, Joseph straining his eyes, hoping to see two barefoot boys on mules coming through the darkness. Listening for sounds of their voices, hearing only tree frogs and katydids.

Inside the office, the staff had gathered to once again plan their escape. Joseph could hear their voices, rising and falling. Urgent voices. Experienced and business-like.

Dill was saying they mustn't wait too long to leave, as they had done in Jackson. "We'll get packed and be prepared this time."

"What about some of us remaining behind with the proof press?" Mack asked. "A few volunteers could stay and put out some more issues. Then when the Yankees enter the town we'd have only a few things to pack and we could skedaddle out the other side."

Some favored this idea. Others thought it too dangerous. Joseph listened to their discussion but remained detached. The only thing he knew for sure, for absolutely sure, was that he would not be leaving Atlanta until he found out what had happened to Ryan and Nate.

CHAPTER THIRTY

S HAUGHNESSY COULD NOT BEAR the sight of Joseph pacing in front of the building. He brought two chairs out and set them on the wooden sidewalk. "Here, you might as well be resting yourself. Sure, walking up and down won't bring them back any sooner."

Joseph shook his head and continued to pace, shoulders hunched, hands shoved deep in pockets, his eyes scanning the darkness. Shaughnessy waited a moment then settled himself in one of the chairs. "The boys will be coming back," he said. "And won't they be bursting with tales of their adventures?" He was attempting to reassure himself as well as Joseph. He must remain calm, for he felt fragile, as if the slightest thing might open the mental floodgate he'd erected to keep his emotions from sweeping him away.

After Molly's death, he had shut down somehow, forced his mind to remain blank, his body numb. He remembered Joseph urging him to eat, telling him he hadn't eaten in days, and himself feeling not the least bit hungry. Like a fire turned to ashes, he was, no longer needing fuel. He had a sense that he was falling, with no end to the falling.

In recent weeks, he had gradually surfaced, but only to a certain level. He had often heard others speak of the pain of losing someone dear to them, but he had thought they meant mental anguish. He was unprepared for the very real pain in his gut. Time ceased to exist for him. Days passed and he was unaware of their passing. He clung to his work, thinking that his only hope for survival lay in keeping busy. But when he attempted to read even the shortest passage, the words slid by, leaving no impression, sentences were read over and over and still not retained. He found himself playing endless games of solitaire, a game he had always considered a waste of time. But it soothed him now, the way it occupied his thoughts without requiring more than automatic reactions.

Now, with a new concern facing him, he fought for control.

He tilted his chair back against the wall and closed his eyes. He had so many memories of Ryan and Nate as small boys, happily fishing or splashing about in the shallow part of Wolf River, or gathering twigs to build a shelter for their pet turtles. Another memory came -- himself holding Ryan when he was a baby, sleeping limp and trusting against his shoulder. And he had never had babies of his own.

Careful, he told himself. He must step back again, make himself unfeeling, efficient, a comfort to his friend.

Through the long night they waited, hoping, despairing. At first light, Joseph insisted he must go search for his boys. Shaughnessy protested.

"Stop and think, Joseph. If they're able to get back, wouldn't they be coming here as soon as possible?   One of us should stay and wait. Decisions may be required of--" he paused, swallowing the words 'family members'--"Anyway, I think I should check around the city. Find out if anyone has seen or heard of them. We have to consider -- just consider, mind you -- that they could be among the wounded."

Whatever color remaining in Joseph's face drained away. "Aye." He sank into the chair Shaughnessy had brought for him hours ago. "One of us ought to stay."

Shaughnessy hurried away before Joseph could say more.

He was glad he had talked Joseph into waiting at the *Appeal's* office, Shaughnessy thought, as he checked one hospital, then another. He was informed that the Medical College Hospital was overflowing and not taking in new casualties. The same was true of the Concert Hall and the City Hotel. He was directed to the many makeshift centers set up about the city. He wandered among the tent-filled parks where the newly wounded lay on blankets beneath white-grey tents. Flies swarmed everywhere and the smell of sweat and blood and disinfectants replaced the once fragrant aroma of the flowers that grew in the park. Shaughnessy ignored the sights and smells but was overcome by the sheer numbers of the casualties -- hundreds of them -- so young, so hurt. He hurried on, looking into every face, wanting to find Ryan and Nate, yet dreading what might face him.

When Shaughnessy had checked for information from every possible source, he headed back toward the office. As he turned down Ivy, he heard the scream of a shell, then a rattling sound directly overhead, followed an instant later by an ear-shattering blast. He stopped, momentarily stunned. Had a shell landed within the city limits?

A man ran past him. "Need a doctor," he shouted. "A little girl's been hurt bad."

Shaughnessy hurried toward the corner of Ivy and Ellis where a crowd had gathered. Several men bent over a man and woman, attempting to aid them. It was apparent that the child lying beside them was beyond help.

Another shell rattled above them, then fell on the street, sending cobblestones flying in every direction. Had the siege of Atlanta begun, Shaughnessy wondered. It's first victim a child?

CHAPTER THIRTY-ONE

DAYS PASSED, THEN A WEEK, THEN TWO, and Ryan and Nate did not return. The *Appeal's* staff and their many friends joined in the search. Joseph and Shaughnessy visited hospitals daily, met every train that rumbled into the depot carrying wounded. Though terribly overworked, doctors who were acquainted with the boys promised to keep an eye out for them.

For once, Joseph was grateful there was no way to get mail out of the city. Maybe by the time they could write again, they would have only good news to relate to Bridget.

The siege, which had indeed claimed a child as its first victim, now rained death from the sky. The scream of incoming shells blended with the boom of cannons. Shrapnel tore through the air. Homes and buildings were riddled, some destroyed entirely. Church spires tumbled. Grapeshot rattled in the oak trees and shells sent limbs crashing to the ground. Could Hell be worse?

Shaughnessy wondered. And yet, in the midst of the grimness, he found a source of amusement. Dill.

Each morning Dill, portly and impeccably groomed as always, walked down Whitehall toward his office. While others around him screamed and sought cover whenever a missile hissed overhead, Dill continued on, unflinching, eyes to the front, as if daring the shells to single him out. Occasionally, he shook his gold-handled cane toward the unfriendly sky. Ah, thought Shaughnessy, wasn't he the one? No fearful skittering about for Dill. And didn't it seem reasonable that the owner of the newspaper Sherman hated most would behave with such dignity? Shaughnessy was surprised to find himself chuckling, and it had been so long since he'd laughed.

In mid-July, General Johnston was relieved from his command for failure to stop the Yankees. He was replaced by Hood, a General who was known to be an aggressive fighter. Shaughnessy and Joseph were upset by the change. Hood, they felt, would stir things up so Ryan and Nate would find it even harder to make their way back into the city, if that was what they were trying to do. But the change in leadership brought hope to others. Daily editions of the Appeal breathed fire. Hood lived up to his reputation and the battle around Atlanta intensified.

"Time for us to get out of here," Mack said. "I hate to leave under these circumstances," – he gave Joseph a look of sympathy – "but as you know, the *Appeal's* ability to torment Sherman, then escape just as he has us in his sights has given our fighting men a great deal of encouragement. Think what it would do to Southern morale if we allowed them to capture us now. We must leave as soon as possible."

"Would we keep someone here to run off a daily bulletin on the proof-press as we planned?" Joseph asked, his question a plea. "Shaughnessy and I will stay,"

Mack hesitated. "I know we talked about doing that, but I'm not sure you and Shaughnessy are the ones for the job. Could I depend on you to get out of here when the time is right? Even if you haven't found your boys? How about it, Joseph?"

"I'll see that he goes," Shaughnessy said.

"I don't know." Mack closed his eyes, rubbed the bridge of his nose with two fingers. "I'm thinking one other man should remain with you to make sure you get out in time. I could stay, I suppose."

"That won't do," Dill objected. "If either you or I are taken, the Yankees will crow that they've captured the whole *Appeal.*"

The rest of the staff hastened to volunteer, claiming to be best qualified, for one reason or another.

Mack studied each face. "I believe Ed Goins is my choice, if he's willing."

Joseph drew in a quick breath and turned away to look out the window. Shaughnessy frowned. Goins wouldn't be concerned about the boys, he thought. Or, for that matter, about anyone but himself.

Goins seemed not to notice they were less than happy to have him. "Sure I'll stay. Be glad to, for the sake of the *Appeal.*"

Mack nodded. "It's settled then."

"We'll leave the smaller wagon to carry the press out," Dill decided. "And one horse. Belle, I think. But you'll have to keep a sharp eye on her. Horses and mules are getting mighty scarce in Atlanta. Lot of stealing going on. Do you men have guns?"

"I have a pistol," Goins said. "Got it off a Yankee who's sure not going to be needing it."

"And Joseph and I have a pair of old rifles. Only I think Joseph ---" Shaughnessy paused, let Joseph finish what he was going to say.

"I gave mine to Ryan the day he left. He claimed he wanted to help Joshua with the foraging."   Joseph frowned. "Do you suppose it would have been better if I hadn't let him take it? If they hadn't been armed? Do you think ---"

"No use torturing yourself with supposing."   Mack's usually gruff voice was soft. "You did what you thought best."

When the other members of the staff were aboard a train bound for Montgomery, Shaughnessy, Joseph and Goins put their personal differences aside and got on with their work. They were the only newspaper left in Atlanta and people were starving for information. With communications down, scrounging up enough news to fill even a one-page bulletin was a challenge but they did their best, reporting on enemy advances, while assuring everyone that Rebel troops were fighting back, advising people of the need to conserve the city's dwindling water supply, mentioning the few structures which appeared to have escaped damage so far, telling sadly of those destroyed or deserted.

One day, Shaughnessy walked past the now empty office of one of their former rivals, the *Intelligencer*, and on impulse he entered through an unlocked door. Inside, the abandoned building was dark and silent. Only the fact that the place smelled of printer's ink and contained a few stacks of tattered newsprint gave evidence that a great daily newspaper was once printed there. Ah, the pity of it, he thought.

All through August the battle raged on. Though the Confederate flag still flew over Atlanta, it seemed only a matter of time before Sherman marched into town. He had the advantage of superior numbers and better weaponry, as everyone knew, so what was keeping him from attacking? Was he playing a waiting game, perhaps thinking he would accomplish the same ends with less casualties if he first brought the city to its knees? No one had an answer. And the siege continued. Each day, long lines of wagons and ox carts bearing wounded men streamed in from the front and doctors struggled to tend all who could be helped.

Near the end of August, another puzzling and ominous silence replaced the shriek and thunder of war. This time, rumors had it that the Rebels were withdrawing from the breastworks surrounding the town and marching south.

"Time for us to get out of here," Goins announced. "And I promised Mack I'd see to it that you two left with me."

"No. I'm not leaving yet." Joseph's red-rimmed eyes had a wild, desperate look. "I know it's hopeless, that what I'm doing doesn't even make sense any more. But I can't just – leave. Not until I know what happened. No use asking me to."

"Be reasonable, Joseph," Shaughnessy urged. "Remember you have others depending on you. Have you thought of that? Bridget and the children will need you when this war ends."

Joseph shook his head. "I know. But still, I – I can't leave here yet. You all go ahead without me."

"If anyone stays, it should be me." Shaughnessy said. "I have no one depending on me. I don't even want to go back to a Memphis without my Molly in it? No. I'll be the one to stay."

"For God's sake," Goins shouted. "Will you two stop arguing and help me get this press on the wagon? Haven't you heard that the Rebels are planning to blow up eight carloads of ammunition to keep the Yankees from getting ahold of it? Hell, there won't be nothing left of us, if we don't get moving. And I don't intend to get myself blown up."

As Goins talked, he packed. Grudgingly, Shaughnessy began to hitch the mule to the wagon. When they were ready to go, Goins walked over to Joseph who stood watching, refusing to take part in the packing. "Come on now." Goins was gruff. "Get aboard. I'm not waiting forever."

Joseph folded his arms across his chest, didn't move. "I told you to go on without me. You just don't understand. You have no one who ---"

A blow from Goins fist landed on Joseph's chin, cut off his words, sent him reeling backwards.

"Hey." Shaughnessy grabbed Joseph, tried to steady him. "This isn't necessary."

"You know of another way to convince a stubborn Irish man? Here, help me put him on the wagon."

Shaughnessy put his arms around Joseph's waist and Goins grabbed hold of his legs. Together, they lifted the still groggy man to the bed of the wagon. Then, Goins jumped into the driver's seat, gave the mule a good whack with the reins and yelled, "Let's move."

Shaughnessy rode in the back of the wagon with Joseph in case the effects of Goins' punch wore off. They joined the steady line of people who were fleeing Atlanta in all manner of vehicles. Exhausted soldiers marched along beside the road. The going was slow and they had barely reached the southern edge of town when a huge explosion split the air. The ground shook and flames shot into the sky. The noise was constant, deafening, as carload after carload of ammunition exploded.

Joseph opened his eyes, struggled to sit up. "Got to go back," he murmured. Shaughnessy's big arms tightened around him and he slumped back, defeated.

CHAPTER THIRTY-TWO

JOANNA WATCHED IDLY as a fat bumble bee careened around the veranda, lit on the edge of the table, tried out the arm of a wicker chair, then zoomed out through the shimmering heat and disappeared amid the leaves of a magnolia tree. Such a carefree existence, she thought, flying about with no petticoats and long skirts to weigh you down, with no worries, or chores to be done. Or cheerful letters to write to a brother when it was getting harder and harder to sound cheerful. Oh well. She would do her best. She smoothed a wrinkled square of brown paper out on the table, dipped her quill in a small jar of ink and began her letter.

September 7, 1864

Dear Ryan,

Another week has gone by and still no letter from Atlanta. The Argus is printing disheartening news, saying that Atlanta has fallen. According to them, Sherman is ordering all its citizens to leave even though most of them have no place to go. Sounds cruel, but very like Sherman. But perhaps it's not true. Everyone here knows the Argus prints only what the Yankees allow them to print. Reading it, I sometimes feel disloyal, yet it's the only way to know what's going on in the world, unless friends are lucky enough to receive mail and generous enough to share it.

How I would love to be so lucky, to receive a letter which would let us know you and Papa and Nate and Shaughnessy are safe and well. But we haven't gotten a single letter since before the siege of Atlanta began. Yesterday I sent a box of apple-cinnamon cookies -- your favorite – addressing the package to the Appeal office on Whitehall. I'm hoping that if you're no longer there, some kind soul will send it on to you. See what a foolish optimist I am?

Every day, I stop by the post office on my way to work. It is so hard to see how disappointed Mama is when I return empty handed. And Nate's mother is mighty anxious because she hasn't heard from Nate. Will has left us to search for his sons again. Do you remember how Viney's singing could stir our hearts, even in happy times? Well, now her songs, spirituals mostly, are so full of sadness, we can hardly bear to listen.

And poor Mama. She looks so thin and worn. She has not been her cheerful, busy self since we lost dear Molly, but concern for her loved ones keeps her going. As I've written before, all the younger children, from Emilie down to Clare, have had the measles -- one at a time, wouldn't you know -- which has meant practically a whole summer of cross, itchy little patients. Now, they all have colds and Mama frets over them constantly. Already, she has had to help three of her friends bury a child, a heart scalding task women must help each other through, since fathers are often away and, in most cases, not even aware they have lost a child. Mama remains fiercely determined to keep us all well so this will not happen in our family.

Connor, Viney and I are doing our best to help her. Connor has taken over most of the chores you used to do. However, he still grumbles about being left back with the women folk. Last week, two of his friends joined the Army of Tennessee and he tried to talk Mama into letting him go with them. Mama was firm, saying that he wouldn't be draft age for another two years and she had no intention of allowing him to go to war before then. Connor has been in the most difficult mood ever since. From where I sit on the veranda, I can see him chopping kindling for the cook stove. His shirt is off and his shoulders are broad as a man's. You would be impressed with the way his muscles stand out as he lifts the axe and gives each stick of wood a fierce whack that sends pieces flying, a whack he no doubt wishes could be aimed at the enemy. I sympathize with him in a way. You cannot imagine how Memphis has changed ---"

Joanna scratched out her last sentence, put her quill down and leaned back in her chair. As usual, she was allowing her letter to wander as if she were talking to Ryan, telling him things he would be happier not knowing. He would not want to hear that his home town had been a captured city so long that it hardly seemed to be connected with the war any more. They'd been shut off from the rest of the world for over two years now and their first fine righteous indignation was wearing thin. The young people especially were eager to get back to normal, to have a social life. That certainly didn't belong in a letter, she thought. In fact, most of what she had written so far would be better not said. She ought to tear the letter up and begin over but then, paper was so dear. She settled for apologizing for the mood she was in and assuring Ryan they were really getting along quite well. "And if Papa is worried about us growing short of money," she added, "assure him that Mama is making do splendidly, stretching out the savings he left her and spending the money her father sends to best advantage. We really have few needs. Mostly we eat vegetables from Viney's garden and eggs from her little brood of hens. So in spite of my complaining mood, please rest easy about us. I love you and miss you. When you get home, we'll have a grand celebration."

She slipped the letter into an envelope and sealed it, planning to mail it on her way to work. Letters were so unsatisfactory, she thought. As she went upstairs to put on a dark dress and white apron, her uniform for working in the hospital. How she wished Ryan was here so they could talk as they used to do, saying whatever came to mind, sharing anything that concerned them. Ryan was the one who understood her best. She longed to tell him about Andrew. She hadn't mentioned Andrew in any of her letters which, she supposed, was proof of how guilty she felt. But what would Ryan think of her if he knew that, while he was off fighting Yankees, she was home making friends with them? And what would he have to say about the way she had deceived Mama so she could go to the ballet with Andrew?

Joanna hadn't meant to fool Mama like she did. She had fully intended to ask her permission to attend the show and had brought up the subject while they were setting the table for supper one evening. She had begun by oh so casually mentioning the fact that all the young people in town seemed to be pining to have a normal life again. "They've been organizing dances, or so I hear," Joanna had said. "And there's been hay rides, taffy pulls, anything that's fun. It's for the cause, you know, because they sell tickets to the events to raise money. And most think it's only good manners to allow the Yankees to attend if they have the price of admission. After all, most of the troops occupying Memphis are just home-sick boys and ---"

Bridget had interrupted this outpouring. "Joanna, I know all this. Whenever I go to the hospital to help or have women over to wrap bandages, I hear my friends discuss it. Some claim to understand and excuse the young people, saying it's only natural that they should be bored and want to have fun. But," -- she set a pitcher on the table with a firmness that caused the tea to slosh about -- "that doesn't make what they're doing right, does it now?"

Joanna had realized she would never get her mother to accept the fact that her own daughter was fond of a Yankee. She gave up and turned to Sarah for help.

Sarah had been a true friend, inviting Joanna to spend the night at her house, lending her a lovely blue satin dress with matching slippers to wear. When Sarah's mother became curious, Sarah had told her Joanna would be attending a party with friends. Joanna hated lying and was sorry to involve her friend. But it had been worth it. It had been such a long time since she had enjoyed anything and the night was magical. Going to the theater, with Andrew looking very handsome in his uniform and herself dressed like a fine lady, seemed the grandest thing she had ever done. After the show, they had walked back to Sarah's house, holding hands and humming bits of the music they had heard. It was a memory she would always treasure.

She had agreed to go out with Andrew again sometime, maybe to see East Lynne at the Olympic theater. But then the children had come down with the measles. Also, Bridget had gotten word that her own father was very ill. Joanna scolded herself for doing something that might cause her poor mother more worry. She had promised herself she would put this Yankee, this enemy, out of her heart.

But it wasn't that easy. Though she had told Andrew she must not see him anymore, she continued to be attracted to him. Whenever he was present at a social gathering, everything seemed brighter, more interesting and exciting. When he looked at her with longing, she wondered if everyone could see the pulse pounding in her throat.

Though she did not allow herself to go out with him, she saw him almost every day. He knew the places she went often and would just happen to be there and they would stop to talk. He would inquire after her family in the most proper way. He seemed eager to talk to her, if only for a few moments. She would tell herself each day that she would say they mustn't continue to meet, not even for short talks, but whenever she saw him waiting, looking so eagerly in the direction she always took, her good intentions deserted her. Eventually, she gave in and consented to continue their walks beside the river.

Bit by bit, they became better friends. With Sarah's help, they were able to attend dances, go on hay rides and to parties at homes of their friends. When she had to work late and planned to ride Kilkenny home, he would ride along with her, saying his horse loved evening strolls. And also, he would point out that it was dangerous for her to be riding alone at night.

"Don't tell my mother that," she had told him. "I've assured her it's perfectly safe. And she's always worrying about me."

"She sounds like a very good mother. When do you suppose I might meet her?"

"Not until I let her know about you. And I haven't been too brave about that. I'll have to get my courage up and to be honest, I don't know when that will be."

One night, as Joanna rode Kilkenny up the driveway and around the house, she found Connor sitting on the bench outside the carriage house. In the bright moonlight, his face looked troubled. She dismounted and hurried to him. "Is anything wrong? Has there been bad news?"

Connor shook his head. "Nothing like that but could you just sit here a minute? I think we should have a talk."

"Well, I have to take care of Kilkenny first."

"I'll do it for you in a minute. After we've finished discussing something." He stretched his long legs and patted the bench. "Come on, sit down beside me."

A bit reluctantly, she sat. "What is it you want to know?"

"It's not something I want to know, but something I already know. I've been hearing about you and how you're getting so friendly with a Yankee. With the enemy."

She lifted her chin. "Don't call him the enemy. His name is Andrew. Andrew Bradley."

"But he is a Yankee, isn't he? And I've learned a lot about him that you probably don't know. People are saying he comes from a very wealthy family up in Pennsylvania. His grandfather was once the mayor of Philadelphia, in fact. And his father is a Colonel in the Federal army. I don't mean to butt in, Joanna, but I can't help but be concerned. What do you think a family like that would have to say if he came home with a Rebel bride? An Irish Catholic bride at that."

Joanna rose from the bench. "And who said I was going to be his bride?"

"Well, I just figure ---"

"Well don't just go figuring when you don't know what you're talking about. I'm not planning to marry him. I'm not planning to marry anyone. At least not for ages and ages. Andrew and I are just friends. Do you hear me? Just friends."

"They say some of the girls who have married Yankees didn't plan to do so at first. Joanna, don't you see how risky what you're doing is? You're going to break Mama's heart. And your own." Connor sighed. "I just wish Ryan could be here to talk to you. You'd listen to him."

Joanna sat down again. She looked up at Connor but a cloud had passed over the moon and she could no longer see his expression. She patted his hand. "I know. We both need to talk to Ryan. But stop worrying. I'll think about what you've said."

"Then I'll put Kilkenny away so you can start thinking."

She could sense his smile in the darkness. She gave him a hug and started toward the house. Poor Connor. He had always been the carefree little brother with Papa and Ryan taking care of things. Now they were gone and Connor seemed to feel the weight of everything concerned with the family. And though he was young, there was truth in what he had said. Obviously, there was no likelihood of a happy ending for her and Andrew. But what Connor didn't understand was that she wasn't like those other wishy-washy girls who had married Yankees. And she would certainly never be like the girls who couldn't keep themselves to themselves and ended up in disgrace. Didn't Connor know she had better sense than that?

And now, Joanna thought, as she put the letter she'd written to Ryan that morning in the pocket of her uniform, it was fall once again. Almost two years had passed since that November day she and Andrew had met out by Fort Pickering. And they were closer than ever. When she was away from him, she could hardly wait to see him again. She wished she hadn't volunteered so many hours to the hospital. With her mind always on Andrew, she was forgetful, unmindful of her duties. She wanted to be with him every minute and she didn't care what people thought. Or how it would end. She just wanted to be with him. Now.

One night she got off work and found that he was in the stable and had already saddled Kilkenny. "To save time," he told her, with the grin that reached into her heart.

She did not want her time with him to end and when they reached the place where they usually parted, she suggested that they ride a bit more. She led the way across the meadow and into the woods.

"This is where my brothers and I used to play when I was younger," she said. She led the way to the creek and showed him the willow tree where they'd read books to each other and acted out many favorite scenes.

"Ah," he said. He never seemed to grow tired of hearing about her family, her friends, her life. He dismounted and went over to the creek. "It's beautiful here." They stood admiring the way the willow limbs reflected in the clear water. "Did you go wading here, you and your brothers?"

"Of course."

"I'll bet it was lovely on a summer day." His voice was wistful. "I wish I could have been there with you. I hate it that I've missed so much of your life."

"We could wade in the creek now, if you wish."

He laughed at the idea but sat on the creek bank and began to remove his boots. She laughed, too, then took off her shoes. Holding her skirts up, she entered the creek. "It's a little cooler than it is in the summer," she said.

"I like it. It makes me feel more alive." He splashed water her way and she splashed back. For a while they played, splashing one another as if they were children.

When they returned to the edge of the bank to put on their shoes, they were a bit damp. Joanna shivered. He put his arms about her and before she could move away, he leaned down to kiss her. A gentle kiss at first, then suddenly fierce. Her heart raced and her blood seemed to be singing through her veins. Alarmed, she forced herself to push him away. She had thought she would be in control of such a situation. No one had warned her of the sweetness of being close to someone you cared for, of the over-powering urge to be closer. "We -- we have to leave here," she said, sounding desperate.

"Don't be afraid," he whispered. "I wouldn't do anything you don't want me to do."

Tears gathered in her eyes. "That's the trouble, I do love you so. I want you in a way I don't understand. And I won't become one of those women left to raise a fatherless child. A woman scorned by everyone."

"I wouldn't want that for you either. Do you think I would allow such a thing to happen? It's just that" -- he paused as if trying out words in his mind -- "we're going to have to get married."

"We couldn't do that."

"Yes, we could. And we will. My Captain will marry us. He's married several others of my troop to Southern girls. If we can't get your mother's permission, you'll just have to lie about your age. Say you're twenty or so."

More lying, she thought. "No," she decided. "Getting married is -- serious. I won't go sneaking around and lying about it. We'll have to tell my mother."

"Well then, we will. I love you, Joanna. Nothing is going to keep us apart."

Taking her hand, he stepped within the circle of the drooping willow limbs, then pulled her close to him. She felt her heart race once again, felt his lips trembling on hers. Would she have the strength to push him away again? She must, she told herself. But he touched her hair, traced her lips with his finger, then kissed her again, and she felt her strength, her resolve slipping away.

And her mother would never, never allow her to marry a Yankee.

CHAPTER THIRTY-THREE

A S SHAUGHNESSY AND GOINS took turns urging the old horse across the dusty red roads of Georgia, Joseph remained dazed. Groggily, he grumbled at them for dragging him from Atlanta, insisting he would return first chance he got. They journeyed onward, through Columbus, across the Chattahoochee River, into Alabama and on toward Montgomery.

When at last they arrived at the Appeal's new office in Montgomery, a relieved staff abandoned their tasks and came out of the little frame building to greet them.

"We were worried about you," Dill said. "Did you have trouble getting out of Atlanta?"

"Aye, we did," said Shaughnessy. We'll give you the details after we're settled."

"Are you hungry?" Joshua asked. "I cooked up a fine batch of field peas and some corn pone. Could build a fire and hot it up again if you like."

"That's kind of you, Joshua." Shaughnessy smiled. A tired smile. "And we'll surely take you up on that. But I think we need rest more than food at the moment."

"I know just how you feel after that long ride. Felt the same myself." Doyle led the way to a room in the back of the building. A half dozen bedrolls were scattered about on the floor. "Just fall into one of these. Sleep as long as you want."

When Joseph awoke, he heard Shaughnessy snoring softly. He sat up and looked around, wondered what time it was. Most of the other bedrolls seemed to have acquired occupants. He felt around for the britches he'd left beside his bed, pulled them on, then put on his shoes and crept quietly from the room. He was surprised to find the rest of the building empty and dark, but he saw Mack standing in the moonlight just outside the front door and joined him.

"Ah Joseph," Mack said, you're awake. And about time."

"How long did I sleep?"

"About ten hours or so. How are you feeling?"

"Hungry."

"A good sign. Well, what shall we feed you? Shaughnessy and Goins woke up and ate the rest of Joshua's field peas and corn pone, then went back to sleep again." Mack looked at the sky, considered "And I'd say it will be an hour or so before any cafes open up, but the saloons are open all night and some serve some kind of food. I just don't know what."

"Anything will do. My insides are empty as a drum."

"Come on then. Let's take a walk. There's several places located a few blocks from here." They walked along the boardwalk, the thump of their shoes echoing on the quiet street.

"Heard they had a bit of trouble getting you out of Atlanta." Mack sounded amused.

Joseph rubbed his chin, still a bit sore. "I guess you got the details from Goins. He would make a good story out of it."

"Well, yes. But he served his purpose. Actually, I chose him to stay because I knew he wouldn't be too soft to do whatever needed to be done. Someone had to get you out of there."

"I suppose. But I didn't speak to Goins until we were halfway to Montgomery. And several times I had a strong urge to return his punch. But I finally realized he was following orders. And you're right. I got kind of obsessed there for a while, couldn't think straight. But I've had a lot of time to think and I'm figuring those boys were smart enough to hide out and let Sherman's troops pass by them. There are a lot of refugee families around Atlanta who dug holes in the side of hills – bomb proofs, they call them – and maybe the boys found something like that and afterwards just decided to take off in the opposite direction. It would have been the sensible thing to do, actually. They probably learned a thing or two from watching our escapes. Why, they're probably on their way home now. May be there already."

"Sure," Mack said. "That does seem quite possible. As you said, they're smart boys."

Joseph took a deep breath, felt better than he had in a long time. "Sure am hungry."

"Let's see if something is open over by the capitol." With a nod of his head, Mack indicated a large building which rose above other structures, its tall marble columns gleaming in the moonlight. "Dill thinks it's an omen of sorts that our office is now located in the shadow of the very building where Davis took his oath as President of the Confederate States. Odd, isn't it? After all our traveling, here we are in the place where it all started. Somehow it's given Dill the notion this may be the end for us."

"Do you agree?"

"Well -- who knows? We're still putting out a daily paper. And it's still in demand. But not many people can afford to pay for it these days. And our staff has shrunk considerably."

"Yes, I noticed. Where is everyone?"

"Well, Mr. and Mrs. Dill have a room in the Exchange Hotel across from the office. We figured we couldn't ask Mrs. Dill to bunk with the men, could we? The rest of us sleep wherever we find it handy. Those who are still with us, that is."

"Do we still have Linebaugh? And Latke and Vernon?"

"Linebaugh took a position in Richmond. Latke and Vernon went home. They're past forty-five so they don't have to worry about the draft any more. Most of the crew sort of scattered after we left Atlanta. Dill and I couldn't afford to pay them anyway. Money is a problem."

"Joseph sighed. "Hasn't it always been since we set out to be refugees?"

"Not to the extent it is now. But let's not dwell on that at the moment." Mack paused to re-light his cigar. "Here, turn down this side street. I see the lamps are still burning in one of my favorite saloons. And they sometimes serve fair-to-middling food."

As the days passed, Joseph's strength returned. He was glad to get back to work, though the pressroom was only a shadow of its former self. In Atlanta, it had taken twelve men just to keep up with the requirements of the composing room. Now their daily edition contained only two pages. Even so, getting material to fill the little paper was a major problem with the wires down and mail deliveries rare. Army couriers traveling across the southernmost states sometimes dropped off packets of newspapers from other cities. Mack gleaned what news he could from them.

One day they were delighted to receive a paper telling of Sherman's plan to march across Georgia toward the sea. A celebration erupted in the pressroom, with a great deal of hurrahing and back slapping. Wasn't it grand that their old enemy, the general who had nipped at their heels for the last three years, was now heading in the opposite direction? He would not likely come their way again.

Through a dreary rain-drenched winter, the staff tried to remain optimistic in spite of the dark news they were forced to print. The Yankees were gaining on every front, pushing the Rebels back from one stronghold after another. They received two messages from General Lee and printed them, messages that underlined the sad state of affairs. The first pointed out that Confederate soldiers faced a choice between renewed fighting and abject surrender. "To such a proposal brave men with arms in their hands can have but one answer," Lee stated. A later announcement, signed by General Lee, proclaimed that all Confederate deserters who returned to their commands within twenty-one days would be granted pardons. Clearly, desertion was a growing problem among Rebel forces. Men were giving up the fight against the overwhelming odds and returning to their homes and fields.

After that, they heard nothing from Lee. Nor did they know where Grant or the other Federal generals were fighting. The lower part of the Confederate states might as well have been a distant planet.

Spring finally arrived, bringing more rain, more grumbling and complaining from the staff. Years of war had ravaged the land and, even with Joshua's skills as a forager, they often went hungry. The days passed slowly, uneventfully.

"I sort of miss having old Sherman on our tails." Billy said. "I wish we could at least have a little excitement."

In March, he got his wish. They learned that they had a new enemy: Major General James H. Wilson of the Third Iowa Volunteer Cavalry. General Wilson, a young man still in his twenties, was often referred to as the "boy general". It was rumored that he commanded over twelve hundred men, cavalry men who knew how to fight as well as ride. Most ominous of all was the report that they were armed with the new Spencer rifles. The Spencer, a .52 caliber carbine which fired metallic cartridges loaded into a seven-round magazine, was considered a marvel. Rebels referred to it as "that Yankee gun that could be loaded on Sunday and fired all week."

How sad and unfair, thought Joseph, to have all those fresh young Yankees, riding fine horses and armed with shiny new rifles, galloping across the land in pursuit of ragged, poorly mounted, badly armed and often hungry Rebel soldiers.

Wilson fought his way south, defeated General Forest at Selma, Alabama, then headed for Montgomery. Once again, the Appeal's men packed hurriedly. They now had only two wagons, having traded two others for a fresh team. The larger wagon would carry the main press, boiler and steam engine, the smaller the proof-press and remaining supplies. Mr. and Mrs. Dill would travel in the dray, pulled by old Belle.

As soon as the wagons were loaded, they set forth, struggling through muddy, rutted roads and across rain-swollen creeks. Joseph noticed that Mrs. Dill, who had helped with the packing as she usually did, now sat bundled in blankets on the seat of the dray. She looked tired and pale.

Back through Alabama they went, back toward Georgia. Now that Sherman had marched on, they would seek refuge in Macon. Others who fled Montgomery traveled with them. And soon, the retreating Rebel army was riding past them. A Rebel who stopped to water his foam flecked horse near the Appeal's camp one night, informed them that Montgomery had surrendered without resistance.

"City officials rode out to meet Wilson," the soldier related, "and turned over the city to him. He rode into town like a damn king, excuse the language," – he tipped his hat toward Mrs. Dill – "Anyway, he's now headed for Columbus. You folks better move along a lot faster than you have been."

They took his advice and decided not to stop for rest but to continue on through the night. By noon the next day, they crossed the Chattahoochee River and entered Columbus. There, they went to the sheriff's office and asked if he could offer a place to hide their equipment and supplies.

Sheriff Osgood was a plump man with a round face and a huge gray mustache. Though obviously in his later years, he moved with energy and spoke in a strong voice. "You bet we can give shelter to the *Appeal*," he said, in answer to their request. "Be an honor. I've heard a lot about your newspaper, heard that both the Yankees and proud Southerners often speak of it as the greatest Rebel of them all. Yes indeed, it would be a privilege to help you. Folks in Columbus will be proud to know you're here."

"What do you think of Columbus' chances of holding off against General Wilson?" Mack asked.

Osgood shrugged. "We've got three thousand men and cannons in place beside the bridges. But Columbus is filled with factories and munitions. The Yankees want us bad, consider us a prize. To tell the truth, I can't guarantee anything."

"Maybe we ought to continue on," Mack suggested to Dill.

For a moment no one spoke. Joseph recalled the days when there would be no 'maybe' about it. Threatened with capture, they would have taken off pell-mell, intent on escaping. He looked at the faces around him, saw a deep tiredness, discouragement.

"I don't know," Dill said. "Mrs. Dill is not well and ---"

"Why don't I go on to Macon with the main press and the engine and boiler?" Mack asked.

"You mean split up? I don't know. We've always---"

Mack interrupted. "Actually, it would be for the best. If we traveled in a smaller group, it might make us less conspicuous. Suppose I take one other man? Make a beeline toward Macon? We could get there in time to hide the big press before Wilson catches up."

Dill looked at his wife. Her face was flushed with fever. "All right then. We'll follow your plan."

Joseph moved toward the large wagon. Mack had said only one man would go with him, and he wanted to be that man. But much to his dismay, Ed Goins shoved him aside and jumped into the seat beside Mack. Mack flicked the reins over the horses' backs and the wagon was soon out of sight.

"God be with him," Dill murmured. He turned to the sheriff. "I was wondering – my wife is not well – do you know of anyone who might offer her a place where she can rest?"

Osgood squinted his round face, thinking. "There's Mrs. Sudbury, the mayor's sister-in-law. She has a small rooming house and would likely take her in if she has the space. Anyway, wouldn't hurt to stop and ask. I'll get my horse and show you the way."

Mrs. Sudbury greeted Mrs. Dill with sympathetic clucks. "Of course I'll put you up, you poor dear. You look like you're done in." She gave Mr. Dill a disapproving look. "And your mister can stay to look after you if he's a mind to."

"I could show the other men where to hide your stuff," Osgood said. "If you think they can handle it without you."

"Of course we can," Shaughnessy said. "Stay with your wife. You look exhausted yourself."

"And if you need it, Mrs. Dill, we could leave your trunk here," Joseph offered.

She hesitated. "I hate to be a bother, but maybe a bath and fresh clothes will give me strength."

With the trunk removed and the Dills settled, Joseph took the reins of the dray and the others rode along in the wagon. They followed Osgood through the streets crowded with military vehicles, wagons, Confederate troops.

A confederate soldier rode up and hurriedly spoke. "Pardon me sir, but we've just learned the Yankees have hauled into sight across the river. We're planning to remove planks from the lower bridge and force Wilson to use the more heavily fortified upper bridge. Do you think you could bring some of your prisoners to help out?"

"Well, as soon as I---" began Osgood.

"Go ahead if you're needed," Joseph told him.

Osgood reached in his pocket, took out a key and gave it to Shaughnessy. "Keep going straight ahead," he directed, "until you come to a big warehouse on the left side of the street. It's loaded to the rafters with bales of cotton but I think you'll be able to hide your things in the basement."

"We'll manage," Joseph said.

Osgood turned his horse, called back over his shoulder. "When you're finished go back to the jailhouse. I'll tell my deputy to scrounge up a meal for you."

"Come on," Joseph told the others. "We want to unload while we have daylight."

When everything had been carried into the warehouse basement and hidden under tarps, Billy, one of the crew told Joseph that he and the rest of the boys would take the horses to a stable to be cared for. "I saw one down near the end of Main. Jake's stable, it was called. And we were thinking we'd have a look around the town when that's done. See some sights before all Hell breaks loose. We can drop you off at the jail so you can enjoy that meal the sheriff said would be waiting for you and then come back about midnight."

At the jailhouse, Osgood's young deputy hobbled about on crutches, one empty pant leg pinned above the knee. "Call me Corporal Miller," he said. "'Course I ain't rightly a corporal no more since I'm discharged, but I figured I traded my leg for the title so might as well keep it." He fed Shaughnessy and Joseph beans seasoned with salt pork, baked yams and a hunk of cornbread.

Joseph ate heartily, called it a meal fit for a king.

"My wife's the cook," the deputy said, looking proud. "She made the corn bread special when I told her earlier who she would be cooking for."

Later, Corporal Miller passed out cigars. "We might as well relax. The Yankees won't have time to mount an attack before dark. They'll likely wait until first light tomorrow."

The four men sat outside the jail, leaning back in chairs, smoking and watching the sun go down. It was 8:30 p.m. Maybe, thought Joseph, they could have a bit of a nap---

A shot echoed down by the river, followed by more shots, then cannons boomed.

"Son of a bitch!" said Miller. "Looks like Wilson isn't going to wait for morning."

Shaughnessy stood, looked off down the street. "I just wish we hadn't let the others go off. They ought to be here with us."

"No matter," Miller told him. "Ain't no one place safer than another at a time like this."

"Could we go up on the balcony?" Joseph asked. "Maybe get a good view of what's happening?"

"Go if you want to," Miller said. "I've seen enough battles to last a lifetime."

Joseph and Shaughnessy climbed the stairway to the balcony in front of the jailhouse. From there, they saw artillery light up the sky. The roar and crash of battle echoed in the dark, moonless night.

Gradually, the enemy advanced until they were fighting in the streets just below Joseph and Shaughnessy. The people of Columbus, who had apparently not expected the fight to begin until dawn, were scrambling to get out of harm's way. Women clutched children and flattened themselves against buildings. Galloping horses pounded by. Joseph saw men raise their rifles to shoot, but it was so dark he couldn't tell which men were Yankees, which Rebels. Men fell to the street, wounded or dead, to be stepped over by other men.

By eleven o'clock that night, it was over. The street was cluttered with abandoned guns, haversacks, spent shells. Shadows danced in the glow cast by burning buildings. Then, ambulance corps arrived, carrying stretchers to pick up the fallen.

Osgood returned. "I released my prisoners in return for their help removing planks from the bridge," he told Miller. He suggested that Shaughnessy and Joseph try to get some sleep. "Just bunk in one of the cells. Nothing else to do until morning."

Exhausted, both Shaughnessy and Joseph stretched out on the narrow cots, fell asleep immediately.

When they awoke the next morning, Osgood was gone.

"A bunch of Yankees came in and took him away," Miller told them. "Made him bring all his keys. They're searching buildings to see what bounty they've captured."

"Searching buildings?" Joseph gave Shaughnessy a look of alarm. "What if they find the *Appeal*?"

"And what could we do about it if they did?"

"I don't know. But maybe we can divert them, cause some kind of excitement that would get their attention away from the warehouse." Joseph grabbed his jacket, ran out the door and down the street. Shaughnessy followed.

But they were too late, for the warehouse doors stood open and Yankees were pulling the *Appeal's* proof-press from the building with cries of triumph. It's the famous Memphis Appeal, they shouted. The Rebel sheet wanted by Sherman. Hadn't they escaped capture a half dozen times or more? And now they had captured them. Wilson would sure be pleased. Gleefully, the Yankees began to pound the press with crowbars.

Joseph leaned against a lamp post to steady himself. For a moment, he had become a five-year-old boy again. The voices of the Yankees became the yelling, cursing voices of the men who had killed his father. The smashing blows against the hand-press were a sound he'd hoped never to hear again. He turned away from the destruction of the Appeal, his heart aching.

When the press was destroyed completely, the Yankees emptied cases of type, scattered them on the street, added ledgers and supplies to the pile and set it all afire. The smell of melting metal and burning paper lingered in the sultry morning air.

Shaughnessy put a hand on Joseph's shoulder. "At least they didn't get the main press and boiler. Thank God, Mack got away."

"But what about Dill?"

The two men stared at one another. "We'd better get him out of here fast," Shaughnessy said.

As they walked down Main toward the stable, Osgood came riding up. "I need to tell you it's all over town that Dill's here. Someone recognized him and it won't take the Yankees long to find out where he's staying. Unfortunately, there are people who would point out their own grandmother for a few Yankee dollars."

"We're on our way to get our horses now," Joseph said.

"Where are they?"

"In Jake's stable down the street."

"Well, if you hurry, maybe you'll get there before the Yankees do."

But once again, they found that the blue coats were ahead of them. "They took the good horses and all the carriages and wagons they fancied," Jake told them. "Only left some old wagons out behind the building. One is yours, I think."

"Do you know what happened to the young men who brought our horses in?" Shaughnessy asked Jake.

"Don't know as I do. Seems like the last I saw of them was just before the battle began last night."

When Joseph located their wagon, he climbed into the rear. "Looks like they pawed through all our knapsacks and bedrolls."

Shaughnessy joined him. "Yeah, the scoundrels helped themselves to our guns, damn 'em." He looked at Jake. "You say they took all the horses?"

"All of them 'cept a sad looking little mare. She's laid out in the rear of the stable."

Joseph and Shaughnessy hurried inside, certain they would find Belle.

"Ah, 'tis her," Shaughnessy said. "Is she alive do you think?"

Belle was lying on a pile of straw, her eyes closed. Joseph bent to examine her. "I don't know. Hand me that bucket of water." He poured water over Belle's head and neck, speaking to her as he did so. "Come on, Belle, old girl."

Belle opened one eye, looked at them, and whinnied softly. Joseph held out a handful of oats and she lifted her head. After a moment, she began to nibble. They persuaded her to struggle to her feet by holding a bucket of grain just out of reach. When she'd eaten the oats, they took her out to the water trough. She lapped up water as if she'd been lost in a desert.

Shaughnessy rubbed the little horse's ears. "Poor Belle. Do you suppose she'll be able to pull the wagon by herself now that the Yankees have taken our other horses?"

"She'll have to. Damn those Yankees. They take whatever they want."

"Spoils of war, Joseph." Shaughnessy hitched Belle to the wagon. "Come on, let's lead her along for a while. Show her she can do it."

They walked down the street until Belle gained confidence and then they climbed on the wagon and went to Mrs. Sudbury's boarding house.

Mr. and Mrs. Dill were waiting on Mrs. Sudbury's veranda, dressed and ready to go. Their trunk was on the floor beside them.

"We heard that the Yankees had found the Appeal's equipment and destroyed everything," Dill said, "and we knew we'd better get out of town. Fortunately, Mrs. Dill is feeling a little better after a night's rest." He put on his hat. "Come on, let's go." He helped Mrs. Dill into the wagon.

As Joseph was loading the Dill's trunk, he heard heavy footsteps behind him. He turned and saw that a Yankee squadron was moving to surround them. Instinctively, he looked about for a means of escape. Guns rattled into position and he found himself looking into the barrels of a dozen rifles, the first Spencer rifles he had ever seen. Out of the corner of his eye, he saw Dill put a protective arm about his wife, saw Shaughnessy's fists clench.

They had been so intent on outrunning the Yankees, as they had many times before, that they had been careless, unprepared. Their only weapon was the small hand-gun Dill had carried in the pocket of his waistcoat. And what good would that do against a dozen Spencer rifles. Joseph set the trunk down.

The leader of the squadron – Colonel Minty, the men called him – touched the trunk with his toe. "Let's have a look in here. I want to be sure I've got the right men."

Two soldiers held the trunk steady while another pried it open with a crowbar. They pawed through its contents, tossed articles of clothing aside, examined papers.

"Here, look at this." The Colonel was handed a newspaper clipping, a picture of Dill standing in front of the *Appeal's* Atlanta office. The Colonel looked at Dill, then back at the picture. "Aha, it's him all right." He turned to his men. "Looks like the hornet's nest of the Confederacy is ours at last. General Wilson will be elated."

CHAPTER THIRTY-FOUR

JOSEPH HELD HIS HEAD HIGH as he, Shaughnessy and the Dills walked through the streets of Columbus surrounded by soldiers. In all of Joseph's nightmares about the Yankees capturing the *Appeal*, in all the times he had imagined what it might be like, he had pictured violent scenes with every man resisting until overcome by force. Never had he thought their years of exile, their grand adventure, would end in a calm, orderly surrender. Yet, he had to admit, they were being treated in a very civilized manner. It would have been much more humiliating if they'd been forced to march through the streets with their hands bound like criminals. He tried to distance himself from what was happening but he could not shut out the sound of the soldier's boots tramping the hard earth with military precision, nor the rattle of their artillery. He was glad when the soldiers turned to guide them up a short flight of stairs and across a porch. Two guards stepped aside to allow them to enter into the hallway of a small clapboard house.

Undoubtedly, someone's home, thought Joseph, looking about at the pleasant rooms they passed. Someone's beloved home taken over to be used as headquarters for a Yankee general.

Colonel Minty dismissed his squadron. "I'll take them into the General's office."

They entered a paneled room lined with book shelves and furnished with a large desk. Joseph was surprised to see a General and another officer kneeling on the floor, a large military map spread out before them.

"Allow me," began Colonel Minty, his voice triumphant, "to introduce you, sir, to Colonel Benjamin F. Dill, editor of the *Memphis Appeal.*"

The General jumped to his feet. "Have we caught that old fox at last? Well, I'll be damned."

A confused moment followed. General Wilson and Dill stared at one another. Dill stood tall, proud, confronting the younger man without flinching. Both, Joseph realized, were men who had made their mark on the world, men to be reckoned with. He saw a hint of mutual respect in their eyes.

"So at last we meet," General Wilson said. He put out his hand. Dill hesitated, then accepted the gesture. They shook hands firmly.

"And this lovely lady must be your wife," the General said. "Someone bring a chair for Mrs. Dill."

Joseph and Shaughnessy stood at the edge of the room, ignored for the most part.

General Wilson seated himself behind a desk, shuffled papers, played with the corner of a large handsome mustache, smoothed his balding head. "We have matters which must be discussed," he began, then stopped, rearranged the papers again. Obviously, he was attempting to conduct the proceedings in a business-like manner. But the jubilant atmosphere in the room could not be denied. Undignified whispers escaped staff members, traveled about the room. Officers came from other parts of the house, peered through the doorway to have a look at the famous editor of the *Memphis Appeal*. Wilson's men congratulated him, told him how proud they were to serve under the General who had captured the famous rebel newspaper, the newspaper which Sherman and Grant had failed to subdue.

General Wilson beamed at one and all, said, "I believe this calls for a drink."

Aides quickly produced glasses and a silver flask. A bit of bourbon was poured into each glass and passed around.

"You'll join us, of course," Wilson said to his captives and, though Mrs. Dill, Joseph and Shaughnessy declined the drink offered them, Dill accepted graciously. "Hmmm," he said, after taking a sip, "I believe this is the finest bourbon I've had in years." He swirled the amber liquid around in its glass and added that it was almost worth getting captured for.

A round of good-natured laughter followed.

Later, when the whiskey was gone and the other men had returned to their tasks, General Wilson leaned forward in his chair, put his hands flat on his desk. "Now," he said to Dill, "we really must get down to business. What shall I do with you, now that you're my prisoner? After all, your newspaper has caused a great deal of trouble for the Federal government. May have prolonged the war. That's a very serious matter. I can't overlook it, but" -- his hand went back to the mustache –- "maybe I should talk this over with my associates." He rose from his chair and gestured for two of his men to follow him into the next room.

Dill reached out to take Mrs. Dill's hand. "There now. It's not going to be so bad. Wilson is not like Sherman. I don't think he hates us."

After much discussion among his aides, General Wilson had his adjutant draw up a long-winded document filled with fancy legal phrases binding the Appeal editor, asking that he recant the fake doctrines he had professed and "as long as he might live to conduct himself in deed and word as a loyal citizen of the great Republic." The document also placed Dill under a $100,000 bond, a bond to guarantee he would not publish another issue of the *Appeal*. He was given the choice of signing the document or going to jail. Under the circumstances, Dill signed. The bond, covered with Confederate funds, the only money Dill had left, was accepted, and the Dills, Shaughnessy and Joseph were set free.

When Joseph and Shaughnessy returned to Mrs. Sudbury's boarding house, the Dills were already there. Mrs. Dill was indignant. The Yankees, she told them, had taken Belle and their wagon, as well as their trunk, their collection of silver quarters and dimes and all their clothing. Bristling with anger, she added that they had even taken Dill's hat.

"That's a shame, ma'am," said Shaughnessy. "Have you reported it to General Wilson?

"Yes, but he says he doesn't know anything about it." Mrs. Dill said. "He insists that he doesn't approve of looting but it's a hard thing to control. Oh, those Yankees, they're full of excuses.

"Now, dear," Dill soothed. "You mustn't let it upset you so. You'll be feeling poorly again. And it could be worse, you know.

At least, Mack has probably hidden the main press by now. And we have an offer" -- he paused looked at Joseph and Shaughnessy -- "but of course, we can't accept it unless it includes all of us and --"

"Wait a minute," Shaughnessy said. "What offer are you turning down?"

Reluctantly, Dill told them that, to show the city's appreciation for the *Appeal's* wartime efforts, the mayor of Columbus had made arrangements to have them escorted back to Memphis. However, the offer didn't include Shaughnessy and Joseph, and so was unacceptable.

Shaughnessy frowned. "Nonsense. Of course, you're going to accept. Mrs. Dill has been through enough and should be taken home.'

"Aye, we insist that you go while you have the chance," Joseph agreed. "Shaughnessy and I will find our own way home."

CHAPTER THIRTY-FIVE

JOSEPH AND SHAUGHNESSY ASSURED the Dills once again that they would be fine, that they would have no trouble finding their own way home. Looking doubtful, almost guilty, Mr. and Mrs. Dill left Columbus in a fine carriage, accompanied by a military escort, just as the mayor of the city had promised. After they were gone, Joseph and Shaughnessy wandered about, looking for Billy, Doyle and Joshua. They found Billy and Doyle camped beside the Chattahoochee River discussing ways to, as Billy put it "get their asses back home." They sat on the river bank beside them. No one said much for a while.

"Now, that's what we need," Doyle said suddenly, pointing to a raft that was approaching from the north. "If we floated down to the Gulf, we could maybe find a boat that would take us over to Mobile. I have kin there who could help us get over to New

Orleans. All we'd need to start out with is a raft. Where do you suppose we can get one, Billy?"

Billy didn't answer. He was staring at the raft. "That looks like--- It is. It's Joshua."

They all stood, waved, then waited as Joshua steered the raft to the edge of the river.

"Where'd you get that thing?" Doyle asked.

Joshua gave them his widest grin. "Found it upriver."

"Found it?"

"Well, let's just say, there's some mighty mad Rebels up there that were planning to use this here raft to desert their post. Heard 'em talking about it"

Billy stepped onto the raft. "There's all kind of stuff stashed here. Some blankets and food. And Hell, this looks like a jug of moonshine."

"Well that's actually whiskey," Joshua said, trying to look modest. "Good whiskey. Got it from the hospital stores."

They stared at him.

"Well," -- he shrugged —— "the Yankees were going to get it anyway. They're taking everything they can get their hands on. So I beat 'em to the whiskey. It's a good-bye present to you folks."

"Aren't you going with us?" Joseph asked.

"Naw, I'm staying in Georgia. Don't have folks in Memphis anyway. And I heard a rumor about the gov'mint handing out a mule and a patch of land to every freed slave." He paused, looking wistful. "Don't exactly believe that, but if it does happen, I want to be waiting someplace handy, standing in the front of the line."

"But what if we need you to forage for us?" Doyle asked. "What if we run out of food?"

"You'll get along." Joshua handed Doyle a splintery oar. "This old oar was the best I could get hold of for steering the raft. Ought to have two, but this one will have to do. You can push the boat out into the current with it. Just stay in the easy water next to the bank and you'll move right along. And one other thing, there's a rope hitched to a corner of the raft. If you stop for any reason, tie up to a tree." After giving them this advice, he urged them to get going. "Those men I acquired the raft from might be along any minute, looking to take it back."

They thanked Joshua, hugged him, wished him a fine life as a free man. Then, Doyle pushed off with the oar until they were caught up by the current.

For the next few days, they floated along, passing the jug around, taking long sips of the excellent whiskey, drowsing in the sun, then waking to sip again. Sometimes they even ate a little of the food -- dried beef and biscuits. It was what their tired bodies and souls needed, they all agreed.

They didn't notice at first that they had run out of food. When their stomachs began to protest, they steered to the edge of the river.

"Tie up to that tree yonder," Doyle told Billy, as they set out to look for berries, or anything edible overlooked by harvesters.

It was late, the sun about to go down, and Joseph cast a worried look around deserted fields. "Wish we had a gun. We were foolish to set out unarmed."

"Maybe we'd better go back to the raft," Shaughnessy suggested. "Hell, I'd rather get along without food a while longer than have someone steal our whiskey."

They headed back toward the river, arriving just in time to see the unmanned raft bounding down the stream at a swift pace.

They chased along the bank – Shaughnessy even jumped in the water to swim after it -- but the raft was soon out of sight.

Doyle turned on Billy. "Didn't you tie it up like you were supposed to?"

"I did. I did. I guess I just didn't make the knot tight enough."

They sat on the bank, mourning their loss.

"Now what are we going to do?" Doyle asked. "How are we ever going to get to Mobile?"

"Walk," said Joseph. "It's the only thing left for us."

"But I reckon it to be almost two hundred miles from here," Doyle said. "And the country is probably crawling with deserters and marauders and the like. We'll be lucky if we don't get ourselves kilt."

"We'll travel at night," Joseph decided. "It won't do us any good to sit here talking about it. I want to get home." They set out, walking from dusk to first light, sleeping each day under bushes, on bare ground or piled up leaves. They were living like animals, eating berries and whatever else they could find. After a while, they lost track of how long they'd been walking, began to despair of ever reaching Mobile.

"I think we're getting close," Doyle told them one day. "Smell that Gulf air."

The others sniffed, smelled nothing but dry earth. But Doyle was excited. He urged them to continue walking although the sun had already risen. "We'll just keep on for an hour or so," he said. "Get us that much closer."

They trudged along, so tired that they were almost asleep on their feet. When a mule-drawn wagon bounded over the hill behind them, they were caught unprepared. They dodged behind a bush. Joseph looked at the men who drove the rig and was surprised to see Negroes in blue uniforms -- Yankee uniforms, clean, neat. The wagon came to a stop beside their hiding place. "You men want a ride?" one of the soldiers asked, smiling. White teeth shone in a black face. "War's over, you know. We ain't enemies anymore."

"What do you mean the war's over?" Doyle asked.

They came out from the bushes, everyone talking at once. "Who told you so?" "Yeah, where'd you hear that?"

"We just come from Montgomery," the man sitting beside the driver of the wagon answered. "Heard about it there. Lee surrendered to Grant back in April sometime."

Joseph was amazed. "What day in April?"

"Don't know. Don't know much more about it. They've been slow as molasses about fixing telegraph wires in this part of the country. Even the big bugs don't know what's going on half the time. Heard that General Wilson fought two battles after the war had ended. But get in, men, if you want to ride. We don't have all day."

"Where you headed?" Doyle asked.

The driver inclined his head toward the boxes and kegs in the back of the wagon. "Taking this here load to Mobile. You can sit on top a keg or box if you want. It won't be easy settin', but it'll get you there."

"Beats walking," said Billy. He climbed aboard and the others followed.

In spite of the fact that their bones were jarred every time the wagon bounced over a rut in the road, the men of the *Appeal* were so exhausted they soon fell asleep propped against one another. When they awoke, they were parked in front of a building and the Yankee drivers were beginning to unload, stacking kegs untidily beside the wagon.

A man standing on the building's loading dock called down to them. "You men take it easy there. Those things could fall over and blow us all to Hell."

"What's in them anyway?" Billy asked.

"Gun powder, mostly." was the calm reply.

Doyle stared at the keg he was sitting on. "You mean we've been bouncing across the country sitting on top of gun powder?"

"That's a fact, sure enough," one of the soldiers told them. "We been ordered to gather up all the gunpowder and shells and such that got taken off the Rebs and we ---"

No one waited to hear more. Quickly, they jumped from the wagon and took off down the road.

Five blocks away, they paused to catch their breath. A bar beckoned and they searched their pockets, found enough to buy each of them a pint.

Inside the bar, there was a roar of conversation. They sat at a table, ordered their pints and tried to determine what all the excited talk was about. It was a while before they could decipher the torrent of words. When they did, they could hardly believe what they were hearing. Lincoln had been killed, the men were saying. Shot in the head. Assassinated by some crazy actor. He'd been dead since late in April. Almost a month.

Beside Joseph, Shaughnessy swore softly. Billy and Doyle looked stunned. Joseph felt a deep sadness. Lincoln was the enemy, and yet he was devastated to learn he was dead. A great loss for the country. A tragedy. One thing about Lincoln, Joseph thought, he was a man who seemed able to keep control of those under his command. Who would take his place? The country was torn apart, the South a great gaping wound. And the man who could make it right again had been shot by a fool.

Joseph nudged his companions, urged them to finish their drinks so they could leave the bar. He wanted to begin the search for Doyle's cousin, get that boat ride to New Orleans arranged so he could go home to his family.

Doyle's relatives welcomed them, treated them like returning war heroes, shared their meager supplies of food with them. They brought out their best booze, toasted the refugee newspapermen over and over. One of Doyle's uncles was a barber and he gave all of them much needed haircuts and paid fifteen cents each so they could bathe in a tub of hot water. An aunt collected clothing from other family members to replace the rags the refugees were wearing. Doyle's cousin got them free passage across the Gulf, an arrangement which included anything they wanted from the bar.

New Orleans was home to Billy and Doyle, but Joseph and Shaughnessy still had a long way to go, and no money to buy tickets on a steamboat. Billy solved their problem, persuading his former boss, Mr. Sinnott, the editor of the *New Orleans Times,* to pay their fare on a Memphis bound steamer, a big steamboat called the *Empress.* "Glad to do it in return for the *Appeal's* contribution to our cause," he said. He also sent a wire to Bridget, letting her know when her husband would arrive.

Once on the steamboat, Joseph and Shaughnessy found yet another generous bartender who served them before they even put in an order, saying it was on the house. And everyone, it seemed, was eager to buy a drink or two for the men who had been a part of "the greatest Rebel of them all."

"Seems like we've floated home on a sea of bourbon," Joseph complained to Shaughnessy.

"A blessing for a man who doesn't want to think," was Shaughnessy's reply.

But Joseph did want to think. He imagined his home-coming again and again, thinking just how it would be, with Ryan waiting there, safe, his children running to greet him, and Bridget in his arms. It would be grand, wouldn't it?

Still, there were times when he looked at himself in the mirror and saw a stranger and he would wonder if he'd find Bridget as changed as he himself was. He recalled a time long ago, when he was a boy of eighteen, standing beside the Mississippi waiting for a bride-to-be he hadn't seen in four years, recalled how he had fretted that they might have grown into strangers who no longer wanted one another. Remembering this, he shivered, looked in the mirror again. And though it was May, the warm breeze blowing down river seemed suddenly cooler.

He decided he would limit his drinking, only have one a day from now on, no matter how many of the *Appeal's* admirers wanted to treat him at the bar. He didn't want to arrive in Memphis all blurry eyed, smelling of spirits. There were, he thought, a lot of habits he'd acquired as a refugee that would need to be cast aside.

CHAPTER THIRTY-SIX

IN THE BOARDING HOUSE ROOM which had been Joanna and Andrew's home for the last six and a half months, Joanna arranged flowers in a vase and put them on a small table. Then she set out two plates with matching cups and saucers, china she had borrowed from her mother. This would be her last dinner with Andrew, at least for a while. She wanted it to be nice.

Everything was ready, chicken and dumplings and baked yams waiting in the warming oven downstairs, a lemon cake with a thin bitter-sweet icing (Andrew's favorite) set out on a small chest beside the table. She looked around the room. Though it was small and furnished with odds and ends, she loved everything about it, even the faded roses on the wallpaper. They had been so happy here. To make their first home pleasant, she had sewn filmy yellow curtains for the bay window. This afternoon, the warm April sun filtered through them. She had set pots of geraniums on sunny window sills, framed her own water colors and hung them strategically to hide worn spots on the wallpaper. Her mother had contributed a colorful red and yellow quilt for their bed, a small table, two chairs and a storage chest. In one corner of the room, an ancient marble fireplace, though an eyesore with its scarred mahogany mantelpiece and cracked mirror, had provided them with cozy wood fires which had kept them warm during the winter months. A bearskin rug, Andrew's contribution purchased from a local store, lay beside the hearth. There, they had shared cups of tea and glorious moments, moments which had made the world fade away leaving just the two of them, together.

For Christmas, they had put up a small tree, decorated it with popcorn and berries. As they sat on the bed on that cold December morning, bundled under their quilt, they had exchanged presents. She had knitted a sweater for him, her first effort at such a domestic undertaking. Andrew had admired it extravagantly, then had given her a small ring with tiny sapphires.

"It's not your real wedding ring," he told her. "Remember, my grandmother left me a huge diamond ring in her will, saying it was for my future wife. It will be yours as soon as you get to Philadelphia."

She had smiled so he wouldn't guess how uneasy she felt when she thought about going North. She would go gladly, of course, for she loved him. She'd do anything to please him so he would delight her with his boyish smile.

Sometimes she was amazed at herself, at how she had changed so easily into the housewife she had once decided she would never be. Her ambition to lead another kind of life -- she had thought she wanted a career of some sort, something challenging -- had been abandoned. When she fell in love with Andrew, she'd realized nature had other plans for her.

When she had finally gotten her courage up to tell her mother about Andrew, she wondered why she'd been so reluctant. Her mother's only concern was that she might have chosen a difficult life for herself, marrying a Yankee.

"Are you sure you want to do this?" Bridget had asked.

Joanna had answered without hesitation. "Oh, yes Mama. I can't let him go away without me, no matter what."

"You're that fond of him?"

"I love him."

"Then he must be a fine lad, for I'm sure you wouldn't love him if he weren't." There had been a silence then, and Joanna saw that her mother was lost in thought. "Aye," she said finally, "I know what you're going through. I know all too well how it is to fall in love with someone your family disapproves of."

"Papa?"

"Yes, your father. Just as you're planning to do, I followed him to a land I knew nothing about, wanting only to be with him."

"I'm glad you understand, Mama. And don't worry. I know Andrew and I are going to be happy together. I just know it."

And so far, Joanna thought now, they had been truly happy. Truly, wonderfully, ecstatically happy. She moved about their rented room, smoothing the yellow curtains into place, watering the geraniums, straightening pictures on the wall. She wanted everything to be perfect when she served Andrew the last dinner they would be sharing until they were reunited. She would not let anything spoil it.

When Andrew returned from taking his bath in the big tin tub in a downstairs room, he grabbed her in a playful hug, kissed her lightly. He was dressed in uniform, a reminder he would be leaving soon. But she pushed the thought aside, kissed him back, put her hands in his hair, a tangle of damp curls.

"I'll go get the dinner while you finish packing," she said.

She hurried down to the kitchen where the landlady allowed her to cook an occasional meal. Removing the chicken and baked yams from the oven, she carried them up to their room and transferred them to serving bowls.

When he came to the table, his curls tamed, sitting tall and handsome, she felt a moment of insecurity. Was she beautiful enough to match such a husband? Unconsciously, she reached up to smooth her long, thick hair.

He noticed the gesture, said, "I love your hair. You wouldn't ever cut it, would you?"

"Not if you don't want me to." She sat down and poured coffee in the delicate cups.

"Hmmm," he said, after taking several sips. "Real coffee. Where did you get it?"

"Oh, I have sources. I'm so grateful to have the war over so we don't have to make-do with those awful concoctions?"

"I'm grateful it's over so I can take you home with me."

She put her cup down, leaned her chin in her hand. "I hope your folks will like me." Why did she keep saying that over and over?

"They'll love you. How could anyone not love you?"

The dinner was the best he had ever eaten, he bragged, after he had devoured two helpings of chicken and baked yams, and several pieces of cake. To last him for a while, he said. "Don't know what kind of food they'll have on this boat I'm taking. I've heard that most of the passengers will be war prisoners on their way home. They'll no doubt be a noisy bunch. And who would blame them if they celebrated all the way?"

She sighed. "I wish you didn't have to go alone. I should be going on that boat with you."

"I know. And I don't want to go without you. I hate leaving you. But truly, it is best this way. Just keep reminding yourself what I said about wanting to have things right for you when you arrive. I want my parents to be properly informed about how wonderful you are. And I'll have our own place, our new home, ready for us to move in so we won't have to put up with any slights or unpleasantness, if there should be any. And I promise, I promise for the thousandth time, I'll send for you as soon as I possibly can."

She began to clear the table, but he reached for her hand, held it. "Let's have a good-bye kiss while we're still alone." He pulled her into his lap and they kissed, a long kiss which, he insisted, didn't seem at all like a good-bye kiss.

"It wasn't. But we'd better go anyway or you'll miss that boat."

"I suppose you're right." He looked about the cheerful room. "I'll always remember this place."

"So will I."

"Shall we leave early so we can walk on the Bluff one last time," he asked.

She put on her bonnet, tried to not let herself get sad. There would be time for that later. She would not let it spoil her last walk by the river with Andrew. Outside, the April air was cool and a light rain fell off and on, but they had walked in the rain before. They lowered their faces against the mist, clinging to one another as they strolled along the edge of the Bluff.

The *Sultana* arrived late. When Andrew saw the boat steaming upriver, he pulled his watch from his pocket. "Here it is, finally. And it's almost six o-clock."

"I was hoping it wouldn't come at all," Joanna said.

They walked down the cobblestoned river bank to wait on the wharf as the *Sultana* approached the shore. From its decks came the sound of merrymaking, wafted across the water by the breeze. Every lamp on board must be lit, Joanna thought, for the old steamboat glowed as brightly as a showboat. When it settled beside the wharf, men leaned over the railings on every deck. Happy shouts rang out -- "We're going home." "No more war."

" -- heading for home."

"Looks like they've had a drink or two of 'Oh be joyful'," Andrew observed.

"It's so crowded," Joanna said. "I don't think I've ever seen so many aboard one boat."

"Can't say as I have either."

They were silent a moment, looking at the boat. The upper decks were actually sagging a bit under the weight of shoulder to shoulder passengers.

Another man who stood beside them waiting to board the boat, remarked, "Looks more like they have a load of hogs aboard than men."

"Oh Andrew, do you have to go?" Joanna exclaimed. "I mean, couldn't you wait and catch the next boat?"

"The next one won't be any better. As long as they're paying steamboat captains five dollars a head to take prisoners home, most of them will be greedy and want to load on as many as possible. Anyway, my father is planning to meet me in Cairo. I wouldn't want him to make such a long trip only to have to come back again."

She nodded, said no more, held his arm as tightly as she could.

The *Sultana* lowered her gangplank and deckhands carried barrels and cases ashore. Some of the passengers came ashore, men shouting to one another, obviously headed for a nearby saloon.

It was almost eleven o'clock before the loading and unloading was done and Army guards had rounded up drunk soldiers to herd them back aboard the boat.

"I understand they have one more stop," Andrew said. "They're supposed to pick up a load of coal over on the Arkansas shore, and we'll be on our way." He gave Joanna one last kiss, ignoring appreciative whoops from the other men. Then, reluctantly, he started up the gangplank, stopping halfway to look back at her. "They're going to love you," he called. She saw his smile once more before he was swallowed up by the crowd on the deck.

She waited, hoping he'd be able to squeeze a place for himself by the railing but she did not see him. She shouted good-bye in case he could hear her, then stood waving. Other soldiers returned her wave for Andrew, calling out in playful imitations of a southern accent.

"Bye now, pretty thing."

"See ya'll later."

A cold damp wind was blowing from the North, but Joanna remained to watch as the *Sultana* crossed the river, docked for a time and then continued up the river. Only when she could no longer see the boat did she turn and walk slowly up the Bluff.

She couldn't bear the thought of going back to their empty room. Perhaps, she thought, they would need extra help at the hospital. She hadn't done any volunteer work in a while, not since she and Andrew had gotten married. She would stop by tonight, see if they could use her. Maybe Sarah would be there and she needed to be near a friend.

But Sarah wasn't working that night, and the hospital was quiet. Almost too quiet. Joanna applied cool cloths to burning foreheads, held restless hands, poured tumblers of water. But the hours passed slowly. Tomorrow, she thought, she would ask Connor to help her pack and move her things back to Mama's house. She was surprised she no longer thought of it as her house.

By two a.m., the patients had settled down, most of them asleep, so Joanna went to stand by a window and looked wistfully toward the North. She thought of Andrew, of the smile he'd given her as he walked up the gangplank. And the happy shouts of the men leaning over the railings of the *Sultana* echoed in her mind. She wondered fretfully if Andrew been able to find a place to lie down and get some rest. Or even sit down. Already, she missed him so much. How would she endure all the days she would have to wait before he could send for her?

She was startled to feel a tremor shake the hospital. And then she saw a red glare on the northern horizon. Men began to run in the street below her, calling out to one another. Was that a boat going up, I wonder. Which one? Joanna fled from the hospital, ran toward the Bluff, stumbled down the cobblestone road to the edge of the river.

CHAPTER THIRTY-SEVEN

WHEN THE *EMPRESS* LANDED at Memphis, Joseph wanted to rush ashore as soon as the gangplank was lowered. He held back, however, matching his stride to Shaughnessy's reluctant steps. They made their way slowly forward, Joseph looking about, wanting to see how years of Yankee rule had changed his city. The sun still shone on the red clay of the bluff just as it always had, but the wharf was new, he noted. He could still smell the newness of its boards. It was much larger than the old one had been. And even busier. Vessels of every kind gathered around, many of them flying stars and stripes. Enemy ships, he thought, then reminded himself they were supposed to be one nation now. Maneuvering through the crowd on the dock, he searched for friendly faces but saw only strangers. More Yankees, no doubt.

"Papa," called a cheerful voice. "Papa, over this way."

Joseph turned to look up at a tall young man. "Connor? Is it you?"

"Yes, Pa, it's me." Connor grasped Joseph in a bear hug, then released him to give Shaughnessy a similar greeting. "Mama's waiting at home," he told Joseph. "She doesn't like to bring the children into crowds."

Joseph took a deep breath and asked the question that had to be asked. "And Ryan and Nate?"

Connor's voice was gentle. "They're not here yet, Pa. But we do have a letter from Ryan. Just got it about a week ago though it was written last fall."

"So long ago. They ought to be here by now."

"I know, Pa. But men missing longer than that are showing up every day. We'll just have to wait. And not give up hope."

"How's your mother taking it?"

"Just like you'd expect. We're all walking softly around her."

"Blames me I suppose."

"Now, Pa. We all know it's not your fault. Now tell me, do you have any bags that need to be picked up?"

"No. Nothing."

"How about you, Shaughnessy? Anything you need to bring to the house?"

"No, lad. Thank you for offering. And I don't think I'll be going home with you."

"But you have to. Mama's expecting you. She had Viney get the spare bedroom ready. And they're making a feast to welcome both of you home."

Shaughnessy managed a smile. "That's kind of them. Tell them I appreciate it. But right now, I think I'll go by Bell Tavern. See if my credit's still good." He turned and walked away.

Joseph called after him, promising that he and Connor would drop by to see him in a few days. Then they hurried to the carriage so Joseph could read Ryan's letter. Joseph paused only to greet Kilkenny, to give his nose a friendly pat and rub his mane. "Do you suppose he remembers me?"

"Sure he does."

"He's gotten a bit older, I see."

Connor grinned. "We all have." He untied the reins. "Climb in, Pa. I'll take the driver's seat. Kilkenny's used to my touch."

Joseph watched his young son as he urged the old horse up the cobblestoned road, skillfully avoiding wagons, carts, drays and carriages rushing up and down the side of the Bluff. He was impressed and said nothing until they reached a reasonably calm side street. Then, Connor reached down to remove a box from beneath the carriage seat, took out a smudged and wrinkled envelope and handed it to his father. Joseph's hands shook as he pulled out a single page.

"Dear Loved Ones," the letter began.

"First of all, Nate and I are fine, so don't worry. Don't know if you've gotten any of my letters and it's a bother to be writing things over and over. When I get home, I promise never to tell you anything twice again. But I do want you to know how sorry I am that Nate and I got caught behind enemy lines. I know Pa must have been frantic when we didn't come back that day in Atlanta and it's all my fault, me and my notions about being a correspondent. Wanting to see everything and then, not noticing when all of a sudden, Sherman advanced and got between us and the city. We were right in the thick of the fighting and I don't know what would have happened if a

kind family hadn't reached out and snatched us into a bomb safe they'd dug in the side of a hill. We huddled there for days while the war howled all around us. When we finally got back to Atlanta, Hood had retreated and Atlanta was in Yankee hands. The Appeal building was gone, just blown up I guess, and we couldn't find any of the staff. Or anyone we knew. We wandered around in a daze sort of, sleeping in abandoned buildings, scavenging for food – boy did we miss Joshua – trying to figure out what to do next. Then one day, we heard that Sherman wanted everyone to get out of Atlanta so he could finish burning it up. He was offering free railroad tickets to Macon or Chattanooga. We figured we'd go to Macon and maybe catch up with the staff. But they only allowed us to have tickets to Chattanooga. When we got there, we decided that since we were in Tennessee we might as well just start walking home. We thought all the fighting had moved to the east of Atlanta but boy were we wrong. First thing we knew, Hood's men were all over the place. When they saw us, they thought I was a deserter. Wouldn't listen to anything we said. Just told us we'd better get back in uniform if we knew what was good for us. They gave me an old dirty uniform with a bullet hole in the shoulder and a no count rifle and said they'd be watching me and if I tried to get away again, they'd shoot me. I tried to tell them I was glad of a chance to fight for my homeland, but I don't think they believed me. At least Nate and I are able to keep together which is a great comfort. I'm running out of paper now and someone is waiting to borrow my quill so I'll write again the next chance I get. When I get home I'll have some great stories to tell. Maybe even write a book. Now don't you all be worrying about Nate and me, you hear? We're going to make it fine.

Love, Ryan.

Joseph finished the letter, leaned back, drained. He tried to recall what he knew about the fighting that had gone on in Tennessee after Atlanta fell. There'd been terrible battles near Murfreesboro, he remembered. And Columbia. And the weather had been fierce, the battles fought between ice storms. Poor Ryan and Nate must have had a bad time of it.

Connor put a hand on his father's knee. "Don't think the worst, Pa. I've heard that when soldiers aren't going to make it through the war, they sort of have a feeling about it. And Ryan sounded positive he would be home, didn't you think?"

"Well, he did. But then, he's so young . . . Joseph's voice trailed away.

After a while, Connor stirred uneasily. "I hate to do this, Pa. But we're almost home and before we get there I have to tell you about Joanna." Quickly, he added, "Now don't go thinking she's hurt or sick or anything like that. It's just that, well, something happened. It's not an easy thing to tell. But it will be better if you know about it ahead of time."

"Go ahead, then."

He did not mind so much hearing that Joanna had married a Yankee, though wondered if she had chosen a difficult life for herself. But when Connor mentioned the *Sultana* and he remembered what he'd heard about it blowing up north of Memphis, he began to suspect that marrying a Yankee was only a trivial concern.

"Joanna wasn't on the boat but her husband, Andrew, was," Connor told him, keeping his voice flat, emotionless. "The *Sultana* was meant to carry less than four hundred, but there were more than two thousand five hundred aboard at the time of the accident, the boat overloaded by greedy owners. When Joanna heard the explosion, she went down to the side of the river. She was still there when the first victims came floating by the river front, clinging to wreckage and hollering for help. She joined a group of people who went out in boats to rescue as many as they could, looking all the while for Andrew." Connor paused, drew in a shaky breath. "It wasn't until several days later that he washed ashore, dead and so badly burned they wouldn't let Joanna see him. Andrew's father came down from the north to claim his body. While he was here, he didn't even bother to come calling on Joanna. Never acknowledged her existence. I don't think Joanna will ever get over this, Pa."

"No, how could she." His lovely, happy Joanna, Joseph thought. And he had believed she was home, safe. "Poor child. How does she go on with such a sorrow to bear?"

"She's still numb, I think. That's why I figured I should warn you ahead of time. Right now, the family is trying not to talk about it too much."

"Yes, I suppose that's best." They rode on, then Joseph looked at Connor, thoughtfully "Anything else I need to be prepared for?"

"I reckon not. Well, come to think of it, yes. You ought to know that Grandpa died. Happened about six months ago and he was sick for a long time before, so Mama has accepted it, though she was very sad for a time."

"Ah well, I'm sorry I couldn't have been here to comfort her. These are difficult times, it seems." His eyes returned to Ryan's letter. Please God. Bring Ryan home to us.

They rode on, then Connor tugged at the reins and turned Kilkenny toward the long driveway which led to the familiar gray house on the hill. Looking ahead, Joseph saw Bridget standing on the veranda, a hand shading her eyes. He heard shouts from within the house, shouts of "Papa's home." "He's here." Children burst out the front door and ran to gather around him as he climbed from the carriage. He leaned down to embrace each child, felt the tug of small arms about his neck, shy kisses on his cheek, but all the while his eyes were on Bridget. She remained on the veranda, waiting, smiling. As soon as he could disengage himself, he hurried up the steps, took her in his arms, kissed her.

"I'm going to take Kilkenny to the carriage house and feed him his oats," Connor announced. "Anyone want to help?"

None of the children accepted his invitation. They couldn't take their eyes off Joseph.

"Papa, you're here." Joanna came out of the house wearing a high-necked black dress, a color she never wore. But her hair shone in the sunlight, refusing to be somber. "Oh, Papa, I'm so glad you're home." He took her small face in his hands, tilting it up so he could see her. Such a sad little face. He wanted desperately to help her. She moved into his arms and he held her close for a long moment. Then she turned away and returned to the house.

"Where's Shaughnessy?" Bridget asked.

"He wouldn't come with us. I think he needs to be alone at first."

"Well, we must let him know he's welcome any time."

"I'll tell him."   Joseph saw Viney standing just inside the doorway. He knew she had not wanted to intrude. As if she could. As if she weren't part of the family. He held a hand out to her, patted her shoulder.

"Where's Will? Joseph asked.

"He's gone to look for our boys again. Maybe now, he can find them," she told him. "Now, I set out a nice cool glass of lemonade beside the sofa in the sitting room. You just go drink it and rest yourself."

"Thank you. You're a comfort, Viney."

The lemonade tasted delicious, more refreshing than anything he'd drank in a long time. And the old horsehair sofa yielded to his body's contours. The children gathered at the doorway, crept into the room one by one. Quiet now, having lost the momentum of their first burst of excitement, they stood back, regarding him with wondering eyes, as if he were a distant relative they hadn't seen in years.

He returned their gaze, trying to decide which was which. They had all grown so. How old were they now? He didn't dare ask Bridget. For some reason, she got very upset when he forgot the ages of his children. Clare, the baby Bridget had carried about on her hip when he left, must be three by now. Or thereabouts. The boy, Patrick, was a sturdy lad, no longer a baby. Emilie was quite tall now, he saw. And then there was the thin, dark child, who was peeking from behind Emilie. Had to be his Molly Kate. How could he forget her? In an attempt to revive their special relationship, he coaxed her into his lap. "You remember me, don't you? I'm the one who always put your tears back for you."

She looked at him as if he were daft.

"Remember?" he insisted. "You used to get mad if someone wiped your tears away. You'd scowl fiercely and say 'Put my tears back.'" He laughed but she remained solemn. How old was she? He calculated, decided she ought to be about five by now. Maybe six. And he had left a toddler. Aye, if a man didn't pay attention, time itself could do a pretty good job of robbing him of his children. As it had done with Connor, who was now more man than child.

The dinner was obviously meant to be a festive affair. The flowers arranged in a crystal vase, the linen tablecloth, silver gleaming by candle light, all of it spoke of the work and planning gone into providing a special welcome for him. Viney served the meal on Bridget's best china. Joanna had made a lemon cake. And only Viney, Joseph thought, could make yams, field peas, corn pones and collard greens taste like a feast.

But none of this could overcome the fact that Ryan was not there. Or make up for the way Joanna only pushed her food about her plate. There were attempts at conversation, then silence so intense that silver clinking against china seemed to echo in the room.

Joseph made an attempt to lighten the mood, launching into a tale of his trip home. Attempting to make a funny story of it. The raft which Joshua just happened to find for them. Floating down the Chattahoochee River until the raft got away from them and bounded off downstream. Running along the bank of the river trying to catch it. Shaughnessy even attempting to swim after it. Then, the walk across Alabama, and the ride on a Yankee wagon, sitting on barrels all the way to Mobile, leaving out, of course, any mention of gun powder.

Bridget smiled at him from the other end of the table, obviously appreciating his efforts to cheer them. She looked lovely, he thought, even though she was very thin. Just before the meal was ready, she had helped Viney in the kitchen and heat from the old black range had given her more color and curled tiny strands of hair about her face. He wished he didn't have to sit so far away from her. He would like to be beside her. In fact, he was beginning to have a strong desire to scoop her up in his arms and carry her upstairs to their bedroom. But the children ---- He would have to wait. And he had never been a patient man.

CHAPTER THIRTY-EIGHT

THE NEXT MORNING, HE AWOKE, reached out for her, his eyes still closed. She was gone. He heard the bright chattering of children, Viney singing in the kitchen. He continued to lie in bed, remembering the night, feeling content, happy. It was lovely to be home again. He got up, washed and dressed and went to find Bridget.

She was in the nursery, bending over their youngest daughter. "Do you think she has a fever?" she asked, when she saw Joseph.

He came and put a hand on Clare's forehead. He had not done this in a long time, but the routine came back to him. The skin a little warm. But not hot. "If it is a fever, it's a slight one." He was reassuring.

"But she may be coming down with something. It seems I just get one well and another comes down. And I'm not sure what it is this time. I'll have to ask around, see what's going on."

Clare gave Joseph a smile. She appeared alert, free of discomfort. He wanted to point out that she seemed fine to him, but remembered that Bridget did not like it when he took the children's illnesses too lightly. "Do you want me to go after a doctor?"

"I don't think so. Not yet anyway. Oh Joseph, sometimes it's all just too much, with Ryan not yet home and Joanna so grieved she's starving herself to death. And now a little one sick again."

"Could I be of any help?"

She gave him a look of appraisal which made him feel somehow that he was growing smaller, lacking somehow.

"Well, let me think. There's always cleaning to be done but I think Viney can handle that. And it must be done right." Her look was stern. "And the children are more used to me doing things for them. But it would be a help, Joseph, if you could take a look at the household accounts. Just go over the last year and see how we're doing. I'll be down later and we can talk about our financial problems."

The last thing he wanted to do on this lovely morning was discuss financial problems. Especially when he was going to have to admit he had no money. And no salary to be counted on in the foreseeable future. But she had asked him to help with the only thing she seemed to think he was capable of handling. He would of course do his best.

After a breakfast of oatmeal and peaches, he went into the little room they used for an office and removed a ledger from its customary place in the roll-top desk. He pored over monthly expenses, recorded in neat rows of figures. He almost hoped he'd find that she had things in a mess so he could point out, gently of course, the way things should have been done. But he was impressed by her thoroughness, how she'd kept a careful record of every transaction.

"You did a fine job here," he told her when she finally found time to join him. She merely nodded as she settled into a chair opposite him. "It had to be done."

He looked at the ledger. "I see that your father sent you money every month or so."

"Aye, he did. Until his death."

"Ah drat it, where has my mind been?" Joseph put his head in his hands. "Connor told me you'd lost your father. I meant to tell you how sorry I am, how I wish I could have been here to comfort you. It seems you had so much to endure. And all alone."

"She looked down at her hands, clasped tightly in her lap. "It was a time of sorrow. For so long, I've known he was there if I needed him. He was a great comfort. A loving father. But he was very ill and I knew I couldn't keep him forever. His death was a blessing, for him anyway, a natural end to a full life. Unlike the way it was with dear Molly."

"I know. Such a tragedy. A great shock to all of us. I don't think Shaughnessy will ever be the same. He'll never stop missing her."

"Nor will I. For her sake, we must do what we can to ease Shaughnessy's pain. I was hoping he'd consent to stay with us, at least for a while."

"I'll ask him."

"Tell him Viney is making an apple cobbler today. Maybe that will tempt him."

"Aye, Viney's apple cobblers are that hard to resist."

They smiled briefly. Then Bridget reached into the pocket of her apron, took out a letter and laid it on the desk in front of Joseph. He picked it up, examined it, a long white envelope with a lawyer's name and return address printed in the corner. It was addressed to Mrs. Bridget Anna Harrigan, with no mention of a mister. The envelope had been neatly slit open and he could see a folded paper inside.

"Take it out and read it," Bridget urged. "It's about a small inheritance from my father."

Removing the letter, Joseph leaned back in his chair and began to read. A moment later, he was sitting straight up. "Holy Moses," he said softly. He read the letter again, not trusting his first reading. "Holy Moses," he repeated. Bridget's inheritance was substantial. Eight thousand dollars, the lawyer reported, plus some stocks and bonds estimated to be worth another three thousand. Apparently, Bridget's father had made some wise investments. Joseph contemplated the total amount. It was more than enough to take care of their living expenses until the *Appeal* was in business again. With some left over to be invested, he thought. "What do you want to do with it?" he asked her.

"Well, I was thinking we ought to pay the balance we owe on the house."

"A good decision. But there'll still be quite a bit left. And it's yours, you know."

"Mine, Joseph?" She looked at him, one eyebrow raised. "Why this house doesn't even belong to me."

"Of course it does."

"'Tis in your name. Is that not so?"

"A mere technicality. In accordance with the requirements of the law. Be reasonable, me – me love." He had almost made the mistake of calling her 'pet', then remembered in time that she resented the endearment. "The law knows that the husband is the provider. That he must pay the property taxes as well as provide for all family needs."

"That's true, Joseph. Such matters are a husband's duty. And to tell the truth, I'm very tired of the responsibility. Tired of figuring and fretting, wondering each month whether our obligations can be met. I'll be relieved to have it off my hands. I have my own duties, you know, caring for the children. And managing the household. It may seem easy, but it isn't."

"I'm sure it's not."

"It's a full time occupation, making a home and rearing a family. And an important one." She stood and turned to go. "Which reminds me, I need to look in on Clare again. She's better, but still not quite her lively self. Do what you think best with the money."

She left the room without a backward glance, obviously considering the matter settled. Joseph sat at the desk, staring at the figures in the letter. Well, he thought, she was right. It was customary for the man of the house to manage family finances. He looked at the check once more. He would take it to the bank this afternoon. And then see about inviting Shaughnessy to visit them.

But Shaughnessy resisted, saying it brought on too many memories of the four of them together. Memories he couldn't face as yet. Maybe later, he said. He did want to see Bridget. Or the children. But for now --- He confided that only alcohol could dull his pain. It was, he said, what kept him going. Since Joseph felt it was unhealthy to drink alone, he considered it his duty to drink with him as often as he could. And when Joseph mentioned that he didn't like to pay for drinks with Bridget's inheritance, Shaughnessy said not to worry, he'd just put it on his tab. Paddy didn't seem to be concerned about when the bill might be paid. Also, since Memphis was proud of its Rebel newspaper and considered them heroes, there was always someone eager to buy them a drink and toast their return.

It was a temptation to Joseph. He was drawn to the dark rooms, the conversation spiced by the experiences of returning warriors. There, hidden away from a world he no longer seemed to fit in, Joseph felt a sense of belonging. He knew what was expected of him. At home, he was frustrated by the things he couldn't make right. No matter how many letters he wrote, how many people he contacted, he had been unable to find any trace of Ryan and Nate. He had prayed until the words echoed hollowly in his head, unanswered. Still, he felt besieged, seeing the silent questions in Bridget's eyes, the wondering if he had done all that could be done.

Nor was he able to comfort Joanna. When he noticed that she spent a great deal of time walking along the bluff, he offered to walk with her but she insisted she needed to be alone with her memories. There was nothing anyone could do, she said.

Bridget had flung herself into a flurry of house cleaning, something she had always done when she was disturbed. Joseph was accustomed to burying himself in his work, too. But now he had no work. No job to go to. When he was home, he knew that he was only in the way. Nowhere to go, except the Bell Tavern.

CHAPTER THIRTY-NINE

"I'M GOING TO A MEETING of the Appeal's staff," Joseph announced, his voice revealing a great improvement in his mood. "Dill wants to talk about getting the paper back into production."

Bridget glanced up from the cake she was stirring. "Well, tell the Dills and everyone hello for me. And would you be coming straight home after the meeting?"

"Of course," he said. As if he always came straight home. He hurried out of the house, his step light. Maybe soon he would have a job to go to every day.

Dill scheduled their first post-war staff meeting on June the sixth, the date on which they had fled Memphis three years ago. He sent out word that they would meet in Mack's room at the Gayoso Hotel since poor Mack had returned from Georgia feeling so ill he was unable to leave his bed.

"I can't imagine Mack being anything but healthy as a horse," Joseph said to Shaughnessy as they climbed the stairs to the third floor of the Gayoso.

"It is unlike him," Shaughnessy agreed.

But Mack, they discovered, was indeed a sick man. He was in bed, propped on pillows. As each staff member entered the room, he greeted each man with a slight wave of his hand. Joseph was dismayed to see how unwell the usually vigorous Mack looked. His skin was gray with a pale tinge of purple.

"We'll make it a brief meeting," Dill said. "I don't want to tire Mack."

"Don't worry about me, I'll just lay here and take it all in," Mack said. He stirred restlessly on his pile of pillows. "Can't seem to get enough air when I lie flat," he complained. "Don't know why that is."

"Possibly need to drain the lungs," Dill said. "Probably nothing to worry about."

"Sure. Sure, it's nothing to worry about. So stop looking so glum all of you. I'll be up and about in no time, spreading hate and discontent with the best of them."   He attempted a laugh, but it was only a faint echo of his old devilish chuckle.

Though the room with its flowered wall paper and oak wainscoting was large and pleasant, it contained only two chairs. Mrs. Dill was given one and the men insisted that Dill take the other. Shaughnessy and Vernon claimed the window sills and Joseph, Ed Goins and Seth Latke propped themselves against the wall, resting their elbows on the wide trim above the wainscoting.

Dill looked around the room. "I guess we are all here. We'll build the staff back up later."

Wanting to cheer him, Joseph said, "Billy and Doyle said they might come up from New Orleans and join us when we get going again."

"If we get going," Goins said.

"Not if, when," Mack growled from his bed.

Dill opened a ledger, balanced it on his lap, and studied it for a few minutes. He didn't look too good himself, Joseph noted. The war seemed to have robbed both men of their health.

"Here's where we stand," Dill said. "Thanks to a brave and devoted staff, the Appeal has earned itself a great deal of respect. There's hardly a soul who doesn't know about our exploits."

"I'd say we're plumb famous," Ed Goins put in.

"Or at least well-known," said Vernon.

Goins snorted in exasperation. "That's the same as famous."

"Now men, let's move on. Fame, or whatever you want to call it, doesn't take the place of operating funds." Dill paused, smiled briefly. "There is one bit of good news to report. The bond forced on me by General Wilson can be forgotten since Lee had already surrendered by the time we were captured. Actually, we evaded the Yankees throughout the entire war, a feat we can be proud of." He paused again while this bit of news was digested and enjoyed, then he continued, his voice somber again. "Still, the fact remains that the war has ruined us financially. It cost Mack and Mrs. Dill and I our personal fortunes. The *Appeal* now owns little more than its name and the good will of its readers. Even our building was sold during our absence and I don't know whether we'll get it back or not. We have nothing but the press and boiler and the thirty-seven boxes of tobacco taken as payment for a debt. These items are still hidden in Macon."

"So we fooled the Yankees one more time," Latke interrupted.

"Good for the *Appeal*," said Joseph.

"Indeed," said Vernon. "One more feather in our caps, I'd say." Dill waited a moment until the room grew quiet again. "Yes, we have much to be proud of, but back to our problems. We still must figure a way to get the press home. Now the tobacco might bring in a couple thousand, but we can't sell it until we get our hands on it. And without money how can we go after it? So how in blazes are we going to get our press home? We have no newsprint, type, ink--nothing. Gone, all of it. Gone. Why I even lost my genuine wool hat."

There was appreciative laughter at the attempt to lighten the grimness of their situation.

"If the Appeal is to survive," Dill continued, "we're all going to have to give it our continued devotion--above and beyond the call of duty. And after all we've gone through, I don't know how many of you want to continue sacrificing. I'd understand if you went on to other things."

"Not me," said Goins. "You won't get rid of me with talk of doomsday. After all I've put into this paper, I'm not about to quit now."

"Nor I," said Latke.

Vernon, who was familiar with the figures on the books, said he'd have to think about it.

"What about you, Shaughnessy?" Dill asked.

Shaughnessy shrugged. "I don't know what else I'd do with myself."

"And you, Joseph?"

"Me? Of course." He was surprised Dill had even asked. Didn't everyone know he would never desert the *Appeal*? For a brief moment, he had an urge to take the floor and remind them that he had been with the *Appeal* since it put out its first scrawny weekly edition, to even reveal to them the long ago promise he'd

made beside the Colonel's grave, but he told himself they didn't
have time for flowery speeches. He merely added quietly, "You
can count on me to make any sacrifice required to get the *Appeal*
up and going again."

"Hmmm," Dill said. "And how would Bridget feel about
that?"

"I'll have a talk with her." He tried to sound as if that would
settle it.

The meeting broke up shortly after that. They must give their
problems thought, Dill said, then they would meet again and
perhaps make some decisions.

After they left the hotel, Shaughnessy persuaded Joseph to
walk home with him. "You'll come in won't you?" he asked. "I
have a bottle of fine old whiskey on hand I'd like to share with
you."

"Sounds tempting but I promised Bridget I wouldn't be too
late tonight. Maybe some other time when we –" Joseph's words
grew less firm. Shaughnessy looked so hopeful and his small
house seemed dark and forlorn. "Well, just one small drink
wouldn't hurt, I suppose."

They went inside and Shaughnessy began lighting lamps.
"Place is in a mess," he warned. "Haven't had much inclination
for cleaning."

Joseph felt a sudden stab of regret. Since they usually met at
bars, Joseph hadn't seen the inside of the house in a while. He
peered around in the dim light and concluded it was indeed a
mess. Something else was different too, something he couldn't put
his finger on. Then he realized that most of the furniture was
missing from the parlor. In the dining room, the big round table,

the sideboard and the chairs Molly had upholstered with intricate needlepoint were also gone.

"Been selling furniture to raise money to live on," Shaughnessy said, before Joseph had time to ask questions. "Anyway, what do I need with a parlor or a dining room? Who would I entertain?" He led the way into the kitchen, lit a lamp there. "Have a seat and I'll see if I can find a couple of clean glasses."

Joseph moved a stack of newspapers from a chair and sat down at the cluttered table. The condition of the kitchen Molly once kept spotless amazed him. Dishes containing half-eaten food, pots and pans, spilled and congealed substances covered every surface. Muddy footprints trailed across the floor. Even a bachelor should live better than this, Joseph thought. He considered giving Shaughnessy a lecture, pointing out that he would feel better if he made the place livable, but he hadn't the heart to scold him. After all, would he himself do any better under the circumstances?

He took a sip of the whiskey Shaughnessy had poured into a smudged glass, murmured, "Mmmm. Good whiskey."

Shaughnessy grinned. "Traded the sideboard for it," he said, obviously proud of himself. He emptied his glass in several gulps and poured himself another, drank a few swallows, then asked, "Aren't you a bit depressed after tonight's meeting? The Appeal's future doesn't seem too promising with Mack laid up. And I thought the Dills looked almost as poorly as Mack. Did you notice?"

"I did. But, maybe they're just tired. The both of them need a good rest I'm thinking. You know, it's occurred to me that, in a way, it's a blessing we're facing so many problems. Maybe it'll fire Mack up. He's never been able to resist a challenge."

"True. Hadn't thought of it that way."

Joseph sipped his whiskey, looked for a clean place to lean his elbows on the table. "I want to get your opinion about something that concerns me. When Dill was talking about the *Appeal*'s situation, about its sad lack of finances, I couldn't help but wonder if I ought to invest Bridget's inheritance in the paper. After all, I earn my money as a newspaper man. It's the only thing I know. If the *Appeal* failed --- But still, I don't know. The money is Bridget's and I'd feel guilty if I didn't invest it wisely."

Shaughnessy thought for a moment, then pointed out that the Appeal could hardly be considered a wise investment at the moment. "Maybe you should think that over," he suggested. "Just wait and see how things go."

"I suppose you're right," Joseph agreed. He would hold onto the money for a while, he decided.

As they talked, Shaughnessy continued to pour more drinks for himself. Joseph allowed himself one more, then sipped it, making it last. Bridget hated it when he came home all tipsy.

When Shaughnessy's head drooped, Joseph helped him to his unmade bed, covered him, blew out the lamps and left.

When he got home, the house was dark, the children apparently asleep in their beds. Only one lamp burned in Bridget's room. He tiptoed up the stairs.

She was at her dressing table, dividing her hair into sections, preparing to braid it. Well, he thought, he would unbraid it. She shouldn't be wasting their time being stand-offish, not after they'd been apart so many years. And they weren't getting any younger. They should be taking advantage of every moment. He continued to stand in the doorway, watching her hands fly in and out, completing the braid and tying it firmly with a ribbon.

When she was done, she turned and acknowledged his presence. "Well, decided to come home, did we now?"

He winced, knowing he was in trouble. He cast about for ways to soothe her. The meeting had lasted quite some time, he told her, then changed the subject, telling her about how poorly Mack was doing.

"And Mr. and Mrs. Dill?" she asked. "Are they well?"

"Er, I believe so." He didn't want to worry her, to have her think he wasn't going to have a job. "I'm sure they'll be fine after they've rested."

"And Shaughnessy? Has his mood improved?"

"Not much."

He decided he would tell her about the condition of Shaughnessy's house. Maybe it would prove to be a diversion.

"Maybe I ought to go over tomorrow and help him clean it."

He thought she would think it generous of him to consider helping his friend, but she only shrugged. "Do so, if it pleases you, but sooner or later, Shaughnessy is going to have to begin taking care of himself. After all, you have a family to see after."

"I know. I know. And I intend to do better." He walked toward her and she backed away.

"And where have I heard that said before? I've been thinking. I've been thinking long and hard. And I believe we should have separate bedrooms."

He looked at her, startled. "What are you saying?"

"I'm saying that I think it's foolish of me to risk having another child when you barely take note of the children you have. I suppose you forgot today was Emilie's birthday. Remember, I told you last week?"

He nodded. Truth was, he had forgotten. She should have reminded him again, but he didn't dare say so.

"We were hoping you would at least get here in time to have cake and ice cream with us."

"But that's no reason to – for us to have separate bedrooms. Just because I forgot one birthday."

"Not one, Joseph. I could make a book of the things you've forgotten. You love your children, I know. But you don't care enough to be a proper father. Other things are of greater importance. If this were not so, we'd probably have Ryan home with us and ---"

She stopped and a great silence filled the room. So there it was, out in the open at last. Just as he'd suspected, she did blame him.

"That's not fair," he said. "I was as concerned for my son as any father would be."

"Were you Joseph?" Her eyes flashed. "I didn't want to say anything because I know you do love Ryan and you're hurting, just as I am. But what were you thinking, letting him wander about among the enemy? Where were you when he disappeared? In some saloon with your cronies?"

"Indeed I was not."

"Well, you didn't keep your promise. You said you'd keep a watchful eye on him at all times. You had only one child to look after, Joseph. I had six here at home. And you'll notice I didn't lose one of them."

His temper flared to match hers. For a moment they glared at one another.

"I didn't mean to say all that, Joseph," she said, after a moment. "It's just been inside of me all this time. Anyway, I was serious about our having separate bedrooms. I asked Viney to freshen up the guest room for you."

That she had talked to Viney about this private matter seemed to him the last straw. He was humiliated. He lifted his chin, then turned away from her. His anger mounted as he left the room and marched down the hallway. He certainly wasn't going to stay where he wasn't wanted.

CHAPTER FORTY

THE NEXT MORNING JOSEPH DISCOVERED that all his belongings had been moved to the guest room. His razor, strap and shaving soap were set out beside the wash basin; the clothes he'd left behind when he went to war were hanging in the closet. Though this indicated that Bridget intended the arrangement to last, he was confident her anger would fade in a few days and she would want him once again. However, days stretched into a week, then two. He and Bridget began to speak of the two rooms as her bedroom and his. Worse yet, the children were calling the guest room "Papa's room." With each passing day, Joseph realized that moving back into his own bedroom was becoming more of a hurdle.

He tried to talk to her, to make things right again, but she was unreachable. When she wasn't cleaning, she sat in the wicker rocking chair on the side porch, watching the road Ryan would likely be coming down on his way home. Bare strips had appeared on the floor of the porch, the paint worn away by days and nights of rocking. And she didn't want to talk, she said. About anything.

To regain her favor, he stopped going to Bell Tavern to meet Shaughnessy. He wandered aimlessly about the house, went to bed early. One night, as he undressed, he noticed a great thirst. He was alarmed. When had the pleasant drinks he shared with friends turned into this terrible need. Would he become like men he knew who got the shakes when they didn't have a drink in their hand? The thought repulsed him.

He put his clothes back on and went to Bell Tavern, determined to have an understanding with Shaughnessy, to convince him they must slow down their drinking. Maybe even stop entirely for a while. It would be the sensible thing to do and would perhaps make Bridget feel kindly toward him again. But as soon as he stepped inside the tavern, the smell of stale beer and damp sawdust brought irresistible longings. He decided to allow himself one pint, just one, then have that talk. He couldn't find Shaughnessy, however, even when he went from table to table asking if anyone had seen him. This started a spirited discussion which eventually included everyone in the tavern, some claiming to have seen Shaughnessy in one place, some another. During all this lively talk, one of the men thrust a glass of whiskey into Joseph's hand. He drank it in thirsty gulps.

"A shame about Shaughnessy," a soft-voiced man observed, "losing his darling little wife like that while he was off at war."

They all got melancholy over the poor soul's rotten luck. Another whiskey found its way into Joseph, then another, and the next thing he knew, Paddy was snuffing the lamps and announcing it was time to close.

"But Shaughnessy was supposed to be here," Joseph protested. "We always meet here."

"He was in earlier this evening," Paddy told him. "Left saying he'd had enough. Was talkin' about goin' back to Ireland."

"Why didn't you tell me?"

"You didn't ask me. Besides you were all having such fun speculating about the man."

"But I'm supposed to be looking after him." Joseph felt confused. He finished his drink and left.

Mist filtered through moss-hung trees as he staggered out of the tavern on legs which threatened to fold up beneath him. He stood at the edge of Smokey Row, blinking in the hazy pre-dawn light, trying to get his bearings. Wasn't it odd now that a road he had traveled so many times could take on the look of a foreign land? He shook his head to clear it.

He must find Shaughnessy. See if he was all right. Why, he was probably near death if he hadn't shown up for an evening of socializing. Maybe he was home in bed, ailing like Mack. Aye, that was where he might be found. But, thought Joseph, looking up and down the road, which way would that be?

Ah, no matter. His senses would come back to him after he'd walked a bit. He set out, toddling along in the wake of a riverboat captain and his lady friend. To keep his mind from drifting farther away, he concentrated on the sight before him, concentrated on the way the man's big hairy arm encircled the girl's waist, on the way it almost disappeared into the soft flesh above her backless gown. He had no wish to pry but he was walking so close behind the pair that he couldn't help overhearing the business transaction they were making.

"My you're the pricey one." The captain's voice was intimate, playful. "What makes you think you're worth it?"

Her answer was a tinkly laugh and a toss of curls that sent perfume adrift in the air. Joseph held his breath but a wave of nausea washed over him. He lurched forward, putting out a hand to steady himself. To his dismay, his hand shoved itself into the lady's bare back. The captain whirled about, glaring down at him.

"Beggin' yer pardon," Joseph stammered, swallowing hard to keep the contents of his stomach out of the conversation. "Sure and I meant no disrespect to the lady. 'Tis just that I'm having trouble staying perkindicular."

With a snarl, the huge boatman made a threatening move, but the lady held him back. "Leave him be, Boris. Can't you see he's soused? We've got better things to do than waste time on an old drunk." The captain shrugged and let her lead him away.

Joseph stared after them, incensed. Old drunk, indeed. He wasn't that much older than the both of them. And he might have had a wee bit too much of the drink, but he was sober now. Sober enough to realize he'd been in danger of a thrashing. He knew better than to mess around with boatmen. It was one of the first things Shaughnessy had taught him when he arrived in America.

Shaughnessy, he thought. His friend these many years. And now he might be needing help. Joseph straightened his shoulders and set out down the dusty road. At least, he now knew which direction to take.

When he got to Shaughnessy's house, he found every lamp lit. And Shaughnessy was sweeping a pile of trash out the door. Joseph was startled to see that he was crying, tears running silently down his face, dripping from his chin. He had never seen Shaughnessy cry before, though he'd supposed he cried over his loss in private moments.

"Come in," he said to Joseph. "I'm cleaning Molly's house. Don't know what I was thinking of, letting it get like this. She always kept it clean as a whistle."

Alarmed, Joseph said nothing about the tears, just pitched in and began helping with the cleaning. He gathered a huge pile of clothes, tied it in a sheet. "You can take them to the laundry," he suggested.

Shaughnessy wiped his face with his hand. "Why didn't I think of that? Molly hated for her house to be messy. Why didn't you tell me it was getting so bad?"

Joseph thought it best not to answer. They continued to work on the house, Shaughnessy pouring drinks of bourbon to sustain them. Eventually his tears stopped. When the house was done to his satisfaction, he collapsed on the sofa, was asleep in a second.

The sun was now rising, Joseph saw. He was going to be lucky if he made it home before everyone was awake. But he was tired, so tired. He would rest. But only for a moment. He sank into a chair. His eyes closed.

When he awakened, the sun had traveled to tree-top level. It must be late. Nine, maybe, or even ten. He was rumpled and bewhiskered. Must be a sorry sight. The family would be through with breakfast by now, he estimated. Maybe he could sneak up the back stairway without being seen. He began to walk, distressed to see how unsteady he was on his feet.

He took back roads home, crossing fields to approach his house from the side, then keeping close to the shrubbery which grew along the back of the house. He stumbled once, fell into a snowball bush with giant blossoms. Their pink petals showered over him. Peering into a window, he decided the kitchen was empty. He stopped by the pump to wash his face, then smoothed his hair and clothes. He would walk right in, looking as natural as possible, as if he might be returning from a meeting. But when he stepped inside the kitchen, he found it was not empty after all. He moved along the wall, creeping toward the staircase as quietly as he could. But it was no use.

Several small daughters surrounded him. Their eyes widened as they looked him over.

"Papa got whiskers," Clare observed.

Molly Kate wrinkled her nose. "And he smells funny."

"Why do you have flowers all over you?" Emilie asked.

Joseph moved away from the wall, looking for an escape route. As he crossed the kitchen, he stumbled and fell against the table.

"Papa fa' down," Clare said, sounding sad.

Joseph scowled. "Papa didn't fa' – fall. He just stumbled a bit. Long meeting last night. Now go play somewhere."

"Joseph." Bridget entered the room, a look in her eyes he had never seen before.

He hurried toward the stairs. He stumbled again on the bottom step, reached for the railing, missed and fell to his knees. He heard the sad little voice again, "Papa fa- down."

CHAPTER FORTY-ONE

SOMEHOW JOSEPH MADE IT to his bed, where he fell into a deep sleep. When he awoke, a bright sun sifted through the lace curtains. His head pounded and he had never been thirstier. The pitcher on his dressing table contained only a few swallows of lukewarm water so he considered taking a sip from the bottle of bourbon he kept in his highboy. But when he opened the bottle, its odor made him shudder. He returned it to its hiding place. Coffee was what he needed.

The house was strangely silent as he went down the back stairway. Where was everyone? And what time was it? Morning? Afternoon? He was thoroughly disoriented. The coffee on the back of the stove was stone cold. Why hadn't Viney kept it warm for him? He drank a cup anyway, then drank another. After that, he walked through the house, wondering again where everyone was. Finally, in the upstairs parlor, he found Viney, her feather duster flicking rapidly over the furniture.

"Good morning, Viney? Where's my family?"

Viney continued to concentrate on her dusting. "They're not here. Mr. Joseph."

"But how did they get off so early? It is early, isn't it?"

"It's way in the afternoon. You slept plumb 'round the clock and then some. I guess you were mighty tired."

"Aye, Viney, I was. But where has everyone gone?"

She hesitated. "Well, Miz Bridget, she took all the young'uns and went down to the Gayoso Hotel."

"The Gayoso? They've gone to a hotel?"

"Yessir, like I said."

"But why would she do that? The Gayoso is no place for a woman with all those children."

"Maybe so, but that's where she told me she would be."

For a moment, Joseph was at a loss for words. He looked at Viney. Funny thing about her. She could be as polite as ever, her face a mask and her eyes unreadable, but still you could tell when she was all puffed up with disapproval. "Well---" he said several times. Then, "Did she leave a message?"

"Not that I know of. But between you and me, I'd say you ought to be making plans to go after her,"

"I don't understand." He heard his voice rise like a fretful child's. "Why has she gone to a hotel of all places? Didn't I provide her with a fine home when she was wanting one so bad? Why can't she stay put?"

Joseph's eyes remained on her firm back as he waited for – for what? For her to say it was all a mistake, a prank. For her to make another, sensible suggestion about what he should do. He finally turned away. He knew very well what he had to do.

Joseph shaved, bathed, dressed in clean clothes and set out for the hotel. As he entered the Gayoso's lobby, the explorer, De Soto, and his men looked down from the large mural on the wall, looked down on an elegant room which seemed to be swarming with young Harrigans. They were running about, hiding behind the skirts of fine ladies, crawling under chairs occupied by sedate, frowning gentlemen. Connor was trying to capture them and settle them down but that only added to the confusion.

Maybe no one knows whose children they are, Joseph thought. Maybe he should leave and come back to get them later – when they were asleep, perhaps. But before he could make his escape, a child spied him.

"Papa," Clare cried out. "Look, Papa's here."

Joseph was immediately surrounded by his children who flung their arms about him, greeting him as if he'd been missing for years. The girls were dressed in Sunday finery – curls bound back by large taffeta bows, crinoline dresses stiff and starchy, every lace-edged ruffle and puffed sleeve lovingly ironed. Patrick wore a blue velvet suit.

As their cries grew shriller, everyone in the room looked their way.

"Where have you been, Papa?"

"Wanna see me slide down the bannisters?"

"Mama's upstairs reading and she says she doesn't care if she sees you again ever, ever, ever."

Joseph winced. Why did the Lord give children such piping voices?

They led him upstairs to a room they called theirs. Bridget answered their knock. She too was wearing her best, a lovely gray silk dress. She greeted him with silence, which somehow bothered him more than words of anger.

"Did you know they have room service here, Papa?" Molly Kate asked. "You can just pull that cord and they'll bring you anything you want."

"We had lobster for lunch," Connor said. "And I ate a half dozen eggs for breakfast. You wouldn't like to stay and have dinner with us, would you?"

"Indeed not," Joseph said. "We're leaving immediately." He looked at the baggage stacked in a corner of the room. "How did you get all these bags down here? I don't see how they ever fit in the carriage."

"I brought everyone down first," Connor said, "then went back to get the bags."

"Well." Joseph looked doubtful. "I'll leave it to you to get the carriage and bring the baggage home. I came down in a taxi and I guess the rest of us can go back that way."

Bridget spoke for the first time. "Connor, would you take the children downstairs?"

"But, we were just down there. And they were –"

"Connor." Bridget spoke softly, but some note in her voice was effective. In minutes, the children had left the room.

"I can't imagine why you brought all the children down here," Joseph said. "They're raising Cain down in the lobby."

"You don't know why I brought them here, Joseph? Well, you may not want to hear this but the truth is, I didn't want the children to see you, the way you've been behaving. I didn't want them to be ashamed of their father."

"But ---" began Joseph, then was silent, and his behavior of the day before came back to him, each detail an embarrassment. For the first time, he was ashamed of himself. He would do better, he promised her fervently. "As a matter of fact, just last night, or was it the night before, time has escaped me, but anyway I went down to Paddy's to find Shaughnessy and tell him we ought to slow down our drinking."

"But that wasn't what you did, was it?"

It wasn't, he acknowledged, and he wasn't sure why he hadn't. He remembered something about not being able to find Shaughnessy, then finding him crying and staying to help him clean his house. She would never believe that. He found it somewhat unbelievable himself. But he would do better in the future, he said. Only when he promised over and over that he would never again make a spectacle of himself in front of the children would she agree to return with him.

Once he had his family home, Joseph examined his feelings. Hurt pride. Resentment. She had humiliated him in front of the whole town. He felt a need to show everyone he was still the man of the house.

After a few days, he returned to Bell Tavern. He would show her – and himself – that he could have just one pint and leave, like a sociable man. He looked for Shaughnessy, once again couldn't find him, so he sat alone at the bar. Alone until Ed Goins settled himself on the stool beside him. Goins was the last person Joseph wanted to see. That headache of a man who took such pleasure in other's misfortunes.

"Well, Joseph," he said, "I didn't think we'd be seeing you around here anymore."

"Why not?" Joseph growled.

"Talk gets around in a town like Memphis. People's tongues have been wagging, I'll tell you. It makes a great story, how Mrs. Harrigan marched in the hotel, all those children following along like ducklings. And weren't you the embarrassed one when you came to fetch them? People are getting a huge chuckle out of it."

"You seem to be enjoying it."

Paddy brought Joseph's pint, said, "It's on the house. And Joseph, if you haven't seen Shaughnessy lately, he's been looking for you. Maybe you'd better stop by and see him. Said he had something to tell you."

Joseph took his pint to a table, drank it before anyone else had a chance to join him, then left.

He found Shaughnessy in his bedroom, clothes and various possessions scattered around an old wooden trunk. "Would you believe, I'm using the same trunk I arrived with to be going back home?" he asked.

"You're going home? To Ireland?"

"I am. I know that won't please you, but it's what I'm planning to do. Here, hand me those shirts."

Numbly, Joseph did as he was told and Shaughnessy continued to pack. "My mind is made up," he said, "so don't try to change it. You'll see when you have time to think it over, that it's all for the best."

"How could it be for the best?" Joseph stared at the pattern on the rug at his feet. He could remember when Molly and Shaughnessy had bought that rug. He tried to think of something to say, some reason to give Shaughnessy for staying. But every reason had a selfish ring to it. "You'll be missed," he ventured. "Everyone will miss you. How can you just go away when your whole life is here?"

"*Was* here."

"But there's still – how about the Appeal?"

"The Appeal will go on without me." He turned his back on Joseph and bent over to rearrange things in the trunk. His voice sounded different coming from its wooden depths. "I'm leaving for two reasons, Joseph. First, for myself. I can't stay here without Molly. Not without destroying myself. And you with me. And that's the other reason I must leave. Can't you see I'm not good for you anymore?"

"No such thing," Joseph protested.

"Joseph, I'm pulling you away from your family." He stood up, looked down at Joseph. "If we continue to behave as we have, you'll be losing your own sweet wife."

"But Bridget will be upset about you leaving. She promised Molly we would look after you. Make you part of our family."

Shaughnessy stopped packing, wiped an arm across his sweaty forehead. "I'm sure you meant well, all of you. I'll come to dinner one more time, to tell Bridget and the children good bye and assure Bridget that I have five sisters and numerous nieces and nephews who'll be happy to have me back among them. Not to mention Molly's father and the rest of her family. That's where Molly and I began, Joseph. We were sweethearts in Ireland, just like you and Bridget. "Tis a funny thing. Recent memories are so painful, but long ago memories, ah, they can be sweet, like buried treasure.'

Joseph watched as Shaughnessy closed his trunk, locked it. "Will you be coming back?"

"I don't know. But you'll get along without me. That is, if you'll promise to do one thing for me. Will you promise?'

What is it you're wanting?"

"Just this. I've seen the drink take over a man before and I know there is only one cure. And that is to stop completely. Do you understand me?"

"Aye. But we've been at it pretty steadily since we left Columbus. It might be hard to stop."

"It might be. But it's the last thing I'm going to ask of you, Joseph? Will you do it?"

Joseph promised he would try.

CHAPTER FORTY-TWO

STAYING OUT OF PUBS did not tax Joseph's will power as much as he expected. With Shaughnessy gone and Mack still confined to his bed, stopping by Paddy's for a bit of cheer only depressed him. Nor did the bottle of Irish whiskey hidden in his highboy tempt him. Whiskey was meant to be shared with friends. There was a sadness about solitary drinking, and he didn't need any more sadness.

His nerves were raw, accustomed to spirits as they were, but he was sure they would recover in time. And there must be other ways a man could occupy himself if he put his mind to it.

He wished he could go back to work, but Dill had only called three meetings so far, and none of them had been productive. They were still stuck on the problem of getting the press back. Sometimes Joseph felt guilty, listening to them talk of their need and knowing he had money to invest. He wanted to discuss it with

Bridget, point out to her that the newspaper was their source of income. After all, what other skills did he have? But would it be fair to put it like that? Shouldn't he let her know that, as Shaughnessy had said, the *Appeal* couldn't be considered a sound investment in its present condition. Also, another thought had begun to trouble Joseph, a thought which grew more and more troubling as the days passed. Owning a share of the *Appeal* had been a lifelong dream, but if he bought that share with Bridget's money, would that not make her the true owner instead of himself? Once that question had taken root in his mind, he couldn't seem to find the satisfactory answer. If only Shaughnessy were still here to advise him.

If he hoped to talk it over with Bridget, he would need to approach her when she was in a friendly mood. And she was definitely not being friendly. She was civil, polite, but nothing more. And they were still sleeping in separate bedrooms. He had thought, at first, that she was being unfair, but now that he was sober – terribly sober – he was beginning to see her side. He looked at himself the way she must see him, so changed by the past years that he was barely recognizable. She had said goodbye to a reasonably serious and dedicated family man and had gotten back a man who was acting like a deckhand on shore leave. It would take time, he knew, to erase that image.

As the hot days of July crept by, he wandered around the house, feeling lost and useless. One morning, he lounged in bed, unable to muster the will to begin the day and he found himself contemplating the changes in his children. Bridget's disapproval seemed to be rubbing off on them, for they had become stand-offish. They no longer greeted him with hugs and noisy chatter. Now, when he entered a room, they seemed subdued, uneasy.

Well, that was something he could work on. He rose and dressed, a purpose in mind.

He went down to the kitchen where Patrick and the smaller girls were sitting around the table eating their breakfast. He put a hand on Clare's bright curls. "And how's my Molly Kate this morning?" he asked her.

There were tentative giggles and Molly Kate said, "Papa, I'm Molly Kate. Don't you remember?"

"Oh," said Joseph, pretending to look closer at Clare. "Then you must be Patrick." This time there were peals of laughter. He was making progress.

Encouraged, he went to the hardware store, bought needed supplies and began making repairs on the house. Each day he worked on a project, with the children following him about eager to help. Patrick insisted he should carry Papa's toolbox since he was the boy. The younger girls protested until Joseph gave them an old hammer and let them have turns hammering nails into scraps of wood. Emilie he found, could be counted on to offer suggestions.

Connor still remained aloof, busy with his friends, his job, his own like. Perhaps, Joseph thought, he should have begun paying more attention to him years ago. He had never been quite as close to Connor as he had been to Ryan. From the start, Bridget had laid claim to their second son. Joseph recalled the day the child had been born, prematurely, alas, but still squalling and healthy. Bridget had insisted he was delicate, had fretted over him much more than she had the others. She was still attempting to tie him to her apron strings, big strapping lad that he was. Now Joseph regretted not making more of an effort to claim his share of the boy's affections. But there was no going back. He had missed his chance.

He thought about this as he went about his repair work, grateful that he had found a way to keep busy during the long days. The nights were another matter. He would fall asleep, exhausted from a day of labor, only to awaken again before the night was half over to lie, tossing and sleepless, the humid heat of summer pressing down on him. In the morning he would arise feeling more tired than ever. He decided to try sleeping outside in a hammock as Shaughnessy had done, but there, mosquitoes buzzed, crickets chirped, and his insomnia grew worse. Perhaps walking would help. He began with strolls around his property, then about the neighborhood, and finally, all around town, carefully avoiding the streets where he might be tempted to enter a saloon. When the rest of the world began to stir, he would sometimes stop by Mack's hotel room for a short visit.

He arrived early one morning to find Mack up, shuffling about the room. "Can't find things anymore," he mumbled.

"What is it you're needing?" Joseph asked.

Mack peered about him sadly. "I've forgotten now." He gave up, crawled back in his bed and sank back on his pillows, panting from the effort. "Never thought I'd come to this."

"You'll get better."

"Sure."

He seemed to be nodding off so Joseph edged toward the door. "I'll go and let you get some rest."

"No, stay. I get too much blasted rest." He looked at Joseph, his eyes watery and unfocused.

Joseph recalled that there was a time when, if you got Mack riled up, those eyes could nail you to the wall with a fierce black glare. "You'll be yourself again soon," he assured him, keeping his voice cheery. "You'll be back at your desk, raring to go, eager to – what was it you used to say? – to stir up the complacent and puncture the pompous."

Mack attempted a smile. "That was my specialty, wasn't it?"

"Sure, and you'll be at it again. All you need is rest. And I don't want to be staying too long and tiring you."

"You won't. Sit down,"

Joseph sat.

"No word from Ryan?" Mack asked, then answered his own question. "Of course not. If you had heard, would I have to ask?"

Every now and then, Joseph's longing to have his son back hit him so hard that it took his breath away. So hard that he thought he couldn't bear it. He struggled for composure.

"Hurts doesn't it?" Mack asked gently. "Well, don't be giving up. I heard that the Willard boy got home last week. Just walked right in while they were at dinner."

Joseph nodded. "I've heard tales of things like that happening. I'm hoping it will be the same for us,"

"It will. It's happening every day. They say Rafe Parker even made it home and he's nearly fifty. He'd walked hundreds of miles, using a tree limb for a crutch. Said you couldn't slow down an old mule who was headed for the barn. Good way to put it ---" Mack lapsed into silence, obviously exhausted by so much talk. Joseph sat beside him for a long time, waiting until his raspy breath took on a regular cadence, then he left quietly.

Outside, the sun was shining, the river breeze stirring the leaves of the trees. A bright summer day. After the time spent in Mack's dim room with its odor of sickness, Joseph was relieved to be in the open, to be able to stride briskly along. He chided himself. How could he disconnect himself so easily from his friend's suffering? He ought to be – well, what? What could he do about Mack? About anything?

He decided to take a walk along the river bank. There was reassurance in the way the old Mississippi kept rolling along, ignoring mankind's daily problems. As he neared the Bluff, he saw Joanna standing in the distance, looking out over the river.

The sun glinted on her hair and a breeze tugged at her black muslin skirt. He was quite close before she looked up and saw him, saying, "Papa. You startled me."

"I'll go away if you wish. I don't want to intrude."

"No, you can stay. I've noticed that you've become a wanderer like me. You must be frantic about Ryan. As I am. Oh Papa. I miss him so."

He gave her a hug. "There, child."

"I know I shouldn't be causing you and Mama more distress, going around like a lost soul. Mama says I'm just punishing myself coming here so often, living it over and over. But that's not how I mean it to be. It's just that—oh, I don't know—it's hard to explain. They say that life must go on, but my life seems to have ended here. I'm trying to find some way past it, something I can hold on to."

Joseph took her hand in his. "Come on, let's walk."

They walked along in silence, Joseph waiting until Joanna was ready to talk. "I can't just forget Andrew, Papa. I keep seeing his face. The way he looked at me from the boat. Smiling, hollering, 'They're going to love you.' His parents, he meant."

"Of course they would love you," Joseph said. "What's not to love?"

"That's what Andrew always said. But you know how it is. People have dumb reasons for not liking other persons. Especially someone their son has married against their wishes. They weren't too happy, you know, about him marrying a Southern girl. And an Irish Catholic, at that."

"Hmmmph. He was lucky to get you."

"Papa. You're just as prejudiced as they are."

"Hadn't thought about it like that."

"Anyway, it doesn't matter now, does it? I'll never meet them." She stopped walking and looked down at the river. "Andrew and I loved to walk along the river, holding hands and talking. I would tell him how I used to play on the Bluff as a child and think of the people who were here long before us. The explorers, you know, and the Choctaws. I used to imagine I could feel them around me."

"Did you now?" Joseph saw for a moment she had put her sorrow aside.

She smiled, her eyes softened. "I was afraid Andrew would consider me daft, saying I imagined I could feel the presence of people long dead. But he seemed to think everything I did and said was wonderful. Oh Papa, we were so happy. And now – it's over. How I wish there could have been a child. Something to hold onto. Something left of the both of us."

Joseph searched for words of comfort, found none.

"I know I'm not the only person who's lost a loved one in this war." She blinked tears away and lifted her chin. "I'm aware of all the suffering of others, of how the brave ones accept it as best they can and try to get on with their lives. But that's the trouble, Papa. I don't seem to have a life to go on with. I've lost my place in the world. And here in the South, I'll always be that girl who married a Yankee."

"Now don't be feeling guilty about that. You weren't the only one who fell in love with a lad on the other side. It happened both here and in the North, or so I've heard. It just proves that love is stronger than war."

"You put it in a nice light, Papa. And I'm truly not ashamed I loved Andrew. He was a wonderful person. I'm sure everything would have been grand for us if only he were still here with me. But alone---"

Joseph thought he could not endure the look of desolation on his daughter's face. She had always been such a happy person. He thought of her as a young child, so fanciful and busy. So curious about everything, eager to learn. A moment ago, he had seen a brief flash of that eagerness when she was speaking of the history of the Bluff. An idea came to him, a way that he might help. He was quiet as they continued to walk, thinking how it might be worked out. Then he asked, "How would you like to go to college?"

"College? Me? I never thought about it but I guess I would love to go. Not to Memphis Female College though, where they specialize in teaching women to be proper ladies. I'd like to go to a regular college. The kind men attend. But that would be expensive. How could I ever afford it?"

"I think it might be arranged. But first, I'll have to discuss it with your Mama." As he spoke, Joseph realized his dream of ever owning a share of the *Appeal* was slipping away. But this, he decided, was more important. He felt sure Bridget would agree. "Your Mama will no doubt think sending you to college will be money well spent."

Joanna looked wistful. "I do love studying. History, especially. For instance, I'd like to learn everything I possibly can about the people who lived on this earth before us. Even if I am a woman, maybe I could be a professor. Or an explorer, digging up the past. Oh, wouldn't I love to go on expeditions and poke around ancient ruins."

"Well, I wouldn't mention that to your mother. Right at first anyway."

Joseph was pleased with the changes his plan brought to their household. After some thought, Bridget agreed it was just what Joanna needed. Joanna visited with her old school teacher, Mr. Magevaney, and he told her that many colleges had closed during the war, but those planning to reopen soon might be willing to accept women.

"Our supply of young men has diminished," he said. "Such a pity."

Joanna wrote to the list of colleges he gave her. She studied the catalogs they sent, deciding which would give her the classes she found most interesting. She also decided she didn't want to wear black to college – it would depress the other students, she said, and Andrew would hate to be the source of that – so she and Bridget made a trip to the dry goods store, choosing pastel fabrics, bringing them home to plan what would be Joanna's college wardrobe. The voices Joseph heard coming from the sewing room sounded, if not exactly happy, at least busy. For once, he had done something right.

CHAPTER FORTY-THREE

A SUMMER COLD HAD SETTLED in Joseph's chest and all of Bridget's hot poultices and Viney's brew, made of God only knew what ingredients, had not cured it. He sat in the swing on the side veranda, a light blanket draped across his shoulders though the day was hot and still.

Connor came out of the house, eating a peach he had grabbed from the table where Bridget and Viney were getting ready to make peach preserves. "Feeling better, Pa?"

"Not much," Joseph grumbled. "But don't tell your mother or Viney. They've just about pulled all the hair out of my chest with these sticky poultices. And the last concoction Viney forced me to drink was so bitter, my eyes are still watering."

"Well, they're just taking care of you---" Connor paused as he studied a wagon coming down the road. "Does that rig seem to be going slower than usual?"

They continued to watch as an old man drove his mule-drawn wagon at an uncertain pace. The rig came to a stop beside the front gate.

"Hey now," Connor said, tossing his peach aside and taking off down the driveway. Joseph threw off his blanket and followed him.

"This the Harrigan place?" the man called out.

"It is," Joseph answered. He saw a somewhat familiar head rise from the bed of the wagon.

"Nate," yelled Connor. "Nate, you're home." Nate attempted to climb from the wagon, tumbled into Connor's arms.

"And Ryan?" Joseph's voice was a whisper as he pushed forward and searched the back of the wagon. He turned to Nate. "Where is he? Where's Ryan?"

Nate hung his head. "I wanted to bring him home. I tried my best. They wouldn't let me."

"He's in a hospital somewhere?" Joseph made the question a statement.

Nate shook his head. "I'm sorry. Sorry. But I have to tell you this. Ryan's dead."

"Dead?" Joseph put out a hand and clung to the side of the wagon.

"Yes sir. Killed in battle."

The driver leaned down. "You going to be all right?" he asked, eyeing Joseph carefully.

Joseph nodded, an automatic gesture, but of course he wasn't all right. He looked at Connor. The boy's face was now gray, his eyes glazed with shock.

"I tried to take care of him." Nate was trembling. I did the best I could, honest.

"He's been dreading telling you this," the driver said. "Been carrying on about it ever since I picked him up about fifty miles back."

Dimly, Joseph heard what the man was saying. Heard himself say, "It was kind of you to bring Nate here. You ought to stay a while. Rest up before you go on." Ordinary words. Words that might hold off what he wasn't ready to face.

"Thanks for asking," the man said. "But I'm on my way to my cousin's in Mississippi and this ol' mule ain't getting me there very fast. I'd better keep moving along. Sorry about your boy. I'll take Nate on down the road to his family."

"No." Nate detached himself from Connor. "I have to stay here and tell them what happened. Thank you, sir. For everything."

The driver touched his battered hat and flicked a rein over the mule. "Get along now," he shouted. The wagon creaked as it moved slowly forward.

"Is that Nate?' Molly Kate called from an upstairs window. "Oh, it is. It is. Hey, everyone. Nate's here."

Bridget appeared on the porch. The family came from every direction. Their shouts of joy made it clear they expected only good news. Joseph braced himself, forced himself to continue breathing. Somehow he had to live through this. He would be needed.

They all gathered around Nate on the porch steps. Nate sat down, took a deep breath and began to tell what had to be told.

"We hadn't been with General Hood's troops long before Ryan and I figured out we were fighting for a crazy man. He didn't even seem to care if a battle made sense. Fought day or night. Rebels and Yankees just went after one another like they wanted to get it over or die in the trying. Once we even fought hand to hand with a bunch of Yankees." Nate paused, his eyes reflecting the terrible things he'd seen. "Ryan and I, we were scared at first. But after we survived a couple of battles, we got restless. Began telling ourselves those stupid Yankees couldn't kill us. Thinking the things we saw would only happen to others. Not to us. Even beginning to believe it was so. And then one day, something exploded in front of us, knocked Ryan down. I yelled at him. 'You're going to be all right,' I told him. But when I turned him over and saw his chest was all crushed, I knew he was hurt bad." Nate's throat seemed to sort of close up and Viney brought him a glass of water.

Joseph saw his son lying in Nate's arms, his chest bloody. He shook his head but the vision remained. He reached out and took Bridget's icy hand in his.

"I knew I had to get him some help," Nate continued, after a few moments. "I unrolled my bedroll, laid him on the blanket, tied one end around my waist and started dragging him along toward the rear of the line. Doctors were there. Taking care of the wounded. I tugged at their sleeves to get their attention, said I needed someone to help my friend. One of the doctors looked at Ryan, shook his head, said he was gone, told me I'd have to put him over on top of a pile of bodies. Well, I sure wasn't going to do that to Ryan. When no one was looking, I just took off still pulling him along. I don't know how long I kept going. Late at night, I ran into a couple of Yankees, walking along with their guns pointed out like they were expecting to kill someone. When they saw me, I asked them to please not shoot me because I needed to get help for my wounded friend. One of the Yankees bent down to examine Ryan and said real kind like, that didn't I know nothing could be done for my friend? They said I should bury him while I had the chance. I fought with them, said I had to take him home to his folks, broke down crying. I guess they felt real sorry for me because they said they'd help me give Ryan a nice burial. They took the shovel I had tied to my back and began digging. Then they wrapped Ryan in the blanket, covered him, face and all." Nate swallowed hard. "They put him in this grave they'd dug and threw the dirt back in. I asked if I could say something over the grave and they said to be quick about it because we could hear what sounded like another battle breaking out somewhere nearby. I told Ryan, 'Goodbye, my friend' and I asked God to take care of him because we all loved him so much. Then I looked around for something to mark his grave with. But bullets started zinging all around us. The Yankees took off and I decided I better run too, because I couldn't see a thing. I didn't know which side was shooting at me. Only thing is, when the firing died down, I couldn't find my way back to where the grave was. So" – Nate paused, swallowed hard – "that's the worst thing I have to tell you. I don't even know where he is buried. All I know is, it's somewhere in Tennessee. I wandered around looking for that grave until I got shot in my side and passed plumb out. When I woke up, I was in a hospital and everyone was saying the war was over. I didn't see anything for me to do but start walking home. As soon as I could hobble along with a stick, I headed out. I just didn't know what else to do. I just didn't know what to do."

"You did the right thing, Nate," Joseph said. "No one could have been a better friend than you were to Ryan and we'll always be grateful you were with him."

Later, when they had all gone to bed for the night, Joseph lay wide awake, staring at the ceiling. Hours passed yet he felt no need for sleep. His body seemed to have shut down and no longer had need for food or sleep. He heard a rumble of thunder and was grateful for it; rain would be a diversion. Lightning flashed once again and thunder rolled across the sky. A brisk breeze blew the curtains straight out into the room. As he closed his window, he could hear other windows being shut and knew that Bridget was about her usual task of securing the house for a storm. She would look in on each child, he knew, and see that they were all tucked beneath blankets. He ought to be helping her, he thought, though he never had before.

After a while, he heard her go back to her bedroom and then, above the storm, he heard her crying. He sat up. What was this nonsense – this insanity – staying apart when they needed each other so much. He rose from his bed and crossed the hall. Without knocking, he entered their bedroom, climbed into the bed and gathered Bridget into his arms.

She buried her head in his shoulder, tried to muffle her sobs. "I'll have all the children up if I don't quiet down. But oh Joseph" – she moved closer to him, clung to him---"it just came to me. I used to be able to keep all my children safe. And now---"

"I know," he said. "I know."

CHAPTER FORTY-FOUR

ALL THE NEXT DAY THE RAIN POURED down, a steady drumming on the roof, rushing down the rain spouts, making muddy rivulets across the yard. The Harrigans wandered about the house, despondent, desolate. The trouble, Joseph decided, was that they hadn't prepared themselves for an unhappy ending. They had been so sure that one day Ryan would return safely. They wanted Ryan home, longed desperately to have him resting in his bed, sipping broth, smiling at them, telling of his adventures.

Joseph was sure they were all keeping their emotions under control because they knew it would make it harder for the others if they didn't. He had forced himself to shave and dress though he felt more like lying in bed. He was still fighting off his cold. His chest felt tight and painful but he wasn't coughing as much so he assumed he was better. He ought to be doing something. Bridget had risen early and was going about her tasks in a trance, refusing all offers of help as if she feared running out of things to keep her busy. The children were subdued, their small faces forlorn. Molly Kate read to them for a while, then gave up and they sat huddled together on her bed, watching the rain fall. Joanna had spent the morning in the sewing room and when Joseph went in to talk to her, he made no mention of the damp drops on the pale green dress she was sewing.

Toward noon, Joseph looked out the window and saw that Connor had returned from town. He had gone to get himself excused from work, saying he couldn't think straight and would probably deliver all the telegrams to the wrong addresses. Now, he wandered about the yard, ignoring the rain. Joseph supposed he wanted to be alone but Bridget would be upset if she saw him with his thin shirt so wet that it was sticking to his skin. He put on a slicker, grabbed another one and slipped out the side door.

He caught up with Connor, draped the waterproof coat over his shoulders, then walked beside him as he cried softly, his shoulders mixing with the rain.

"Shouldn't you come inside? You'll worry your mother if she sees you all wet."

Conner shook his head sending drops of water flying. "I just don't feel like coming in yet."

"I understand, but, well then, if you don't want to come in why don't we go out to the carriage house? We could be alone there."

The carriage house was dank and quiet, with only the sound of Kilkenny munching his feed. Joseph and Connor climbed into the carriage and sat side by side on the leather cushion, saying nothing. It occurred to Joseph that there was something to be said for Irish customs, for wakes with the loved ones laid out among family and friends and everyone speaking fondly of the dead, some giving in to their grief with keening and wailing, some partaking of the drink or eating the food set out for hospitality's sake. There were many who considered wakes outlandish, he knew, but for all that, they did have a way of getting you through, of sharing the pain.

But there would be no old-fashioned wake for Ryan. Perhaps a somber memorial mass, but no funeral. Joseph winced at a sudden vision of Ryan lying alone in an unmarked grave. He didn't realize he had begun to shake, until Connor touched his shoulder and said, "Pa, we'd better go."

The next morning, Joseph was burning with fever. He lay in bed listening to Bridget tell Connor to fetch a doctor and not to take no for an answer. After that, he slipped into blackness, awaking now and then to see concerned faces beside his bed, a strange doctor leaning over him. He lost all sense of time.

When he finally awoke, his mind clear again, he was amazed to learn he'd been lying there, drifting in and out of consciousness, for almost three weeks.

"But you're much better," Bridget said, "You've been cool to the touch for several days now. The doctor says you're going to be fine, that you're a strong man and all you need now is to sit up so your lungs can drain. He also wants you to walk around for a little each day."

But Joseph didn't feel like sitting up and walking around. He turned his face to the wall. When Bridget brought up a tray containing a bowl of broth and a bit of tapioca pudding, he realized he was causing her concern and extra work. He must not do that. He took a few sips of the broth, a few bites of the tapioca, then pushed the tray aside.

"Tomorrow," he promised. "Tomorrow, I'll eat and get out of bed for a bit."

But somehow, he just couldn't.

Connor shaved and bathed him each day, pulled fresh night shirts over his head, tucked him under a sheet, watching him anxiously all the while. "You've got to get up now, Pa," he urged.

"I will. I will."

"When?"

"Soon now." But once again, he'd turn his face to the wall. He lay there for another ten days, feeling used up, unwilling to go on. Then, one day Bridget came bustling in. "I've brought you a visitor," she said. "'Tis Mr. Dill."

Dill stood in the doorway. "May I come in?"

Joseph nodded.

Bridget brought a chair, put it beside the bed, and left them alone to talk.

Joseph watched Dill as he settled in the chair, shocked at his appearance. Dill had always been portly but solid. Now his flesh sagged as if it were losing its hold on the bone structure beneath.

"Glad you're better, Joseph," he said. "I've been concerned about you."

"I'll survive," Joseph said. "But Mack. How is he? And have you gotten the press back yet? Are you ready to get out a paper?"

Dill held up a hand. "Whoa. One thing at a time." He paused. "I'll start with the press. No, we don't have it back but I've made plans to get it. We still have that thirty-seven boxes of tobacco hidden away and a friendly dealer in Nashville has agreed to accept it sight unseen as a basis for a credit of two thousand dollars. Also, several steamboat lines have offered free transportation. If all goes well, we should have a paper out as early as October. November, at the latest. That is, if you're willing to help. I need you to go with me to bring back the press."

"Isn't Mack well enough to go?"

Dill looked away from Joseph. "I'm afraid we can't count on Mack. Truth is, Joseph, and we might as well face it, the doctor says that Mack isn't going to recover. Says, in fact, that he doesn't have much time left."

"Ah no. We mustn't lose Mack. What would we do without him? He was always so ---" Joseph couldn't go on. Too many losses, he thought. It was just too much. He wished Dill would go away so he could close his eyes, try to stop thinking.

"Joseph, don't turn away from me." Dill sighed. "The thought of going on alone overwhelms me. As you can see, I'm old and tired. The war has taken its toll. But we mustn't give up. Not now. The *Appeal* is needed more than ever. The sword has torn our land apart, now we have only words to put it back together again. And I just don't think I can get the press back without help from someone."

Joseph struggled to sit up. "Dammit, look at me. I'm weak as a kitten. I doubt I can even stand."

"I won't be leaving for another few weeks. Plenty of time for a young man like you to get your strength back. Don't say you're not young either. Compared to me, you are."

"But I have to think of my family. I couldn't leave Bridget. Not now."

"Talk it over with her. See what she says. I'll be back in a day or so to get your answer."

After Dill left, Joseph settled back on his pillow. He turned toward the wall again, but this time it did no good. He could no longer shut out his concerns. It was true, of course, that the *Appeal* would be needed more than ever. He thought of Colonel Van Pelt, how he had started the newspaper to give the people a voice, and of the promise he'd made by the Colonel's graveside. And he thought of his father. He would not approve of a son who gave up when he was needed. Joseph sighed. He knew what he must do, though he halfway hoped that when he talked to Bridget, she would insist he was needed here with his family. And he wasn't going to risk getting on her bad side again. Joseph swung his feet over the edge of the bed and stood up on shaky legs.

CHAPTER FORTY-FIVE

IN MID- SEPTEMBER, JOSEPH AND DILL set out to bring the *Appeal's* press, steam engine and boiler back to Memphis. The journey would be long. They would travel three rivers, up the Mississippi, across the Ohio and back down the Tennessee River into Alabama. From there, they would go by wagon to Macon.

As they headed northward up the Mississippi, Joseph spent his days lounging on the deck of the steamboat, hoping the gentle September sunshine would restore his health. It would soon be fall, he reflected, his favorite time of the year, but the thought did not inspire him as it once had. He was tired. Still a bit shaky. And he was worried about Dill, who was staying in his cabin most of the time, saying the river dampness bothered him. He worried, too, about leaving Bridget although she had assured him she would be fine. She and Joanna would be busy, she told him. Joanna had chosen a college in North Carolina – Trinity College, it was – and she would soon be leaving by stage coach to see about getting registered for the next term. Joseph was happy for her. It was the only good thing that had happened to the Harrigan family lately, he thought, realizing he was taking a dark view of almost everything these days.

His mood had not improved by the time they reached the Tennessee River and began to travel through Tennessee. Watching the war-scarred landscape glide by, he was appalled by the devastation. He saw the charred skeletons of burned-out farms and plantations, acres of scorched earth, dying trees with limbs lopped off by shells. Cannons and other weapons had been abandoned to rust and deteriorate. He saw bleached bones of horses, old wagons sunk in mud, some overturned with their splintery wheels moving slowly in the wind, spokes half gone like missing teeth. The unending desolation got to him. Instead of feeling rested, he realized he had grown wearier. If only Mack were with us, he thought. Or Shaughnessy. And his heart ached for his son. He realized just how essential a part Ryan had played in all his dreams of the future. Somehow he had to let go of those dreams and move on.

When he and Dill finally arrived in Macon, they received a warm welcome. The mayor thanked them for the Appeal's war efforts. There were many eager hands to help them pack press, engine and boiler in new crates. The tobacco was shipped to Nashville and they received a credit of two thousand dollars.

"Everything is falling into place," said Dill.

They loaded their machines and equipment on wagons for the trip across land, back to the Tennessee River. There, they boarded a steamboat called the "Blue Bayou" – more free transportation. The owner of the boat told them the *Appeal* had brought him comfort during the long months he had stood guard on the outskirts of Atlanta.

"Amazing," Dill reflected. "Everywhere we go, we meet people who found us a comfort during the war."

Joseph nodded. "It's good to know we were appreciated."

"Indeed it is." Dill lit one of the few cigars he allowed himself. He was in an expansive mood. "Well, we have one more stop – Cincinnati – and then we'll head home to get our first post-war edition out, probably by November. We ought to be on our way to recovery in a year or so. The small office I rented on Madison is just temporary, of course. We'll get our own building back some day. Mark my words. We'll---" He began to cough and had to snuff his cigar out.

"Should you go rest now?" asked Joseph.

Dill nodded, he couldn't stop coughing. Joseph watched him walk slowly back to his cabin, realized for the first time that he hadn't seen Dill use his cane since they left Memphis. It occurred to Joseph that the cane might have been sold. The thing had a gold handle, would probably bring a good sum. He decided not to ask about it.

Once again, they traveled across Tennessee, the scenery as depressing as ever.

A passenger strolled down the deck and stopped to lean on the railing beside Joseph. "War really tore things up," he noted.

Joseph answered with a nod.

As the man lit a pipe, the breeze caught its smoke and carried it towards Joseph. Joseph coughed and the man moved downwind. "You're not a smoker, I see?"

"I'm recovering from a bout with lung fever, or something. Damn near did me in. I'll wait a while before I smoke again."

"A wise decision. Where you from, friend?"

The man's easy ways and pleasant, casual voice lured Joseph into conversation. Better to talk than think. He told the man he was from Memphis, added his name and put out a hand.

"I'm Jessie," the man said, as they shook hands. Jessie Paxton. I have a farm up on Missionary Ridge. Say, I watched when they were loading your press. You one of the owners?"

Regretfully, Joseph admitted he wasn't. "Thought of buying in a number of times but – it never did work out."

"Is that a fact?"

Joseph found himself opening up to the stranger, telling him how it had been his life's ambition to own a part of the *Appeal*. Telling him about Joanna. And finally, telling him that he had a son buried out there – he indicated the deserted landscape they were passing. "Don't even know where his grave is."

"A shame," Jessie said. "A dadblamed shame."

Joseph drew in a breath. He needed to talk about Ryan and somehow it seemed easier to tell the story to a stranger.

Jessie listened in silence, then said, "It's a sorry thing to think on, the way we lost so many boys. I come across graves often, a lot of them unmarked. Have a dozen or so on my own property up on the ridge. There's no doubting what they are. They sink a little, you know. Wind and rain carry off the mounds and the soft dirt settles about ten or twelve inches. Makes the graves permanent. Even without a marker. T'other day my granddaughter was playing and stumbled into one. Her older brother told her what it was and now she brings flowers to put on the soldier's grave."

Joseph was quiet, so he continued.

"They say the country's pock-marked with such graves. They're everywhere that battles were fought. Most of the time, you can't tell whether a Yankee or a Reb lies there, but it doesn't matter. You know it's the final resting place of a brave and good man who gave his life fighting for what he believed to be right. I'd say you can be proud of your son. No matter where he lies.

Joseph inclined his head and moved away.

"Hope I didn't say anything that made you feel worse," Jessie called after him.

"No," Joseph said. "Just need to go lie down awhile."

He went to his cabin because for the first time, he was crying. The aching knot he'd carried inside for so long seemed to be melting and tears rose to the back of his throat, filled his eyes. When he could cry no more, he blew his nose and washed his face in the basin of water he kept on a washstand in the corner of his cabin.

It was dark when he went back to the railing to look out over the land. He was glad to be by himself again, to think. He seemed better able to handle the vision of Ryan lying alone. He knew now that Ryan was buried among thousands of graves filled with brave and good men. One grave might be forgotten, but thousands delivered a message as permanent as any carved in marble or etched in bronze. It was not what he had wanted for his son, but he must accept it.

At Cincinnati, Dill spent eighteen hundred dollars buying equipment from the Franklin Type Foundry. He told Joseph he hoped they could get enough donations in Memphis to buy their first supply of newsprint and ink, for he had spent the last of the tobacco money.

Another offer of free passage got them as far as Cairo. But the steamboat turned north at Cairo and they had to disembark. The press, boiler and newly acquired equipment were unloaded at the landing. Dill and Joseph sat on a bench beside the wharf, hoping someone would offer to take them back down the Mississippi to Memphis.

Dill fretted. "Maybe I shouldn't have depended so much on free transportation. We're too far north to get help. No one up here has probably heard of the *Appeal*."

But to their surprise, they found that, even in the North, people knew of the *Appeal's* war time reputation and spoke admiringly of "that scrappy little paper." They were soon on their way down the Mississippi. Before they left Cairo, they sent wires to Bridget and Mrs. Dill letting them know when they might expect them to arrive, that is, if the steamboat kept to schedule.

When they arrived in Memphis, they were surprised to find a large crowd waiting at the wharf. Friends of the *Appeal* greeted them with shouts of 'welcome home' and congratulations for a job well done as they descended the gangplank. Joseph saw that everyone seemed to be dressed up in their Sunday best, the men wearing dark suits and tall hats, the women looked bright and colorful in beribboned bonnets, with their skirts flowing almost as extravagantly as they had before the war. Evidently everyone considered it an occasion deserving a celebration.

Joseph looked for Bridget, found her surrounded by all of the children and hurried to greet them. Viney was there, too. And Nate was there, hobbling about on a cane, a grand cane with a gold head.

Joseph gave Dill a questioning look. "So that's where your cane went?"

"I never actually needed the thing," Dill said brusquely. "Just liked the way it felt in my hand. I decided to give it to someone who could put it to better use."

Nate overheard the conversation, and grinned. "Don't I look mighty fine?" he asked, holding up the cane.

"You do indeed, Nate," Joseph told him.

The crowd gathered closer about them, asking questions, wanting to know if they'd had any difficulties getting the press home. Joseph saw that Dill looked very pale. "Are you all right?" he asked.

"As a matter of fact, I'm exhausted. I wonder, could you supervise the unloading. I'd like to go home and rest."

Joseph told him to go along, not to worry. "I'll take care of everything," he called as Dill walked away, Mrs. Dill beside him.

Someone aboard the steamboat shouted, "Move back everyone. We're going to put the press ashore."

There was a hush and a few "ahhs" as a crate was swung out over the dock like a bale of cotton. The voices of the youngest Harrigans could be heard clearly, shouting, "There's Papa's *Appeal*." "Papa's *Appeal* is home."

"Yes," Bridget said firmly, putting her hand on Joseph's arm. "Papa's *Appeal* is home.

Joseph had heard his children refer to "Papa's *Appeal*" many times through the years – but to have Bridget say as much, ah, hadn't he longed to have such approval from her? He thought about what she and the children had said as he saw to it that all the *Appeal's* equipment and supplies were unloaded with care. And as he thought, an idea came to him, took shape. Wasn't it a fact that devoting a lifetime of energy and sweat to something made it belong to a man far more than the giving of money? Didn't the *Appeal* belong to him in the same manner that ships belong to the men who take them to sea? He walked over to supervise as machines and supplies were loaded on a large freight wagon, and put a proprietary hand on the crate containing the press.

When all was loaded, Joseph climbed into the wagon, took the reins in hand and gave them a shake. A team of mules strained, began to move the heavy load forward.

Going up the road to the top of the Bluff, Joseph was painfully aware of the empty seat beside him. He felt a great, wrenching loneliness – for Ryan and Shaughnessy and Mack. Without them, putting out a paper would lack excitement. It would never be the same again.

"Wait, Pa," a voice called, when the wagon reached the Bluff's crest.

Joseph halted the mules and turned to see Connor running toward him.

"Wait, I'm going with you, Pa" His long legs sprinting over the cobblestones, Connor caught up with the wagon, grasped its side and swung himself aboard. "I've decided to go into the newspaper business."

Joseph looked at him, taken aback. "When did you decide this?"

"Thought about it a lot while you were away. Talked to Mama some about it. And just now, well, it came to me. This is what I want to do."

"And what does your mother have to say about it?"

"Ah, she didn't like it too much at first, but I convinced her it was better than going wandering around in Indian country."

"You rascal."

"Yeah," Connor agreed, grinning. He leaned back in his seat and propped a big foot on the front of the wagon. "So. Let's get moving. I want to try my hand at – what is it Mack always says –

at stirring up the complacent and puncturing the pompous. I just might be good at it."

"You might at that." Joseph flicked the reins and the mules continued on. They traveled down Main, then turned on Madison where the limbs of great elms entwined over the avenue. The trees were bright with patches of red and gold leaves.

THE END

Acknowledgements

Many thanks to all the friends and relations who helped me complete Harrigan's Appeal. Special appreciation goes to Maralys Wills, my professor who generously devoted countless hours guiding me with her talented editing. Also, my son, Michael Van Buskirk, applied his many skills to getting the book ready for publication. Daughter, Lynn Guinn, a fine writer herself, had many helpful suggestions for me. Daughter, Pegi Crook, a natural-born sales person began promoting the book before it was finished. John Van Buskirk sent words from Texas that he could hardly wait to read the book. And, of course, Barbara Deatherage was invaluable with her many hours of research and aid in creating new chapters. She also helped to recover lost chapters as the book was moved about several times. I'm certain **Harrigan's Appeal** never would have been completed without her assistance.

I also must give credit to my grandfather, Patrick Douglas Egan, who worked as a foreman for the Commercial Appeal at the turn of the century. He is known to have invented the process to add color to a continuous web press, something other pressmen has thus far not been able to do. I had planned to write an article about him and this process, but while researching old newspapers, I discovered a much larger and intriguing story and the novel I'd always wanted to write.

www.ingramcontent.com/pod-product-compliance
Lightning Source LLC
Chambersburg PA
CBHW051318250626
47155CB00007B/2375